PROLOGUE

Nothing felt right to Helena. The location, timing, odd message… none of it. She ached for a cigarette. But it had been hard enough shaking the habit after finding out she was pregnant sixteen years ago. No way was she going through that again. But the ache was there.

Doheny State Beach officially closed at 10 p.m., so she turned left down Puerto Place, drove alongside the parking lot, turned around, and pulled up to the curb. The last thing she needed was a parking ticket, but it was either park there or drive to the harbor and walk all the way back. She hoped this wouldn't take long.

Sitting in her 2003 Chevy Venture minivan for a few minutes, Helena wondered what could possibly require all this cloak-and-dagger nonsense. She sighed. Some people simply couldn't keep themselves out of trouble.

Opening the door made the warning beep echo around the deserted beachfront, drowning out the sounds of the waves and the distant traffic on Pacific Coast Highway. She took the key from the ignition, and the beeping stopped. Why she felt the need to be quiet was beyond her imagination, but stealth seemed to fit the circumstances.

Grabbing her phone and the sticky note from the cup holder, Helena checked for texts or missed calls. She saw none, but a low battery warning informed her she had less than five percent remaining power. Cursing herself for forgetting to plug it in at work, she left the phone and got out.

Closing the door, she locked the minivan, and under the yellow glow of the streetlight, stared at the handwritten note one more time. She then glanced at her cheap Walmart watch. It was almost 10:30.

Stuffing the sticky note in her pocket, Helena crossed the sidewalk, passed between two coast live oak trees, and headed toward the beach where she was able to hop across the stream dividing the day parking from the rest of Doheny. With her tennis shoes sinking into the soft, grainy sand, she trudged toward the grassy picnic area, searching the dimly lit grounds for a familiar face. Ahead, a late-night jogger went by on the pathway, lost in their thoughts and whatever played through their earbuds. The sounds of teenage kids' muffled laughter filtered her way in the darkness from farther down the beach, bringing back a flood of memories.

How many times had she come down to this beach at night? Helena felt stupid and embarrassed for her current trepidation and the knot twisting in her stomach. She couldn't recall feeling scared when she and her two best friends from high school had shared what was undoubtedly a very expensive bottle of wine one of them had smuggled from her father's collection. Unlike Helena, her friends had wealthy parents with fancy cars and even fancier wine collections. It was the first time she'd ever been drunk.

A few more firsts had taken place nearby with her boyfriend from her sophomore year. Helena laughed to herself and tried to shake off what now felt like a silly sense of unease, but the anxiety was reluctant to leave.

Sitting on a concrete bench by the picnic area, she shivered and blamed it on the cool, late spring chill from the ocean breeze. Her slight build provided little insulation. She was always the first to get cold. Feeling untethered without her cell phone, she considered

WHY SHE HAD TO DIE

INVESTIGATOR KAT CROMWELL MYSTERY - BOOK ONE

NICHOLAS HARVEY

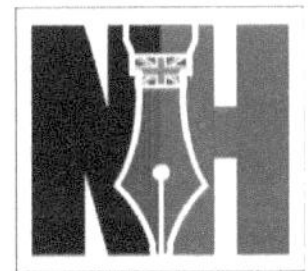

going back to the minivan for her sweatshirt and getting the phone, even if it was about to die. But she didn't intend to be there long enough for either to matter. She'd be fine. Pretty soon, a park ranger would come by to shepherd the kids from the beach and, in due course, Helena from her bench. The idea of a ranger close by eased her concerns a little, unwinding one small twist from the knot in her stomach.

Glancing at her watch once more, she tilted her wrist toward the path light but was still unable to make out the hands. She rose and stepped from the shadows of the palm trees until the meager light illuminated the dial. It was already 10:40 p.m. Helena fought the temptation to examine the note once more, but having read it a dozen times, she knew what it said. She was in the right place, at the right time.

Walking back to the bench, she told herself *five more minutes*, and then she'd leave. Her bed was beckoning. Helena's bed was always calling. It was hard to remember a time when she hadn't felt thoroughly worn out. Closing the restaurant at ten meant home by 10:30ish after reconciling the registers and helping clean up. Getting up at 6:30 a.m. for breakfast and running Scarlett to school gave her the precious hour she could spend with her daughter each day during the week. Scarlett's grandparents picked her up from school and dropped her home after dinner, but she'd be in bed by the time Helena came home and checked on her girl.

What she would do in a year when Scarlett could drive, she had no idea. The minivan with over 200,000 miles on it was hard enough to keep running, so the cost of adding a second vehicle didn't bear thinking about.

Helena would face that hurdle when she reached it, as she'd done for the past sixteen years since finding out she was having a child… and Scarlett's father had decided it was time to bow out of their relationship. She'd made it this far, and had raised a good kid, so she'd continue doing whatever it took to keep their heads above water. Scarlett might have to wait for a car, but that would be okay.

Her daughter was smart and knew their circumstances. She'd understand.

The breeze blew a little harder, and Helena shivered again, annoyance beginning to supersede her trepidation. She'd been here on time, just to be left alone. *Typical.* The palm fronds swished as they brushed against each other, and she stood, hearing the light crunch of twigs from behind her.

"I was about to leave," she said, keeping her voice down.

Helena turned but saw no one, and her stomach knotted once more.

"Hello?" she called.

She held her breath and listened, but what she'd perceived as footsteps seemed to vanish amongst the rustling of branches and waves washing up the gently sloping shoreline. Turning in a circle, her eyes struggled to adjust to the darkness of the trees and picnic area beyond as she contemplated what to do next. Memories of nighttime adventures in the park and on the beach evaporated from her mind, replaced once more with uneasiness and a sense of dread. Beginning with the note, nothing had felt right. Out of character. Even for one so unpredictable and scattered.

Lifting her arm, Helena tried to read the time on her watch once more, but it was too dark. She took a step toward the light and immediately felt something fall against her chest. She jumped, but was too late to prevent the line being pulled tight against her throat.

The little Helena had learned over the years about self-defense was lost to the belief that this couldn't be happening to her. Paralyzed by fear and panic, she writhed and clutched at the cord around her neck. Her attacker violently shoved forward, sending Helena to the ground. Her cheek and nose smashed against the concrete, and an agonizing pain consumed her face. She tasted blood in her mouth and felt the warm fluid flow from her crushed nose.

Above her, grunts and groans conveyed her attacker's efforts and complete commitment, which added to Helena's feeling of helplessness. A bony knee in her back pinned her to the ground while the force on the cord increased with newfound leverage. Helena scratched her own neck as she clawed at the line embedded into her flesh, to no avail. Her head throbbed, and the desperate urge to breathe was overwhelming.

The realization that she'd drawn her final breath made her want to scream and cry, but she could do neither. With the feeling that her throat was being irreparably crushed, Helena's mind swam through a dark swamp of confusion. She felt herself go limp a moment before she lost consciousness.

It could have been a few seconds or several hours—Helena had no way of knowing. Her face throbbed in pain, her head pounded, and her stomach churned with nausea. Desperately dry, her throat constricted as she fought the urge to gasp and cough.

She was alive but instinctively knew to be quiet. Her ordeal wasn't over.

Consciousness felt like the world beyond a spinning merry-go-round—swirling by so close, yet she couldn't step off. It was right there, and still out of reach. Her body jolted, and she realized she was in a vehicle that had just come to a stop. The rumble of the engine vibrated through the surface she was lying on, which was cool and hard, like metal. She was face-down.

A door opened. A few moments later, more hinges creaked and her foot flopped, released from a restriction she hadn't been aware of. Hands roughly clutched her ankles, dragging her body across the steel surface until her legs dangled beyond what she guessed to be the tailgate of a pickup truck. With her lips slightly parted, Helena tried to breathe in soft, easy sips so her chest didn't heave with each inhalation. Water lapped close by, and she caught the tangy scent of the shoreline.

Barely opening one eye, she struggled to focus and take in her surroundings. It was dark, with a hint of light from somewhere nearby, vaguely defining the details of the inside of the truck bed. A hand pushed an object away with a metallic clunk, and for a split second, she glimpsed bare skin below a rolled-up shirt sleeve. Instantly, she knew who it was.

But why was this happening to her? It seemed unfathomable that the secret Helena knew could lead to this. And yet, it had.

The hand wrapped under her neck, and another shoveled forcefully under her thighs as she felt herself gingerly lifted from the vehicle. Helena held her breath and squeezed her eyes tightly closed. If she could feign death for a few more moments, she was sure her limp body was about to be thrown into the ocean. A surge of inner strength came her way as she thought of her daughter. Of staying alive. For Scarlett's sake. She willed herself to surrender to what was coming next and fought the instinct to tense her muscles.

With a guttural groan from her attacker, who struggled and staggered a few steps, Helena felt her trim body being spilled from her captor's arms, falling through the night air. She wanted to scream and flail her arms and legs, but her body didn't respond. In the brief moment of weightlessness, she noticed her left wrist felt oddly bare. Her watch had gone.

Yearning for the comforting embrace of the water, she pictured herself finding the strength to swim away. All she had to do was make it to the beach and call out for the park ranger. She'd wrap her arms around Scarlett and tell her she was fine. That everything would be okay.

But Helena never knew the cool, welcoming embrace of the ocean below.

1

Sweat flew as I punched the heavy bag. My taped and gloved hands ached, but I kept hitting. Jab, jab, cross. My legs were beginning to feel heavy, and the bounce was fading in my step, but I kept going.

"Kat," my dad's gruff Londoner's voice called to me. "That's enough, girl."

I dropped my hands, panting and wondering why he'd called me over. My father was usually happy to watch me tire myself out on the bag so I wouldn't bug him about letting me spar.

"If you tell your mother, I'll have your guts for garters. Understand?" he said, his deep voice menacing. As if I didn't know better.

He stood by the ring with Cisco, a nineteen-year-old featherweight division fighter he trained. That meant the kid weighed between 122 pounds and 126 pounds. At least that was his pre-fight target. Cisco was probably 130 or more, which put him ten over me. I didn't care.

My dad had been firmly against me sparring with anyone since the day I took an active interest in the sport he'd built his life around. *Everyone's goal in life should be to avoid getting smacked in the head, love,* he'd repeatedly told me, *especially you.* But eight months ago, things had dramatically changed in my life, and I needed an outlet. Being smacked in the head seemed like a good fit.

"Go get your sparring gear," he told me, and I jogged to the locker room, hurrying back with the shiny groin guard and headgear that had never seen use.

"Alright, do you need protection for your…" he stammered, pointing in the general direction of my chest.

I'd never fully shaken my tomboy tendencies, but my slender, 5'-6" frame had finally developed curves late in high school. So even with my bob-cut brown hair, I'd long since moved on from being mistaken for a boy.

"I'm good," I replied, trying not to laugh at my dad's awkwardness.

Some female fighters wore a padded protective sports bra, but my regular gym bra under my tee would have to do. I wasn't about to pass up this opportunity by giving Dad time to reconsider.

He helped me switch from the lighter bag gloves into the sparring gloves, which looked similar to those used in competition but with extra padding. He then fastened my headgear for me. I'd bought the regulation style used in amateur competition, but now wondered if I should have gone for one with the chin guard and nose protector. Or perhaps a full-face crash helmet.

Dad turned to Cisco. "Work on defense, but keep her honest." He then waggled his finger at us both. "Break when I say break, or so help me, I'll cuff the pair of you 'round the bloody ear. Right?"

Cisco grinned and nodded. "Yes, sir," he responded in accented English, slipping through the ropes that Dad held apart for him.

My dad held out my mouthguard I'd paid to be molded ages ago but never had cause to use. I used my tongue to push it in place and chomped it around with my teeth, trying to get used to its strange presence in my mouth. My heart was pounding. He rested a hand on my shoulder and leaned closer.

"This kid's weak spot is shorter fighters coming at him underneath, so I need you to work him up high, then sneak a few under his guard, alright?"

I nodded, but I was more worried about keeping my face intact than the subtleties of Cisco's defensive flaws. Last I knew, the kid was unbeaten since he'd turned eighteen. My whole sparring obsession was starting to feel like a bad idea, and my legs were quivering as I stumbled through the ropes into the ring.

Before I could come up with an acceptable reason to bow out of the one thing I'd relentlessly pestered my dad for, I heard the words "Fight on," and Cisco was on his toes and moving toward me. I jabbed to check him up at the edge of my reach, which he comfortably absorbed with his glove, and we both began bobbing and rotating counterclockwise around each other. I jabbed a few more times, inching closer with each attempt until I was one quick step away from the sweet spot for my punching power.

Cisco's eyes were laser-focused yet somehow soft and relaxed. It was then that I realized he'd done little but jab my gloves in return, which was undoubtedly what my father had told him to do. The kid, whose family hadn't been able to make his training fees in months, wasn't about to thump his trainer's 25-year-old daughter. I stepped away and dropped my hands.

"Bloody hell, Dad," I lisped through my mouthguard. "It's not sparring if you've told him he can't sock me."

I glanced over at Cisco, who was trying to follow our conversation. Generally, having grown up in America, I used US terms. But being raised by English parents meant my accent had stuck around and the odd UK word or two found their way into my speech. My dad teased me whenever I sounded American. My sparring partner had no doubt been raised in a Spanish-speaking home, so our accents were making it hard for him to follow along.

Although, Cisco grinned, so I supposed he got the gist of things.

My dad scratched his head, finally looking up to meet my gaze. "Why are you so bloody hell-bent on getting smacked in the face?"

I spat my mouthguard into my glove. "Because I need to be ready. Out on the streets, some drug-dealing wanker won't care that I'm a girl. He'll try to knock my head off. I need to be ready to dodge or take it."

My reasoning sounded solid to me, despite it all being a lie.

"You work in Dana bloody Point, love," he retorted. "This ain't downtown LA, is it? You're hardly investigating shootings and gangbanging, or whatever they call it."

"No, but you never know when some drunk will take a swing," I countered, as he'd brought up a valid argument.

Dana Point is a sleepy beachfront town in South Orange County, California, and the only town I'd worked in after graduating from the Sheriff's Department training program. With the constant escalation of house prices, the only criminals who could afford to live there had either been in town their whole lives, or were lawyers and business executives with dubious morals committing white-collar crimes. Most calls were domestics and DUIs. With only a handful of roads leading in and out through densely populated, upmarket towns like Laguna Niguel and Aliso Viejo, it made little sense for petty criminals to wander this far from their home turf.

"Fine," I heard my dad say. "But don't come whining to me when your face starts leaking."

"When was the last time I came whining to you about anything?" I pointed out, popping my mouthguard back in.

It was true. I was Daddy's little girl, and an only child, but I'd never been the sort to run to my parents in tears, despite being picked on my whole life. Which happens when you're a little different from the other kids. Having an English accent I'd never lost, despite living in America longer than I'd been in the UK, was part of it.

And my *other oddity*, which most people couldn't understand.

Anyway, I preferred to hit back at whatever hurt me. Sometimes that was a merry-go-round, and one time it was a kid named Bobby Garcia, a chubby brat our junior year who thought he'd help himself to a fondle as he passed me in the hallway. He had a permanent kink in his nose after they did their best to straighten out the broken pieces, and I was suspended for two weeks.

Cisco's eyes had changed as we danced around each other once more, tapping the other's gloves with little jabs before stepping clear. I couldn't tell if his new expression was concern or fear. If it was fear, it was of my father, the former British heavyweight champion, not of me.

His next jab flew above my gloves and hit my forehead, fortunately protected by my headgear. My head shot back, feeling like it had been smacked with a baseball bat instead of the extended jab from Cisco. Bloody hell, I thought as I managed to keep my feet moving and duck away from him. *That wasn't even close to a fully thrown punch, and he about knocked my head off.*

I warily kept him a little farther away from me and forced my mind to stay focused on his movements, remembering all the little comments I'd heard my father make over the years. How he coached his fighters to read their opponents and work their weak spots. Which, of course, he'd already spoon-fed to me when it came to Cisco. But to get a punch underneath, I needed Cisco to throw a punch at me first, which he'd just done, and I'd had no idea it was coming. The kid was lightning-fast. He also outreached me by a good amount.

Trying a different strategy, I began dancing more from side to side, hopping from the ball of one foot to the other. My legs ached, but I knew I had to keep on the move, stay ahead of any plan he was forming. I feigned a left uppercut and saw the spark in Cisco's eyes. He really wanted me to do that again. I felt like I was playing with fire, even if the flames were turned down to their minimum. His fear of hurting the trainer's daughter was the only reason he hadn't put me on the canvas by now.

Dipping on my left side, I made like I was going for the left uppercut, but quickly threw a right cross under his left arm. Just as my glove landed, some kind of steam train ran full force into my head.

The canvas blew all the wind from my lungs, and the lights in the ceiling spun circles above me.

"You okay?" I heard Cisco's voice above me. "I'm sorry, Miss Cromwell."

I found my breath, and the room came back into focus. I spat my mouthguard out in a stream of slobber and gasps.

"Don't ever apologize, kid," I heard my father say. "She asked for it."

Thanks, Dad. It was true, but for fuck's sake, he didn't have to start me off with a fighter who had a shot at being state champion this year.

I reached up, and Cisco hooked my forearm, dragging me to my feet.

"You alright, love?" Dad asked, and I looked his way and nodded.

"Best be heading to work, though," I mumbled, and reached out my gloves to Cisco.

He tapped them in return. "Thanks for sparring with me, Miss Cromwell."

I managed a laugh. "Yeah. Showed you a thing or two, eh?"

"First sparring partner to get my chin in the past year," he said.

I leaned against the ropes and held out my hands for my father to unlace my gloves. He had a grin on his face.

"That didn't teach me to know better, if that's why you look like the cat who ate the canary," I told him between pants as I slowly regained my breath.

He shook his head and spoke as quietly as Frankie Cromwell's voice could ever get. "Bin telling that kid someone's coming underneath on him one day, and I knew he didn't believe me. If I'd known all I had to do was stick you in there with him, I would have done it months ago."

"Glad to be of help," I grumbled sarcastically, although I was secretly rather proud of at least connecting with the kid's jaw. I may have only knocked a hair out of place, but at least he knew I reached him. "Are you gonna let me spar properly next time?"

"What wasn't proper about that?"

"You know what I mean, Dad. You had him playing with me. Why can't I spar with one of the newer blokes? Someone with similar experience."

He finished untying the laces and wriggled the gloves from my sweaty hands. "Because they're unpredictable, and that can be dangerous, love."

"You let them spar against each other," I complained as he unwrapped my hands. I felt the relief of the constriction coming away.

"Yeah, but they pay me to let them smack each other. Plus, I promised your mother," he replied, dumping the wad of wrappings into my hand. "I faced some scary buggers in my time, but I'm smart enough not to go up against her when it comes to you. Besides, she's right. Who knows what it'll do to your wiring?"

I scoffed. "Might fix it."

He held the ropes apart, and I jumped to the floor. I turned and gave Cisco a wave. "Thanks for taking it easy on me," I said, and the kid grinned back.

I gave my dad a kiss on his cheek. "Find a non-crazy one for me."

He grunted, and I walked away, glancing up at the clock on the wall between various banners celebrating champions my father had trained over the years. There were a lot. It was 6:35 a.m. If I hurried, I'd catch the sun making its way above the hills and throwing its gorgeous light across the ocean.

Showered and changed, I hurried outside to Doheny Park Road, threw my smelly gym bag in the trunk, and got in my department-issued car. Most of the traffic was heading out of town, but I eased into the flow making its way onto Pacific Coast Highway, which appeared to be backed up from the light at Dana Point Harbor Drive. I switched on the news radio and shuffled along with the rest of the commuters and a handful of surfers making a late start. I made my way over to the left lane and got lucky with the turn signal, barely coming to a stop before catching the green.

I could already see that the coast was clear of the June Gloom morning mists as peeks of the ocean flashed by between the trees in the park at Doheny. It was May, but the fog often defied its name, beginning earlier in spring and annoyingly lingering until summer.

I turned left on Puerto Place, then left again into the parking lot, where my seasonal parks pass allowed me to skip the meter. The surfers had taken most of the spots facing the water, so I parked in the second row and got out, soaking in the sound of the waves on the beach. The cool, salty breeze would frizz my hair, but I didn't care. It was one of the many reasons I kept it short.

On the pathway, I saw a familiar figure, although his movements seemed more peculiar than normal. Erratic. Unsettled.

"Dennis? You okay?" I asked, strolling toward the homeless man.

He startled as if he hadn't heard me arrive, which wouldn't surprise me, given the many voices he appeared to converse with in his head. From the little I'd managed to glean over the years, Dennis had once been married and worked as a manager in a shoe store. An addiction to pain pills after a cycling accident had spiraled his life out of control until he'd ended up on the streets. They say most people are only a paycheck or two away from poverty, and Dennis was a sad example of how that could easily occur when the wrong chips fell a certain way.

"I didn't do nothing," he yelped. "Didn't do it. Not me. Didn't, you know?"

He continued pacing in a circle on the path, muttering and shooting occasional looks my way as though he hoped I'd disappear.

"What didn't you do, Dennis?" I asked, looking around for anything suspicious.

I couldn't see anything except a beautiful morning. Rich colors spread across the water, sparkling off the crests as the long, easy rights rolled in for the longboarders.

"She there," he said, shaking his head while continuing to pace. "I didn't. She there. Already there."

A sense of dread fell over me. The poor man was a few slices short of a full loaf, but I'd never seen him like this.

"Show me, Dennis," I urged patiently, and he pointed to the corner of the beach by the rocks. "Over there? Is there someone over there, Dennis?"

He nodded vigorously and hid his face in his hands, stopping by his shopping cart full of his earthly possessions, such as they were. Walking in the direction he'd pointed, I took the narrow path to the sand alongside the creek leading to the beach. I still couldn't see anything out of the ordinary. I kept walking to where the creek blended into the sand and the incoming waves met the freshwater stream.

And then I saw her. Dropped amid the seaweed where the high tide had reached, nudged up against the rocks, was the body of a woman. I ran over, but from the color of her skin, I knew she was already dead. I took my cell phone from my back pocket and dialed the station.

"Hey, Sarge, this is Kat."

"To what do I owe this honor, Cromwell? If you're calling in sick, you'll be on my shit list until the end of time."

Sergeant Derek Martinez was a career cop after a dozen or so years in the military. He was firm, efficient, and ran the Dana Point Sheriff's Office like a precision Swiss watch. No one knew if he loved, tolerated, or hated them, as he treated everyone like they were always on his shit list. Not sure why, but I kinda liked the guy.

"No, sir. I'm afraid I'm looking at a body washed up on Doheny by the breakwater."

"That's not the way I like to start my day, Cromwell. Think she's a partygoer fallen off a boat?"

"Hardly my favorite way, either, sir," I replied, "But you'd better send forensics."

"What are we looking at, Kat?" he asked, his voice softening.

"I see marks around her neck, sir."

"Secure the scene," Martinez ordered. "I'll get back to you."

Once we'd hung up, I studied the corpse for a few moments, taking in the details and my first impressions. Knowing I needed to lock in this moment, I took my compact instant Polaroid-style camera from my other back pocket and carefully snapped a picture.

2

To my relief, someone had produced coffee amongst the chaos of emergency services, crime scene crew, and pop-up tents erected on the beach. The early morning tranquility had been destroyed by sirens, lights, a gathering crowd, and now news vans arriving.

"Cromwell," someone called to me, and I turned to see Hugo Fuentes, my fellow investigator, waving me up the beach.

The sergeant had dispatched him to join me, which had undoubtedly ruined Fuentes's morning regimen of a breakfast burrito from one of the food trucks on his drive to work. He was a veteran of the force, which made him a lot older than me, considerably more experienced, and pissed off he was even having to deal with someone who he considered a newbie. My three years in the deputy sheriff program, followed by six months under my belt as an investigator, didn't mean squat to him. And never would, from what I could tell. Especially as he was a homicide investigator, and I was assigned to cover any and all major crimes. Except homicides, despite my repeated requests.

The only reason our paths crossed at all was because we were the only two investigators based out of the small Dana Point Sheriff's office. Everyone else reported to the main Santa Ana department headquarters, but first Fuentes, and now me, were an experiment in allowing a few of us to operate closer to the areas we covered. Weekly meetings in Santa Ana kept our leashes tight, for which Fuentes always had an excuse not to carpool with me.

"Her car's parked outside the lot," he told me as I reached him. "Been broken into."

When I'd rolled the body carefully over before the cavalry had arrived, I'd been sure I recognized the woman. Several other deputies confirmed my suspicion. We all knew Helena from a local restaurant where she'd worked for years. Still, we'd need official confirmation from prints as she had nothing on her person to verify her identity. Only her car keys.

We walked across the corner of the park toward Puerto Place, which ran alongside and down the edge of the harbor parking and boat storage to a dead end. The rock jetty continued from there, forming the southern boundary of the harbor itself. Fuentes looked as perfectly put together as he always did. Not a hair out of place, clean-shaven, his shirt ironed, and his suit a perfect fit. I often wondered if he had them tailor-made, but I'd never plucked up the courage to ask.

Uniformed deputies were setting up crime-scene tape on tall orange cones around a minivan as we approached. I'd passed the vehicle when I'd arrived but hadn't paid it any attention. The broken window was on the passenger side facing the park, which explained why I hadn't noticed it. That and the poor early morning light.

"Helena Redman," one of the deputies told us, holding up the registration he'd pulled from the glove box.

I peered in through the driver's door, which the deputies had left open. Apart from the scattered pebbles of tempered glass, the interior looked unmolested. The radio was still in the dash—not that it looked worth stealing—and a sweatshirt lay on the back seat. Fuentes used a gloved hand to open the tail door, which swung up on creaky hinges.

"Empty grocery bags, an umbrella, and a beach chair," he announced unenthusiastically.

"Bit odd, really, isn't it?" I commented. "If she was attacked—"

"She was attacked," Fuentes interrupted. "She has strangulation marks around her neck, and her skull is crushed in."

We were trained to talk about cases in terms like "probable" and "suspected" until the fact in question was proven by evidence or testimony that would hold up in court. But my partner was right, and we both knew it. Still, he was being a prick, as usual.

"So, what's odd?" he pushed after I didn't continue.

"Well, the perp didn't smash the window to take her from the minivan, right? So why smash the window?"

"How do you know she wasn't inside?" one of the deputies asked. He was a younger guy, probably mid-twenties like me. I'd seen him around the Dana Point station, but I had to glance at his tag to recall his name. Ripley.

His tone was interested rather than challenging, so I pointed to the two front seats.

"There are pieces of undisturbed glass across both seats."

"So, there couldn't have been anyone sitting there," he said, nodding slowly.

"You two start searching the bushes," Fuentes ordered the deputies. "All around here, and toward the crime scene."

"What are we looking for?" Ripley asked.

Fuentes stood with his hands on his hips and stared at the younger man. "Evidence. We're cops. That's what we do."

Ripley's mouth began to open, but he kept himself in check. His partner muttered something under his breath as he walked away.

"In particular, we're looking for a purse or handbag," I explained. "Maybe a cell phone. There isn't anything in the vehicle, and only keys in her pockets."

Ripley nodded his thanks to me, then followed his partner and began searching amongst the trees and bushes surrounding the park. Fuentes used his radio to request another deputy to come guard the minivan now that he'd sent the first two away. Once I noticed one heading our way, I began walking down Puerto Place. Fuentes fell in step next to me.

"Break-in could be unrelated," he said as we stayed by the edge of the curb.

The roadway sat atop the landfill used to form the south side of the harbor. Parallel to us on our left, the beach gently sloped away toward the water, and we passed by the crime scene, now six feet below us at the foot of the huge rocks used as riprap.

"Fits, I suppose," I replied. "The minivan's parked in an odd spot, and by her body temperature, she died more than a few hours ago."

I chewed that over in my mind and shivered as I recollected touching the woman's cool, clammy skin. The cold water of the Pacific Ocean would have expedited the drop in body temp, but I was still sure the medical examiner would come up with a time of death in the middle of the night.

"Maybe she caught the perp breaking into her vehicle?" I suggested. "They struggled, and she wound up dead."

We carefully surveyed the rocks as we walked, looking down at the ocean below us. The jetty formed the breakwater throwing up the long, gentle waves Doheny Beach was renowned for, and surfers bobbed astride their longboards in the lineup a hundred yards to our south.

"Then why was she here?" Fuentes asked in return.

I wasn't sure exactly why the man was conversing with me at all, as it went against all our interactions to date, but I was happy to ride the wave until it would undoubtedly come to a condescending end.

"Meeting someone?" I responded.

He nodded as we strolled on, stopping every few yards when we noticed trash wedged in the rocks. The carelessly lost or discarded detritus of boaters and fishermen.

"She parks. Meets someone. The killer leaves on a boat?" he offered.

"Doubtful," I replied. Fuentes wasn't a waterman, but I'd grown up in Dana Point and spent my life in and on the coastal waters. "Doheny is a long, shallow beach. Hard to bring a boat even close to shore. Maybe a kayak or paddle board, but they're not exactly the best getaway vehicles."

He paused and looked back at where the deputy now stood near the minivan. I followed his gaze, shifting to the beach where they were finally moving Helena Redman's body on a gurney that had to be carried across the sand. We both pivoted and stared toward the end of Puerto Place, where the narrow road made a tight loop around a public restroom building.

"So, they met in the park, or on the beach," Fuentes hypothesized. "She was attacked near the water, then dumped there against the rocks. High tide washed any evidence away."

We continued walking.

"It's possible she came down to the beach, perhaps after leaving work," I said, making a mental note that someone should drop by the restaurant when they opened. "Looking for a little peace and quiet at the end of the day, and she was jumped by a complete stranger."

Fuentes made a low, thoughtful groan, but I couldn't tell whether it was in agreement or opposition.

"She's clothed," he finally said.

"True," I agreed, and not because of the fact that she was wearing clothes. That point was obvious, but I knew what he meant. The medical examiner, or ME as we referred to them, would confirm the fact, but it was unlikely Helena had been sexually assaulted. Putting clothes back on corpses was a time-consuming and clumsy business that perps rarely stuck around for, or had any interest in.

If her attacker had been a stranger, the city could have a bigger problem. Helena may have been his first victim, but she wouldn't be his last. That's how serial killers got started. We also needed someone to check the database for similar MOs back at the station in case he'd found a taste for killing somewhere else.

"It's possible the attacker found a rope or something handy on the beach, but my guess is he came prepared," Fuentes said as we came to a stop at the loop. "Autopsy should narrow down what was used. Didn't look like a belt mark to me, though."

I nodded my agreement and stared at the rocks between us and the water, now eight feet below. I stepped closer and almost tripped over the brightly painted red curb. My foot landed on the top of the first of the dark gray boulders, angling steeply toward the ocean. My eyes flicked to my planted foot, which had saved me from falling. My thighs ached from my workout that morning. They both complained more when I crouched down, used a wadded-up nitrile glove in my hand, and reached between the smaller rocks filling the gaps between the boulders. I pulled out a black plastic wristwatch. Its band was broken away where it should have attached to the watch casing by a pin.

I stood and showed Fuentes.

"Hasn't been there long," he commented.

He was right. It looked clean. Anything left out in the elements near the ocean quickly discolors and or corrodes. There were no inscriptions on the cheap timepiece, and it was still working, showing the correct time.

Fuentes turned and began studying the roadway for tire marks or other items. I stared at the rocks below me. Seagull droppings in various states of decay peppered the riprap, giving the seawall a lighter and mottled tone.

"These on all night?" Fuentes asked, and I spun around to see he was pointing to a streetlight on a concrete pole with a decorative bell-shaped shroud.

I thought for a moment. I'd been on Doheny Beach late at night, after the park had officially closed. Every local kid had at some point in time. I recalled it always being pretty dark.

"I don't think so," I replied, making another mental note for someone to check with the harbormaster's office.

I glanced to the boat storage yard on the far side of Puerto Place. Vessels of all shapes, sizes, and ages were sitting on trailers, some covered and some exposed to the elements, such as they were in

Southern California. I spotted several more poles with modern-looking light fixtures attached.

"I expect those over there stay on," I said. "Or at least operate on motion detectors."

Turning back to the rocks below me, my eyes immediately fell on a darker marking. I wrapped the watch in the nitrile glove, set it down on the ground, and began picking a path down the boulders. I remember my mum yelling at me when I was a kid while we'd walked the same road, telling me to stop playing around before I fell in. The descent did seem more precarious than I recalled it being as a ten-year-old.

"What the hell are you doing?" Fuentes asked, watching me from the road.

It dawned on me that I couldn't picture him doing the same thing. He'd order a uniform to do it rather than mess up his carefully manicured nails. Hugo was divorced, and while we'd never discussed our personal lives—we'd never really discussed much of anything before—I had the impression he was playing the field pretty hard. South Orange County certainly had an abundance of well-maintained divorcees filling the internet dating sites.

Had this been an internet date gone wrong? So far, we'd not found a cell phone, but I notched up another note in my head about checking for a computer at Helena's home. I needed to write these thoughts down before I forgot them. Although, I doubted Fuentes would have any interest in my input on his case. Quite why he was humoring me now was still a mystery.

My foot slipped, and I banged my knee on a boulder, letting out a grunt. It made me wonder if my head might be bruised where Cisco had clocked me, but now wasn't the time to check. One more step down, and I reached the mark I'd seen from above. I grunted again, this time for a different reason.

"Better get forensics here next," I said, looking up. "We may have found the kill site."

As Fuentes called it over the radio, I looked back at the sticky mess of blood, hair, and what I guessed to be skin on the corner of the rock. It was just above the high tide mark where the water stained the rocks.

Glancing back and forth from the road above to the water below, I realized something. Helena had been one rock away from landing in the ocean. Someone had launched her body from the edge of the road, and going by what I could see, her head had been the only part of her to hit the rocks. Although she'd been strangled, so I doubted she was alive when it happened.

Climbing a few steps back up the riprap, I took the instant camera from my back pocket and recorded the scene.

3
______

Once uniforms cordoned off the rocks, we walked back to the park, where several deputies gathered around an area near a bench. Fuentes had fallen silent, which I assumed meant he was sick of the sand getting in his overpriced shoes and was ready to leave. Or he was simply done humoring me.

"Found what appears to be blood," Deputy Ripley said as we approached.

"You don't know blood when you see it?" Fuentes fired back.

Ripley wisely ignored him and looked at me. "Could be from the vic. I saw the head wound."

"We have more blood along the jetty," I replied, crouching down to examine the stain on the concrete. "Can we put a fast-track on forensics to see if they all match?" I added, looking up at Fuentes.

He nodded. "Have you turned up anything else?" he asked, still focused on the deputies.

They shook their heads.

"Seriously? We have blood here, and 200 yards away, a body on the beach, and a minivan 100 yards over there," Fuentes ranted, pointing across the parking lot. "And you guys have found nothing else?"

Ripley's partner shrugged his shoulders, unintimidated by the investigator. I noticed his badge read Hanson.

"Can't find what ain't there, sir," the deputy snapped back as I knelt and took an instant picture of the blood, making sure to include the park in the background. Framing the scene was important to me.

Fuentes groaned as he looked in the direction he'd just pointed. "Shit," he mumbled.

I stood and saw Captain Roberta Bradley purposefully striding our way while my picture took its forty-five seconds to develop. She was diminutive, maybe four inches shorter than me, but filled the height she'd been given with a full figure. The woman carried herself with an air of authority and confidence I admired. Hugo probably disliked her for the same reason, and for the fact she was a female holding a position of authority over him, although I'd never heard him say as much. From all I'd seen, Bradley had earned her way into the rank and did a solid job in a difficult role, which everyone above, below, and all around wanted to throw darts at.

I figured I'd like her even more if she didn't seem to have it in for me.

"Don't suppose this is a slam-dunk case with the perp handing himself in?" Bradley said as she reached us. "You found the vic, Cromwell?" she added.

I figured her first question was rhetorical. "Yeah. Homeless guy I know was acting weird, ma'am. He led me to the body washed up on the beach. Strangled, by the marks on her neck. She's also suffered a head wound, and I think her nose is broken. Traces of blood here and down the road on the rocks."

The captain looked around in the general direction of the places I'd mentioned. "The minivan?"

"Belongs to the vic," I replied. "We think it was broken into after she'd gotten out."

"You already have a positive ID?" she asked a little more pointedly. "I was told she didn't have any identification on her."

She was still looking at me, so I answered but dared not look at Fuentes. I was certain he'd be steaming. He was the homicide investigator; I was only there because I'd been first on scene by chance.

"I believe Fuentes has asked for her prints to be run asap, ma'am," I answered. "But I recognize her, and the minivan is registered to Helena Redman. She's a local. Works at Capistrano Bay Tavern."

Bradley nodded, then looked from me to Fuentes, who I could now see was doing his best to appear uninterested.

"Anything else worth mentioning, Hugo?" the captain asked.

"No, ma'am," he replied. "Once we get verification from her prints, we can drop by her residence and check with the restaurant."

Bradley nodded again and turned back to me. "You found her, Cromwell, and I spoke with the chief at homicide. We agreed this can be your case."

My mouth fell open, and I stood there speechless.

"Seriously?" Fuentes challenged, hands on hips, towering over the captain.

"Seriously," Bradley barked back. "And don't puff your damn chest out at me, Hugo. Someone gave you your start years ago. Now she's getting hers."

Fuentes eased back a step and muttered something incoherent in Spanish behind gritted teeth. The captain returned her attention to me.

"Press'll be up my ass, but that's my problem, Cromwell. Wrap this one up tightly, okay? Make sure you've buttoned everything down before the DA gets the case. Don't rush things, but hurry up and get on with it, if you catch my drift."

I caught her rather loaded and broadly targeted drift. *Solve the case quickly and don't bugger it up* was the gist.

"Yes, ma'am," I replied, finding my voice.

"She's lead?" Fuentes asked, making no attempt to cover up his displeasure.

"You'll work the case together, but yes, she's lead. To begin with, at least." Bradley replied with a stern look, but a hint of amusement in her voice. "It'll be a good experience for you both. Cromwell needs to show us old-timers what she can do, and you can demonstrate your mentoring skills, Hugo. Keep me looped in as well as your chief."

Bradley strode away without another word, leaving Fuentes clenching his jaw and me wondering whether the captain was showing faith in me for once or setting me up. The only people seeing the lighter side of the situation were the two deputies, who couldn't hide the smirks on their faces. I felt comfortable assuming their glee was aimed more at Fuentes than me.

My cell rang, and I saw it was the station calling. "Cromwell," I answered.

"We have the prints back already," Sergeant Martinez informed me. "She was in the system as a witness from years back. Matches the registration of the vehicle. It's Helena Redman."

"Can you send me—" I broke off as a vibration through my phone told me my question was moot.

"Texted the address," the sergeant confirmed, then the line went dead.

"Confirmed ID," I said to Fuentes, passing the phone to him. He seemed to have unlocked his jaw and reconciled the situation enough to at least look at me without daggers in his eyes. "I have the address," I added.

He grunted and walked away, which I took as our plan to visit Helena Redman's home and do the toughest and most unpleasant part of our job: the death notice. Many times, a uniformed deputy took care of the task, but I refused to shy away when it was a case I worked.

It was a rare occasion when a police cruiser parked outside somebody's house and a cop knocked on the front door to deliver good news. Unless the missing child or dog was with the deputy, of course. But seeing a deputy at your doorstep looking like they'd rather be anywhere else was a dead giveaway. Rightly or wrongly, I felt like it softened the lead-up to the inevitable gut punch if two people in sport coats walked up the driveway.

Of course, I'd also never informed anyone that their loved one had been murdered before. We'd been taught that the act of delivering the worst news of someone's life was cripplingly heart-breaking, but every once in a while, you stared a guilty party in the face, and their poor theatrical reaction gave them away. Partners and lovers were the go-to first suspects in murder cases, so I wondered who would open the door at the Redman residence.

Fifteen minutes later, after Fuentes drove us to the apartment on Olinda Drive, leaving my car at Doheny, he let me take the last step towards the front door and knock. *Your case. You're up.* He didn't say it, but I could read as much from the way he hung back.

The apartment was what I guessed to be a converted double garage next to an older two-story home. If Helena Redman was living here, then she either knew the homeowner or someone else was contributing. Not a chance that a waitress's salary could afford even this pokey little place in Dana Point anymore.

My heart sank when the door opened to reveal a teenage girl who already looked like she knew. But not in the guilty-partner way. The kid was scared of what we were about to say, even without us wearing uniforms.

"Is this Helena Redman's residence?" I asked, trying my best to keep an even voice as I held up my badge. "I'm Investigator Kat Cromwell with the Orange County Sheriff's Department, and this is Investigator Hugo Fuentes."

The girl's brown eyes flicked between the two of us and our badges, which never failed to garner a reaction. Fear, contempt, joy —the list went on, but I'd never pulled the badge and been met with an impassive expression.

"Is it my mom?" the girl stammered.

"Are you Helena's daughter?" I asked, cautious of being swept into a circle of confusion.

The girl nodded. "Mom didn't come home last night."

"Is that unusual?" Fuentes asked, and I wanted to punch him in the face.

"May we come inside?" I quickly intervened, and the girl stepped back, allowing us to pass.

I understood the need for first reactions. People out of their comfort zones were more likely to speak the truth or lie poorly. But damn, give the kid a break. I was confident she didn't strangle her mother and launch her off the sidewalk into the ocean.

The inside of the apartment was old but clean and tidy.

"What's your name?" I asked.

"Scarlett," the girl replied, her voice still shaking. If I judged the look in her eyes correctly, she was on the verge of panic.

"Is your father home?" I asked, already knowing her reply as I surveyed the décor. Too many candles, no men's shoes by the door, and the TV wasn't nearly big enough for a man to be living there.

Scarlett confirmed it with a shake of her head.

"Anyone else home?" I continued while Fuentes walked around the living room, looking at photographs and making the poor girl even more nervous.

"No. It's just mom and me."

"Do you have any other family nearby?"

I fought to keep the relief from my face when she nodded.

"My grandparents. They live up the hill. What's going on? Where's my mom?"

"How old are you, Scarlett?" I asked. My guess was fourteen, but it was hard to tell with kids sometimes.

"Fifteen."

"No school today?"

Scarlett frowned at me. "My mom didn't come home. I didn't know what to do."

"Have you called your grandparents this morning?" I asked.

She shook her head.

"May I ask why? If you were worried about your mum, how come you didn't call your grandparents?"

I expected an eye roll, but to the kid's credit, she just frowned again and looked down. Okay, now was a more appropriate time for Fuentes's question. If there was ever an appropriate time to question a kid whether her mother sleeps around.

"Does this happen often?" I asked, and heard Hugo scoff behind me.

"No. Never," Scarlett replied with a certainty in her voice. Almost an urgency. *Was she covering for her mother? Or hating the idea we'd get the wrong impression?*

"Let's call your grandparents," I suggested, but Scarlett didn't move.

"Where's my mom?"

"I'd like to speak with your grandparents and see if they can come by, and then we can discuss what's going on," I explained, hating the way I sounded.

Scarlett pulled her phone from her pocket and scrolled through her recent calls until she found a number and hit redial. She'd had to scroll a long way to get past what I imagined to be all the unanswered attempts to her mother's cell.

"Nana, it's me," she said. "The police are here, and they won't tell me what's going on."

I could hear a raised voice on the other end, and I held out my hand. Scarlett handed me the phone.

"This is Orange County Sheriff's Department Investigator Kat Cromwell. Who am I speaking with?"

"This is Shirley," the woman replied in a flustered voice. "I'm Scarlett's grandmother. What on earth is happening? Is Scarlett in some kind of trouble?"

"Not at all, ma'am," I replied. "But would it be possible for you to come here right away? Or can we bring Scarlett to you?"

I could hear a man's voice in the background as Shirley mumbled and bumbled for a moment.

"Either, I suppose," she finally managed. "Could you please tell me what's going on?"

"We'll bring Scarlett to you, ma'am," I decided, figuring I'd expedite the process. "We'll be by in a few minutes."

I hung up with the grandmother and ignored Fuentes's disapproving glare.

"Does your mum have a computer?" I asked Scarlett.

She pointed to a well-used laptop on the end of the kitchen counter. Hugo nodded and left to get an evidence bag from the car.

"Is your mum's cell phone here?"

Scarlett shook her head. "She has it. She always responds to texts within a few minutes."

"You've texted and called her last night and this morning, right?"

"A bunch. I woke up at midnight and noticed she wasn't home when I got up to use the bathroom. I called, and it went straight to voicemail. Been the same since then. I left messages."

"Do you two have a tracking app to see where you are?"

Scarlett nodded. "Yeah, but her phone's not showing up."

"Okay," I responded. "Can I look in her room?"

Scarlett led me from the living room into a short hallway with three doors, which were all open. On the right was the girl's room, which was only big enough for a twin bed and a dresser. The bedroom on the left was larger with a neatly made queen bed, dresser, and full-width mirrored doors to a closet.

I moved inside and looked around. Apart from a pair of jeans and a lightweight sweater draped over the end of the dresser, the room was spotless. On the bedside table sat a picture of Scarlett, a clock radio, and a paperback novel.

"Where does your father live?" I asked.

"I'm not sure," Scarlett replied. "We never see him."

I wanted to dig further, but it would have to wait. I hadn't taken a picture yet, and I could feel my anxiety rising.

"Bring your phone, and the keys to lock the door," I told her.

We returned to the living room, where Hugo had bagged the computer. Before walking out, I stood by the doorway and took a picture of the little apartment. I figured it ought to be enough, but I could never really tell. No two situations were ever the same.

With the girl directing my partner between awkward periods of silence, we drove a couple of miles up Golden Lantern to an older home off Camino Del Avion. When we arrived, both grandparents were waiting in the driveway. As far as death notices went, this one was turning into a train wreck. It took several minutes to shepherd the family inside the house and park their arses in chairs. By the time I'd accomplished that much, the grandfather was the only one not in tears. Adding to the chaos, their golden retriever flitted between everyone, sensing the trauma in the room. Fuentes was of zero help, and was probably enjoying the shit show, notching up the marks against me.

Looking around the living room, pictures of Scarlett were prominent, suggesting she was their only granddaughter. I guessed they were very involved in the girl's life. Of course, they probably hadn't planned on being as involved as they were about to be. I also spotted pictures of Helena at various ages, some with a boy I assumed to be her brother. There was only one picture of siblings as adults.

My focus shifted back to the family, who stared at me expectantly, and I took a deep breath.

"I'm sorry to inform you that we found Helena's body at the beach this morning," I began, continuing despite Shirley's wails of grief. "Her death is being investigated as a murder."

"Who?" Helena's father demanded. "Who did this?"

Wrapped in her grandmother's arms, Scarlett stared at me, stunned, tears streaking down her cheeks. It was a typical reaction for many people, even when they knew what was coming. Somewhere deep inside, disbelief held the news at bay until the words were finally spoken. Meanwhile, her grandfather had skipped directly to the anger stage.

"We don't know as of yet," I responded. "Our first question for you is the obvious one. Who might have had a reason to harm your daughter?"

"The beach? You found her at the beach?" he fumed, ignoring me. "How was she killed?"

I glanced at Scarlett, then back to the man who'd identified himself as Bob Redman when we'd arrived.

"We can't speculate on the cause of death until an autopsy has been performed, sir," I replied, which wasn't always true. In this case, we didn't know if Helena died from strangulation or the vicious head wound that I assumed came from the rocks, so it gave me an excuse not to discuss any of it in front of Scarlett.

"Can you think of anyone who might have had reason to harm Helena?" I asked again.

Shirley picked her head up and wiped her face. Fuentes finally participated by handing over a box of tissues, which he found on an end table by the sofa. Shirley blew her nose and handed a tissue to Scarlett, who'd freed herself from her grandmother's embrace.

"Our poor girl," Shirley said, fighting back the sobs. "I can't imagine anyone wanting to hurt her."

"Scarlett told me her father isn't around much," I queried. "Is there any animosity there?"

Shirley squeezed Scarlett's knee. "He's long gone. We never even discuss him."

"Darian Rutherford," Bob offered. "They were high school sweethearts, but he took off when…" He trailed off and checked himself, running a hand over the bald spot parting the sea between his short gray hair. "He came around a few times afterwards, but to my knowledge, it's been years since Helena has seen him. Works fishing and crab boats up Oregon way, I believe."

"Was she dating anyone lately?" I asked, making a note of the father's name.

Scarlett and Shirley both shook their heads, but Bob groaned and leaped to his feet.

"That son of a bitch, Wendell," he hissed, and the two women swung their heads his way.

"Chris?" Shirley responded. "He would never hurt Helena."

"The hell he wouldn't," Bob rebutted, stomping back and forth across the living room. "Damned stoner."

4

Fuentes started the car and turned on the AC. It was 70 degrees outside, typical for late spring, but the sun was intense through the windshield. I would have just rolled down the windows, but he probably didn't want to ruffle his hair.

I waited while the latest instant picture I'd taken finished developing. Snapping a photograph of a room full of grieving family felt incredibly invasive, so I'd hopefully nonchalantly taken a pic while holding my camera as I'd walked out. The camera I used these days wasn't actually the Polaroid brand. Someone had made an instant camera that was the size of a modern smartphone, just thicker to accommodate the print heads. It fit into my back pocket. People often thought I was using my cell phone until the picture began spooling from the slot.

"Well?" Fuentes asked, looking down the street rather than at me.

What was the saying? "Teamwork makes the dream work." Clearly, Hugo's idea of teamwork on this case was for me to make every decision so he could point the finger at me if I failed to make an arrest. Apparently, he was content for his mentoring reputation to take the hit. Not that he had a positive rep for helping anyone out or guiding young investigators, so a hit to something already on the canvas didn't make much difference.

"I'll call in the ex-boyfriend and see if we can get an address if you'd like to drive us to Capistrano Bay Tavern," I said. "See if we can start piecing together her movements from last night."

Hugo responded by driving away from the grandparents' home, so I called the sergeant and requested anything he could dig up on Christopher Wendell. I also gave him Scarlett's father's name to see where he showed up these days. It was tempting to have a go at guessing Helena's password for her laptop, but the IT guys had a conniption the last time I did that. I was convinced it was because they were pissed off I'd cracked the password without their fancy software, but they insisted on quoting pages of protocol BS in response.

The Capistrano Bay Tavern was the latest name for a restaurant that had been a Dana Point fixture for as long as I could remember. It used to be called The Renaissance. Why it was called that, I had no idea, but they served good food and had a small stage where bands played on Friday and Saturday nights. I also didn't know why they'd sold the place, as it had always seemed busy to me. But the new owners rebranded, as the marketing people called it. They'd added a bar outside on the patio and continued doing stellar business. At least that was how it appeared from the line waiting to be seated at the weekends. A few of the old staff had stayed on, which was why I'd recognized Helena, although I hadn't recalled her name until I'd been reminded.

The lunchtime patrons were all seated on the patio, so we walked inside and approached the long bar where one waiter cleaned glasses and smiled our way.

"Lunch is served outside," he said. "The hostess can seat you."

I flashed him my badge, which quickly sent his smile running for cover.

"Is the owner or manager here?"

"Sure. Just one moment," the guy replied, and scurried into the back.

I always wondered exactly what it was someone like that thought they'd done that made them nervous of two police investigators. Forgot to pay a parking ticket? Ran a red light last week? Or maybe this guy knew something about Helena Redman being strangled? The average citizen generally reacted with a look of guilt when the badges came out, so it was hard to know.

A tall, auburn-haired lady in her late forties appeared from the back with a concerned look on her face. No doubt the bartender's message of cops in the restaurant hadn't been received lightly.

"I'm Caroline Russo, the owner," she said. "How can I help you?"

"Cromwell and Fuentes with the Orange County Sheriff's Department. Is there somewhere private we could speak?" I looked over at a table in the corner, well away from the customers outside.

"Certainly," Caroline replied.

She came around from behind the bar. She was taller than me, with an exceptional figure, which I caught Hugo admiring as she led us to the table. Going by her toned legs, I'd say the woman certainly made good use of a gym membership. Once we were seated, I opened the conversation.

"Does Helena Redman work for you, Mrs. Russo?"

"Yes, she does. Is everything okay? Is she in some kind of trouble?"

"Could you tell us when you last saw Helena?" I asked, keen to get a few crucial questions in before delivering the bad news.

Caroline thought for a moment. "Last night, I suppose. Helena closed for me."

"You were here when she closed up?"

"No. I left around 9:45. We close at ten."

"Who was still here when you left?"

Caroline looked off into the distance, considering the question. "Helena, one of our other servers, and a couple of busboys, I think. The kitchen had closed, and the chef had already left."

"How did Helena seem to you?"

"Is she okay?" Caroline pressed, but I didn't respond, waiting for her to answer my question, which she finally did. "Normal, I'd say. I didn't notice anything unusual."

"Did she mention where she was going after work?"

"No. She usually goes straight home. She has a teenage daughter."

"Has she been seeing anyone lately?" Fuentes jumped in. Which surprised me. I'd already become accustomed to him sitting there like a spare part.

Caroline shook her head. "Not to my knowledge. Between work and her daughter, I don't think Helena has much time for a love life. Can you two please tell me what's going on now?"

I figured we'd held out long enough.

"I'm afraid we found Helena's body at the beach early this morning," I said. "We're treating the case as a murder inquiry."

Caroline gasped and clutched her face with both hands. "No!" she exclaimed through her fingers. The woman's body visually shivered, and her cheeks turned red. "Poor Scarlett. I can't believe this."

I gave her a minute, and Hugo went to the bar, returning with a handful of paper napkins. He was showing himself to be useful when the tears started.

"You hadn't noticed anything out of the ordinary in the past few days or weeks?" I asked once Caroline had settled down and wiped her eyes.

She shook her head. "Helena was the best employee. More than that," she corrected herself. "A friend."

"You spent time together outside of work?" I asked.

"Well, not really," she admitted. "Work friends, I suppose. But we talked, you know? She shared things with me. It wasn't your normal boss-employee situation. We were more like coworkers."

"But she hadn't talked to you about any particular problem lately?"

Caroline paused and contemplated again. "No. I think she was in a good place. I mean, it's been months since she finally kicked her boyfriend to the curb."

"Are you referring to Chris Wendell?"

She nodded. "He used to work here part-time behind the bar. He's a charmer. Chris doesn't even try, but he's just one of those guys who makes everyone around him smile and have a good time."

"Why did they break up?"

"They were good together for a while, but it was the same as why I had to let him go from here. When anything gets serious, Chris flakes. He's simply not wired to hold down a routine or responsibilities. They dated for over a year before Helena let him be involved with Scarlett. He was supposed to pick her up from school, but he forgot. Or the surf was up, or band practice. Who knows? She let it go the first time, but when it happened again, she realized their relationship was heading nowhere. Just like Chris. He'll always be the fun, good-looking, carefree guy, but nothing more."

I wasn't sure what to make of Caroline's detailed description. It certainly supported the fact that she and Helena had discussed things on a personal level, but I was yet to hear any reason Chris Wendell had for brutally murdering a woman he broke up with many months ago.

"Did Chris ever threaten Helena?" Hugo asked, so it appeared we were thinking along the same lines even if we weren't discussing anything.

"Not that I'm aware of," Caroline replied. "But I did hear that he took the breakup badly. He smoked a little weed, like everyone else, but I heard he'd moved on to more serious drugs after they split." She shrugged her shoulders. "But that was gossip, so I can't say for certain."

She looked across the restaurant as a tall, well-groomed, gray-haired man walked in.

"Felix," she called out.

The man approached our table and we all stood.

"It's Helena. She's been murdered," Caroline blurted, and he paused short of the table, looking stunned.

"Helena? My God. Who would ever harm Helena?"

I introduced us both, and he shook our hands with a firm grip.

"I'm Caroline's husband, Felix," he said, then dropped into the fourth chair next to his wife.

"How well did you know Helena?" I asked, carefully observing his reaction.

The question was unsubtly loaded, but the man didn't flinch.

"Not as well as Caroline, but she's worked here since we bought the place a few years back, so I've spent time around her in the restaurant. I run our other businesses, you see. Caroline heads up the tavern."

"Other businesses?" I questioned.

"We have a couple of liquor stores," Felix replied. "One here, one in San Clemente."

"Do you know Chris Wendell?"

"Sure," Felix replied. "He's the bartender who worked here for a while, right?"

He looked to his wife, who nodded but didn't meet her husband's eye.

"Is he a suspect?" Felix asked, turning back to me.

"Early days," I replied. "But we intend on speaking with the bloke. Any other former boyfriends you could tell us about?"

"You're sure it was someone she knew?" Felix asked. "I mean, I know the spouse or lover is always the first suspect, but Chris seemed harmless enough to me. He's not the kind to go out of his way for anyone or anything. He's a lover, not a fighter, as the saying goes."

I glanced over at Caroline, who sat there passively. Except her left eye twitched, and her forearms tensed for a moment before she forced herself to relax. The definition in her muscles was still clearly evident, and I upgraded my theory from simple gym membership to regular sessions with a personal trainer. Her physique came from a long-term commitment to being in amazing shape, especially at her age. I wondered if I could stay committed to working out for that long.

"The other staff who were here last night," I said, moving on, "we need to speak with them. Are they working this evening?"

"Yes," Caroline replied. "They'll be here at four if you'd like to drop by again."

"As close to four as possible would be best," Felix added. "At five, we get busy for happy hour and then dinner."

I rose from my chair. "Thank you both for your time. We'll be back to speak with your staff."

Fuentes began walking away, but I paused. "May I take a quick picture of the two of you?" I asked. "Just for my own notes. We speak to a lot of people, and it helps me keep everyone straight."

Felix shrugged his shoulders, but Caroline frowned. By the time I held my camera up, her expression had softened. She didn't smile but lifted her chin into a well-practiced and elegant pose.

"Thanks again," I said, and jogged to catch up with my new partner.

Taking a quick glance back, I noticed Caroline began crying once more. Her husband put his arm around her, and she didn't brush him away.

"What do you make of those two?" I asked Fuentes once we were back in the car.

"Somebody's been screwing the staff," he scoffed.

"Yeah. That was my impression."

"Doesn't really connect us to Helena Redman being strangled on Doheny Beach, though, does it?" Fuentes added.

I thought for a moment. He was probably right, but the timing would be interesting to know. Before I could further the conversation, Fuentes waved a hand at the picture developing in my hand.

"What's the deal with the pictures?" he asked. His tone was more challenging than curious.

"They help me remember," I replied. Which was true.

"What's wrong with the camera on your phone?"

I tried to keep my voice even and not be baited. "Nothing. I like having the snapshot."

He was staring at me. "You realize it freaks people out, right?"

Outside of talking about my fiancé, my strange picture-taking habit was the last thing I wanted to be discussing with anyone, but especially Fuentes.

"Maybe Helena was about to tell somebody about it," I said, completely ignoring his statement that he'd loosely phrased as a question.

He took a beat, then thankfully responded about the case. "Seems to me like they both already know, and they know that the other knows. If you get what I mean."

"Then perhaps Helena just spilled the beans, and someone was mighty upset about it," I suggested.

Hugo shrugged his shoulders. "We have an address for the bartender?"

"Yeah. Sarge texted it while we were in there. Head for the Beachwood Trailer Park."

"Figures," Hugo grunted.

As we left Capistrano Bay Tavern, two things struck me as noteworthy. Something had certainly happened in the Russo household involving the man we were hoping to see next, and I'd just had a brief conversation with my new partner that could almost be construed as productive.

5

Most of the trailers in Beachwood Park were newer modern units. Some were even what I believed they called modular homes, but a few hailed back to the days of basic single-wides and showed their age.

Chris Wendell's unit was one of those. A Hispanic man answered the door, opening it a crack to ask who we were, and seemed relieved when we asked after Wendell. A dog barked from inside as the man went to find his roommate, who appeared after a minute, shushing the dog before looking us over.

"Can we speak outside, Mr. Wendell?" I requested as the unmistakable scent of weed wafted out of the open door.

He closed the door behind him and walked down the steps as I introduced ourselves and we showed him our badges. He seemed relatively unfazed, but it wasn't his first time having the police knock on his door. The rap sheet Sarge had sent showed several possession charges before cannabis became legal, an old DUI for booze, and one receiving-stolen-goods charge, which appeared to have been dropped.

He was as I'd pictured from Caroline's description. A lean surfer's build with broad shoulders, shaggy, sandy blond hair, and something more than a five o'clock shadow but not quite a full beard. Chris exuded a laid-back California vibe that most of us who grew up here moved on from after high school, but it was easy to imagine how for some, an evening of tequila and charm could wind up as a night in a trailer park.

"Can you tell us where you were last night, Mr. Wendell?" I asked as we stood behind an older Jeep with faded yellow paint and no top, parked under a carport attached to the mobile home.

"I worked a shift at Salty's, then came home," he replied, edging over to block our view of the expired tag on his license plate.

"What time did you leave Salty's?" I asked.

He ran his hand through his hair, thinking too long about the question.

"It's not a trick question, Mr. Wendell. Salty's closes at eleven. Or is it twelve?"

"Eleven during the week, midnight or so Friday and Saturday," he replied. "So, I guess I left after I cleaned up. Would have been around 11:30."

"You don't sound sure?" I countered.

"Hey, what's this all about?"

"When was the last time you saw Helena Redman?" Hugo asked, and his timing was perfect. He'd been silent until this moment so his pointed question had an impact, which was clear by the mixture of shock and concern on Wendell's face.

"Is Helena okay?" he replied. "I haven't talked to her in ages, maybe a month or more."

"Her body was found on Doheny Beach this morning," I responded, hoping Hugo would take another jab. He didn't disappoint.

"So, perhaps you'd like to be more specific regarding your whereabouts last night. Was your roommate home? Can he corroborate your story?"

"Oh, shit," Wendell gasped, and leaned over with his hands on his knees. For a moment, I thought he was about to vomit, but he straightened up with tears forming in his eyes. "This can't be," he muttered.

"Let's get your roommate and see if he can support your story," I suggested, but Wendell held up a hand.

"Manny works nights, man. He wasn't home." Wendell wiped his face and pulled himself together. "I was home before midnight, but you guys can't possibly think I had anything to do with hurting Helena. I loved her, man. Seriously, things didn't work out with us, but I would have done anything for that woman."

"You must have been pretty pissed off when she dumped you, then," Hugo said, fully embracing the bad-cop role.

Wendell gasped and shook his head. "Come on, man. Sure, I was bummed, but that's how shit rolls sometimes. I loved her enough to want her to be happy. I tried being what she needed, but I'm no good at the parenting and partner stuff, man. I get it."

"This your vehicle?" I asked, pointing to the Jeep.

"Yeah."

"Any plans to leave town?"

"No, man. I've got work lined up for weeks."

I didn't bother asking for permission before I snapped an instant photo, then handed him a card with my number.

"Okay. Thanks for your time, and sorry for your loss," I said, although after the verbal beating we'd given the guy, I couldn't blame him for looking at me like I was full of shit.

"He didn't strike me as the violent type," I said as Fuentes drove us out of the trailer park.

"Killers aren't all facial tattoos and the aggressive, up-in-your-grill types, Cromwell. Don't underestimate what a jealous lover can do in a fit of rage," he replied.

I choked back my initial reaction to his condescending response. "I was going to add that he's hiding something on the timeline," I said instead. "He was either too stoned to remember, or he didn't go straight home from closing the bar."

"Yeah, I caught that."

"Maybe we can catch him on CCTV from last night. That Jeep is distinctive," I suggested.

Fuentes grunted a response. Even though we didn't have access to many cameras in Dana Point, searching through footage was still monotonous and time-consuming. We could put in a request to the tech department, and they'd run it for us using recognition software, but we wouldn't get anything back for weeks with their backlog. So, if we wanted answers quickly, we had to sit down at a computer and roll through the footage ourselves. I couldn't see my new partner doing that.

"I'll drop you at your car," he said, turning left on Doheny Park Road, then taking the slip road onto PCH. "I'll take the computer by the station."

"Okay," I replied, although slipping away at 3 p.m. on day one of a murder case didn't seem appropriate to me. "I'll swing by the restaurant at four and speak with the other staff."

"I have paperwork I need to finish and turn in," he added.

That was still a shitty excuse in my book. Maybe he wanted to update the captain in person and let her know I was absolutely nowhere on the case. But there was nothing I could do about either of those things except keep pursuing the leads we turned up.

"Her cell phone and purse, if she had one, are still missing," I said, thinking aloud and hoping my partner would act like a partner. "We know the phone is turned off and probably already has the battery and SIM pulled, but maybe the killer is hanging on to them as trophies."

"More likely, they're in a random dumpster or city trash can," Fuentes replied, turning left on Dana Point Harbor Drive. "Besides, we'd never get a warrant to search Wendell's place with the little we have so far."

I thought that over for a minute as we waited for the turn light at Puerto Place. He was right. Unless forensics turned up something, we were thin on evidence of any sort.

"You know what's puzzling me?" I said.

"Couldn't even begin to guess," Fuentes replied.

"Why her minivan was broken into. If the blood near the bench in the park belongs to Helena, then it would appear the killer attacked her, or at least struggled with her there. Maybe she ran, and he caught her down the road," I continued, pointing to where we'd found the watch and more blood on the rocks along the harbor jetty. "Strangled her, then threw her in the water. Body washes onto the beach with the incoming tide. Sound about right?"

Fuentes parked next to my OC sheriff's-issue black Ford Fusion. "Something like that."

"So why break into the minivan?" I asked again.

My partner just looked at me and didn't say anything.

"Her keys were still in her pocket. Why didn't he take them and just unlock the doors?" I pressed on.

"Maybe he broke into the minivan before he attacked her?" he finally replied, dragged into participating. "Or he didn't check her pockets before he threw her into the water."

"Let's assume the uniforms did their part, and neither a purse nor the cell phone are in the park or along the jetty," I said, preempting his customary critique of the boys and girls in green.

"Could be in the water," he reluctantly admitted.

I nodded.

He grinned. "You want to call out the divers?"

"I think we should."

"You're the lead. It's up to you," he said, still smiling.

I got out of the car and closed the door. It was good that Fuentes was going his own way for the rest of the day. I was getting close to punching him. Which would finally convince the captain I was indeed a hothead who couldn't keep herself in check.

One incident in uniform, and I'd carried the reputation with me ever since. And then there was my fiancé, of course. An accident, at least that's what it had been ruled, but I knew what they were thinking behind the looks.

Maybe they were right. I couldn't remember, and boy, had I tried. None of my usual tricks could pull the details from the depths of my broken mind. A self-protection mechanism, the shrink had told me. But she didn't know about my faulty wiring.

I sat in the car with the door open and called Sergeant Martinez.

"Busted the case wide open, Cromwell?" he said in way of a greeting.

"Not yet, sir," I replied. I was out of energy to play any more games with the swinging-dick club. "Can we put a couple of divers in the water along the jetty, sir?"

"I was wondering when you'd ask," Martinez commented, now making me feel like I'd screwed up for not asking earlier.

"Thanks. Fuentes has the vic's computer, sir. He's on his way. Email and dating sites would be the priority."

"Anything else?" he asked, and I honestly couldn't tell whether he was being facetious or just asking me.

"Not at the moment, sir. Oh, wait. Could you run background checks on Caroline and Felix Russo, please? They own the restaurant where the vic worked. Capistrano Bay Tavern."

"Suspects?"

"Unlikely, but there's a connection involving them and Helena's ex-boyfriend, who we just interviewed. I'm heading back to the tavern now to meet with the rest of the staff from last night."

"Alright. Check your email in a while," Martinez responded.

"Oh, and one more thing, sir," I said quickly before he hung up. "Any chance uniforms could drop by Salty's and verify Chris Wendell's movements last night? He worked bar and said he left after cleaning up once they closed."

I heard a deep sigh. "I'll see what I can do," he replied before the line went dead. I still didn't know whether he'd been taking the mickey or just being helpful.

My next call was to the harbormaster's office, who bounced me around a few times before a guy in a maintenance division was able to tell me the lights along Puerto Place stayed on all night. And no, they didn't have any cameras facing the street, only the boat storage and the marina itself.

While I was on the call, my mum texted me.

"Heard about the Doheny woman on the news. Very sad."

At least she hadn't heard about Dad letting Cisco punch my lights out.

I typed a reply. *"Yeah. My case. Won't make it this evening."* My mum liked to longboard in the late afternoons if she didn't have after-school classes.

"Good for you. Tough case, I would think, but you'll get them."

Typically optimistic. My mum saw the bright side of everything, which made her a great drama teacher at the high school.

Thinking about my old school gave me a thought.

"Know Scarlett Redman? Freshman."

"Yes. It's Scarlett?"

I could feel the dread radiating from my phone. Not from the words, but from knowing how much my mum cared for her students. For everyone.

"No. Her mother. Good kid?"

I didn't even know why I asked that. I couldn't imagine it was relevant to the case. Curiosity, I suppose. Or caring about the kid. I hoped I inherited some of my mother's empathy even if I didn't get either parent's height or her stunning looks. Although people told me I did—her looks, that is. To me, though, she was drop-dead gorgeous, and I was average. The really hot blokes in school had never pursued me.

But that could also have something to do with punching guys who grabbed my arse.

"Quiet. Not in my classes."

"Thx. Gotta run," I texted back, to which I received a heart emoji.

I laughed to myself. My mum understood that I was at work and had shit to do. Dad would have kept on asking questions until he found out whatever he wanted to know. They were chalk and cheese in so many ways, but somehow it had worked for thirty-two years of marriage.

By the time I'd driven up the hill to Capistrano Bay Tavern, it was a few minutes after four. I spoke to the waitress and both busboys. None of them recalled anything out of the ordinary, and they'd all left by 10:15 p.m., leaving Helena to lock up. According to the staff, the victim mentioned nothing about going to Doheny or anywhere else. I asked Caroline to check the alarm records, which showed Helena's code was used at 10:27 p.m. It would be days before we had the ME's autopsy report, but I already knew it would give a time of death with a relatively wide window. Partial submersion in water played havoc with a corpse's body temperature.

The hours following a crime were considered critical. Perps were running, cleaning up, or panicking. After two days, if serious progress hadn't been made, it was generally considered to be a long-haul case with an increasing chance of going cold as time wore on. But just like Fuentes's bullshit, I couldn't let the pressure get to me. As the uniform had said that morning, I couldn't find what wasn't there.

I sat in my car and checked my email. Nothing yet from Sarge, which surprised me. He was usually quick, or, to be more accurate, he was usually quick at having one of the office staff get the reports out.

My phone rang in my hands, showing one of the station numbers.

"Cromwell."

"It's your lucky day," Martinez offered.

"How come?" I asked. Nothing about the day had felt lucky for anyone so far, starting with a punch I hadn't seen coming. It had gone downhill from there.

"Rideshare driver just came by with dashcam footage from last night."

"No shit? Does it show Helena?"

"Nope. But it shows a guy breaking the window of her minivan," Martinez replied.

"And the driver didn't think to call that in?"

"Says he didn't see it. Caught the news and realized he'd been in the area last night. I can tell him we can't use it if you like?"

Okay, now I knew he was being facetious.

"Got an ID on the perp?" I asked.

"No clue. I'll send it out for facial recognition, but I think it's too grainy to tell. Sending you the clip now."

My cell buzzed. I put Sarge on speaker and opened the text he'd just sent. He was right—the video was terrible quality. The man was on the backside of the minivan, and as the camera went by on Dana Point Harbor Drive, it only caught a brief glimpse, although it was clear the thief was swinging something at the window.

"Wait," I blurted. "The white pickup parked up the road. Can you get anything from that?"

"Look at you, Miss Nancy Drew," Martinez ribbed. "Or whoever the British Nancy Drew is. Anyway, one step ahead. No license plate legible, but it's a Ford Ranger extended cab. Fuentes is here, and he ran all the names connected to the case so far through the DMV."

"And?" I dutifully asked after the sergeant left me hanging.

"Helena Redman has a brother. White 2008 Ford Ranger registered to Travis Redman. Gave the parents' address."

"No shit?" I muttered again, trying to visualize the Redmans' living room and coming up blank.

"No shit," Martinez echoed, and hung up.

I dropped the phone on the passenger seat and pulled my photos from my pocket. Shuffling through them, I found the one I'd taken that morning. The Redman family in various states of torment, in their perfectly put-together suburban living room. Everything we'd spoken about came rushing back to me like an avalanche of sounds, smells, and visuals.

I sat back in the seat and clearly saw the photograph I'd noticed of the man I'd presumed was the victim's brother. Travis Redman.

6

———

Warrants don't magically fall out of the sky like confetti at a Hallmark movie wedding. The process took time. We had to fill out a sworn statement showing probable cause and then get a judge to agree and issue the warrant.

Contrary to popular belief, judges weren't readily accessible outside court hours. By the time I arrived at the station, Fuentes had filled out the paperwork, but the duty judge was gone for the day.

It wouldn't be until 8:30 a.m. when we'd get the final signature needed to proceed. The warrant would cover Travis Redman's vehicle and place of residence. All we had was the address on the registration, which matched his driver's license, but I had a hard time believing a 26-year-old guy still lived at home. Especially one with a DUI conviction for weed on his record, as well as a breaking-and-entering charge. Or maybe they were the reasons he was forced to still live with Mummy and Daddy. He was sitting on two strikes under California law. One more felony conviction meant mandatory jail time. I wished I'd asked the Redmans about him that morning, but it hadn't sprung to mind while I was delivering the death notice.

I checked that Helena's phone records had been requested, then spent some time searching open cases that could have a connection. Nothing jumped out at me. I couldn't rule out a random act of violence, but then why did she drive herself to Doheny after work? A question we were yet to answer.

Next was social media, hunting for anyone who'd made a scathing comment on Helena's page. She didn't post much, so it didn't take long. Occasional pictures of Scarlett's activities, and shares from the restaurant. I then searched for as much background information on the victim as I could find. Again, she was a law-abiding citizen who wasn't in the media, so I spent far longer searching than learning much.

Moving on, I burned through a couple of hours looking at CCTV recordings we had immediate access to in Dana Point. It was laborious, and none of them gave me anything interesting. I was focused on the white pickup, of which there were plenty, but had no luck spotting the one belonging to Travis Redman. Or Chris Wendell's yellow Jeep, for that matter.

Some might consider it suspicious that two vehicles we knew had driven around the town late that night had avoided all the cameras, but with so few camera locations, it didn't seem strange to me. I'd asked Caroline Russo about cameras at the restaurant, but she'd told me they didn't use them, which was unfortunate. Seeing Helena leave might have given us some indication of her state of mind through body language. Although twenty minutes earlier, all had seemed fine, according to her co-workers.

One thing we did have now was a slightly better timeline, and I began plugging what we'd learned into a spreadsheet. We knew she'd set the alarm at 10:27 p.m., and the timestamp on the rideshare driver's camera showed the minivan being broken into at 12:10 a.m. Scarlett's call went straight to voicemail at midnight. Unless Helena had turned off her phone or ran out of battery, it pointed towards her already having been attacked. If the police divers found her phone in the water, it would further support that theory.

I had my pictures spread out across the desk in front of me, in the order I'd taken them. Of the six, three scenes were already clear to me. Two others surged back when I studied the pictures. The last photograph, of the blood on the ground at the park, came back slowly. I recalled the deputy sheriff and the tense conversation with Fuentes, then the man's name. Hanson.

It took me a minute before all the details fell back in place. That was the way it worked sometimes.

Why was Helena's blood, if it was her blood, found in two locations?

I sat back in the chair and let out a long breath, reminding myself once more to let the evidence speak to me. It was human nature to plug in pieces of which we had no proof if they felt like a good fit. Travis Redman murdered his own sister, then broke into her vehicle to retrieve something he didn't want anyone else to find. From what little evidence we had, it certainly seemed like the best fit. But what about motive?

Shutting down my laptop, I stood and stretched. According to my Tag Heuer Carrera watch that Dad went crazy and bought me after I became a deputy sheriff, it was five past eight. I'd put in a long day. Not long enough to do Helena Redman justice, but at least we had a lead to follow in the morning.

I packed up and walked outside to the car. The evening had already cooled off, and the ocean breeze felt chilly through my blouse.

Driving home, I couldn't stop thinking about Scarlett. What a day for that kid. Her father appeared to be out of the picture, but that was another loose end I needed to follow up on. Out of the picture didn't necessarily mean the guy didn't have a beef with Helena. Maybe we'd caught a lucky break with the dashcam footage and Travis, the brother, was our guy. But I couldn't forget about other leads and lines of inquiry until we knew for sure.

I arrived home and parked the car on the street. Under normal circumstances, I would never have been able to afford a home in Dana Point. In fact, I doubted I could afford a home anywhere in

California with the prices such as they were. Mum and Dad bought two old fixer-upper beach cottages on Copper Lantern when I was only ten. The housing market had crashed, and they saw an opportunity to pick up the properties to refurbish and rent out. They told me the plan had always been to give me one of them when the time was right. Graduating from USC and diving straight into the Deputy Sheriff's Training Program had apparently been the right time.

I'd been grateful every day ever since. The cottage was only 800 square feet, but it was mine, and I loved it.

My fiancé, Paul, could never understand why I wouldn't let him move in so he could give up his apartment and save himself a ton of money. After all, he already stayed with me most of the time. It wasn't easy to explain that it was my space. My sanctuary. I'd be forced to let the drawbridge down to my castle and relinquish my independence when we were married, but for a reason I wasn't completely sure about in my own mind, I wasn't ready yet. So I lied. I told him my parents were old-fashioned when it came to living together, but I wondered if he'd ever truly believed me.

Of course, that didn't matter anymore. Paul was gone, and I still had my castle.

I hated cooking. I didn't consider myself a foodie and would be content to live on fish tacos and wine for the rest of my life. Which was reflected by my fridge and larder rarely being well-stocked. Sprinkling a double helping of slightly stale Raisin Bran into a bowl, I threw not-quite-expired milk over it and called it dinner. My mum enjoyed good wine and had attempted to pass on her sommelier knowledge to me, but four years at university on ramen noodles and now living on a county cop's salary meant my Chardonnay came from a box.

I switched on the TV and found a rerun of an old series I'd always loved. I could remember each episode from all ten seasons and often found myself reading the lines along with the actors. Such was the weirdness of my stupid, broken brain. It had an amazing capacity for retaining information, and most of the time, it let me access that detail. *Most* of the time. Watching the show, I chuckled a few times and almost forgot about my day while I ate my cereal.

Throughout all the training, coaching, and mentoring they throw at you when you're becoming a cop, one message they hammer home relentlessly is figuring out how to switch off. Police officers at all levels burn out at an alarming rate. If you can't find a way mentally to step away from the job after your shift, the scumbags and tragedy will eat you alive.

That's what they say.

In reality, the best investigators take their work home and never completely leave it behind. Some of them grind out a career and make retirement. Some don't. I knew I should work harder at balancing the job with life outside of the badge, but work was all that had kept me going over the past eight months, and I still wasn't ready to face the real world.

I finished my glass of wine and turned off my friends. As I went to bed, I wondered for the umpteenth time if I should get a cat. It would feel good to have someone pleased to see me when I came through the door. Dogs were reliable for that, but my life didn't lend itself to the routine required for a dog. A cat made its own routine, which, with my luck, would probably result in it completely ignoring me when I came home. Resulting in me feeling worse.

As I lay down and closed my eyes, I decided for the umpteenth and one time that I was better off alone.

It was almost always the same. It's dark, although it wasn't actually nighttime when the accident happened. A tempest rages, whereas the reality was closer to four-foot swells and a nasty rain shower.

We're adrift with engine trouble. Which was accurate. And we were fighting. Which was probably also true. Everything else could be exactly as that dreadful day played out, but I had no idea.

The nightmare was so familiar to me by now that truth and fiction blended amongst the pieces I thought I remembered. The farther I got from the event, the more the lines blurred, and the more I distrusted my fragmented memory.

It's a nightmare, so nothing works like real life. Sometimes we're on a sailboat, other times it's a floating lorry. Once, it was my third-grade classroom thrown around by the violent seas instead of the Four Winns cuddy cabin cruiser belonging to Paul's parents. Regardless of how the dream plays out, one thing I know beyond all doubt: I come to with a sore face, a nasty cut on the back of my head, and my fiancé is gone.

I jolted awake, and the clock read 4:58 a.m. If I tried going back to sleep, the nightmare usually returned in some shape or form, which I couldn't face. I had another nightmare to deal with today.

For a while after the accident, I couldn't shake the only snippets I could recall in my mind. I think that's how the dreams began. Exhausted, I'd finally fall asleep with the vision already playing in my head. These days, it would only return every few weeks. Typically, when I was completely stressed and most needed rest.

My alarm would have gone off at 5:15 am, anyway, so I swung my legs out of bed, used the bathroom, then put on my gym clothes. Running a few minutes early, I made coffee before throwing my work clothes in a duffel bag and heading for the car. I really needed to buy a hanging bag of some description to put my jacket, pants, and blouse in instead of the gym bag, which didn't smell great. But I hated shopping nearly as much as I hated wearing slacks and a jacket, so I'd perpetually procrastinated.

Working out sucked, but it felt good. Given that I'd grown up around a boxing gym, exercising was in my DNA. I couldn't imagine life without it, but it still sucked. Boxers trained hard, though, so I had plenty of motivation around me and usually came away feeling inadequate but better prepared to face the day.

"Mum told me you got your first murder case," my dad said, leaning over me as I bench-pressed a respectable amount for my size. A weight he could lift with his little finger.

"Yeah," I grunted as I finished the set.

"How's it going?" he asked, sliding five more pounds on each side and standing behind the rack to spot me.

"One promising lead," I told him. "We'll find out more this morning."

He knew by now I couldn't discuss case details, but I also knew he wouldn't talk about it with anyone except my mum. Telling either one of them anything meant they'd both know within hours. I swear, sometimes it was like they were telepathically linked.

He nodded, which meant he understood. It also implied I should do another set. He didn't know I'd already done three sets. Or then again, perhaps he did.

"Two more," he said when I struggled on the eighth rep.

I grunted and groaned but squeezed out two more. He took the bar from me when I finished and placed it gently in the rack as though he were moving a toothpick. My dad wasn't all cut and bulging muscle like a bodybuilder. He was simply brawny. He still worked out every day but was careful not to injure himself, telling me he kept it up because he'd never known a world in which he didn't.

I loved being around my dad. He had a way of calming me and making me feel like everything would be okay. Except when he'd stuck me in the ring with Cisco. Actually, that wasn't true. He'd even made me feel like that would be alright. Otherwise, I wouldn't have done it.

Showered and dressed, I drove along PCH and pulled through PC Beans, the little local coffee shop that had been there ever since I could remember. Officially, the place was Pacific Coast Beans, but no one in Dana Point ever used the full name. Even the signs inside read PC Beans. My order came out with a drawing of a sheriff's badge on the paper cup instead of my name, so I knew Joanna, a girl I went to school with, was the barista.

I left the parking lot with a smile and drove up Ruby Lantern to La Cresta, then across to Golden Lantern, where I turned left. Continuing up the hill, I passed Dana Hills High School and wondered if Scarlett Redman had slept last night. The thought caused a lump to form in my throat. Partly for the poor girl, and partly from the crushing weight of responsibility I felt to find her mother's killer.

I pulled into the station more motivated than I could remember being in a long time. In at least eight months, anyway.

7

___

Warrant in hand, I knocked on the Redmans' front door. I heard voices inside, no doubt wondering who was interrupting their grief. Perhaps a neighbor with a casserole and sympathies. The news I had for them was going to be far less appetizing.

Shirley opened the door.

"Detective?" she said, her expression quickly switching to one of hope. "Have you arrested someone?"

The woman's desperation to find a positive in the wake of her daughter's death hit me harder than Cisco's right hook. For a moment, I was stunned into silence. Fuentes stood behind me and didn't offer any relief.

"I'm sorry, Mrs. Redman," I finally managed, not bothering to correct her term "detective" to "investigator." "But that's not why we're here."

Her face returned to one of devastation. Her husband joined her from inside the house with their dog in tow.

"Come in," he offered. "How can we help you?"

His eyes moved from Hugo and me to the two deputies leaning against the patrol car blocking the driveway beside the house. Bob had offered for us to come inside, but was yet to move and allow us to do so.

"Is your son Travis here?" I asked.

Both parents looked at me, and I watched their bodies tense.

"No. Why do you ask?" Shirley responded.

"Does Travis live with you?" I persisted.

"Here, and at a friend's place," Bob replied, his brow furrowed in confusion. "If he works late, then he usually stays with his friend."

"Did Travis stay here Tuesday night?"

Bob shook his head, moving a leg to one side to block the golden retriever from exiting the house. "Why are you asking about Travis?"

My optimism about having our killer in custody this morning was rapidly dwindling. If the apartment was in Travis's name, we'd have a strong argument that the warrant extended to include a second residence, but a crash pad in someone else's name was a separate warrant. By the time we had it signed, Travis's parents would have called their son. If not to warn him, then at least to ask their boy what could possibly be going on.

"Have you spoken to him in the past two days?" I asked.

"Of course," Bob replied, his voice becoming angry. "His sister was murdered yesterday. I called him after you left."

Shirley began sobbing, and Bob put his arm around her.

"You need to tell us what the hell is going on," Bob challenged, no longer looking as though he'd like us to come inside.

Which was too bad, because the paperwork in my hand was all the invitation we needed. Except now I was certain we'd find nothing useful here.

"We have a warrant to search your house and Travis Redman's Ford Ranger pickup truck," I explained. "We have reason to believe he has information pertinent to your daughter's case."

Now the Redmans looked like Cisco had been let loose on the pair of them. Stunned into open-mouthed silence, they stared back at me in disbelief. But I knew from yesterday's interaction that it wouldn't last long.

"That's ridiculous!" Bob blurted. "Travis would never have anything to do with hurting Helena. She's his sister, for God's sake."

I held out the warrant paperwork, and he shooed the dog back inside the living room before snatching it from me.

"Can you give me the address of his friend's place, Mr. Redman?"

"I've no idea what the address is," he snapped back, shaking his head and muttering between sentences. His caring arm around his wife raised to wave in the air as though it could swipe all the chaos away. "Do you know, Shirley?"

His wife sniffled and caught her breath. "I've no idea. It's in San Juan Capistrano somewhere."

"Friend's name?" I asked.

"Johnny," Bob replied.

"Got a last name?"

They both looked at each other and shook their heads. The picture was becoming a little clearer. Travis was their problem child. No doubt they'd grasped at every straw a parent turns to when they're desperate to get their kid's life on track, from loving embraces to kicking them out. He probably bounced in and out of their lives as it suited him, and they were glad of the time they had with their boy, praying all along that it would work out in the end.

"I don't know the address, but I know where it is," came Scarlett's voice from behind her grandparents.

They stepped aside, and the girl maneuvered forward around the hovering dog.

"It's near the mission, back toward the creek," Scarlett added, looking at me. "What did Uncle Travis do?"

Shit. Now what was I supposed to do? The kid could be our only current option to track down the guy, but we'd have to take her along.

"You need to come with us," Hugo said, finally speaking up when I'd rather he stayed out of it.

"Wait a second," Bob started, moving around his wife and blocking the door. "Scarlett's not going anywhere until we know what's going on and why you're looking for our son."

I sensed Hugo moving toward them behind me, and I held a hand out to stop him.

"Here's what we're going to do," I said firmly. "Mr. Redman, you'll stay here while our deputies serve the warrant. They'll search Travis's room. Mrs. Redman, you and Scarlett will come with us so she has a guardian with her."

I turned and waved for the uniforms to approach the house. Bob began complaining again, but his wife cut him off.

"Let's just get this over with, hon. The quicker they realize Travis has nothing to do with—" she broke off, her voice cracking. "The sooner they can move on to whoever really murdered our girl." She turned to Scarlett. "Come on, dear. Hopefully, we won't be long."

The grandfather stepped aside, and the two women joined me outside the house. I recognized Deputy Ripley from the day before at Doheny Park, and I pulled him aside.

"Don't let the old man call his son, okay?" I whispered.

"Can we stop him from making a phone call?" Ripley wisely asked.

"Technically, no. But ask if you can hold his cell phone while you conduct the search. Hopefully, he'll comply without too much fuss. Take your time and let him stand outside the room."

"And watch us search?" Ripley questioned.

"Yeah. It'll keep him busy," I replied quickly, needing to leave. "I don't think you'll come across anything here tying the son to the case, but I bet you'll find stuff his father wouldn't approve of in his house. That'll help keep him distracted so he doesn't call the bloke and warn him we're coming."

"I gotcha," Ripley replied.

I hurried to the car where Hugo had shepherded Shirley and Scarlett into the backseat.

"You know the warrant doesn't extend to the friend's place," Hugo said, standing on the sidewalk after closing the back door of the Fusion.

"Yeah, but if he's there, his truck will be, too, and we need to get our hands on that," I replied, keeping my voice low so the two women in the car couldn't hear. "And you never know. Maybe Travis will invite us in."

Hugo scoffed. "Two chances. And we should call for uniform backup."

I got in the driver's seat, and while Hugo sat down and buckled himself in on the passenger side, I took care of a little housekeeping. Turning to Shirley and Scarlett in the back, I showed them a picture from the evidence file of the watch I'd found at the jetty.

"Recognize this?" I asked.

They both leaned forward.

"That's Mom's watch," Scarlett answered without hesitation.

"Thanks," I replied, and started the car.

"Feel free to call for backup on the way," I told Hugo as I pulled away from the Redmans' house, U-turning in the residential street.

"Tough without an address for them to meet us, Cromwell," Fuentes rebutted.

"Good point," I replied, looking out the side window to hide my grin. I preferred the small, tactical, and stealthy approach rather than rushing over the hill with an army. I had no plans to wait for backup.

***

True to her word, after a brief hesitation and one wrong turn, Scarlett directed us to a quirky, curving, narrow street between the railroad tracks and the creek, which ran parallel to each other west of downtown San Juan Capistrano. The bungalow on Ramos Way was a modular home, like most of its neighbors, except the others were clean, tidy, and well-maintained.

Johnny's was not. The ten feet of front lawn between the street and the porch was a mixture of dirt and overgrown weeds, while the home was long overdue for attention to the grubby, faded blue paint.

I spotted two vehicles parked alongside the rectangular house on the driveway leading to a rickety carport. A white Ford Ranger sat nearest to the road.

I drove past and turned the corner, stopping out of view of the home.

"Stay in the car, no matter what happens. Okay?" I said, looking over my shoulder at Shirley and Scarlett.

They both nodded nervously. The Fusion's rear doors wouldn't open from the inside, but if they became motivated enough to clamber over the seats to the front, they could get out. Our unmarked cars didn't have cages like those in patrol cars. Hopefully, there'd be no need for one.

Hugo radioed in our position and asked for two uniforms in the area to drop by but stay out of sight of the home. We both got out and closed the doors, meeting a few yards behind the car so we were out of earshot of the Redmans.

"Don't suppose you want to wait for the uniforms?" Hugo asked.

"I'm too worried about the father calling the kid," I replied. "We don't need this guy in the wind."

Fuentes didn't argue the point, but he didn't indicate any form of agreement, either.

"I'll cover the back if you want to knock," I offered.

He thought it over for a moment. "We should stay together. He's a murder suspect."

"Then we can't cover the back," I pointed out, knowing what was coming next.

"Which is why we wait for backup."

"Then I'll knock. You cover the rear," I said impatiently.

Groaning, Fuentes shook his head. "I'll knock," was all he replied before he walked away, turning the corner toward the house.

I jogged in the other direction. None of the immediate homes had fences dividing the lots, so I slipped behind the next house over and found myself behind Johnny's carport. Some long-abandoned vehicle sat under a filthy tarp, surrounded by unidentifiable piles of junk. I moved to the corner nearest the building and listened. Footsteps on creaky wood told me my irritated partner was walking up the steps to the front door. Staying low, I made my way across the back of the house, careful to avoid the empty beer cans lying in the dirt of what a realtor would describe as a "cozy backyard."

There was no back door. Poking my head around the far side of the house, I could only see two more windows. I heard Fuentes rapping on the front door, so I moved back to the corner by the carport. From inside the home, hushed and panicked voices grunted back and forth, although I couldn't make out what was being said.

"Hello, sir, are you Johnny?" I heard Fuentes ask after the front door's hinges squeaked upon opening.

"Who are you?" came a sharp reply.

"Orange County Sheriff's investigator, Hugo Fuentes."

"What do you want, man? I'm busy."

"Are you Johnny?" Hugo asked again.

We'd both looked at Travis's mugshot again on the drive over, so I figured whoever had answered the door did not resemble the crappy picture we had.

"Yeah," I heard Johnny reply. "Those Bible-punching fuckers down the end complaining again?"

"Are you the only person in the house, sir?" Hugo asked.

"Yeah," Johnny lied.

I'd heard two voices.

"Really?" Fuentes questioned. "Travis Redman, who owns the white Ford Ranger parked in your driveway, isn't here with you?"

"No, man, I don't know where the dude is," Johnny lied again.

At that moment, I heard a window slide open. I'd been banking on Travis making a run for his truck, but the sound came from the far side of the home. I might never have heard the window moving in its track if Johnny bothered to clean his home every once in a while.

Sprinting across the back of the house, I turned the far corner as Travis Redman landed in the overgrown weeds below a window twenty-five feet away from me.

"Police! Hold it right there, Redman!"

The young man looked tired, disheveled, and terrified, but that didn't stop him from bolting.

"Bollocks," I muttered, taking off after him as he headed around the back of the neighbor's place.

He angled my way, which allowed me to quickly close the gap, but then I realized why. Travis ducked between two stands of trees where the trodden-down path soon evaporated, and he dodged left when shrubs blocked the way. I was only five or six steps behind, but I'd already lost sight of the man beyond brief flashes of color between foliage. Fortunately, I could still hear his feet pounding on the ground over my heavy breathing.

"Don't make this worse, Travis!" I shouted between gasps as a dangling branch smacked me in the head and scratched my ear as I slid by.

We burst into a small clearing, but he kept running, aiming between another home and more trees. A dog barked from my left, but I didn't have time to check whether it was restrained or joining the fray. Ahead, a wooden fence stood in our path, stretching between the house and another one a hundred feet to my left. The sun-faded red slats didn't look sturdy, but they reached at least four feet above the mowed grass of a far neater backyard we were now crossing.

Travis didn't hesitate. Leaping from several feet away, he vaulted the fence, which shook and rattled from where his left hand catapulted him over. With no time to ponder what lay on the other side, I copied his move and vaulted, swinging my legs to the right while planting my left hand on the top of the fence. Pain shot through my palm as splinters pierced the skin, and my tennis shoe grazed the wood as I cleared the fence. Looking down to spot the landing, my eyes went wide, and I would have shrieked, but there wasn't time.

Both feet landed on top of Travis's prone body, which was crumpled on the ground amid the furrowed ruts of a vegetable garden. Momentum carried me over, landing in my best attempt at a shoulder roll, which didn't quite work out as planned.

Winded, I came to rest wrapped in what I guessed were tomato plants and their trellis-like stick frames. Pushing myself up to my elbows, I sucked in a sharp breath when I saw red splotches all over my slacks, jacket, and white blouse. It took me a moment to realize it wasn't blood. Under my feet, Travis groaned and wheezed.

I clambered up and brushed tomato splatter and pieces of plant, dirt, and sticks from my body.

"Get up, Travis," I barked. "You're wanted for questioning in connection with your sister's murder."

"You broke my fucking ribs," he hissed, clutching his chest.

"Good. The day's not a total loss, then," I replied as I pulled my instant camera from my back pocket.

8

———————

Standing under my shower, I let the water wash away the remnants of the shit show my morning had become. We had the perp in custody, but there would be a standard inquiry into the arrest as the suspect had been injured. And the neighbor lady had threatened to sue over the damage to her vegetable garden. Apparently, a handful of plants were far more important to her than the capture of a murder suspect. A sad commentary on our times. I'd bet money that her stupid garden had its own Instagram account.

If that wasn't enough, Hugo had snapped a picture of me standing in the mud, covered in tomato juice. That delightful moment would no doubt be widely circulated throughout the district before I even made it back to the station.

Toweling myself dry, I did my best to push those thoughts from my mind. Travis would be available for an interview once he'd been discharged from the hospital, where they'd verify he had a cracked rib or two. Perhaps I was supposed to feel bad about that, but I didn't. Annoyed. Angry. Frustrated, I guess. But he chose to jump out of the window and run. What I needed to do now was focus on why he broke into his sister's minivan. Travis Redman had the opportunity and potentially the means to kill his own sister, but what was his motive?

Checking my cell, I noticed I had seven new text messages. Two were from Sergeant Martinez, so I clicked on the first he'd sent.

"Blood matched from both sites at Doheny. Helena Redman."

For a moment, my jumbled brain had me wondering exactly what the message meant, and I rushed to the living room. As soon as I spread my pictures out and saw the one with the bloodstain at the park, everything came back to me.

Despite a lifetime of dealing with my affliction, these moments still sent a wave of panic through me. My biggest fear was being separated from my pictures. A couple of class clowns screwed with me once in high school, taking my camera and pictures away, hiding them from me. I'd been pissed off but unaffected until the next day when a teacher asked me to review for the class what we'd discussed the day before. I had nothing. A blank space in my memory.

The two kids were suspended for two days. I, on the other hand, was suspended for a week for beating the shit out of the pair of them.

I returned to the bathroom and refocused my mind on the case. After getting verification that the watch had belonged to the vic, I'd been confident of the jetty location being where her body had been dumped in the water. But confirmation of the second site near the bench in the park added a layer of complexity to the killer and victim's movements. It also meant they'd spent more time in the area, which opened up the opportunity for someone to have seen them. The park rangers on duty had already been interviewed and as of yet, no member of the public except for the rideshare driver had come forward. But maybe we'd still get lucky.

Sarge's second text informed me the divers had combed the base of the rock jetty and removed three trash bags full of garbage from the water, but there was no sign of any personal effects or cell phone belonging to Helena Redman. The hits kept on coming. Now I'd take shit for ordering a worthless search, although I doubted the captain would take issue with this one as I'd hardly strayed from protocol. But it would be more fodder for my so-called colleagues. More importantly, it meant the items were still at large, along with whatever was used to strangle the vic.

Travis's truck had been quickly searched for anything obvious, then towed to our lab for forensics to conduct a thorough examination. The third text was from Fuentes telling me that apart from spotting a few tiny pieces of glass in the footwell of the Ford Ranger, they'd found nothing worth mentioning and moved on to the house after the extended warrant came through. The other texts were from co-workers sharing Fuentes's picture of me with plenty of laughing emojis and teasing remarks.

Famished by the time I left the house, I dropped by Buena Vista Market in the shopping center and marketplace between PCH and La Plaza, trying not to spill the contents of the two tacos I'd bought down my clean shirt. It was almost 1 p.m. when I parked at the station, took a few moments to compose myself, then walked inside.

"Interview room one," Sergeant Martinez informed me without preamble. "I was about to text you."

I thanked him and messaged my partner, asking him to join me. He didn't reply, but showed up outside the interview room a few minutes later.

"Turn up anything at the house?" I asked.

Hugo shook his head. "Place is a dump. Plenty of weed. Legit prescription antidepressants. Nothing tying him to Doheny from what I found."

"Okay," I said, although I'd been hoping for something more to run with. "Let's see what he has to say."

Travis Redman looked just as bedraggled as when I'd seen him climb from his friend's window. He clearly took the tousled-hair look seriously or simply didn't care about his appearance. The stark gray interior of the small interview room and the caged overhead white light didn't help his pallid complexion.

Travis leaned forward in the chair with both arms wrapped around his chest.

"Ribs hurt like a bugger, yeah?" I said, taking a seat on the opposite side of the table.

I'd cracked one when I was a kid, doing something dumb on a skateboard. The boy who lived four doors down had dared me to jump the ramp he'd built so I didn't have a choice. It sucked. Breathing made me want to cry for the first few days.

Travis looked up at me and nodded. "I need a lawyer?" he asked, his voice low and wispy as he winced in pain.

"Up to you," I replied. "You're here on our request to answer questions regarding your sister's murder. If you think you need a lawyer for that, then of course it's your right to have one present."

"I'm not under arrest?" he asked.

It was hard to tell, as he was speaking quietly to minimize the pain from his lungs on his ribs, but I swear he seemed surprised.

"No, sir," I replied, because he wasn't. Yet.

I gave him the standard spiel about the interview process and recording, which he verbally agreed to after some prompting.

"Let's start with a few basics, Travis. Where do you work?" I began.

"I do day work, so it varies."

"I see," I replied with a smile. "Give us an example. Where's the most recent place you've worked?"

"Last week, I helped out a guy doing a renovation in San Clemente."

"And your place of residence?" I followed up, despite his evasiveness.

"Mail goes to my parents' house."

"But you stay with your friend, John Gerard, a lot of the time."

"Sometimes."

"Great," I said, and smiled again. "Would you mind telling us where you were two nights ago, Travis?"

He didn't look up. "At my buddy's place."

"Gerard's in San Juan? Where we found you this morning?"

He nodded.

"What did you have for dinner?"

His head jerked up to look up at me. "What?" he wheezed.

"I'm curious. What did you have for dinner?"

"I don't know."

"It was two nights ago," I reacted with a chuckle. "Surely you can remember that far back?"

"Pizza, I think," he mumbled.

"Nice. Everyone loves pizza. Where from?"

His eyes shot from me to Fuentes, who stared back with disinterest plastered all over his face. It was either a great ploy, or my partner was truly bored out of his mind.

"No worries, I'm sure the box was still in the rubbish bin," I said as Travis seemed paralyzed to reply. "We collected everything from the house."

"What?" he muttered again.

"It would be a superb way to prove where you were, yeah?" I continued. "Pizza bloke delivers at a certain time, and if you paid for it, we'd know you were there. Your mate Johnny bold-faced lied to my partner here this morning so we can't trust a word he says, you see. If you two hadn't played your silly games, we'd have no reason not to believe him. So, did you pay for the pizza?"

I had a feeling Travis wasn't as dumb as his actions and words suggested, but his paranoia and confusion over what we already knew was spinning his head like a merry-go-round. I didn't wait for a response.

"Were you close with your sister, Helena?" I asked.

Travis nodded. His brow knitted in pain, but I sensed it wasn't his ribs this time. This might be my first homicide case, but I'd paid attention in training and studied on my own. Hurting over her murder didn't make him innocent. Plenty of killers regretted their actions when they realized what they'd done, but it helped me gauge his emotions.

"Do you have any idea who killed her?" I asked.

"It wasn't me," he answered far too quickly. "I loved my sister."

"Did she help you with stuff? You know, be there for you and all that?"

He nodded again. "She's the only one I could rely on. She was always there for me."

His voice cracked under the words, and his eyes turned moist. He sniffled and wiped his face, wincing again when he moved his arm.

"So, who do you think would want her dead?" I asked.

"I've no idea." Travis gently rocked back and forth in the chair, his eyes down.

"You don't seem too keen on helping us find her killer," I pointed out.

"Of course I am," he said without looking at me.

"How about jealous boyfriends?" I suggested.

He shrugged his shoulders. "I don't think she'd been dating anyone lately. She may have hooked up with her ex a time or two, I don't know."

"Her ex? Who's that?"

"Chris. He used to work at the restaurant with her," Travis muttered. "You should talk to him," he added with more conviction.

"Okay, that's good, thank you," I replied, writing Chris's name needlessly in my notebook on the table. "So, let's see if I have this straight. You were at your friend's on Tuesday night. You ordered pizza at some point in the evening, and then what?"

Travis rocked a little more. "Went to bed, I guess."

"About what time?"

Gone were the days when you could quiz a suspect over what they watched on television, as no one watched scheduled programs anymore. Everything was streaming on demand.

"Eleven, or maybe a bit later," he replied.

"And you were tucked up in bed the entire night?"

He frowned at me. Occasionally, my English accent and phrasing were useful for throwing people off.

Travis hesitated as though he was processing what I'd said before he nodded. I had him worried that I was trying to trick him. That was good. He was off-balance.

"Help me understand something, Travis," I said, switching approaches again. "Your sister has been murdered, so naturally, the police show up at your door to chat with you about it. But your reaction is to run. I don't get it."

More rocking and averting eye contact. "I don't know. I've had trouble with cops before. Maybe I panicked."

"It really appears like you don't want us to find who killed Helena," I responded. "I'd have thought you'd do anything within your power to help us."

"I'm here, aren't I?" Travis snapped back.

"Only because we brought you here after apprehending you. What didn't you want us to find?"

"I've got nothing to hide," he replied. He attempted to sit back in the chair defiantly, but groaned, clutched his ribs, and leaned forward again.

I lowered my chin toward Fuentes and waited. He took the hint.

"Then why this stream of bullshit and lies?" he asked.

Travis flinched, surprised by the quiet guy now grilling him. Fuentes's question seemed to hit Travis right between the eyes, as he wheezed and coughed again. It was as if my partner had actually punched the guy.

We waited two full minutes before Travis settled down enough to even speak. I hoped the camera was recording properly. The audio alone might sound like we were beating the living daylights out of him.

"I don't know what you're talking about," he finally groaned.

"The hell you don't," Fuentes rebutted. "We know you broke into your sister's minivan at Doheny Beach."

For a second, I thought we'd be waiting for the coughs and convulsions again, but Travis kept it together.

"You're making shit up," he grunted.

"We have video footage of you smashing her window," Hugo replied. "So quit all the lies, and let's talk about what really happened."

Travis had no idea where to look.

"Your sister was murdered about a hundred yards from where you broke into her minivan," I said, then sat back for Fuentes to bring it home.

"Why on earth did you kill her?" he demanded, tapping a finger on the table.

"I didn't!" Travis shouted. "I want a fucking lawyer, man. I'm not saying anything else."

His attempt at folding his arms to demonstrate his point ended in a pained whimper, so he slumped forward once more and stared at the table.

"Just to be clear, Travis," I responded, "rather than help us understand why you were breaking into Helena's vehicle, you're choosing to lawyer up. Is that correct? You're happy letting us put all our efforts into building a case against you rather than sharing your side of the story, or offering us an alternate theory."

"I don't know who killed her," Travis mumbled. "But it wasn't me. I would never."

"But breaking into her minivan is fine with you?" my partner challenged. "Does that fall under some kind of deranged sibling code of conduct?"

Travis shook his head. He looked like he was about to say something several times, but never actually spoke.

"Come on, Travis. Pull your head out of your arse," I urged. "You're smarter than this. Tell us why you were there and why you broke into her vehicle."

He finally stared right at me. His eyes were the darkest green I'd ever seen, riddled with pain and confusion. I could tell he was on the verge of crying, and his jaw quivered. His truth lay vulnerable and naked behind a fierce but wavering shield of distrust and fear. I was so close to reaching him, if only I could make him believe that he'd be better off confessing. But would he?

"Lawyer," he whispered, and looked down.

I wanted to slam the table with my fist. Travis had been on the brink of talking until surely he'd seen the doubt in my own eyes. We currently had zero presentable evidence to place him at the murder scene itself, and any decent lawyer would tear apart the blurry dashcam video. I let that notion hit me at exactly the wrong moment, and I'd exuded my uncertainty.

"A deputy will be right with you," I said, and followed Fuentes out of the room.

I tightly clenched my jaw and desperately wanted to punch something as we walked down the hall in silence, but abruptly stopped when Captain Bradley came through the door ahead.

"I thought he might break at the end," she said, stopping in front of us.

"Yeah. Sorry," I responded, and wondered how to phrase my explanation for screwing up, but I didn't have a chance.

"You did well," Bradley shocked me by saying. "Are you booking him for breaking into the car?"

"That was my thought," I responded, feeling off-balance myself. "Might be a bargaining chip, and at least we can hold him a little longer."

"Good," she said with a firm nod. "And you never know. Some lawyers are smart enough to advise their clients to come forth with more information. Maybe we'll get lucky."

If the lawyer realized how little we had, he'd be an idiot to advise Travis to say much more, but I nodded in return. Bradley turned to leave us, but as she opened the door at the end of the hall, she paused and looked back.

"You two make a good team."

I watched the door swing closed behind her before Fuentes shoved it open again without saying a word.

9

———————

The rest of my day evaporated with an endless stream of paperwork. The arrest report took four times as long as usual. I deleted and rewrote every line multiple times, overthinking my wording, continually reminding myself that it was worth it. A little extra time now was better than days lost in court defending my arrest while some smarmy lawyer painted me out to be an angry cop using overzealous force. A fence, a vegetable garden, and gravity had all conspired to crack Travis Redman's ribs. I was merely a pawn in their plot. Initiated by the prat running in the first place.

My mum texted, inviting me to dinner. I weighed my options of stale cereal, stopping for food I couldn't really afford, or a home-cooked meal, and made the easy decision. I knew it was my mum's way of ensuring I didn't completely neglect myself, which I often resisted under the guise of rejecting her fussing. But tonight, I was ready for a non-combative environment.

Like half of California, I doubted my parents could afford to buy their house in today's market. My dad ran a boxing gym, and she taught at the high school. Neither brought in great money, but it was what they enjoyed. They'd been afforded the luxury of choice on the heels of having been smart with their former careers and careful with their money. Dad had been a professional boxer and parlayed his British heavyweight championship into endorsements and then a commentator gig in the US. Mum had been a model, then an actress. Her childhood was the reverse of mine. Born in California, her parents moved to the UK when she was three. My mum and dad moving to America was partly to be around her family, who'd returned after Mum had left home.

Growing up, I'd only known two homes, and the first in England was a faint memory kept alive by photographs. Like many things. We'd moved to the States when I was only six years old, so my parents' house on El Camino Capistrano was a place of great comfort and familiarity. It also had an amazing view from the south-facing bluff across the harbor to the Pacific Ocean, with Catalina Island in the distance to the west. On a clear day, we could even see the profile of San Clemente Island, nearly sixty miles away.

I parked in the driveway and walked through the gate to the left of the triple garage. From the street, the house had a humble and less-than-stunning appearance. Garage doors and an entryway filled the width of the lot under a red Spanish tile roof. But through the gate, a courtyard filled with flowers and small trees stretched to the house itself, a single-level, three-bedroom abode with a similarly tiled roof. Simple, practical, and maximizing the location without being pretentious, which happened to perfectly describe my father.

"Hello, love," Dad said as I opened the sliding glass door we always used instead of the formal front entrance. He was sitting on a bar stool at the kitchen counter while Mum made dinner.

"Hey," I greeted them, dropping my backpack by the door so I wouldn't forget it.

The backpack was my version of a briefcase, which I never left in the car in case of a break-in. There wasn't always vital or confidential paperwork in it, just usually my notebook and computer, which didn't need to end up in the wrong hands. My security measure was sensible, but it meant I always had to remember to take it whenever I left places. So after forgetting it several times, I'd discovered tripping over it helped.

Truthfully, it was now an ingrained process so my broken brain could remember every time, but I could still overlook things like anyone else.

"I made pasta. I hope that's okay?" my mum asked, knowing full well it was more than okay with me.

When I did cook at home, pasta was my go-to, but that was mainly because it was fast and simple. My sauce came from a jar, whereas Mum's would be homemade and much tastier.

"Glass of wine?" she asked as I dropped onto one of the bar stools.

"You can bung it in a glass or hand me the bottle," I said. "Either's fine."

"That kind of day, then?" Dad chuckled.

I stared across the kitchen and through the windows, where the orange hues of sunset mixed with the glow of lights emanating from the harbor below.

"I landed on my head in a bunch of tomato plants before lunch," I moaned. "That's how good today was."

"Are you okay?" Mum asked, concerned.

Dad laughed. "The bigger question is what the tomato plant did to get arrested."

"Frankie!" Mum scolded. "Your first concern should be about the health of your daughter."

"She walked in here, didn't she?" he retorted, still chuckling at his own joke. "Looks fine to me. Apart from that scratch on your ear," he added, pointing to the side of my face.

"I'm going to have a beauty of a bruise on my thigh, too," I said, pressing the tender spot. "But it wasn't like I was punched in the head," I added, raising an eyebrow at my dad.

"The trick to not being smacked in the head," he replied, grinning, "is to read your opponent so you know it's coming."

"Sometimes, when you're fed to the wolves, you don't have time to sort that out, Dad."

"Should I consider this to be whining? Or regret, perhaps?" he said, barely keeping a straight face. "I seem to recall someone asking, no begging, and now all I hear is whining."

I glared at him, but couldn't keep it up for long. We both cracked up laughing, and he reached over with his big paw and ruffled my hair.

"We're not still talking about tomato plants, are we?" Mum questioned, putting two plates of food on the counter. "And I'm pretty sure I should be mad at the pair of you, but dinner's ready. Take your food and drinks to the table."

We did as we were told, still chuckling under our breath. It felt great to smile and laugh, even if it was only a brief respite from the murder case. And everything else on my mind. I was glad I'd accepted Mum's offer.

We ate for a while with small talk about Mum's school and the gym, steering clear of my work, but when I pushed my plate away, too full to eat anymore, Dad couldn't resist any longer.

"I bet that new case of yours is a tricky one."

It was one of his typical queries. Not really a question, but more of a line, carefully phrased and spoken in a supportive manner, cast into the water to see if he could get a bite. I was sure he didn't plan or scheme it that way; it was simply his nature. Curiosity mixed with concern. If I threw him back a "Yes," he'd do his best to resist asking anything more, and Mum would intervene if he tried.

In an ideal world for my dad, there'd be a bad guy he could grab by the scruff of the neck and shake the meanness out of them so he could fix things for me. He still saw me as his little girl, but life didn't work that way anymore. It wasn't like third grade when Sean Jackson shoved me to the ground and Dad scared the kid so badly, the little bugger peed his shorts. Which was a shame. Sean Jackson deserved what he got. But let loose, maybe Dad could shake a confession out of Travis Redman.

"Yeah," I replied, and considered stopping there, but found

myself continuing. "We have a suspect, but no evidence that would hold up as yet."

"Is that Mr. Tomato Plant?" Dad asked.

His question was humorous, but his expression told me he didn't intend it to be.

"Yeah," I said. "It's the vic's younger brother."

"Oh no. How awful," Mum responded, and looked thoughtful. "I think I remember a Redman boy from a few years back."

"In your class?" I asked, surprised that the man I tackled today would be in drama. Although he certainly created plenty for me.

"No. But I recall the last name for some reason. Maybe it's because I've been thinking about poor Scarlett Redman."

"Her uncle is Travis, if that helps," I suggested.

"Yes, that's him. Travis Redman," Mum replied. "Unfortunately, I'm pretty sure I'm recalling the name for the wrong reasons. He was suspended, if I'm not mistaken."

"Sounds like the guy," I confirmed. "I saw Scarlett today."

"How is she holding up?" Mum asked.

I shrugged my shoulders. "Keeping it together, I think. She helped us find her uncle."

Mum shook her head, her eyes full of pain. If empathy was an Olympic sport, my mum would have more medals than Michael Phelps. It still amazed me how she married a man who made his living punching people in the face.

I guess the gene pool split down the middle when they had me. I sympathized with some people and punched a few of the others.

"Any idea when she's coming back to school?" Mum asked.

I hadn't asked Scarlett, but it was an interesting question. If I were her, I'd go back as soon as I could just to get away from Shirley and Bob, who I sensed were imploding from their own grief.

"I don't know," I replied honestly. I finished my wine and eyed the bottle sitting in the middle of the table.

"Coming by in the morning?" Dad asked.

I sighed and pushed my empty glass away. "Probably. I should get home."

I hadn't realized how much I'd needed a little family time to remind me the earth was still on its axis. But I knew I'd be running the case over in my head before I went to bed. The longer I stayed here, the later that process would finish and allow me to attempt rest.

"Sorry to eat and run," I added, getting up and taking my plate to the kitchen.

My dad rose, too, and left the living room.

"That's okay, you're busy," Mum said, clearing the other two plates. "It's good to see you."

"Best meal I've had in ages," I said, intending to compliment the cook, but Mum looked at me with the sad-eye thing, and I wished I'd phrased it differently.

Paul, my fiancé, had been an excellent cook. Eight months can seem like forever, but in other ways, it felt like we were still together just a week or two ago. An image flashed through my mind of Paul in my little cottage kitchen, making dinner for us both while I studied files on the sofa.

I walked back to the living room and met my dad, who'd returned from his office in the back of the house.

"Here," he said, handing me an old photograph.

It was of me, standing by a tent next to a river with mountains towering in the background. Yosemite. The memory of our camping trip when I was in fourth grade came back to me in a steady stream of almost overwhelming senses and moving pictures. I could hear the water rushing by and the birds calling overhead. My mother's laughter. The smell of pine trees and the flowers in the meadow.

For a moment, I felt completely enshrouded in the memory. Transported to the past and returned to the banks of the river, where I relived the soft touch of the breeze on my face. I slowly turned in a circle, taking in the magnificent scenery, lost in the purest joy reserved for a child. That all-encompassing elation born of innocence before life's stresses invaded, never to be completely shoved aside again.

As smoothly and methodically as the memories had flooded back, they receded, and my senses returned to the present. I quickly handed the picture back to my father, who immediately tucked it into his back pocket.

My parents had a limited supply of similar pictures that we'd learned could be brought out once every three or four years and would, most of the time, remain effective. My dad knew to use them sparingly. Once a more solid connection to my long-term memory took hold, the effect was lost. Sure, it was nice to recall those moments whenever I wanted, or parts of them at least, but nothing like the onslaught of happiness I'd just felt.

I wrapped my arms around the big man.

"See you tomorrow, love," he told me, holding me for a few extra moments.

I knew what that extra squeeze meant.

"I love you, too, Dad," I told him when he let me go.

"I'll walk you out," Mum said, and I knew I'd be wasting my breath telling her not to bother.

Grabbing my backpack, I slid the glass door open, then closed it behind my mother. She looped her arm through mine as we walked across the courtyard. Her tall frame elegantly and effortlessly glided as she always had, towering over me by three inches. She moved with a natural grace I'd long ago given up on emulating.

"You must still miss him, I'm sure," she said before we reached the gate.

It was mind-boggling to me how she knew Paul had been in my thoughts, but it didn't surprise me anymore. Her uncanny knack had often kept me from descending into dark places. But I didn't want to have this conversation right now, even though it might be the best thing for me. I had too much else going on, so I unlocked our arms to open the gate latch.

Paul's death was devastatingly tragic, but my parents didn't know the whole story. I missed being engaged to a man I deeply loved and believed I could spend the rest of my life with. A man I'd been prepared to share my home with. My precious sanctuary.

But I no longer missed Paul himself.

Without another word, I gave my mum a quick hug in the driveway, then hurried to my car.

I'd never seen an upside to telling them the whole story. One that I didn't fully understand myself.

10

Nothing got the morning off to a better start than reviewing an autopsy report. It wasn't for anyone with a weak stomach. I ate my chocolate croissant and sipped my vanilla latte with a badge drawn on the cup while I sat at my desk and studied the details.

Cause of death was most likely the blow to the head. Clearly, Helena had been strangled, but the medical examiner's conclusion leaned towards her having been rendered unconscious but not asphyxiated. His reasons might as well have been written in Sanskrit, as the medical terminology meant nothing to me. His conclusion also stated that she certainly didn't drown.

The attacker's method of strangulation was a 3/8-inch double-braid nylon rope, which made me release a long sigh.

"Great. We're looking for a piece of marine rope," I said, somewhat to Fuentes, sitting at the opposite desk, but mainly just to voice my frustration.

"Should be easy in a beach town," he muttered in reply. "It does say dirt, hair, skin, and other fibers were present in the neck abrasion."

"Which means it was probably an old, used line, which would rule out recent purchases," I pointed out.

Fuentes leaned to the side so he could see me around our computer monitors. "Are you saying you don't want to check the marine supply stores?"

What a loaded question. I certainly didn't want to, as it had a low-percentage chance of getting us anywhere, but the box needed ticking.

"We'll take a photo of Travis with us," I responded.

That earned me a grunt, and Fuentes swayed back behind his monitor.

"And Chris Wendell, I suppose," I added as I thought it through. "Nothing close to the rope the ME described was found yesterday, right?"

"No," Fuentes confirmed.

As it stood, Travis Redman was the only person we could place at the scene, which gave him opportunity. And while he theoretically had the means, without the rope or forensic evidence tying him to the murder, we still had nothing.

Motive was another issue. I was an only child, so I hadn't experienced firsthand the dynamics of sibling rivalry, but I'd seen plenty of it. Still, falling out with your big sister was a far cry from strangling her and tossing her into the ocean.

The autopsy also showed that fingernail scrapings revealed a mixture of food, blood, skin, and dirt. Food from Helena's work. The blood and skin were her own, consistent with the scratches on her neck as she tried to free the rope. Apparently, she'd been unable to claw her attacker.

"Anything stand out to you?" I asked my reluctant partner.

"I hope the poor woman was still unconscious when she was dumped on the rocks," he commented. "Otherwise, no."

I glanced at the pictures lined up on my desk from my instant camera to make sure I wasn't missing anything before I spoke again.

"Do you think the killer thought she was dead when he threw her over the rock jetty?"

I heard a faint scoff from behind the monitors.

"If you catch the killer, you can ask him. Otherwise, I doubt we'll ever know," Fuentes finally replied in a bored tone. "We need the forensics on the hair and fibers."

It was still hit-and-miss on my partner acting like a partner. Currently, it appeared to be a miss. The point I was working towards running by him was why the killer went to all the trouble of moving Helena. He could have left her where he'd first attacked her and probably strangled her. Why take the time and risk to be seen moving her unconscious body down the road to throw her into the sea? My guess was that the killer didn't realize they'd left DNA in the park and thought tossing her in the water would hide other evidence. Which was somewhat true. The killer may also have gotten the tides wrong and thought the body would be taken out instead of dumped on the beach.

It would be nice to hear an experienced homicide investigator's take on the matter, but that wasn't happening, so I let my point go.

"The hair could be a winner if there's a follicle attached," I said as I stood and closed my laptop, disconnecting it from the monitor. "Want to divide and conquer the marine shops?"

"Sure," Fuentes replied, rising from his chair. "I'll take the one on Del Obispo."

I was glad to be out of the office and back in the sunshine now that the marine layer had burned off, revealing the Pacific Ocean spread out before me as I crested the hill on Golden Lantern. If I had my way, I'd drive around all day in my 1979 Volkswagen bus, but the department had insisted on supplying me with the most boring car ever made. The only pluses were the siren and red and blue flashing lights hidden behind the grill, which came in handy occasionally.

The marine supply shop on Pacific Coast Highway belonged to a nationwide chain. While it wasn't the biggest store, it had stayed in business for as long as I could remember and was a handy place for anything boat-related. I pulled into their parking lot, grabbed my phone, and headed inside.

Behind the counter were two men who couldn't have been more

opposite. I recognized the older man, who I guessed to be in his sixties. I didn't know his name, but he'd worked there for years and had the look of an old salt. The other man was probably in his early twenties, but if he told me he was seventeen, I'd believe him. Skinny, pimples, pale skin, and he immediately appeared uncomfortable when I walked into the store. It was hard to say if he was simply that nervous, if I'd arrived while he was doing something he shouldn't, or if humans of the female variety generally threw him for a loop.

I passed the young man and approached his older counterpart, showing my badge and introducing myself.

"Carl," the man replied. "How can I help?"

"Would you mind if I showed you a couple of pictures? See if you recognize either of these chaps."

Carl shrugged his shoulders. "Sure. Let me put my glasses on."

I brought up a photograph of Travis Redman and held it before him. He squinted, despite the glasses, which didn't bode well for his court appearance testimony if it came to it.

He shook his head. "Can't say I know that one."

I looked along the counter to where the younger man stared at me as though I might be a creature from another planet who threatened to eat him alive.

"Mind taking a look, sir?"

The young man scooted our way and peered at the phone screen, dipping and moving his head from side to side. I wasn't sure if he had trouble focusing with both eyes at the same time, but he didn't produce any glasses. He, too, shook his head.

I switched pictures to Chris Wendell and tried again. The young man did his head movement weirdness before saying "No," so I held the phone before Carl. He squinted even harder at this picture.

"I might have seen him," Carl said.

Though surprised, I was careful not to display a reaction.

"Plays guitar at Hennessey's some nights, I reckon."

I was careful not to laugh. "But not in the store?" I checked.

"Don't think so."

"Okay," I said, putting my phone in my pocket. I pointed to two security cameras aimed at the aisles of goods from the corners of the store behind the counter. "Are they recording?"

"I think so," Carl replied.

"Do you know how long the recordings are kept?"

"No clue," he replied, and I believed him. It was easy to picture Carl struggling to master his TV remote.

"A week," the younger man mumbled, almost sounding apologetic. I should have guessed he'd be the tech-savvy, video game-playing superhero behind closed doors type.

"Cool," I said while I formulated a plan. "I'm looking for someone who bought 3/8-inch nylon double-braid line. Could we check sales for the week prior to Tuesday evening and grab the time of day from the transactions? Then I could look at those times on the security tape."

The older man's expression was dubious. "We sell a lot of 3/8 rope in a week. Besides, we'd need to call the manager in to go over the sales stuff."

"I can do it."

Carl and I both turned to the younger man.

"What's your name?" I asked.

"Jeremy," he replied shakily, as though he wasn't certain.

Two customers walked up, ready to pay, so Carl moved to another register to help them.

"How long will that take, Jeremy?" I asked.

His eyes flicked up to meet mine, then instantly shot away again. He glanced toward his counterpart at the register. I realized there was a good chance Jeremy was on the spectrum in some way. I instantly felt guilty for having viewed his oddities with humor. After all, very few people harbored a stranger quirk than I had. This guy was holding down a job, which undoubtedly wasn't easy, and with the way he'd looked over at Carl, I guessed he wasn't given much leeway.

"Only a few minutes. I could do it on my lunch break, if that's okay?" Jeremy replied.

"When's your lunch?" I asked.

"Eleven."

What I wanted to do was tell Carl that he should cover the front while Jeremy helped the sheriff's office out with a murder inquiry, but I figured that would only cause Jeremy more grief in the long run.

"I bring my lunch, so I just sit in the back, anyway," he added.

"I appreciate you doing this, Jeremy. It'll be a big help. Alright if I come back at eleven, then?"

He nodded.

"Thanks," I said. "I'll see you in a while."

My cell buzzed as I left the marine store. It was a text from Fuentes. He was finished at the other shop, where he didn't have any luck. I knew the place he'd gone to. It was more of an automotive parts store with a small marine section.

It was 10:20 am, and I was already hungry again despite eating the croissant earlier. My morning workout had been enthusiastic after a restless night, so I figured I'd burned enough calories to deserve an early lunch. I called my partner.

"Hey, I have to come back here at eleven, so I was thinking of grabbing a bite to eat."

"Where?" he asked in reply.

I hadn't thought about what or where yet. "The taqueria on PCH just down the hill from the marine shop," I told him after a beat, knowing I could walk there.

"Okay," he replied, and hung up.

I looked at the phone in my hand. I had no idea if that meant "Okay, enjoy your lunch," or "Okay, I'll be right there." Shoving the phone in my pocket, I started walking and shifted my thoughts back to the case, as I really didn't care what Fuentes did.

The taqueria was a small place in a row of shops lining the hill alongside PCH. I ordered a couple of Baja fish tacos and grabbed a water while I waited for my order to come up. My mind was busy arm-wrestling itself over what direction to head the case next when Fuentes surprised me by walking through the door. I'd figured he'd take the opportunity to be anywhere I wasn't.

He ordered, then came over and sat opposite me. I was about to ask him whether the automotive shop had cameras, but decided to stay away from work talk as he'd chosen to join me for once.

"You're not married, are you?" I asked, which came out more abruptly than I planned.

He held up his left hand and wiggled his bare ring finger.

"You used to be, though?"

He nodded.

"Kids?"

"No."

They called my order number, and I gladly left the table to get my food. When I returned, I settled for asking Fuentes about the cameras at the automotive store.

Carl had exaggerated. Once we narrowed the sales down to black 3/8-inch double-braid rope, there were only six sales over the time period in question. The line was sold by the foot, and for most marine applications, I'd expect the sale to be for at least twenty feet or more, so one transaction stood out. Someone had purchased four feet. I was antsy to get to that one, but we systematically moved through the recordings in the order of the sales.

Jeremy gave Fuentes all kinds of odd looks when we walked in, so I was pleased when my partner chose to remain in the shop instead of cramming into the small office with us. Jeremy was far calmer with a keyboard in front of him, swiftly moving back and forth between the transactions to get the times, then back to the video recordings. I had to concentrate on picking out the names on the transactions for each one in turn as he scanned the screen remarkably quickly.

I didn't recognize the first four by name or face, and noted no name was recorded for the fifth transaction. The one I'd been waiting for. I eagerly watched the screen as a woman stepped to the counter and paid cash for her four feet of black marine rope.

"Replay that again," I asked, and Jeremy did as requested.

The resolution wasn't high-definition, but it was reasonable enough to identify someone.

"One more time," I asked, and watched the transaction at the register with Carl.

I didn't recognize the woman at all.

"Can you send me a screenshot of this, please?" I asked.

"Of course," Jeremy replied, and clicked like a demon before pausing and looking at me. "Can I have your email?" he asked, then rocked in his seat. "I'm sorry, I mean…"

"It's okay, Jeremy," I said, wanting to put a hand on his shoulder to let him know everything was okay, but I stopped myself, respecting his personal space. I read off my sheriff's department-issued email address.

"Okay, thank you. Sorry about that," he said as he speedily typed in the address and hit send.

"I really appreciate all your help, Jeremy. Let's check the last one, and I'll be out of your hair so you can eat your lunch."

While Jeremy cued up the last timeline, I remembered to snap a quick photograph of him working at the computer. The association with the footage was vague, but I hoped it would be enough for me to access these memories later if my wiring didn't comply.

Distracted, I forgot to look for the name on the transaction, but the video played, and I watched a man with dark hair and a shaggy beard walk up to the counter. He placed several items down along with a coil of line. It definitely wasn't Travis Redman or Chris Wendell, and I sat back in my seat.

"Need to see it again?" Jeremy asked, and I was about to say no. But there was something slightly familiar about the bloke.

"Yeah, go ahead."

The tape ran again and I sat forward once more.

"Fuentes!" I called out, now certain I recognized the man from the background files I'd studied on our victim. "One more time, Jeremy. Can you freeze it when I say?"

My partner shuffled into the little office. "What have you got?"

Jeremy started the video clip over, and Fuentes watched as I hunted for an email on my phone.

"Okay," Fuentes grunted. "Am I supposed to know this guy?"

I found what I was looking for and held my phone screen next to the computer monitor.

"Freeze," I told Jeremy as the customer glanced up toward the camera.

"Could be the same guy," Fuentes admitted, looking between the two images. "So, who is that?"

"That is Darian Rutherford. Scarlett's father."

Darian Rutherford had let his California driver's license lapse ten years ago in favor of an Oregon license. His records showed five different addresses over that decade, but his cell number had remained the same with a Southern California 949 area code.

Outside, by my car, Fuentes stood next to me while I called the number.

"Yeah," came a gruff greeting.

"Have I reached Darian Rutherford?"

"Who's this?"

"This is Investigator Cromwell with the Orange County Sheriff's Department. Can you please verify your name?"

For a moment, the line was quiet, and I expected the man to hang up.

"This is Darian. Are you calling about Helena?"

"That's correct. I take it you've heard?" I asked.

Her name had been released to the media that morning, so I wasn't surprised. He'd have to be hiding outside of Orange County to avoid the news. Locally, it was a big story.

"Yeah."

"Are you here in Dana Point?" I asked, curious to see if he'd lie.

In all honesty, I still wasn't one hundred percent certain it was him in the video. I'd compared a DMV record photograph to security camera footage. Neither were glamor shots.

There was another long pause. "Yeah."

"Great. Where can I meet with you?"

"What for?"

"This is a murder investigation, Mr. Rutherford. I'd like to see if you can shine any light on who might have been involved."

"You're wasting your time. I can't help you. I haven't had anything to do with Helena in years."

"You never know what may help us, sir. Where are you now? I'll come to you."

More prolonged silence, so I waited. I didn't want to threaten him with coming to the station at this stage, as I preferred him to think we were carrying out routine inquiries.

"In the harbor," he finally replied. "I'm staying on a friend's boat."

With a little more prompting, he gave me the slip number, and I told him we'd be there in twenty minutes.

"We'll be down the hill in five," Fuentes pointed out as we got in my car.

"I know," I replied, starting the engine. "But I'd rather he thinks he has time, just in case he plans on leaving."

My partner didn't respond. I'd gotten used to working alone as an investigator after often having a partner when I was a Deputy Sheriff. But homicide investigators usually operated in pairs, so I wondered how Fuentes had survived this long by being such an arse. Then the thought occurred to me that he might not be… when he had a more senior and male partner.

I drove us north on PCH, then left on Golden Lantern, which took us down the steep grade to the harbor, where restaurants and tourist shops lined the marina. I continued to the west parking lot, closest to where the live-aboard slips were located, having recognized the section from the slip number he gave me. We walked to the top of the jetty, where a metal-railed fence and locked gate prevented non-owners from accessing the boats.

I looked east and spotted a golf cart trundling our way along the wide concrete pathway and waved to the driver. The Hispanic maintenance man waved back, although his expression indicated he'd rather motor on by than have us bother him. But he stopped, so I showed him my badge.

"Mind letting us in, please?"

He studied my badge for a moment and then looked at Fuentes. My partner rolled his eyes but pulled out his badge and showed the guy.

"Hurry up," my partner told the man in Spanish. "We have a suspect we need to question."

At least, that was my best guess at a translation as my Mexican-Spanish wasn't perfect.

"Okay, okay," the maintenance man replied. He punched a code into the keypad, pushing the gate open.

"*Gracias,*" I told him as we went through and walked down the jetty, turning right at the third spur and checking the slip numbers on the pedestals containing the power and water connections.

Arriving at the correct number, I studied the Beneteau sailboat. It was somewhere a little over thirty feet, by my estimation, and in good condition. Probably more than ten years old, but it could be twice that if it had enjoyed an easy life with lots of care.

"Hey," I said quietly to Fuente as I pointed to a new line at the bow. It was black and 3/8-inch in diameter.

I walked along the side of the slip to the cockpit, where a cover shrouded the helm and wheel.

"Mr. Rutherford?" I called.

I heard movement inside, and a few moments later, a man appeared dressed in a well-used sweatshirt and cargo shorts. I recognized his dark hair and thick beard from the video.

"Permission to come aboard?" I asked, using boating manners rather than police insistence.

"Alright," Darian replied, and sat down on the bench lining three sides of the cockpit.

I noted the boat's name on the stern. *Gone with the Wind*, registered in San Francisco.

"Have you seen or spoken with Scarlett?" I asked, taking a seat opposite him after showing him my badge. My partner remained standing.

Darian shook his head.

"You live in Oregon, don't you?" I asked. "What brings you south?"

"Clearing a few things of mine out of my stepmother's house. She sold it. I'm driving back tomorrow."

"Not staying for Helena's funeral?" I asked, trying to keep my voice casual.

He shook his head again. "Don't want to cause any drama."

Having been raised in a stable home with parents who stayed together for all the right reasons, it was beyond my comprehension how the man could turn his back on his own child, both back then and now. But he was undoubtedly right. Amongst the emotional turmoil the family was going through, his presence would do little more than complicate matters.

But none of that was my problem. Our concern was whether Darian had a motive to kill Helena. We knew he had the matching style of rope, and Doheny was less than a mile on foot from where we sat.

"What do you do for work?" I asked.

"Crew on fishing boats. Sometimes crab boats. I've delivered and moved a few craft for people."

"That's a tough way to make a living these days," I pointed out.

He shrugged his shoulders. "Some gigs work out better than others. I get by."

"Let's clear up the routine stuff we have to ask, Mr. Rutherford. Can you tell us where you were Tuesday night?"

"Driving," he replied. "Didn't get here until daybreak Wednesday."

"Must have caught terrible traffic from LA to here in the early hours," Fuentes chimed in.

"When is it not terrible around here?" Darian replied.

"You drove all night?" I asked.

"No. Slept in my truck for a while."

"Where was that?" I pressed.

"Over the Grapevine somewhere. One of the rest stops."

Based on the timing of the video we'd just watched, he was digging a deeper and deeper hole for himself.

"And that was Tuesday night?" I asked, giving him a chance to correct his story. "You sure?"

Darian nodded, his expression remaining as surly as when we'd arrived.

"We have you on security tape buying supplies at the marine store on Tuesday afternoon," I said. "If that helps straighten out your calendar."

Darian groaned, lowering his head and letting out a sigh. "For fuck's sake." He lifted his head back up. "Look, I got here Tuesday morning, but I knew you'd be looking at me if you found out I was in town, alright? I've had nothing to do with Helena for years. That's the truth. And I certainly had nothing to do with whatever happened at the beach."

"If I measured that shiny new rope at the bow, would I find it's the full thirty feet you bought on Tuesday?" I asked.

"What the hell are you talking about?" he demanded, looking at me like I had two heads.

"What was the rope you bought on Tuesday for?"

"Mooring the boat," he snapped back. "The old line was frayed, so the least I could do was replace the damn thing. This guy's letting me stay here for nothing."

"So my question remains," I countered. "If I measure that new line, is it still thirty feet long?"

Darian glared at me. I wasn't sure if he was mad at being called out or simply for being challenged. Either way, he looked ready to brawl over it. His eyes were full of cold, hard disdain.

"Measure all you fucking like, but you can do it while you're leaving," he grumbled. "We're done here. I'll not be stitched up for this shit."

I stood. "You're not being stitched up for anything, Mr. Rutherford, but we'd appreciate it if you'd change your travel plans. We'll have more questions for you."

"You have my cell number," he grunted. "I have business up north."

Contrary to threatening lines in Hollywood movies, we had no way of restricting the man's travel without a warrant or court order, and he undoubtedly knew it. We stepped from the boat and walked along the slip to the jetty. I looked again at the new rope.

"Don't try to measure it," Fuentes said, and kept walking.

I caught up to him, wondering why we wouldn't want to know. I didn't feel like giving my partner the satisfaction of asking him a dumb question, but I couldn't understand why we wouldn't grab the opportunity while we had access to the line. Darian could easily remove it and toss it away as soon as we left.

"Why are we not checking the rope?" I finally asked, stumped.

"Because that's our only chance at a warrant," he replied.

I felt like a chump as we pushed through the gate and walked to the car. I should have thought of that. But things still didn't add up right with Darian. What did he stand to gain from Helena's death? There was no money. He didn't seem to care about his daughter.

"We now have three suspects and not one motive," I said as we got into the car. "And Travis is the only one we can place at the scene."

"The rope could be a breakthrough," Fuentes considered.

It seemed like he might be in a partner-like mood, so I kept going.

"Certainly a chance," I agreed. "But by the dirt and other deposits found on Helena's neck from the rope, my guess is the murder weapon was secondhand, not new."

"The rope wasn't the murder weapon," Fuentes reminded me. "It was the attempted murder weapon."

Well, I'd hoped he was in a partner-like mood. I looked over, and he grinned at me, which actually made me laugh. I wasn't sure how to handle the man when he showed a sense of humor.

"Maybe it was dragged through the dirt in the park," he added more thoughtfully.

I began slowly driving back to PCH, where he'd left his car. "I should have asked him what vehicle he drove down here in, but we can check the one he has registered with Oregon DMV, then look at the little CCTV we have available. See if he was driving around Tuesday night."

"There is a camera in the harbor, looking across the parking lot," Fuentes replied. "But I'm not sure it'll see Dana Point Harbor Drive."

"I looked at that one the other night, but I was searching for Travis Redman's Ranger. Most traffic drives up and down here," I said, referring to Golden Lantern, which we were currently taking to the top of the bluffs. "But it might catch a glimpse of a vehicle going west on Dana Point Harbor Drive."

"Worth a look," he agreed.

When I came to the stoplights at the top of the hill, my phone rang. I checked the caller ID and saw it was Captain Bradley. After hitting accept, the call automatically came through the car's hands-free system.

"Hello, ma'am," I said. "We have a new suspect. Just heading to the station to see about a warrant."

"Okay, good," she replied, though with less enthusiasm than I'd hoped to hear. "You can tell me about them when you get here."

"Will do, ma'am," I replied, about to end the call.

"But that's not why I called," the captain continued. "I need to give you a heads-up."

"Okay," I replied.

"Part of a male body washed ashore earlier this morning at Three Arch Beach."

I winced. That was a wealthy area just north of Dana Point,

which fell under Laguna Beach police territory. But as Orange County investigators, it could well be sent our way.

"You want us to take a look?" I asked, a little miffed she'd pile on a second case only three days into a high-profile murder.

"No, Cromwell. In fact, the opposite. We'll need DNA tests to confirm, but the initial theory is that the remains might belong to Paul Michaels."

The light turned green, but I didn't move and couldn't speak. Horns honked.

"It's green," Fuentes urged.

"Oh… my apologies, Kat," Captain Bradley added. "I didn't realize you weren't alone. Perhaps it's better if you come see me when you get here."

The line went dead, and by some kind of automatic process, I drove the car forward and turned right on PCH.

Of all the crazy things I could possibly have imagined my day containing, my fiancé's body showing up on a beach hadn't been on my bingo card.

12

Sitting in Captain Bradley's office, I stared at her blankly while she tidied up the already tidy papers on her desk.

"I apologize for telling you that way," she began. "I didn't realize Fuentes was in your car."

Delivering bad news while someone was behind the wheel of a car was also less than ideal by most standards. The whole thing had been clumsy, and I could probably make noise up the food chain, which would saddle Bradley with a series of management and sensitivity-training courses. But that wouldn't help anything, and I didn't really care. Fuentes had already made up his mind about me, and my goal was to get the captain on my side rather than alienate her further.

"My reasoning for contacting you as soon as possible was simply to give you advance warning," Bradley continued. "I know how quickly things trickle down, and I didn't want it reaching you via office chatter."

"You mentioned a body part washed up," I said, keen to move on from the arse-covering BS. I didn't blame her. It came with the territory, but I didn't have time for this dance. "Can you be more specific?"

The captain sucked in a breath and considered my question with a pained expression. I had a good reason for asking, and a decent idea what the answer would be. From her seat, she was probably wondering how much to share about a case that could be reopened with additional evidence surfacing. Or, she was thinking I had a sick curiosity.

"An arm," Bradley finally revealed.

"A left arm, ma'am?" I responded.

She frowned, but then nodded.

Paul had broken his left wrist in a mountain biking fall, which had required a pin and screws. I figured there wouldn't be much they could learn from a heavily decomposed arm, beyond the ID from DNA, but it was disturbing to think of the fate of the rest of a man I once loved. When I thought of his final resting place at sea, I wasn't expecting the parts to be in constant limbo, redistributed throughout the Pacific Ocean.

The accident had happened no more than a few miles offshore. The rains had persisted for two more days, and rough seas further hampered search efforts, which had eventually been halted after five days. Where was the rest of Paul? There was a chance that other parts of his body could tell more of the story. I couldn't recall what had happened, so I didn't know for sure, but my gut was telling me it would be best for me if the other components remained on the sea floor.

"That's all we should discuss at this stage," the captain said. "I'll update you if anything more progresses." She leaned forward and eyed me sternly. "I'm obligated to point out that you cannot question anyone about the case, Kat. Please don't put your co-workers in that position, and don't force me to take action."

"I get it," I said, pretty certain I meant it.

"Good. Then get me up to speed on the Redman case."

I took my growing stack of instant pictures from my pocket. Holding them below the level of the captain's desk, I shuffled through them quickly to make sure nothing surprised me. I had to pause for a moment on the blood splatter from the park, but then the information came back to me.

"We discovered the daughter's father, Darian Rutherford, is in town," I began explaining. "Arrived the day before the murder and purchased the same type of rope used to strangle the victim."

"Seriously? Have you interviewed him?"

"We have. He's staying on a friend's sailboat in the harbor, and I've seen the new rope. He replaced one of the tie lines with it."

"Can we match them?" Bradley asked.

"We'll need a warrant to search the boat, and from DMV records, we see he owns a pickup truck, ma'am, so we'll search that as well. Fuentes is filling out the paperwork now."

"Motive?" the captain asked. "Is he trying to get his daughter back, or is there insurance or property involved?"

I shook my head. "According to everyone we've spoken to, including Rutherford, he's had nothing to do with either of them in years. From what I've seen, Helena was scraping by. There's nothing of value."

"Maybe it was a reunion that went awry," Bradley suggested.

"We've requested her cell phone records, but you know how long that can take sometimes. No one else seems to know Rutherford was here. We lucked out seeing him buying marine supplies on a security tape."

Bradley sat back once more and looked out her window for a few moments.

"Where are we with the brother?" she asked.

"We can place him at the scene breaking into her minivan, but we've got nothing tying him to the actual murder, ma'am. No weapon or motive, so far."

"Are we still holding him?"

"No, ma'am. We did overnight. Had to arraign him this morning, as we couldn't keep him over the weekend."

"How did he plead?"

"No contest, apparently, ma'am."

"Hmm," she murmured. "Odd, don't you think?"

"Surprised me. If they knew all we had was an iffy video identifying that his truck was there, and a brief, blurry image of a bloke who looks somewhat like Travis smashing the window, I doubt they would have done that."

"Very strange," Bradley reiterated.

"My guess is he wants it all to go away as quickly as possible, and by cooperating, he'll look innocent of the murder," I suggested, although I was equally perplexed by the move.

"But he's the only one we can place near the scene, correct?"

"Rutherford was less than a mile away, and Wendell was in town somewhere, but Travis Redman is the only suspect we can prove was in Doheny near the time of the murder."

"You've ruled out the homeless guy who found the body?"

"Dennis? He has arthritis so bad, he can barely hold a beer bottle, ma'am," I replied after rolling the idea over in my mind in case I'd missed something. "I don't think there's any way he could have strangled the vic, let alone dragged her down the road and thrown her in."

"Which I can't wrap my head around," Bradley said, looking past me to the wall of her office, as though the governor's framed picture on the wall held the answers. "Why did the killer go to all the trouble of moving the body? The victim was petite, but it's still not easy to move a dead body several hundred yards."

"Unconscious, ma'am," I couldn't stop myself from correcting. "Whether the killer knew it or not, we believe the vic was alive but probably unconscious from strangulation. Hitting the rocks on the way into the water finished her off."

Bradley frowned at me. "Regardless, dead or unconscious, it would have required effort to move her. Have you considered an accomplice?"

An accomplice to whom? I was yet to find a prosecutable suspect. But her point was valid. The only reason I could come up with for moving the body was a bungled attempt at concealing evidence, which wouldn't be a stretch, especially if the murder wasn't premeditated. People often panicked when they realized they'd just killed another human being. But the killer would need to either be a strong man, had help, or used a vehicle to move the body.

"I skimmed the preliminary autopsy report," Bradley said, apparently tired of waiting for my response and moving on. "No signs of sexual assault. Unlikely to be a passing stranger, don't you think?"

It felt odd that the captain had phrased that as a question, but perhaps she was testing me in some way.

"Can't rule out anyone at this stage, ma'am, but if the killer didn't know her, then we could be looking at a far worse problem."

Her brow knitted. "Have you checked the database for a similar MO?"

"Yes, ma'am. Nothing close enough to call it a pattern," I replied. "Right now, I'm hoping forensics from the neck wound will give us something better to work with."

Captain Bradley shuffled in her chair and sat upright, picking up a pen. Her body language for *We're done.*

"Get the warrant for the father, but keep pressure on the brother," she said.

I nodded and hurried from her office. I guess it made bosses feel better to point out the obvious, as though we'd have no idea what to do next if they didn't say the words. Or perhaps it was another ass-covering move. Either way, I wasn't about to take the weekend off to sit on the beach and read a good book. The case was too important to me. That, and I knew I'd end up watching the shoreline in case any more body parts washed up.

I sat at my desk with a fresh cup of coffee. When I say fresh, I mean the tar in the carafe that had sat on the hot plate for goodness knows how long. Fuentes, hidden behind his monitor, seemed to be ignoring me as he clicked away with his mouse.

"Are we waiting for the warrant?" I asked him.

I heard his chair slide back. "Come look at this."

I got up and walked around the desks to his side. On his screen was CCTV from what I recognized to be the harbor. The image was grainy, lit by the streetlamps scattered around the area, with the camera mounted on one of the buildings along the marina facing across the parking lot.

"Rutherford owns a dark green Chevy pickup," Fuentes said, and clicked play on the footage. "Look at the road."

I squinted to make out the top of a large, pale-colored van heading east on Dana Point Harbor Drive. Parked cars, shrubs, and the distance all conspired to make it tough to see any detail, and I wasn't sure a car would be seen at all beyond a sense of movement between obstructions.

"Here," he prompted, and I watched the screen.

What I thought might be the upper part of an extended cab pickup drove east. The time was Tuesday night at 10:21 p.m.

"I'd say that's a pickup truck," I responded. "Which could be dark green. Or any other dark color, I suppose."

Fuentes didn't say a word, but fast-forwarded the footage to 11:17 p.m. and let it play. What appeared to be a very similar blurry, dark-colored pickup traveled west in the direction of the parking lot in front of the sailboat Rutherford was staying on.

"I'd hate to rely on that video in court," I admitted. "But he won't know that when we talk to him again."

"Exactly," my partner said, standing, unplugging his laptop, and grabbing a file from his desk. "I have the warrant."

"Does it cover the boat and his truck?"

"Yup," was all he replied as I rushed to gather up my things and catch up with him.

I left the coffee behind.

"Hey," Fuentes grunted as we got out of the car and started toward the gate for the slips in Dana Point Harbor. "Green truck."

I looked along the first row of vehicles to where a well-used dark green pickup truck was parked. Fuentes walked that way to check the license plate, and I was about to follow until I looked down the jetty and spotted Darian Rutherford. Who'd apparently just seen me.

"Fuentes," I called out. "I don't think he wants to chat with us again."

Rutherford immediately turned and walked briskly to the spur down which *Gone with the Wind* was moored. I jogged to the fence, looking around for anyone who could let me in. I spotted a couple sitting in the cockpit of their sport fisherman, but they were too far away. Grabbing the top of the metal gate, I put my left foot against the sturdy support post and swung my right leg up, hoping my planted shoe wouldn't slip on the smooth metal. Just as my right foot wedged between the fence posts above the upper rail, my left foot slipped, but I pulled as hard as I could with my arms and hauled myself on top of the gate. I unhooked my right foot and dropped to the marina side.

"Hey!" someone yelled. "What are you doing?"

I took off running, pulling my badge out and holding it up in the air, not bothering to locate where the voice had come from. Behind me, I heard my partner calling for support over the radio. Rounding the corner of the spur, I sprinted to the slip and found Rutherford about to step into an inflatable tender.

"I can call harbor patrol if you want to be a twat about this," I said, plucking my radio from my belt. "I don't think you're outrunning them in that thing."

"What the fuck do you want now?" he groaned, swinging his legs back into the cockpit. "You ain't coming aboard without a warrant."

"Good job we have one, then," I told him, wishing I had the paperwork with me.

But Rutherford sat down on the bench and shook his head. "Whatever. Let's get this over with."

"Why were you taking off when you saw us?" I asked.

"Because you're a pain in the ass, lady," he spat back. "And you're wasting your time and mine."

I glanced toward the bow and was relieved and slightly surprised to see the new black line still mooring the boat to the cleat on the dock.

"Got another line we can trade for that one?" I asked.

"I still have the old one," he replied. Begrudgingly, he lifted the hinged top of one of the bench seats and pulled out an old rope. He tossed the coiled line, which landed at my feet. "Knock yourself out."

I grinned to myself. He wasn't the first man to underestimate me. Especially around boats.

Someone must have opened the gate as Fuentes arrived while I was freeing the mooring line. I looked up as he approached. "Want to take a look around inside while I check the rope?"

He nodded and continued to the stern. Over the radio, I heard a uniform calling to let us know they'd arrived. Fuentes replied and told them we'd contained the situation.

"Have a tape measure in your car? Over," I asked using my radio.

"I think so," came the reply.

"Bring it down to the slip, please. Over," I instructed, having realized we'd rushed out of the office without any means of measuring the line.

I fixed the old rope in place, noting it was indeed frayed and tatty in places. Deputy Ripley grinned when he saw me. He held out a tape measure.

"What have you got going on here, miss?" he asked.

For a moment, I left him holding the tape, which was one of the larger outdoor reel models, and laid the new black rope out along the side of the slip. I then took the tape and handed Ripley the end tab.

"Hold this at the other end, please," I told him.

He did as instructed, and we measured the length while pulling the rope tight. It was 29 feet and 2 inches. Rutherford had purchased 30 feet. Winding the tape measure back in, I handed it to Ripley, then picked up the line and studied the end. It had been cut with a hot knife, and a short section of electrical heat shrink had been applied to prevent fraying. You could buy lines that came that way, but I knew this rope had been cut from a large reel at the marine shop. They may have used a hot knife to cut the length, but Rutherford must have applied the heat shrink to both ends.

I coiled up the rope but didn't have an evidence bag big enough, so I left it on the jetty and thanked Ripley for his help.

"This guy a suspect?" he asked quietly.

"Rope like this was used," I replied. "So maybe. But it's a common mooring line, so maybe not. He's the vic's ex from a while back. If he didn't do it, he picked a shitty time to arrive back in town."

"Need us to stick around?"

"Nah. I think we're good. Cheers."

Ripley joined his partner, Hanson, who'd been happy to stay back and stare at the proceedings through his dark-tinted sunglasses. As the two of them walked away along the jetty, I turned back to the boat as Fuentes appeared from inside. He subtly shook his head as he stepped to the dock to join me.

"Has it been cut?" he asked me in a hushed voice.

"He bought 30-foot, and this is 29-foot-2 inches."

"She wasn't strangled with ten inches of rope," Hugo pointed out.

"No, but when you buy rope, they usually give you a little extra. But we have no way of verifying the length when he left the shop."

"So, he could have walked out with 31 feet and cut off a 22-inch piece?"

"It's possible," I said. "He's cleaned up both ends, too, so we have no way to know if he made a cut after leaving the shop. Could have been closer to 30 feet, and he cleaned up both ends himself." I looked at Rutherford. "You did a nice job prepping the line."

He shrugged his shoulders. "I told you, working boats is what I do for a living."

"Why did you shorten the line you'd bought?"

The suspect let out a long sigh. "Because the dumbass kid used cutters instead of a hot knife, so I had to waste six inches off each end."

Fuentes looked at me, and I gave him a subtle nod. Rutherford's story was believable, although I didn't care for him calling Jeremy a dumbass.

"Perfect," Fuentes muttered. He turned to face Rutherford, who stared up at us from the cockpit. "Warrant also covers your truck. Bring the keys with you."

"Don't have them," Rutherford replied.

Great, I thought to myself. *He's going to play more games now.*

"Drop them overboard?" Fuentes asked sarcastically. "No problem. I'll call a tow truck."

Rutherford shrugged his shoulders. "Knock yourselves out, but it'll cost you a fortune."

Fuentes frowned at the man. "What are you talking about?"

"My truck's in Oregon getting a new transmission. I rented a car to drive down."

13

We went through the motions and searched Rutherford's rental car, which gave us nothing beyond evidence that the man tossed every used fast-food wrapper and container into the backseat. And he ate way too much fast food. With rope in hand, we gave the car keys back to the suspect.

"Thanks for your cooperation," I said. "You'll get the rope back when we're done with it."

"Lot of good that'll do me," Rutherford grunted. "I told you I'm leaving tomorrow. Now I have to buy another line for the boat in the morning before I leave. You gonna pay for that?"

"Enjoy the rest of your stay, sir," Fuentes said as he walked away.

"You guys should try a little harder to find whoever really killed Helena and stop wasting my time," Rutherford threw out as his parting words.

I paused. Annoyed, but also curious. "Enlighten us, Mr. Rutherford. Give us your theory."

The man looked at me with a mixture of surprise and further irritation. "How the hell should I know? I told you I haven't had anything to do with her for years."

Or your own daughter, I wanted to add, but restrained myself. Scarlett was probably better off without this tosser in her life, anyway.

"We'll be in touch," I said instead, and left him grumbling and swearing under his breath.

I was through the gate before I realized I hadn't taken a picture. I already had one of Rutherford and the sailboat, but I never knew whether that would be enough to recall a second visit to the same location. It was too late now. Fuentes would make a note of it or comment, and that was the last thing I needed.

Walking past the green truck, I stopped again, took out my phone, and snapped a picture of the license plate. As we drove away, I held out my phone with the photo I'd just taken.

"See, those things do work for pictures," Fuentes said, taking it from me.

I thought it best to ignore the comment. "Barmy thought, but why don't we run this plate?"

"Barmy?" he replied.

"Yeah. You know, crazy, or a bit nuts."

"Fitting," he muttered as he took his laptop from his stylish satchel.

I couldn't tell if he was serious or making another attempt at humor. "It's been said," I responded with a laugh, testing the waters.

Fuentes busied himself on the computer, opening the software to run the plate. I figured if he'd been trying to make a point, he'd decided to drop it, but then he spoke again.

"You nearly took yourself out jumping that gate."

Okay, so he wasn't kidding around.

"Never a doubt," I replied jovially. "Cat-like reflexes. Get it? *Kat*-like reflexes."

I cringed inside. My attempts at humor were worse than his. But despite my efforts at levity, I sensed what was coming, and my blood pressure was already rising.

"If you'd just waited a moment, I could have helped you over the gate," he remarked without looking at me. "It's called teamwork."

"Teamwork?" I snapped back. "Are you bloody kidding me?"

He whipped around to face me. I knew I should have let it go, and a voice in my head screamed for me to back down and do whatever it took to smooth this over. But there lies my problem. Or one of them. I never listened to that voice.

"No, I'm not kidding. You're reckless, and you react without thinking," he said in an annoyingly calm voice.

"And you're too worried about messing up your hair," I replied in a less-than-calm voice. "I jumped over a bloody gate, Fuentes. I didn't run blindly into a burning building. If I hadn't, he'd have been gone in the tender."

"And harbor patrol would have rounded him up. That's better than injuring yourself and making a spectacle for no reason."

"A spectacle?" I scoffed. "There you go again. You're more worried about appearances than catching a murderer."

"If you stick around as long as I've been doing this, Cromwell, you'll learn it's not about leaping fences and running around like a chicken with your head cut off," he responded, his voice finally raised. "Solid, logical police work catches these people."

The turn light was red at the corner of Dana Point Harbor Drive and Golden Lantern. That was good, as I realized I'd sped up as our argument had become more and more heated.

"So spreading embarrassing pictures of me around the office is your example of teamwork? I growled. "You learn that from all your years on the force?"

"That would be another example of a spectacle," he countered with no hint of apology.

"Then how about you actually help me with this case instead of sitting on the sidelines and hoping I'll fail?" I blasted, struggling to stop myself from shouting at the man.

"I can't help you any more than I already am, Cromwell," he responded, now fighting to keep his own voice under control. "You were given this case, so it's your responsibility. There's the difference. Not so easy when your name's at the top of the page, is it?"

"You've had it in for me from the bloody start," I growled, accelerating away a bit too hard when the light went green. "You can't wait to throw me under the bus with Bradley. How can I possibly trust you?"

"Trust?" he snorted. "Trust is knowing you can rely on your partner, kid. You're a loose cannon. No one can trust you." He waved a hand in the air. "And what about this picture bullshit? Don't try and tell me you're sharing the whole story about that little habit of yours."

I felt his eyes boring holes into my skull as though my truth had been cut open on a medical examiner's table. Panic joined my anger, and I knew I'd lost all control.

"Then get yourself taken off this case!" I lashed out. "That way, you won't have to trouble your perfect self by dealing with me, and we'll both be happier."

He let out a long breath instead of replying. If he took the higher ground now and sensibly calmed things down, I wasn't sure I could hold myself back from punching him. The irony of proving him right by such an action wasn't lost on me, but that logic, along with my voice of reason, had slipped from my grasp.

"I can't," he said, returning to a measured tone.

"You can't what?" I snapped, too wound up to recall his exact words.

"I can't take myself off the case."

"Why the hell not? You have enough seniority."

He sighed again. "Because Bradley asked me to keep an eye on you."

Suspecting that something was the case was a far cry from having it confirmed. This gut punch knocked all the wind from my sails. Mentoring and assisting were not the same as keeping an eye on your so-called partner, and while in theory they could coexist, the student would never see or feel it that way. I was being tested, monitored, and judged. Of course, we all were. We were public servants, but this was different. *Was I being watched so Bradley could help my progression, or find a reason for my dismissal?*

She had always treated me differently, and I was becoming more and more certain it was connected to Paul's accident. The case had been on her watch, and she'd grilled me hard at the time when I was still a deputy.

We rode in silence to the station, where I parked near Fuentes's car but kept the engine running, waiting for him to get out.

"Ernesto Torres," he said, sliding his laptop into his satchel and opening the door.

"Excuse me?" I asked, at a loss.

"Owner of the green truck at the marina," he said. "Ernesto Torres. Two priors for assault and battery. Both pled down to simple assault."

With that, he closed the door and walked to his car, leaving me still steaming.

I entered the rope into the system as evidence and arranged for it to be sent to forensics. Walking to my desk, I stared at the empty chair where my partner should be sitting. It made me wonder if he'd be there on Monday or if he'd be in Captain Bradley's office explaining how I'd lost my shit with him.

I checked my watch. It was 5:55 p.m. on Friday, but I knew I'd be working all weekend. Screw it, I decided. Torres and his green truck, Rutherford, Travis Redman, and even Chris Wendell could wait until tomorrow morning. I needed to clear my head.

Fifteen minutes later, with my longboard in the back of my VW bus with the windows down and my wetsuit draped over the passenger seat, I left my house and drove down the hill to Doheny. I hadn't taken the time to check the surf report online, but I could see at least twenty surfers in the lineup, which meant conditions couldn't be awful.

Kicking off my flip-flops, I pulled on my faded and shabby-looking shorty, hid my keys in my secret spot behind the rear bumper, and tucked my board under my arm. Jogging across the parking lot and over the creek to the sand felt strange. I was in the middle of my crime scene. Hardly the ideal place to escape the turmoil of work. But long before Helena Redman had been murdered there, it was where I'd learned to surf, and was the closest surf break from my cottage.

The chilly water rushed over my feet as I shielded my eyes from the early evening sun and scanned the ocean. I spotted a few hands waving in my direction as people recognized me from years of catching waves together. Many of them had no idea what I did for a living, and they didn't care. Surfing had a way of uniting people from all walks of life.

As I strode into the water, I finally identified the person I was looking for. The one who'd passed on a love of the sport and taught me soon after I'd landed in California.

Avoiding the larger rocks, I picked my way over the mixture of stones and sand, carefully shuffling my feet to send any stingrays scurrying away. Once I was waist-deep, I pushed my board over an incoming roller, then slid on top and began paddling.

Doheny was a long, easy righthand break, kicked off by a combination of the swells hitting the rock jetty and a reef several hundred yards out, where the change in depth turned the swell to a wave. From there, the gentle slope kept what were usually two- to three-foot rollers going until they petered out near the beach. The spot was ideal for beginners, or anyone looking for gentle conditions and a long, easy ride on a longboard.

I pushed the nose of my Robert August Wingnut model under a mellow wave, feeling the cool water chill my face as the force pushed me and the nine-foot board back toward the beach. Popping out the other side, I swept my wet hair from my face and continued paddling. I could already sense the stress being washed away with each wave I ducked under, and by the time I reached the lineup, my mind was slowly but surely being pulled away from the chaos.

Sitting up, straddling my board, I looked offshore to check if a decent set was heading our way and settled in when I didn't spot anything promising.

"Hey there. Glad you made it."

"Hey, mum," I replied. "How's it been?"

"Getting better," she replied, looking relaxed on her board, her long, silver hair tied in pigtails with the braids draped over each shoulder. "Supposed to pick up over the weekend, so we're seeing the beginning."

"Should glass off soon," I commented, taking another look at the horizon and the sun making its way toward Catalina Island, screened from my view by the harbor jetty.

It was common for the setting sun to still the wind, which consequently smoothed out the ocean's surface until it resembled glass.

Mum nodded and smiled. "Fancy joining me for dinner after this?"

I was about to decline as thoughts of the case flooded my mind, but an older guy twenty yards to our south distracted me. He was someone I'd often seen surfing at Doheny, and he began aiming his board toward the shore, lining up for the next wave. Turning, I checked the ocean surface, noticing the almost imperceptible swell completing its voyage from deeper water.

"Taking this one?" my mother asked with a grin.

"Maybe," I replied, although she knew I wouldn't.

Waves came in sets, and for years, surfers swore they arrived in anything from four to ten waves per set, seven being the popular folklore number. Science had disproven any rule of quantity or where the biggest wave would fall in the sequence, but my mum knew I never, ever took the first wave. Number three was my go-to.

We both let the first wave roll underneath our boards and watched the old guy paddle for it. After three strokes, he backed out and looked for the next one in the set. He glanced our way, and we both nodded, letting him know we weren't trying for the same wave. He paddled hard as the wave reached him, and I saw him pop to his feet as I began stroking ahead of the next wave building behind us.

The swell lifted the tail of my board, and I felt its force begin shoving me forward as I paddled two more strokes with my arms before pushing off the deck of my board and hopping to my feet. I slid my left foot back into my goofy foot stance, keeping my weight rearwards until the nose rose enough to ensure the board didn't pearl. Cutting slightly right, I began gliding along the waist-high curl. Glancing over my shoulder, I saw my mother grinning back at me, riding the same wave. She laughed, which made me laugh like I didn't think was possible on such a shitty day.

When the wave finally closed out, I moved my stance farther back, picking the nose high out of the water, and spun the board around. Dropping to my stomach on the backside of the wave, I paused, ready to paddle back out. My mum soon pulled alongside me.

"Yeah. Dinner sounds good," I told her. "As long as it's tacos."

14

Hosing off my board, I hung it on the rack in the long, single-car garage detached from my house. I stepped back, looking at the dings, knocks, and sun-faded resin. Each scar held precious memories of wonderful days in the ocean. It was strange, but I could recall them all. Perhaps the board itself was the trigger my brain needed, or maybe I was missing some memories and simply didn't know.

The board was nine years old, a high school graduation gift, and I'd be justified in buying a new one, but that would be like saying goodbye to an old friend. My work was filled with reminders of the devastation caused by losing loved ones, possessions, dignity… a fiancé. When I came home each day, my Wingnut with two red stripes down its length was always there for me like a faithful dog. Without the poop to pick up.

I'd had to drop by home as I hadn't taken any clothes to change into after my impromptu surf session, so I quickly showered. The hot water warmed me up, and I was tempted to stay under the spray for another ten minutes and bail on dinner. But I knew it meant a lot to my mum for me to spend time with her. Outside of Christmas, two nights in a row was unheard of in recent years.

I'd never been a makeup kind of girl, even when I'd gradually evolved from my tomboy youth into my mid-teens and discovered a different kind of interest in the opposite sex. Eyeliner was my daily limit, and people tended not to recognize me if I wore blush and lipstick, so I rarely did. Certainly not out for dinner with my mum, as I knew she'd find us a tucked-away, local, best-kept-secret hole in the wall. I pulled on a pair of jeans that passed the sniff test, a T-shirt with a mermaid logo on it from a Cayman Islands scuba-diving operation, and a blue hoodie with Dad's boxing gym logo. I never really shopped for casual clothes, preferring to accumulate them along the way from places and events.

My phone dinged with a text from my mum, so I grabbed my keys and went out front. She was waiting in the driveway behind the wheel of her ten-year-old silver Kia Soul. For a former model and actress, she was the most down-to-earth person, someone who laughed about the parents bringing their children to school in six-figure vehicles. Her humor turned to frustration when they bought similar vehicles for their sixteen- and seventeen-year-olds.

"Where are we going?" I asked as I hopped in the passenger seat and put on my seatbelt.

"Laguna. We haven't been to Adolfo's in forever."

I looked at my watch. It was already late, and traffic along PCH to Laguna Beach was always busy. But Adolfo's did sound good.

"You don't have school tomorrow, but I have to work," I half-heartedly complained.

My mother grinned at me as she drove down the hill on Copper Lantern. "Go in an hour later, Kat. You need a break occasionally."

I considered the surf session my break and didn't feel like I deserved anything more. The case was already three days old, and I was still nowhere close to arresting anyone for the murder. But I relented. She knew I couldn't resist tacos.

The drive took less than fifteen minutes as traffic had died down more than I'd expected, and we even found street parking close by on Anita, the cross-street with PCH. Adolfo's was a small, brightly painted restaurant with a handful of seats inside and more tables on an outdoor patio. We walked in and scanned the large menu on the wall, which, as best I could remember, hadn't changed in years.

Part of my lack of culinary skills or adventurous spirit stemmed from the fact that I had always been a fussy eater. To me, most vegetables tasted like I was chomping on grass and weeds. As a kid, I drove my mother batty as she tried to feed me balanced meals. Breakfast cereal, bread, cheese, ice cream, and tacos covered all the required food groups, in my opinion. Fortunately, I also played football. The original kind, not the American throw-ball version, as my dad would say. And I surfed, and rode a skateboard or bicycle everywhere I went, which kept my figure trim despite my carbohydrate intake.

I'd never been keen on meat beyond cheeseburgers, until another game-changer happened when I was twelve and watched a documentary on how most of the beef and chicken went from clucking and mooing to arriving on our supermarket shelves. After that, I was determined to become a vegetarian, and it took several weeks of negotiations with my mother, already at her wit's end on how to feed me, to get me to compromise on keeping fish in my diet. Mainly because I really loved sushi, as long as it was the basic tuna and salmon rolls. Dad thought I was crazy, but my mum ended up joining me as a pescatarian, leaving him as the only meat eater in the house. As the years passed by, she fed him less and less red meat, using the doctor's concerns over his cholesterol as her reasoning. Nowadays, he'd accepted his fate and only occasionally indulged in steak when they went out to dinner.

Predictably, I ordered fish tacos and a bottle of Corona with a lime. I wasn't a big beer drinker, but sometimes a cold one tasted so refreshing. We took our basket of tortilla chips and dish of salsa outside to a table on the patio. Planters surrounded the area with a variety of flowers and shrubs, adding more color and forming a partial screen to the busy road.

"Should I ask about the case?" my mother said, nibbling on a chip.

"Pretty frustrating so far," I admitted. "Feels like I'm going round in circles."

"It's all so sad," my mum said. "I can't help thinking about poor Scarlett." She took a sip of her wine, then continued, "Do you know why her mother was at Doheny that late? Or was that just where someone dumped her body?" My mother visibly shivered. "It gives me chills just saying those words."

"We believe she was murdered in the park," I replied quietly. "But no one seems to know why she was there. Her cell phone is missing, but I'm hoping her phone records may help us. We've requested them from the phone company, but I doubt we'll see them until next week."

I munched on another chip after lightly dipping the corner of it in the salsa. I loved my wasabi spicy, but didn't care much for hot peppers. Another food-related quirk of mine.

"We're also waiting on forensics from the autopsy. That's probably our best shot at a workable lead."

My mother smiled at me across the table. "You'll figure it out, Kat."

Our food arrived, which saved me from coming up with a response that I either wouldn't believe or would cause her more worry about me.

We ate in silence for a few minutes, and I enjoyed my fish tacos, which were much better than the cereal, toast, or nothing I would have made for myself at home.

"It's important you take some time away from work, Kat," Mum said, which surprised me. She was usually more subtle in expressing her concerns and urges for me to take better care of myself.

"I am," I replied. "I had dinner with you last night, and again tonight. We went surfing. I'm a social butterfly."

She smiled, but the look of concern in her eyes didn't waver. "And I'll take every moment we can have together, my dear, but how about friends? You should be letting your hair down occasionally."

I sensed where this was going and wanted nothing more than to make the conversation head in any direction other than what my mother was really getting at. She'd always been incredibly hands-off when it came to my dating. She didn't pry, but tried her best to give me the support a teenager needs while fumbling their way through a hormonal jungle whilst believing they knew it all already. Neither parent had ever been the type to lay expectations on me to find the right man and provide them with grandchildren to dote over.

"I go out with friends sometimes," I said defensively, trying to recall the last time I'd actually accepted an invitation to do anything beyond catching a quick lunch with a schoolmate.

"Running into one of the girls at the beach doesn't count," she replied, preempting the last occasion I was about to use as an example. "I mean a dress-up-and-go-have-fun type of evening. What about a date, Kat? You know I'm not trying to push you, but I worry you're closing off to the world and losing yourself in your work."

I picked up my second taco, thinking maybe if I kept my mouth full of food, she'd stop asking me the kind of questions I threw myself into my work to avoid. Growing up, I'd always maintained a small but close circle of true friends. I knew loads of people from school, surfing, and growing up in a beach town, but I tended to hang out with a couple of girls I'd grown up with. And then we all went to different colleges. Which was where I met Paul. My trio of friends stayed in touch, but it was mainly email these days, and occasional calls or dinner when they were back in town.

As I thought it over, I realized my mum was right. I'd never added anyone else to my circle. I could see how that looked sad from the outside. It felt sad from the inside if I lingered on the point.

"On the dating front," I said, desperate to derail the topic, "they found what they believe to be Paul's arm on Three Arch Beach today."

Then I took a bite of taco, which barely fit alongside my foot in my big, dumb mouth.

My mum's jaw dropped open, and she carefully put her wine glass down to avoid spilling the contents.

"Oh my God, Kat." She reached over and squeezed my hand. "How absolutely awful. What… I mean, how…" She put her other hand to her mouth. "Goodness, Kat. Are you okay?"

I shrugged my shoulders and finished chewing. "Yeah."

She looked at me in disbelief, which was genuine because I knew she didn't believe me. It wasn't a stretch of her motherly intuition to know my casual demeanor was a charade. Her head tilted slightly, and she squeezed my hand a little harder.

"Kat, you can't gloss over this sort of thing, my love. You'll implode if you keep everything bottled up inside like that."

"Bloody hell, Mum," I responded, more firmly than I'd intended. "What do you want me to do? Have a meltdown in the middle of a murder investigation? It's not like I thought Paul had swum to an offshore island no one had noticed before and was waiting for a passing boat to bring him home. I dealt with his death a long time ago. Bits and pieces washing up on the beach doesn't change anything."

Her look of disbelief didn't go away. But I doubted she knew her reasons were the opposite of mine. I had already dealt with losing Paul, and the sudden appearance of his arm didn't cause me pain or a renewed sense of loss. What it did do was bring me a lot of concern over the investigation being reopened. It had been closed with the conclusion of accidental death. A judgement I could neither dispute nor agree with. I simply didn't know.

"Paul was cheating on me, Mum," I blurted.

They were the words I'd promised myself I'd never say out loud. To anyone, but especially my parents. They'd loved Paul. I didn't know why I'd chosen this moment to break down and tell her, but there it was. Stress, I supposed. Overwhelm, perhaps.

Regardless, the words couldn't be unsaid. I felt my cheeks flush red in frustration at my own weakness. My mother's expression switched from disbelief to shock and then sympathy. She grasped my other hand.

"I'm so sorry, Kat. I had no idea," she whispered, and her eyes welled with tears.

"On the boat," I added, figuring I'd blown the secret so she might as well know the whole truth. Or at least the small amount I'd been able to recall. The key element I'd omitted to share with the authorities. "I'm pretty sure we were fighting when it happened."

"When the accident happened?"

I nodded.

"Have you remembered more from the trip?" she asked.

"I dream stuff," I confessed. "Hard to know if it's really what happened or not. But it fits. I'd found out beforehand. I know I'd planned to confront him about it." I let out a sigh. "Point is, that's why I'm over his death, Mum. I'd already stopped loving him that day."

"But you didn't wish him dead, I'm sure."

I quickly shook my head, but she knew as well as anyone how my temper had gotten the better of me in the past. My parents had dealt with a few of my meltdowns, like the Bobby Garcia incident. Among others. I'd told her about Paul's infidelity to help explain my lack of tears over his arm arriving on dry land, but now she probably couldn't help but wonder if his accident wasn't so accidental. The same way Captain Bradley and the fine men and women of the Orange County Sheriff's Department had wondered for more weeks than an accidental death case should have taken.

"Do you know who it was?" she asked, and I was glad her mind hadn't loitered on the doubt that consumed me.

I nodded, despite my brain screaming at me to stop revealing secrets I'd fought so hard to keep hidden.

She sucked in a breath. "It's okay, Kat. I'm sorry I asked. I don't want to stir up any more bad memories for you."

I forced a smile, recognizing an opening to unwrap myself from the web I seemed to have woven. My parents were always conscious of treading lightly around my broken brain and memory challenges. I knew Mum would be wrestling with thoughts of how much I could recall and what had been disconnected and lost without a trigger.

The irony was that I knew far more about Paul's infidelity than his demise, although I'd been present for the latter. I'd stumbled across his car outside the home of a young woman we'd been watching in connection with a drug case. It was bad enough discovering my fiancé was sleeping around before our wedding, but the fact that it was with the daughter of South Orange County's most notorious drug lord and racketeer had been icing on the cake. Who happened to be a girl I'd gone to Dana Hills High School with.

Initially, I'd been relieved when she didn't come forward and say a word after Paul's disappearance. But then her silence had left me wondering. What could they have been involved in together? Besides the shagging, of course. For the past eight months, that thought had weighed heavily on my mind, but I was yet to come up with a way to look into it without bringing focus back on me and the accident.

"I need to use the loo," I said, attempting to add a physical end to the conversation.

I walked toward the door, glancing across Pacific Coast Highway, and abruptly stopped. On the other side of the road, I saw Hugo Fuentes, of all people. It was like another gut punch. He was the last person I wanted to see, and there he was, sitting in the driver's seat of his personal BMW, which I guessed he'd just parked. I watched him lean over, and although I couldn't see the woman he was with, his movement suggested he'd kissed her.

My curiosity piqued, and I moved closer to the planter by the sidewalk to get a better look. Fuentes sat back, and the passenger door opened. The person he'd just kissed stepped onto the sidewalk, half-obscured by the BMW. But there was no question about one thing. His friend was a tall, handsome man.

My stunned gaze fell back on my partner, and my heart caught in my throat. He was staring straight back at me.

15

——————

Amazingly, with everything going on, I managed a better night's sleep than I'd had all week. It seemed overloaded and overwhelmed overcame my overactive brain. But I woke early and knew there was no chance of going back to sleep, so I rolled out of bed and dug out gym clothes. I'd planned on going straight to the office, but punching the stuffing out of a heavy bag sounded like a good idea before I faced the day.

Dana Point was built on the slope of a west-facing hillside, so at 6 a.m., fifteen minutes after sunrise, the sky above had lightened, but the harbor wouldn't actually see the sun for another hour when it rose above the hills. It made for an extended dawn for our sleepy little beach town to ease into the day, which reflected the coastal lifestyle in South Orange County. Relatively speaking. It was tough to call a town "sleepy" with over 30,000 residents, but compared to the busier beach cities of Newport, Laguna, and Huntington Beach, Dana Point liked to lie in bed in the mornings and go to sleep a little earlier in the evenings.

As I drove to Dad's gym, I rolled the situation with Fuentes over in my mind. Of course, it seemed somewhat obvious now, but I had never suspected that the man was gay. He'd quickly driven away after we'd seen each other, and his friend had disappeared down the street. Not that I'd been of a mind to chase after either one of them, but I couldn't help dwelling on how things would be when I saw him this morning. I hoped he'd realize I didn't give a hoot about his love life or sexual preferences, but he'd clearly gone to great lengths to conceal it from me and everyone else at work, so I wasn't expecting things to be comfortable. Especially after the row we'd had. I knew a little bit about keeping secrets, so I could only imagine the angst he was going through.

I parked and stomped inside the gym, welcomed by the familiar sounds. Men and women working hard, sweating, groaning, encouraging each other, and hitting things as hard as they could.

"Morning," my dad greeted me, looking over from where he was coaching a young fighter on the speedball.

"Hey," I said, and continued toward the locker room to get my bag gloves.

"You okay?" he called after me.

"Yup!" I shouted back, unlocking the metal cabinet to be greeted by the smell of sweat and leather.

"Let me tape you up proper today, alright?"

I took my gloves out and grabbed my wraps, wondering about his special interest. Usually, I taped my own hands if I planned a longer session on the heavy bag, or didn't wrap them at all for shorter workouts. I walked back out to the main gym where my dad appeared to be done with the kid, who was moving on to the weight room.

"Yer mum told me, Kat," he said as softly as his deep voice could manage. "You sure you're okay?"

I wasn't certain exactly what he meant by Mum telling him, as I'd made her swear not to say a word about Paul cheating on me. Dad had really liked Paul, and I hated disappointing my dad.

"I'm alright," I assured him. "Nothing hitting a bag can't cure."

"Figured you'd be ready to hit something," he said with a crooked grin. "Want to spar again?"

"Yeah," I said a little too quickly. "Wait, with Cisco?"

He laughed. "No. I got this nineteen-year-old who's an arrogant little wanker, and he needs knocking down a peg or two. He joined a few months back and thinks he knows it all already. I figured you might be in the right mood this morning to handle him."

I wasn't sure if Dad was complimenting me or supporting the theory that I had an uncontrollable aggressive streak, but I liked the idea of clocking a wanker, so I held out my hands.

"Tape me up, and I'll get my sparring gloves."

With headgear, mouthguard, and the right gloves on, I climbed through the ropes my dad held apart, and looked at my opponent. He was about my height, wiry, and pissed off.

"A tchick?" he complained, lisping with his mouthguard in place. "You want me to hit a tchick?"

"I don't much care if you hit her or not, mate, but I guarantee she'll be hitting you, so I'd keep your hands up if I were you," my dad told him.

The kid walked to the ropes. "No, no, no. Thith ith bullthit."

I bounced on the balls of my feet and jabbed at the air in the corner of the ring to warm up while Dad sorted the kid out.

"You pay me to train you, Aidan. Or at least your parents do, which means you do what I tell you. This isn't a fight. You're sparring. I want you to work on your feet like we talked about. You've practiced on your own, now you need to implement it with a sparring partner. No good if it all goes to shit in the ring, right?"

Aidan nodded. "Okay. But I'm tweating her like any other fighter."

I'm sure he meant the statement as a warning to me, but with the lisp, it was more amusing than intimidating. I reminded myself to focus. The kid had likely sparred far more times than my singular short-lived experience, and the little guys tended to be fast.

"Alright, listen to me, and break when I say," my dad instructed. "Fight on."

We tapped gloves, then Aidan immediately began moving around the ring. His feet were dancing like one of the Irish blokes in Riverdance, and I forced my eyes to stay up high on my target. He jabbed a few times, hitting my gloves, and I noticed his reach wasn't that great.

"You're already getting too busy, Aidan," my dad coached, and I registered a few of Aidan's dizzying foot moves in my peripheral vision.

He jabbed again, and I jabbed back, testing my own reach. My blow hit his gloves but knocked him onto his back foot. He ducked and weaved a little, switching directions a couple of times and shifting from my left to my right. He did it again. I wasn't planted in one spot, and I kept my feet in motion, but I let him do most of the work.

Aidan switched again, moving to my left, and jabbed. My gloves, held high with my elbows in, easily took the blow once again, and now I had a plan. The kid circled a little farther around me and then predictably switched directions, and I knew he'd jab. As soon as he did, I blocked him with my left glove and brought my right over his outstretched arm. Pushing off my rear foot, I gave a solid punch that caught him across his mouth and nose.

Aidan teetered backwards and tripped over his own feet, dropping to the canvas.

"Break!" my dad shouted as the kid scrambled back up to his feet.

"I just tripped!" Aidan shouted, his voice clear, as I'd knocked his mouthguard out. "I was taking it easy on her, that's all."

"Go hit the bag, Kat," Dad said, winking at me. "Twinkle Toes here needs a bit more work on his own."

"No way!" Aidan complained, trying to pick up his mouthguard from the canvas with his gloved hand. "Let's go again. I'll work on my feet, Mr. Cromwell."

Dad looked at me, and I nodded.

"Alright. Do you know what you did wrong, Aidan?" he asked.

"Yes, yes. I know," the kid replied, brushing the mouthguard across the canvas until it was by the ropes.

My dad picked it up and shoved it in the kid's mouth, then

wiped his hands on his sweatpants. I stood in the middle of the ring, and once Aidan joined me and we'd tapped gloves, Dad called "Fight on!" once more.

Two things became evident immediately. Aidan hadn't learned shit from the first round, and now he was frustrated and angry. He did the same back-and-forth he'd done before, and with each change in direction, he left his feet square to me. He threw twice as many jabs and even tried a real blow, which glanced off my left glove and earned him a jab in the left eye.

The sparring had caught the interest of several others in the gym, who took a break from their workouts to watch. Four or five of them gathered outside the ropes and whispered comments amongst themselves. I shut them out of my mind and focused on my opponent, but I could tell by the eye flicks in their direction that the onlookers were getting to Aidan.

After a minute of dancing around and my dad coaching him to no avail, I watched for his direction switch. Instead of waiting for the inevitable jab, I faked a left jab of my own, then clocked him again with an even better right. The ropes stopped him going all the way down this time, and he flew back towards me with a wild swing.

"Break!" my dad called out.

But Aidan wasn't having any of it. There were too many eyes on the kid for him to accept defeat from a girl. I'd dropped my gloves, but quickly dodged his lunge.

"I said break!" my dad shouted.

Aidan still came at me with all control and technique out the window. I kept my arms dropped, but when his glove whistled past my nose as I stepped back just in time, I swung another right, using his own momentum against him. This time, he hit the canvas with a thump, emitting a stunned groan.

The onlookers cheered, and my dad was in the ring faster than a man of his age and size should be capable of. I figured he was concerned if Aidan was hurt, but he skipped that check, reached down, and plucked the kid up to his feet. With one big hand gripping Aidan's shirt, he poked the other an inch from his face.

"When I say break, you break, understand me?"

Aidan frantically nodded his assent.

"Do that again, and you're gone. Understand?"

More nodding.

"Tap gloves, then hit the showers. You're done for the day."

Aidan wouldn't look at me, but he held his gloves out. I paused, waiting with my gloves a few inches from his. He finally looked up, and then I tapped his gloves. The kid couldn't get out of the ring fast enough, making a beeline for the changing rooms. I spat my mouthguard into my glove.

"That go as planned?" I asked Dad with a grin.

Dad scratched his head. "Not exactly. I dare say I lost a client."

"Sorry about that," I replied, unable to make my voice match the words.

Dad smiled and shook his head. "I should have known better. I figured you needed to let off steam, but I didn't think you'd put him on the canvas."

I chuckled. "He put himself on the canvas, Dad. All I had to do was hold a glove in his way. But I do feel better, so thanks."

I held out my hands, and he began undoing my laces.

"I love you, kid," he said without looking up.

I laughed. "Odd time and place to tell me, Dad, but I love you, too."

16

Fuentes wasn't at the station when I arrived a little after 8 a.m. I sat at my desk and ran my own background check on Ernesto Torres, the owner of the green pickup from the harbor. I saw the two priors my partner had mentioned. Bar fights by the look of it. The older one had been in San Clemente, the town to our south, but the more recent altercation eighteen months back had been outside Capistrano Bay Tavern.

I checked the plaintiff, but I didn't recognize the name. However, I noticed a witness statement from Felix Russo. Hardly surprising if the punch-up happened right outside his restaurant, but still worth a conversation.

Seeing the Russo name reminded me to look up the background checks I'd asked the sergeant to run for me, so I checked the database for the Redman case. Neither Caroline nor Felix had any criminal history. A couple of speeding tickets for the husband and a parking ticket from ten years ago for Caroline. They both showed a handgun registration on record, along with Firearm Safety Certificates. It appeared they'd purchased the weapons and taken the required course in the late 2000s. Logical, as they owned liquor stores as well as the restaurant.

It was tempting to drive down to the harbor and find Ernesto Torres, whose address was listed as one of the boat slips, but I decided to chat with Felix Russo first to see if he recalled anything about the altercation. All we had was a grainy video of the roof of a green pickup traveling back and forth on Dana Point Harbor Drive during the timeframe Helena was murdered. I couldn't know for sure it was even Torres's truck, and certainly couldn't prove he'd been behind the wheel. I'd talk to him at some point, but needed something more credible in hand when I did.

I checked the time. It was now 9:30, and still no sign of my partner. I sat for a while with my thumb poised over the keyboard of my cell before I finally typed a text.

"Coming in today?"

Putting the phone down, I pushed it away to stop myself from staring at the screen, trying to determine if the message had been received and watching for the icon showing the recipient was typing a reply. I had just returned to checking the case database for anything else I may have missed when my phone rang. I grabbed it, assuming Fuentes had decided to call me, but the caller ID listed a local 949 number not stored as a contact.

"Cromwell," I answered.

"Hello, this is Bob Redman."

"Good morning, Mr. Redman. How can I help you?"

"We're at the beach, and I think someone is following us."

He sounded slightly out of breath, and I could hear wind and waves in the background.

"Okay," I responded. "Who's with you, sir?"

"My wife and Scarlett. She wanted to stand on the beach at Doheny and talk to her mom."

His voice cracked as he struggled with the last few words.

"I see, and what makes you think someone is following you?" I asked. "Have you seen them?"

"Yes. Well, not entirely," Bob replied hesitantly. "We drove from the house and picked up coffee, then came down here. I noticed a white car in my mirror, then I think I saw it again when we left the drive-thru."

"There are a lot of white cars on the road, sir," I responded. "Can you give me something more? Have you seen the driver? Is the car at Doheny now?"

"The sun was glinting off the window, so I didn't get a good look at the driver," he admitted. "I'm pretty sure it drove by on the road along the jetty a few minutes ago."

"Get a make and model? Or license plate?" I asked, gathering up my things.

Hell, we didn't have any other hot leads or smoking guns, so I might as well respond. There didn't appear to be any imminent threat, and a patrol car would likely run anyone off, anyway, so I headed for my car.

"I didn't, I'm afraid. It was always behind me. Maybe I'm imagining things. We're all at our wit's end, Miss Cromwell, but I'd appreciate it if you could ease our minds and take a look."

"I'm on my way," I said, getting in and starting the car. "Let's keep the phone line open and try to act casually. Do you currently see the car or anyone suspicious?"

We talked back and forth as I drove down the hill on Golden Lantern, turned left on Dana Point Harbor Drive, then right at the light for Puerto Place. I kept my eyes open for white cars and counted twelve in the parking lot alone. This was a wild goose chase, but I welcomed the thought of checking on Scarlett, so perhaps it wouldn't be a complete waste of time.

I got out of the car and scanned the beach. It was a beautiful Saturday morning, and Doheny was already busy with families, surfers, and joggers and bike riders on the pathways. I spotted Bob Redman, which wasn't difficult as he was the only person wearing long pants and a golf shirt on the beach.

"I see you, so I'm hanging up now, Bob," I explained. "I'll take a look around for a few minutes, then join you, okay?"

"Okay," he said while staring straight at me.

If anyone was watching the Redmans, they'd certainly be spooked or put on high alert by the man's obvious concern, but as I doubted anyone was actually tailing them, it probably didn't matter. I hung up and walked to the north end of the parking lot, then across the grass to Park Lantern, the entrance road into the state park itself. A few yards to my right, a pathway returned in the direction I'd come from, but on the east side of the little creek. I followed the trail, which eventually turned left to become the wider path along the back of the beach.

I scanned the larger parking lot and spotted plenty of white cars of all shapes and sizes, but they all appeared to be unoccupied. I paused by the bench and picnic area where we believed Helena Redman had first been attacked. Our police tape and barriers had been cleared, and several families had commandeered the tables for the day, no doubt unaware of the recent tragedy that had taken place at the spot where they now laughed and enjoyed their Saturday.

Turning to face the ocean, I casually glanced across the beach, then to my right, where Puerto Place ran along the top of the riprap rock wall. A white car was moving slowly along the road, heading back toward Dana Point Harbor Drive. It was probably a tourist taking in the scenery, but I hadn't seen anything or anyone else suspicious, so I figured I'd check them out.

If I ran down the path, they'd surely see me and drive away in a hurry if they were indeed spying on the Redmans. Instead, I walked into the park and then ran behind the picnic tables, which garnered attention from the kids playing on the grass, but I doubted the driver could see me from the road.

My problem was the creek. I met the path running parallel to the little gulley, but turning right would take far too long, and going left would put me in clear view of Puerto Place. Cussing under my breath, I pushed through the shrubs and ran down the slope into the ditch, trying not to twist my ankle on the rocks lining the creek. The water wasn't deep, but it still soaked my shoes and socks, and I swore even more as I clambered out to the parking lot. Sprinting across the asphalt, I spotted the car still rolling slowly along the road about fifty yards away.

With my feet making squidgy noises with every step, I stayed behind a row of cars all the way to the far side of the parking lot and ran out into the road, holding up a hand and my badge. I groaned as I watched the driver shake his head and swear at me, but he rolled to a stop. I should have guessed. It was Darian Rutherford in his little white rental car.

I waved him to the side, and he parked. I walked to the driver's window. He manually wound it down. A sure sign he'd found the cheapest rental car available.

"Thought you were all fired up to leave town," I said, panting a little after my run.

"Had to replace the rope you took, remember?"

"Neither the boat you're staying on nor the marine store are down here, Mr. Rutherford. What are you up to?"

"Fuck. Can't I drive around town without you hassling me? Maybe that flies in Australia, or wherever you're from, but not in America, lady. We have rights here."

It was a good job I'd already smacked the shit of someone that morning, or I might have let this guy get to me.

"Sure," I said. "But you don't have the right to follow your daughter around and freak her grandparents out. That's actually harassment."

"I wasn't following them," he replied with less vigor.

"Okay, so you were just returning to the scene of the crime before heading out. That it?"

Rutherford scoffed. "Seriously? You know I had nothing to do with Helena's murder. Why would I? We were over years ago. I've had nothing to do with her ever since."

"So why were you slowly cruising Puerto Place this morning?" I asked again. "Surely you must see how this looks suspicious? This is right where your ex was murdered."

He banged the steering wheel with his hand. "Jesus, lady. I wanted to get a look at my kid, alright? Happy now? I drove to her grandparents' house and hung out for a bit, hoping she'd come outside or something. When she finally did, they all loaded up and drove to a coffee shop, and then came here. I just wanted to get a look at Scarlett before I left."

"The idea of knocking on their door didn't occur to you?"

Rutherford groaned, but at least he'd calmed down. "I told you before, I don't want to get everyone stirred up and confuse the kid. She's going through enough. I don't want her getting any crazy ideas. Scarlett's better off with her grandparents."

For a moment, I considered hauling him in on a harassment charge just to keep him from leaving town, but it felt like a shitty move. We didn't have anything to place Rutherford at the actual crime scene, and zero motive from what I could see. I strongly doubted the rope I'd taken from the boat would provide us with anything more than circumstantial evidence. Even if the fibers matched, there was likely to be ten miles of the same line distributed amongst boat owners in the area. No chance of it holding up in court.

"It would be a great idea for you to stick around a few days," I suggested, already knowing what the answer would be.

"I'm self-employed, lady," he replied. "This trip has already cost me a bundle, and I'm on a boat going out Thursday that I can't afford to miss. If you don't have a court order, I ain't sticking around."

I hoped I wouldn't regret not making it more difficult for him, but even if I hit him with harassment charges, he'd be on his way by mid-morning Monday. I doubted I'd have anything back on the rope by then.

"I was born in England, not Australia," I said. "But I'm an American citizen, and I guarantee I know your rights far better than you do, despite what you think." I tapped the roof of the car a couple of times. "Drive safely, Mr. Rutherford. But I'd be sure to watch the speed limit if I were you."

I quickly snapped an instant picture for my collection as he drove away, cursing me as he went. I allowed myself a smile. Of course, I had no way of organizing police officers to keep an eye out for him from here to Oregon, but I could guarantee it would now be in the back of his mind the whole way.

17

I stood at the back of my car and peeled off my sodden shoes, which were now coated in sand from where I'd walked out onto the beach to speak with the Redmans. Bob was caught between relief at not being paranoid and anger at Rutherford for causing them more trauma on top of what the family was already going through. Shirley fretted, worried, then fretted some more. Scarlett appeared to be numb to the chaos, lost in her internalized world of grief and confusion.

I really felt bad for the kid, but figured Rutherford was right. She was far better off with her grandparents than any life her father could offer.

Tossing my shoes in the boot, I stripped off my equally soaked socks and threw them in, too. My only backup options were a worn-out pair of boxing shoes I'd not gotten around to throwing out and an even older pair of flip-flops I carried in my gym bag.

I chose the flip-flops. After all, it was the weekend.

Pulling my phone from my pocket, I finally got around to checking what all the vibrating and dings I'd missed had been about while I'd been dealing with the grieving family and spying father. Several were unimportant emails, but one was a text from Fuentes. I dropped into the driver's seat and read his message.

"Where are you?"

He'd sent it half an hour ago. I thought about calling him, but figured I'd tread carefully and reply by text.

"Doheny. Heading to Cap Bay Tav."

I sat, staring at the screen, watching the three little dots in the bubble that I'd forced myself to ignore earlier. He was either sending me *War and Peace* via text or taking his time considering what to type. I finally dropped my phone into its dash-mounted holder and drove out of the parking lot. I was already burning up far too much time and energy worrying about dealing with a partner who didn't want to be my partner in the first place.

It took all of three minutes to drive up the hill and park in the tiny lot right outside the restaurant. It looked like they were just getting ready to open as a staff member was sliding back the large patio doors. My phone dinged again, and I removed it from the holder to read the text.

"Lunch at Bonjour Café?"

I guess he'd decided to talk this over. And he'd chosen a quiet yet still public spot, so I assumed he didn't plan on yelling at me too loudly.

"When?" I replied.

This time, he responded right away. *"30 mins."*

That gave me a chance to see if the Russos were around, so I replied with a thumbs-up emoji as I got out of the car, then walked into the restaurant.

"Good morning, Mr. Russo," I said, seeing the man appear from the back carrying a box of wine.

"Detective," he replied, placing the box on the bar. "My apologies. I don't recall your name."

"Investigator Kat Cromwell, sir."

"Investigator? Is that the same as a detective?"

"Basically," I replied, moving to the bar. "I'm with the Orange County Sheriff's Department, who use the term 'investigator.'"

"Guns, badges, and catching bad guys, right?" he said with a smile.

"Something like that."

"Are you looking for Caroline? She should be in the office if you want me to check."

"Actually, I think you may be able to help me, Mr. Russo," I replied, then made sure no one else was within earshot before continuing. "Do you recall an incident outside the restaurant a year and a half ago? A man was arrested for assault."

"Felix, please," he said with another smile. "I do recall the incident, unfortunately. We don't get much of that sort of thing here. Occasional raised voices, but they, or we, usually smooth things over before it comes to blows. We don't really attract the rambunctious types." He paused from removing bottles from the box. "Would you like lunch, Investigator Cromwell? I can have the chef prepare something for you."

"I'm good, but thank you," I replied. I had a lunch date with a porcupine, and I'm sure Russo's chef wouldn't appreciate fixing a dish for my fussy tastes. "Can you tell me what the brawl was about?"

Russo scratched his head. "That, I don't remember, I'm afraid. Something unimportant, no doubt, with a few drinks involved. Why the interest after all this time? Does it have anything to do with poor Helena?"

I was about to give him a vanilla answer and move on when I noticed someone through the door to the kitchen.

"Mr. Russo, is that Travis Redman I just saw?"

"Possibly," the man replied without surprise. "He helps out from time to time."

My first reaction was one of suspicion, but I considered my prior interactions with the Russos and with Travis Redman before saying anything. Unless I'd forgotten something, which it didn't feel like I had, it seemed strange that their relationship had been withheld. But then again, I hadn't given either party a reason to mention it, as best as I could recall.

"What does he do for you?" I asked.

"Odd jobs, mainly. Running errands, maintenance. Occasionally, Caroline has him helping in the kitchen. He's pretty devastated about his sister, as you can imagine."

I forced a smile. "I'm sure. Was Travis working for you on Tuesday night, Mr. Russo?"

He thought for a moment. "Didn't Caroline give you the names of whoever was here that evening?"

"At the restaurant, yes, but you made it sound like Travis does other work for you as well. Perhaps for the liquor stores?"

"When I say he occasionally works for us, Miss Cromwell, I do mean occasionally," he said, then lowered his voice. "The lad isn't the reliable type, if you know what I mean. It was more of a favor to Helena than anything else. We thought after what happened to her, the least we could do was keep him busy and try to help him through this. He's had problems with the law in the past, as I'm sure you're aware."

Travis Redman was still our number-one suspect. He was the only person we could place at the scene, and he'd consistently avoided giving us a reason for breaking into his sister's minivan. It felt like the case might be one piece of forensic evidence away from arresting the young man. But I still couldn't fathom a motive.

"That's generous of you," I commented. "The restaurant must be doing well to afford extra staff out of the goodness of your heart."

Felix grinned and shook his head. "We've kept our heads above water so far, and the weekends are profitable, but Caroline is focused on improving weekday traffic. That'll make or break it for her."

"Her?" I questioned. "Surely the restaurant is yours as well."

"Of course, but this is Caroline's project," he replied. "I agreed to fund it for three years, providing it met certain criteria. After that, it has to stand on its own two feet, or we move on."

His comment made me wonder how a married couple could separate their businesses in such a way, but it wasn't pertinent to

Helena's case, and I was too short on time to be distracted by my own curiosity.

"Back to the incident we were discussing," I said. "Did you know either of the men involved?"

Felix shook his head. "Can't say I did."

I glanced once more through the door into the kitchen, but didn't see Travis. My hope to learn more about Ernesto Torres during this visit hadn't been rewarding on that front, but somehow, the new information regarding Travis felt important. Although I had no idea why.

Thanking Felix Russo for his time, I turned to leave, then thought of one more question.

"Does Travis have a key or alarm code for the restaurant, Mr. Russo?"

He'd returned to stocking the wine bottles, but stopped and shook his head. "Not to my knowledge. That wouldn't be… smart on our part," he added in a whisper.

I checked my watch as I walked out and saw I was due to meet Fuentes in a few minutes. Bonjour Café was farther down Del Prado on the same block as Capistrano Bay Tavern, so I decided to walk. It would take me longer to find another parking spot than to hoof it both ways.

When I was growing up, Del Prado had been the one-way southbound side of PCH, and what was now two-way traffic a block over had been the northbound lanes. In an effort to create a "downtown" feel, the city had made the change a while back, and a lot of new construction had taken place on the land between the two roads. Del Prado had become a quiet street where anyone passing through town had to be aware of a business or restaurant located there to bother stopping, while PCH became a congested mess. Maybe it had worked out for the better overall, but most of the locals preferred the people passing through to keep passing through and leave the touristy chaos to Laguna Beach and Balboa in Newport.

My partner was already there, sitting at a table outside on the café's narrow patio between the sidewalk and the building. It was still early for lunch, so he was the only patron, but I was sure that wouldn't last long come noon.

He glanced up from the menu and nodded as I walked up, then continued reading. A server arrived as I sat down and asked me if I'd like a drink. She was about my height, but with long dark hair, a pretty face, and a busty figure, accentuated by a snug blouse unbuttoned just enough. She also spoke with a sexy French accent. Yesterday, I would have imagined Fuentes making a play for her.

"Coffee, please," I said.

"Latte or cappuccino?"

"Just regular coffee, thanks."

"*Oui, mademoiselle.* Are you still okay with water, *monsieur*?"

"I am, thanks," Fuentes replied, offering the young woman a pleasant smile.

Once she left, he placed the menu down and looked at me. I peeked over the menu I'd just begun looking at, although I already knew I'd be ordering their brie sandwich. If they left the stringy watercress out, it fit my narrow tastes perfectly. It was hard to go wrong with bread and cheese.

"I don't know what you think you saw, but we need to get things clear," he said.

His tone was firm, but there was something else in his voice I hadn't heard before.

"Okay," I replied, happy to let him talk himself down whatever path he chose.

"I suppose you've already spread the gossip around."

"Why would I do that?" I countered, proud of how calm and relaxed my own voice sounded.

He shook his head. "After yesterday's episode, I figured you'd be shouting it from the rooftops."

"What? The thing I think I saw that you say I didn't see?"

"Don't play games, Kat."

"I'm not playing anything, Fuentes," I replied, and placed the menu down. "What you don't seem to realize is that I don't care what you do in your personal life. That's up to you, and it's none of my business. Honestly, I was surprised, but that doesn't mean I'd tell anyone about it. Heck, I didn't even tell my mother who I was having dinner with, and believe me, I could have used a change of subject."

"You want me to believe you're not going to use this against me?"

"I can't help what you choose to believe, but what I can tell you is all I want is for us to figure out a better way of working together. Right now, Helena Redman deserves the best of us, and we're not giving her that when we're at each other's throats and threatening each other with running to Bradley or whatever else."

My voice had risen more than I'd intended, but I took a breath while he stared back at me with piercing eyes.

"And quite frankly," I continued, keeping my volume in check, "I could use all the help I can get. We're over three days into this case with bugger all that'll last more than a minute in court. Whether you start helping me more or not, I have no desire or reason to say anything to anyone about last night. That's not a weapon or leverage in my eyes. I'm asking you as my partner on this case to please help me as much as you can."

"It's not like I've been absent, Kat. We've talked about many of the angles."

I raised one eyebrow at him. "You're telling me you've been fully committed and not holding anything back while you're checking boxes for Bradley?"

That came out sounding harsher than I'd intended, and I winced, waiting for a verbal barrage in return. But he stayed quiet, still looking at me as though his captivating eyes could draw the truth from my soul.

"I owe you in this deal, too," I said, partly to soften my previous statement but more because it was also true. "I know I can get a bit too eager occasionally, but it really crushes me that you think you can't trust me."

"It appears I have no choice," Hugo replied, but his lips curled into a slight grin.

Before I could say anything more and most likely undo the progress I thought we'd just made, the sexy French woman returned to take our order and saved me.

The rest of lunch was spent running over the case and getting Fuentes up to speed on the morning's events. We split the check, and when we rose to leave, I happened to look across the street at a building fifty yards toward Capistrano Bay Tavern.

"Didn't the uniforms canvass the businesses around here for witnesses?" I asked.

"I thought so, yes," Fuentes replied, following my gaze.

"Look at the art gallery over there. Is that a security camera dome near the entryway?"

"I don't recall seeing any footage from an art gallery," he commented.

"Maybe they didn't come this far, or figured the camera couldn't actually see the restaurant."

"Let's go see," he suggested, rising to his feet.

We left the café, walked down the sidewalk, then crossed Del Prado. The gallery had three floor-to-ceiling windows with various paintings and sculptures on display. Its building was divided from its neighbor by a common walkway with a staircase leading to offices upstairs. The camera dome hung from the ceiling of the walkway, close to the front door for the gallery, which was inset into the corner of the building.

"Hi," I said, opening the glass door and spotting an elegant woman in her fifties with high cheekbones, dark hair, and olive skin. "Does the camera out there belong to the gallery?" I asked, showing her my badge.

"Yes," she replied with a slight accent.

"Do you record the footage?"

"We keep it for two weeks, then erase it to make room," she replied. "Has there been a problem?"

"Depending on the camera's view, it may have recorded movements down the road which could be of interest to us," I explained. "Can you access the recording from Tuesday evening?"

"Your people came by the other day, and I explained that the camera doesn't really show Capistrano Bay Tavern," she replied.

"What's your name, ma'am?" I asked.

"I'm Fatemeh," she said, extending a hand. "I'm the owner."

"Nice to meet you, Fatemeh. If you don't mind indulging us, we'd like to take a look, anyway."

"Come with me, but I'm the only one here at the moment so if anyone comes in, I'll need to step out front," she explained before she beckoned us to follow her through a door behind the counter.

The office was clean but cluttered, with framed art leaning against every available section of wall, cabinet, and desk. It only took her a minute to bring up the recorded file on a computer with a large monitor perched on the desk.

"Here," she said, vacating the seat, "you can look for yourself. Press play, then scroll to the time you need."

I thanked her and sat down, using the mouse to start the footage, then sliding the play bar until it reached 10 p.m. on Tuesday night. Fuentes stood behind me and watched over my shoulder. The camera had a wide lens, so the Capistrano Bay Tavern at the end of the block was quite small, and the patio was indeed hidden by the restaurant building itself. I set the playback to 4x speed and watched people move down the sidewalk like Charlie Chaplin in an old black-and-white movie.

When the time reached 10:25 p.m., two minutes before we knew Helena had set the alarm, I slowed the playback to double speed, and we watched carefully. Traffic rolled by, and a few pedestrians moved down the sidewalk, with customers occasionally crossing the road to their cars parked on the southbound side of Del Prado.

When the time passed 10:30 p.m., I hit pause. "I bet she parked in the lot behind the restaurant, or even down the road."

"Probably," Fuentes agreed. "I'm sure employees are encouraged to park as far away from the restaurant as possible to free up room for customers."

I dragged the play bar back to 10:27 p.m. and let it roll once more at regular speed. Any figures were too small to clearly identify, but none drove away in a minivan.

"Bloody hell," I blurted, hitting pause.

My partner leaned in closer as I replayed the footage from 10:28 p.m. one more time. The vehicle we watched was small in the distance and had to have been parked in the last spot before the right-hand side of Del Prado became a turning lane for Golden Lantern, heading to the harbor. But there was no mistaking the color or the make.

"That's Chris Wendell's yellow Jeep," I muttered.

Fuentes stood up straight. "Yup, and he followed Helena to the harbor."

18

Wendell's phone went straight to voicemail, and his roommate, Manny Rubio, told us he hadn't seen him for two days. I checked with Sergeant Martinez and urged him to send uniforms by Salty's bar. By the time we made it to Beachwood Trailer Park, Sarge called back and reported that, according to coworkers, Wendell didn't close on Tuesday night. He'd left shortly after 10 p.m. It was an easy decision to put out a BOLO for Helena's ex-boyfriend.

The yellow Jeep was parked at the mobile home, but according to Rubio, our suspect's mountain bike was missing. The roommate also seemed more worried about maintaining the privacy of his own room than concerned for Wendell or what he'd potentially done, so we left a uniformed deputy at the premises to keep an eye out while we ran around drumming up a warrant. Which Captain Bradley was more than happy to help push through.

We'd also asked for a deputy to visit Fatemeh at the art gallery to collect more footage from her security camera. It was another long shot, but maybe there was something else between the night of Helena's murder and now that would be useful. This time, I agreed with Fuentes that we should submit the large quantity of recordings to our IT department for review.

Once we returned to the trailer park, the tow truck was about to haul the Jeep away. I asked them to wait a moment so I could take a quick look, but I didn't spot any rope. Fuentes and I moved on to the house, which smelled stale, like it hadn't been cleaned properly in years and sweaty clothes had been left lying around for weeks. We began in Chris Wendell's room.

"This place is a mess," my partner complained for the fourth or fifth time.

He wasn't wrong. The only nice thing I'd spotted in the trailer so far was a guitar held in a stand and its amp in the corner of the bedroom. And the dog. A shaggy-haired mutt of some description who seemed eager to be everybody's friend. The kind of dog who'd be perfect for me if someone else could amuse him while I wasn't there most of the time. But then the dog would be more attached to that person than me and barely lift his head when I came home. Like a cat.

"Something's missing," I said, pointing to a second guitar stand with no instrument.

"Who runs away on a bicycle with a guitar on their back?" Hugo replied, shaking his head. "Sounds like a Robert Rodriguez movie."

"I'll have to take your word for it," I laughed.

"*El Mariachi, From Dusk Till Dawn, Machete,*" Fuentes replied. "You've never watched a Rodriguez movie?"

"I don't think so. I'm more of a sci-fi, fantasy fan. For me, modern-day dramas are a mixture of rubbish that couldn't happen and violence we see too much of on the job. At least with sci-fi, you go in knowing it's all make-believe."

"He directed a few of *The Book of Boba Fett* series," Fuentes said.

"Oh," I said. "Then I have watched a Rodriguez show, so you can rest easy tonight knowing that."

He paused from rummaging through a bedside table. "Seriously though, why take a guitar?"

I looked at my partner. The first thing I realized was that he had been far more engaging and chattier since our lunch talk. Which was encouraging, but could have more to do with finally having a positive lead. The other thing was that he had a point.

"Manny!" I called out, and the roommate trudged in from the living room.

"Yeah?"

"How many guitars does Chris have?"

The man looked around the room, then pointed. "There's one."

"No shit, Sherlock," I couldn't stop myself from saying. "Does he own more than that one?"

"I guess. He has an acoustic, too," Manny said. "The neighbors complained about the noise, so he can't play the electric in here."

"You mean he can't play it through the amp in here," Fuentes pointed out.

Manny shrugged his shoulders. "I guess. He usually practices on the acoustic."

"Do you know where Chris plays?" I asked. "Is he in a band?"

"I guess," he said again, which was beginning to annoy me.

"And the name of that band would be..?" my partner prompted.

Manny shook his head. "The Raging something or other, I think. He's been in and out of too many. I can't keep up."

"Any idea where they play?" I asked.

He shook his head again. "Not my thing, and I'm usually working nights."

"Wendell dating anyone?" Fuentes asked.

"I doubt *he* can remember their names, and you're asking *me*?" Manny replied. "Chris gets more—"

He managed to stop himself from saying the obvious, although I wasn't sure if it was because we were cops or because I was a woman.

"Okay, we get it. Thanks for your help," I told him, and he wandered back to the living room.

"We can search the local venues and see if a band name sounds close," Fuentes said, moving on to searching a dresser.

"I guess," I replied with a grin.

My partner actually laughed. "More weed, anyone?"

I laughed with him, and it felt good. Continuing the search, I thought about places in town where bands played, and something nagged in my mind. I took out my instant pictures and quickly thumbed through them. My brain stopped me on the one with Jeremy in the marine supply shop. He was sitting at the desk in the tiny office, but I could picture the store itself, and it was enough to connect the dots.

"I know where we can start," I blurted. "Hennessy's. An old guy at the marine store recognized Wendell from playing there."

Fuentes looked at the pictures in my hand, and I could tell he wanted to say or ask something. But he didn't. Maybe he didn't want to spoil our newfound positive vibe. Whatever his reasons, I was glad to shove my pictures away and move on.

Beyond verifying that Chris Wendell was behind on his laundry and likely never used a vacuum cleaner, we found nothing directly tying him to the murder of Helena Redman. We bagged all his clothes for forensics to check for blood, but I couldn't see any obvious signs as we loaded them. If he still harbored feelings for the victim, there were no traces in his room. No saved notes, cards, or photos, although everybody except me kept all their photos on phones these days, so until we found Chris, we couldn't check his saved album.

"You know, there's a chance he just got lucky and has crashed at a girlfriend's place," Fuentes suggested as we walked outside.

"Phone could be dead, which explains it going to voicemail. Which is full, by the way," I replied. "It all adds up like he could be hiding, though, don't you think?"

"Or he's shut it off so we can't track it. Either way, we need to find the guy," Fuentes said as we walked to my car, having left his at the station. "I'd say he's found his way to the top of the list."

I started the Fusion but sat for a moment, thinking. "Have we seen any signs of a relationship, good or bad, between the brother and Wendell?"

"Not that I recall," Fuentes replied.

"I couldn't think of anything, either. So, we now believe Wendell followed Helena from the restaurant at around 10:30 p.m., and Travis Redman broke into her minivan at Doheny at ten past twelve. But we don't know whether she was attacked between those times, or after, when we know Travis was there."

Fuentes sighed, picking dog hair from his trousers for a few moments before responding. "Which actually keeps the brother at the top of the list, as he's the only one we can truly place at Doheny. All we see is Wendell pulling away. It appears he turns right, but he's so far away at that point, we can't know for sure."

I drove us to the same shopping center as my taco stop, Buena Vista Market, where Hennessey's Irish Tavern sat at the PCH end of the marketplace. It was part of a small Southern California chain of restaurants, and their Dana Point location had ridden the various storms over the years. I could remember my mum and dad bringing me there when we first moved to America.

It was mid-afternoon on Saturday, so I wasn't sure if the patrons were leftovers from late lunches or professional drinkers starting their evening, but the place was busier than I'd expected. We went to the bar, and a young woman with blue hair and an impressive array of piercings asked if she could help us.

"We believe this guy plays in here sometimes," I began, showing her my badge and a picture of Wendell on my phone. "Do you know him?"

"Not personally," the woman replied with a wry grin. "But yeah, I've seen him in here. He also bartends around town."

"With a band?" I asked, deciding not to offer up "The Raging Somethings," mainly because I'd sound daft.

"The Ragged Three," she replied. "He's their new guitarist. They're local. Play here at weekends a few times a month."

"Seen him lately?"

The woman shook her head, causing the accouterments hanging from her ears to clink against each other. "I don't think they played last night. Maybe last weekend, but I'd have to look it up. It all blends together."

We'd seen the man since last weekend, so I was more interested in the last forty-eight hours. "What about the rest of the band? Any idea where we can find them?"

"I know the drummer, Dougie," she replied. "I can text him and ask if you like?"

"Or you could have him come see us," Fuentes interjected. "That would be better."

The woman paused and looked my partner over, her expression tightening. "What's this about? I mean, Dougie's a cool dude. I don't wanna get him in any trouble."

"He's not," I quickly reassured her. "It's Chris Wendell we'd like to speak with. He didn't come home for the past few days, and his roommate is worried about him."

I wasn't sure Manny was concerned about any aspect of Chris Wendell's life beyond his rent check, but Miss Tacklebox didn't know that.

"I have an idea," Fuentes added. "You call Dougie and let us speak with him. Why don't we do that?"

The bartender looked like she'd do anything to be somewhere else right now. "Let me catch up on a few orders, and I'll be right back."

"No, I have a better plan," I said firmly. "Why don't you make the call right now?"

From the glare behind her heavily applied black eyeliner, I knew she was considering her options between telling law enforcement to shove it or complying. I had a good idea what was coming next. The woman pulled her phone from her back pocket, unlocked it, and scrolled to a number. Holding the phone to her ear, we couldn't hear what was happening, but it didn't matter.

"Went to voicemail," she said, ending the call and shoving the phone back in her pocket.

"What's your name?" I asked.

"Cindy," she replied.

I held my hand out. "Show me your phone, Cindy."

"No way," she snapped back. "You can't take my phone for no reason. I have to get back to work." She turned to leave.

"It's called obstruction or impeding an investigation, Cindy," I pointed out, and she stopped. "This is a murder investigation. Now, hand me your phone. Unlocked."

Her eyes grew wider. She quickly retrieved her phone and unlocked it, but didn't hand it to me.

"I know you didn't call Dougie," I said in a softer tone. "But that's what you're going to do now."

She nodded and scrolled again, making another call.

"Hey, Dougie. I'm sorry, dude, but there are cops here looking for your guitarist, and they wanna speak to you."

I beckoned for her to relinquish the phone, which she did.

"…they want with Chris?" Dougie was in the midst of asking.

"Hi, Dougie. This is Investigator Kat Cromwell with the Orange County Sheriff's Department. It's really important that we find your friend, Chris Wendell. Do you know where he is?"

There was a pause on the line.

"Sir, it's vitally important we find Chris as soon as possible. Is he with you?"

"No, no. He's not here," Dougie quickly responded. "Honestly, I don't know where he is."

"When was the last time you saw him?"

"He didn't show up to practice on Thursday night and hasn't answered his phone. We were pretty pissed. It's been over a week since I talked to him."

"Any ideas where he might be staying? Other friends? Relatives?" I asked.

"To be honest, I've known the guy around town for years, but we're not close friends. He has a reputation for flaking, so he's only in the band because we were jammed up for a guitarist. I really don't know much about him."

"He's not mentioned a girlfriend or the name of a friend?" I prompted.

Dougie took a few moments before replying. "A while back, he said something about a cousin in Newport. If he said her name, I don't recall what it was. He said she's married to some rich dude. Maybe you can track her down."

"Okay, thanks. I'm going to text you my number. If you think of anything else, will you call or text me?"

"Sure," he said, but I wasn't convinced.

Helping us when we had him on the line was one thing, but he was probably more worried about filling what now appeared to be a vacant guitarist's spot in his band.

"Thanks, and just so you know, we pressed Cindy into calling you. She didn't have a choice, so don't blame her."

I hung up the call, then texted my number to Dougie. I then forwarded his info to my phone. He was saved in Cindy's contacts as Dougie Sanders.

"Thanks for saying that," Cindy mumbled when I handed her back her phone.

I gave her a card. "Reach out if you think of anything else or hear where Wendell might be."

She nodded and scurried away to catch up on bar orders.

"Worth talking to anyone else here?" Fuentes asked.

"Pretty sure Cindy would have palmed us off if she thought there was anyone else here who knew him," I replied.

Fuentes grunted his agreement. At least I took it as agreement, so I suggested our next move. "Let's see if we can trace the relative."

We walked back to the car, and Fuentes opened his laptop computer. Instead of searching through databases we had access to, he went straight to social media and found Chris Wendell. He hadn't posted anything in the past six days. Before that, it was info and gig dates for the band. He had 832 followers. I watched my partner search Wendell's friends list for anyone with the same last name. Three Wendells, who all turned out to be relatives living out of state.

"A cousin could be from an aunt with a married name, or she could be married herself," I pointed out.

Fuentes added a hyphen after Wendell and got one hit. Sara Wendell-Fenley. Her profile was full of pictures of two young kids, one boy, one girl, both around eight or nine years old. According to her profile, she lived in Newport Beach, California.

19

There was no point going to Newport Beach, then all the way back to Dana Point for Fuentes to then backtrack home to Laguna Beach, so we ran by the station to pick up his car. It was tempting to call the Newport Beach Police Department and ask them to drop by the address we'd found for Sara Wendell-Fenley, but they'd send a uniform in a squad car. If Wendell saw them pull up, he'd be gone before they knocked on the door.

I had to use the loo, so I dashed inside the station. I was about to leave when I saw that Captain Bradley's office door was open.

"We should give her a quick update," I said to Fuentes, who was waiting in the reception area.

He looked at his watch and sighed. "Fine. But let's keep it short."

I knocked on the door, and the captain waved us in. I gave her the briefest rundown on what we knew, which was still a mess of circumstantial crap.

"Could you give us a moment?" Bradley said to my partner once I was finished.

Fuentes sighed. "I'm going to head south. Call me when you're done," he said impatiently and walked out.

Captain Bradley smiled. "How's it going with Hugo?"

I wondered if she knew anything about our row and subsequent discussion at lunch. I'd been with him since Bonjour Café, so I doubted he'd told her about it. Perhaps she was simply asking out of interest or concern, but her timing was suspicious.

"Good, actually," I said. "Wish we were further ahead with the case, but we're working it as hard as we can."

"I'm glad," she responded. "Hugo has a lot of experience to draw upon."

"Yes, ma'am."

"Close the door and sit for a moment, Kat."

I did as she said, but felt like Cindy at Hennessey's. I'd rather be somewhere else doing anything but this. I'd eat broccoli to get me out of this office.

"The remains recovered from Three Arch Beach have been identified as belonging to Paul Michaels," she said in an almost sympathetic tone.

I nodded. This was not a surprise as the serial number on the plate would have been easily traceable to Paul's surgery.

"I'm sure this drags up terrible memories for you," Bradley continued. "Do you need some time? I can have Hugo take over and request someone from Santa Ana to be assigned to help him."

"No," I replied firmly. "I'm fine. I've already dealt with Paul's passing. Pieces of him showing up is certainly disturbing for his family, but I'm okay. I'm completely immersed in this case, ma'am. More than anything, I want to see it through."

The captain sat back in her chair and looked me over. "Do you recall anything further about the incident?"

Her use of the word "incident" instead of accident was not lost on me.

"No, ma'am," I replied, careful to sound relaxed and take my time responding as though I'd thought her question over.

There was no chance I'd share anything about my dreams with her, as they were wholly inconclusive, not to mention I'd sound like a nut job. I also refrained from telling her she'd be the first to know if I did remember anything new. That wasn't a promise I was prepared to make.

I'd tried everything I could think of to trigger my stubborn memory into recalling what took place, but it was simply a blank. All I knew for sure was that we'd gone out sailing as planned, and my intention had been to confront Paul about his infidelity. The seas became choppy, and it started to rain. After that, through a mixture of my own memories and others' comments, I sailed the boat back to the marina. Alone. Where I required attention for the bash on my head, which I couldn't explain. Neither I nor the police could find traces of evidence to show where I'd hit my head on the boat. My weirdly distorted nightmares were my only insight into anything more, and they were hardly a reliable source.

"Well, keep me posted," she said. "Don't try to push yourself if you need a break. Everyone will understand."

I knew that was a load of bollocks, but I kept my cool. "Will do, ma'am," I replied, and rose to leave. "I'll let you know if we find Wendell."

"Don't lose track of the brother," Captain Bradley said as I opened the door. "Unless you turn up something new, he's the only one we can currently place at the scene."

I smiled my acknowledgment and hurried away, checking my watch as I left. Fuentes had ten minutes on me, which, in Saturday early evening traffic, might only mean a couple of miles. When I pulled onto Golden Lantern, I called him.

"What was that about?" he asked in way of a greeting.

My first reaction was to deflect his question, but if I was asking him to be more open with me, it didn't seem right to hide stuff from him. Besides, what did it matter? Not telling him would make more of an issue out of what I hoped would quietly go away.

"The body part on the beach. It belongs to my fiancé."

"Sorry," he replied solemnly. "Why don't we do this in the morning? It's been a long day already, and we probably have a better chance of catching him first thing. I don't see Wendell as an early riser, and I'm sure you have a lot to process with... the other thing."

"No, I'm..." I began, then stopped myself. "Yeah. Maybe you're right. Pick you up at seven in the morning as I drive through?"

"Okay," he replied. "Do you know Dizz's As Is?"

"Sure, I've eaten there." It was a great little restaurant, but too rich for my salary, so I'd only been there with my parents.

"Heading north, the next side road on the right is Solana Way. It's just over the crest of the hill. I'll be on the corner at seven."

"Okay," I said, and we hung up.

I approached the light at Selva and put my left turn signal on to head home. Then, on a whim, turned it off and kept driving down the hill to PCH. Maybe if I had a dog at home, or a cat who acted more like a dog, I'd have done the sensible thing and gone there, but I didn't. I couldn't. The thought of sitting around the house, moping while Wendell could be at his cousin's, made for an easy decision. Staying busy sounded far more appealing to my crazy brain.

The notion that Fuentes would be upset that I'd gone without him rattled around my head as I kept driving. But by the time I passed Solana Way, I'd justified my actions a hundred times over. Few of which would pass muster if spoken aloud, but I avoided talking to myself, so that wasn't an issue.

Loitering in the background where I kept them at bay were the two real reasons I was driving north. Some days, I simply hated going home to an empty house. I didn't miss Paul, because he'd turned out to be an arse, but I missed having someone I loved looking forward to seeing me. And me them. Underneath it all, I was lonely, and throwing myself at work was my coping mechanism. Today, I needed to keep throwing myself a little longer.

And then there was my trait of being a strong, take-charge female policewoman. Characteristics sometimes referred to by others as bull-headed, hot-headed, impetuous, and impulsive.

But why focus on the negative?

The drive to Newport Beach took 40 minutes along PCH, but I

was in no particular hurry. With views of the ocean on my left and fascinating people-watching through Laguna Beach and Corona Del Mar, I didn't mind. The address we had for Sara Wendell-Fenley was on Harbor Island Road, a high-end neighborhood on the bay. Which meant *high-end* even by Newport Beach standards. I drove by the angular, modern-looking home and parked several houses down.

Chris Wendell's cousin's life had clearly taken a dramatically different path from his, either by her own doing or by choice of partner. However, Sara's recent social media posts did not include any pictures of such a partner, although she was still listed as married. I guessed she was mid-divorce, and if the husband was living somewhere else, it increased the chances of her deadbeat relative being allowed to crash at her place.

Getting out of the car, I walked closer and noticed the homes backed up to the bay. From the little I could see between them, they all had boat docks. It was a long shot that Wendell was actually here, but although I'd come without Fuentes, I still needed backup. We never knocked on a suspect's door alone, even one in a swanky neighborhood.

I took a few steps back to ensure I wouldn't be heard and keyed my handheld radio, hailing the local Newport Beach police station. "This is Orange County Sheriff's Department investigator Kat Cromwell," I began, wishing our official titles weren't a paragraph long. "Requesting backup for a home interview."

Dispatch had just begun responding when the front door to Sara Wendell-Fenley's house opened. A woman I recognized as Sara stepped outside with her two children. She closed the door behind her before looking up and seeing me outside the neighbor's place. As our eyes met, a look of panic washed over her face, and I knew the situation was about to unravel.

The daughter had trotted ahead to the sidewalk, where she smiled and greeted me. "Hello."

"Hi there," I responded, returning her smile. "Is Uncle Chris in the house?"

"I'm supposed to say he isn't here," the girl replied with the innocent honesty of a child.

"Libby, come here," Sara urged.

Through the tall glass window by the front door, I noticed movement inside the house. Chris Wendell was exiting the sliding glass door to the rear patio.

"Can I help you?" Sara asked, doing her best to gather her children around her.

"Harboring a suspect wanted by the police would be our first point of discussion," I replied, flashing my badge, but I didn't have time to wait for her response.

20

———————

Wendell looked to have turned right in the backyard, which was north, so I ran up the sidewalk, watching for an opening alongside one of the neighboring homes. His only other option was the bay, but unless he had one staged and ready, it would take too long to launch a boat. His best chance was hopping dividers from house to house.

My problem was the homes were huge and nestled together, with walls and fences joining them all together in an endless barrier. Four houses along, I spotted a gate I could scale if it wouldn't open. The gate wasn't locked, and I charged through, praying a pack of vicious guard dogs weren't waiting on the other side.

The home was an ultra-modern gray and white building with a pathway running alongside toward the water. The place was massive, taking up the depth of the lot to within six feet of a low wall before a boat dock extended into the bay.

Dispatch had been squawking at me, and I finally responded, giving them the address and informing them a pursuit was now in progress. I rounded the corner of the house just as I finished my radio call and looked to my left.

Chris Wendell lowered his shoulder and smashed into me at a full run. I tumbled over a planter into the neighbor's backyard, grabbing at Wendell as he scrambled to stay on his feet. I caught something with my right hand, clutching it tightly while all the wind left my lungs as I landed on my back, hitting concrete.

Wendell wrenched at what I realized was his backpack, trying to pull the strap from my grasp, but he finally let go in order to keep running.

"Dammit, stop!" I wheezed, staggering to my feet.

"I didn't do it!" he shouted, looking over his shoulder.

Seeing he had some distance on me, he came to a stop. He was wearing pale green board shorts, a brown long-sleeved surf brand T-shirt, and flip-flops. I was impressed by how well he'd run in the flimsy footwear. The radio had been knocked from my hand and lay on the patio halfway between us. The dispatch woman's voice echoed off the building as she announced a patrol car was three minutes out.

"I would never hurt Helena!" Wendell shouted.

"Then why are you running?" I called back, catching my breath and trying to ignore the various aches and pains from the fall.

"Cos I'm not getting locked up for something I didn't do."

"If you didn't do it, you won't get locked up," I replied, trying to use a softer tone in the hope of calming the situation down.

If I could keep him talking, maybe the local uniforms would get here and I could still salvage this mess, which had definitely not gone as planned. An image of the disappointed look on Fuentes's face flashed into my mind, and I groaned to myself. I'd be hearing the word *trust* again, and the thought really pissed me off.

"Why were you following her on Tuesday night, Chris?" I asked to keep him talking.

He shook his head and stood there panting.

"Talk to me, Chris. I can help you," I said, wishing I could come up with something more inspiring and original. "We know you followed Helena to Doheny. Tell me what happened."

He glared at me. "I didn't go to Doheny."

"Then tell me your side of things."

"I can't believe she's dead," he muttered, his eyes turning moist as he stared off into the distance.

"You lied to us about closing Salty's, Chris. We have video of you following Helena."

He glared at me again. "What? I didn't follow her, man."

"Okay," I said, thinking about the footage from the art gallery's camera. Fortunately, the memory had stayed with me. We hadn't actually seen him follow Helena's minivan. We'd only seen him drive away. It wasn't even clear that he turned right down the hill.

"So why were you at the tavern on Tuesday night?" I asked.

I wanted to inch my way toward him, but he was so jittery, I was sure he'd bolt again.

He shook his head. "I came by to see her, but she wasn't there, so I left."

Whatever thought went through his mind, I watched his whole body tense. "I gotta disappear," he mumbled, before looking around at the house and then the bay.

"Running won't help your cause, mate," I said. "I promise I'll do everything I can to make sure your version of events is heard, Chris. You can trust me."

I could see his mind was full of things he was dying to say, but he didn't trust me. Apparently, nobody trusted me. And apparently, my little speech was inspiring, just not in the way I'd hoped. He turned, ran down one of the boat slips, and dove into the bay.

Across the short stretch of water was Linda Isle, where the homes were squished even tighter together and worth even more money. I knew the island was horseshoe-shaped, with only one way on and off. I needed to get to the bridge before him.

Picking up the radio, I ran back to the gate I'd come through, wondering how many cameras and motion sensors had been triggered. The explaining and paperwork from this little escapade would keep me mired at my desk for days.

I keyed the mic on the radio as I ran toward my car, but something wasn't right. I glanced down and saw my fall had smashed the plastic casing around where the button was located. It was now a listening device with no way of transmitting.

Sprinting with the backpack over my shoulder, I noticed several people had now gathered in the street, wondering what the ruckus was about. I held my badge in the air as I passed by, hopefully reducing the number of 911 calls I was leaving in my wake.

Reaching my car, I put the lights on but left the siren off as I turned around and sped toward Bayside Drive. Making a left, I drove a hundred yards and then turned left again into the entrance to Linda Isle. A small roundabout with landscaping and a guard shack in the center allowed unwanted callers to turn around before they reached the metal entry gates spanning the road leading to the bridge. I stopped at the shack.

"Hey!" I called out, and an older man in a uniform stepped outside. I showed him my badge. "I'm after a guy who came over from Harbor Island Road. Can you leave the gates closed for a few minutes?"

"No one's passed by me," he said with a Hispanic accent.

"He'll be coming from the island," I clarified.

"One of the residents?"

"No. A suspect in a case."

"Like I said, no one I don't know has come past me to get on the island, and I've been here all afternoon," he announced proudly.

"He didn't come past you yet, mate. I'm saying this is how he'll leave."

"But how'd he get on the island if he didn't come onto the island?"

Apparently, I should have started with that part, as this guy wanted to know every detail.

"He swam. Now shut off the gates so they won't open, please."

The guard stared at me and didn't move.

"Now would be good," I reiterated.

"What if one of the residents wants to leave or comes in?"

To prove his point, I noticed in my mirror that a Maserati SUV had just pulled up behind me.

"I'm chasing a murder suspect. They can wait," I replied, and got out of my car, turning the lights off.

I flashed my badge at the fancy car. A pair of expensive sunglasses stared back at me and waved an annoyed hand in the air. I jogged to the wall lining the road where the metal swing gate was mounted, hopped over, and hid behind a tree so I could see the road.

I called 911 on my cell, quickly explained why I'd gone dark over the radio, and redirected the approaching patrol cars. I requested a helicopter, although I expected to be denied, and asked for the marine unit to watch for a swimmer around Linda Isle.

When I hung up, I let out a long sigh and tried to regroup. *Why the hell did he have to run?* This whole evening had turned into a shit show. Lonely at home seemed like a far more enticing offer at this point.

Hearing a whirring noise, I looked up to see a car driving toward me over the bridge. It slowed for the exit gate, expecting it to open. Which it did.

"What part about shutting the gates off did you not understand!" I yelled to the guard, who was having a conversation with Sunglasses.

He shrugged his shoulders at me as the Maserati pulled around my car and up to the entry gate, which also opened.

"Bollocks," I growled under my breath, and ran past the guard hut to intercept the car leaving.

A man driving one of the sleek, expensive Teslas slammed on his brakes.

"What the hell are you doing?" he mouthed through his windshield.

I marched to the driver's side and showed him my badge. He reluctantly put the window down.

"Are you alone in the car, sir?"

"Do you see anyone else?" he snapped back.

"Did anyone ask you for a ride off the island, sir?"

"What? Of course not."

"Did you see anyone suspicious on the island, sir?"

"No. You want to tell me what's going on?"

"I need you to pull to the side and wait until a police officer tells you it's okay to leave, sir," I said as politely as I could manage.

"I'm going to be late," he replied irritably.

A Newport Beach Police Department squad car pulled into the entrance. I held up my badge and pointed for them to park behind the guard shack in the roundabout so the car wouldn't be seen from the bridge.

I returned my attention to the Tesla. "Pull to the side and wait, sir. Now," I ordered.

The driver did so, complaining under his breath.

"What do we have?" one of the black-uniformed police officers asked me as I met them getting out of their car.

I explained the situation, but I knew we were on a lost cause. Wendell would have easily made it to the bridge by now. He'd likely seen the commotion and chose another option. Which was almost certainly back in the water. Our best chance was the marine unit or a helicopter.

"What about him?" the officer asked me, pointing to the Tesla.

"Oh, he's just a prick, so he's in timeout for another ten minutes, then you can cut him loose."

The officers both grinned. Their radios were lively with chatter, and now I heard dispatch asking for Sam 54, my call sign.

"I assume that's you they're looking for?" one of the officers asked.

I nodded and took the radio he offered me. "Go ahead for Sam 54. Over."

"Sam 54, this is dispatch. That's a negative on the helo. Unavailable for at least two hours. Over."

"10-4 dispatch. Cancel the request. Over."

I wandered over to my car and sat in the driver's seat with my left leg out the door. Total shit show. I looked at the backpack and pulled it over from the passenger seat. Unzipping the top, the nasty smell of Wendell's unwashed clothes hit me for the second time that day. I quickly closed the top, figuring I'd leave that for forensics, and unzipped a pouch on the front. Peering inside, careful not to touch anything, I saw a cell phone, a packet of cigarettes, a couple of pens, and a handful of folded papers that looked like song lyrics or poetry from the section I could see. Under the papers was a pill bottle. I shook the bag until the plastic bottle spun around, then tilted the backpack under the interior light. Fluoxetine. An antidepressant. It was prescribed to Wendell.

At least we had his phone. Maybe we'd learn something from his calls or texts.

I was about to zip the pouch closed when I noticed another zipper along the upper back edge of the pouch. It was one of those pockets within a pocket for extra safe-keeping. I reached over and pulled a blue nitrile glove from the glove box. Scrunching it in my hand rather than taking the time to fight my fingers into the glove, I undid the inner zipper and held the compartment open enough to look inside. I could see a second phone.

"What's this?" I muttered to myself, now taking the time to put the glove on properly.

Carefully, I pulled the phone out and hit a button. Nothing happened, so I held the power button, and the screen lit up. It was locked, but I could still see the home screen picture. Which was a lovely photograph of Scarlett Redman smiling and waving at the camera. A low-battery warning popped up.

"Oh, Chris," I mumbled.

I ran my gloved hand around inside the hidden compartment. My fingers came across a piece of paper, which I pulled out. It was a note written on a page from a pocket-sized spiral-bound notebook, the top edge frayed from where it had been torn away. I unfolded the note.

Meet me at the west benches, Doheny Park. 10:30. It's important.

I carefully slid the phone and note back inside the compartment and set the backpack aside. Slipping off the nitrile glove, I picked up my own phone, paused a moment to collect myself, then dialed a number.

"What's up?" Fuentes answered.

"We have a break," I began, leading with a positive before I'd unavoidably have to circle around to explain how this information came into my possession. "We can now place Chris Wendell at the murder scene."

21

"So, let me get this straight," Captain Bradley said, pacing behind her desk as Fuentes and I stood on the other side like condemned prisoners. Or more accurately, I was the condemned prisoner, and my partner was getting strung up by association. "You two decided not to pursue a murder suspect yesterday evening in favor of doing it the next morning, but Cromwell decides what the hey, she'll do it, anyway, and Wendell subsequently gets away. That about right?"

I waited for Fuentes to protest his innocence, but he stayed quiet. I'd certainly expected a ration of shit over last night's incident in Newport Beach, but I'd hoped to leave him out of my mess.

"It seemed like a long shot, ma'am, and I had the time," I said. The words came out, and right away, I knew I should have just nodded and shut up.

"I see," she responded, far too calmly. "And was it because you considered this lead a long shot that you chose to not wait for backup? Despite the man being our prime murder suspect?"

"He wasn't at the time, ma'am."

Once again, words spewed from my lips before I could stop them. The question had been a perfect trap, and I'd have been screwed however I'd answered, so silence would have been a better option.

"My apologies, ma'am," I threw in, wishing it had been all I'd said in the first place.

"Your apology is of no interest to me, Cromwell. I recognize we often work cases alone, but not murder suspects. There's a reason I put you two together," Bradley fumed. "And it wasn't for you to go off solo-cavaliering, which, in this case, resulted in you losing the suspect."

No, you wanted Hugo with me to report on my every move, I mercifully thought to myself and didn't say aloud.

"With respect, ma'am, I wasn't knocking on the door alone," I said instead. "I called for local support."

"But you didn't wait for them, did you?" Bradley barked back.

"Circumstances escalated when the cousin came out of the house, ma'am."

Bradley shook her head. "It's your state of mind that concerns me more than anything," she continued. "I gave you the chance to take time away to gather your thoughts, but you assured me you were fit to continue."

I couldn't believe the captain was turning this around and making it about Paul when it had nothing to do with the news she'd given me. Although, as I chewed it over, I realized it was somewhat due to avoiding sitting at home alone that I'd driven to Newport. Which could be argued had a connection to Paul. I sensed I was about to be pulled from the case, or worse. I had to do something.

"We did gain valuable new evidence, ma'am," I pointed out, hoping to shine one positive ray of light on the fiasco.

"Which indicates that Chris Wendell is now our primary murder suspect," she snapped back. "The guy you let get away."

So much for my little ray of sunshine. One day, I'd learn to stay quiet. I just hoped I still had a job with the Sheriff's Department at that point.

"Shall we talk about where to go from here?" Fuentes offered.

What a difference a day made. Yesterday morning, he would have piled on and helped Bradley stick it to me. But today, he was urging her to move forward. I smiled inside.

"Oh," Bradley replied, turning her attention to my partner. "You think I'm done? How about you explain to me why you felt tracking down a murder suspect could wait until the next day? Police work getting in the way of a hot date, Fuentes? Well, she can wait next time, dammit. You ought to know better. I put you with Miss Can't Help Herself From Screwing Up so you'd prevent this sort of mess, but you had better things to do."

I figured that was the last time my short-lived partner would bother coming to my defense, but at least the captain used the *she* pronoun so Fuentes would know his secret was safe.

"This is all on me, ma'am," I volunteered, throwing myself back under the bus. "We both agreed to handle it in the morning."

"I understand you were part of that decision, Cromwell," Bradley retorted. "And I've come to expect your impetuous choices. But Fuentes should know better."

There was one of those words with that negative connotation again. And once more, I reminded myself to shut the fuck up.

"Where is the phone and that note now?" Bradley asked, and I quickly responded in the hopes she was finally moving on to something more productive than chewing us out.

"Took them to forensics myself, ma'am. I asked for priority on call activity logs for both phones and fingerprints on the one we believe to be Helena Redman's. I also contacted Scarlett Redman, the vic's daughter, and she knows her mum's password, so that should speed things up. And I requested handwriting analysis on the note to confirm Wendell wrote it."

"And what about finding Wendell?"

"We upgraded the BOLO to urgent and provided a recent photo, ma'am. His bicycle was at his cousin's, so he's now on foot unless he steals or buys a mode of transport. We have a watch on his credit card as his wallet wasn't in the backpack, but it's maxed, anyway, so I doubt he'll try to use it."

Bradley took a deep breath, and I held mine as I knew my sentencing was about to be read. That alone time at home I'd been trying to avoid was about to become unlimited when she suspended me, or even worse.

"I spoke to the chief in homicide, and we both came to the same conclusion," Bradley began, and my legs felt weak. "With one homicide investigator out on medical and another on vacation for another week, we're too short-handed to kick you off the case."

What did she just say? I felt like my brain wiring had taken a new turn for the worse and was now disconnecting me from the present as well as the past.

"But notes have been made in your file, Cromwell, and I don't want you as much as snapping one of your damn Polaroids without Hugo knowing about it. Is that clear?"

"Like gin, ma'am," I couldn't say quickly enough, although her reference to my pictures made me cringe. I didn't need her digging down that rabbit hole on top of everything else.

"Okay," Bradley continued in a calmer tone. "You can partially make up for ruining my weekend by bringing Wendell in so we can wrap this up. I shouldn't need to tell you how much pressure there is to close this case quickly."

I was about to point out that we still had the Travis Redman angle, which remained unexplained, but managed to stop myself. Sometimes I could be a slow learner, but I usually got there eventually.

Fuentes turned and walked away, so I threw out another "Yes, ma'am" and swiftly followed. Once we were back at our desks, I leaned past my monitor and spoke quietly.

"I'm really sorry you got pulled into my cock-up, Hugo, and I appreciate you standing up for me in there."

He slid his rolling chair to the side and glared at me. "I wasn't standing up for you. I was trying to get it over with. What you did was disrespectful and irresponsible. Exactly the shit I was talking about when I said I couldn't trust you."

I felt my arse coming out of the seat as my blood pressure went from idle to pumping like a fire hose in less than a second. Maybe it was because I'd just had to hold myself in check with Bradley, but somehow, I reined in my temper and didn't bite. Instead, I took a few deep breaths before replying as calmly as I could muster.

"I get it. I'm sorry."

"Do you, though?" he challenged. "It's easy to say that, but your actions continue to prove that you don't get it at all. If you were hellbent on going over there last night, you should have said. We would have had options. But no, you lied to me and went, anyway."

"I didn't lie to you," I responded.

"You agreed to go the next morning, Kat! That's what we said on the phone. You lied and kept driving to Newport."

"Bloody hell, Fuentes, I didn't lie to you. When we spoke, I agreed and intended to call it a night. It was after we hung up that I realized I really didn't want to go home, where I'd sit there with my thumb up my arse instead of doing something useful. I swear, I had no intention of that when we talked."

"Then why didn't you call me back to tell me?"

"Because you obviously had something going on, and I didn't want to bother you," I said, hearing how impotent my own words sounded. "I thought I'd be knocking on the door and chatting with the bloody cousin for a few minutes, then driving home. A good way to kill a few hours."

He stared at me, but the venom had left his eyes, replaced by something else I couldn't quite discern.

"Your life is so sad and uninteresting that you'd rather drive around for an evening instead of having time at home?"

Apparently, it was now pity in his eyes.

"No," I replied, but I couldn't come up with anything more constructive to defend myself.

I didn't consider my life to be sad or uninteresting. In transition, perhaps. Somewhat lonely. A dog would be nice. Shit, it was one thing to feel alone, but having someone else point out that my existence was a total non-event felt like a right hook to the jaw.

"I'm throwing myself into this case, that's all," I continued. "This is Dana Point, after all. My hometown. This is supposed to be a safe place where murders like this don't happen. It's a big deal for people who live here."

"Don't forget about body parts washing up on the beach," Fuentes said, looking at me blankly.

If his face hadn't creased into a smirk, I doubted I could have stopped my stapler from becoming embedded in his forehead. But he grinned, instantly splintering my anger, and I laughed instead.

"What a bloody week, yeah?"

"Quite the bloody week," he replied, and slid his chair back in front of his monitor.

The morning wore on. We looked over files and details and things we'd already studied at length. Basically, we were killing time, waiting for Chris Wendell to be spotted and apprehended.

At lunchtime, Fuentes was beginning to gather up his stuff to leave when my phone buzzed with a new email notification. I checked my account on the computer.

"We have Helena's cell phone activity back from the tech guys," I said, opening the attachment with her call log and texting history.

"That was quick," Fuentes commented, settling back into his chair. "Even with the password, that's fast."

"Yeah, I told them it was priority."

He scoffed. "I think someone further up the food chain may have reiterated that for you."

I wanted to feel insulted, but no doubt he was right. Not once in the history of policing has a copper ever dropped off evidence and told the lab or tech guys to take their time. They were always backlogged.

"That's weird," I muttered.

"What?" Fuentes asked, peering around his monitor.

I'd been happy with the opposing desk setup when he was being a dick all the time, but now that he was acting partner-like more often, it was becoming inconvenient.

"No fingerprints on Helena's phone," I said. "Nothing. Wiped clean."

"Probably planned on ditching it," Fuentes suggested.

"There's a whole bunch of water between Dana Point and Newport Beach. If he planned on tossing the phone, why wipe it?"

"Paranoid?" he suggested. "Who the hell knows? The guy's probably in full panic mode."

I scanned through the texts and calls from Tuesday evening. Scarlett's number filled the log. A notation remarked that all the texts dropped in after they powered up the phone. Which meant it had been shut off before Scarlett first tried to reach her mother. There was only one voicemail message from that night, but two more calls had activated the voicemail recording. Those would be Scarlett hanging up without saying anything. She may well have called many more times, but they wouldn't show up because the phone was powered down. Only voicemails registered as they were saved on a server, not the phone itself. The techs, or their software, had transcribed the one message.

"Hey mom, I just woke up. Where are you? I'm kinda worried cos you didn't say anything about not coming home. Call me when you get this."

After that, Scarlett texted eleven more times. They all read the same or similar.

"Mom, I'm worried. Call me."

My stomach knotted at the thought of what the teenager had gone through, all on her own Tuesday night.

"She was attacked before midnight," I said. "Before Travis broke into her minivan."

"That's an assumption," Fuentes replied. "I mean, we already knew the daughter's calls went straight to voicemail, right? Who's to say the vic didn't turn her phone off before her secret rendezvous?"

"Sure," I agreed, "but this is useable evidence that the phone was turned off and left off since then. Certainly suggests Wendell turned it off and kept it."

"Still an assumption, Kat. We can't physically place the phone at the scene." he reiterated. "But a solid one, I'd say."

I nodded. "I get that. She could have left her phone at work, and it was taken from there."

My instant photos were laid out beside my keyboard, and I scanned them quickly. The moment my eyes crossed the one from inside Helena and Scarlett's little cottage, I heard the daughter's voice in my head, and I repeated her words aloud.

"She never went anywhere without her cell phone. Scarlett told us that, remember?" I asked, although I knew it to be true. Scarlett's words were in my head, verbatim.

"Um," Fuentes muttered. "She did?"

"She did," I said firmly. "But regardless, it potentially narrows down our timeline," I continued, drumming my fingers on the desk. "We know she set the restaurant alarm at 10:27 p.m. Wendell followed her, although he vehemently denied it, then took her phone after the attack."

"So Wendell kills Helena," Fuentes said thoughtfully. "Because he wanted to get back with her, or some other love-struck reason."

"Victim of a crime of passion," I said, accentuating a BBC English accent.

"So what was the brother doing there?" Fuentes asked, sliding his chair over again.

"Looking for his sister?" I suggested.

"If you found your sibling's car in a local parking lot late at night, would your first reaction be to smash the window?"

"No, but I don't have any siblings," I replied with a grin.

"That's right," he said, nodding slowly. "You're an only child. It all makes more sense now."

"Firstly, bugger off," I said light-heartedly. "And secondly, no. If I had a theoretical sibling, I don't think I'd be smashing their car windows in the middle of the night."

Fuentes slid his chair back once more, disappearing behind his screen as he spoke. "So, we agree that Travis Redman is still involved in some way?"

"If Helena left the restaurant and drove straight to Doheny, she would have arrived and walked to the benches by…" I paused while I estimated the drive time, parking, and walking in my head. "…10:30, or thereabouts. Travis was seen breaking into the minivan at ten after midnight, which leaves an hour and forty minutes in which Helena was murdered, moved from the park to Puerto Place, transported down the road, and finally dumped in the water."

"I can narrow that down farther for you," Fuentes announced. "At the bottom of the report is a note from the techs. The phone's location was Doheny Park when it was powered down at 10:45 on Tuesday evening."

"So Wendell used the note to lure her to the park, followed her from the restaurant, and likely killed her shortly afterwards. Then he turned her phone off," I summarized. "Travis showed up over an hour later."

"That was swift work to strangle the vic, move her down the road, and dump the body in the water," Fuentes pointed out.

"Wendell must have moved her in his Jeep," I thought aloud. "Forensics have to find a trace. I looked inside, and that thing hasn't been cleaned in donkey's years."

"Shit," Fuentes muttered.

"What now?" I asked.

"Want to complicate it a little more?"

"I thought we'd just narrowed things down, to be honest."

"Look at Helena's phone log from Tuesday afternoon," Fuentes replied. "The four-minute call."

I scanned the list and found the call in question. The number looked familiar. The owner's name was even more familiar.

"Darian Rutherford! That lying prick."

My partner laughed, but I didn't hear much humor in his voice. "We're back to three suspects again."

22

———

To my disappointment, Dad didn't have anyone for me to hit, so I beat the shit out of the heavy bag until my hands and wrists hurt so much, I had to stop. Then I came into the office to face a new day. A new week.

I'd learned in my youth to never say that things can't get any worse, but I truly hoped this week would be better than the last. No bits of fiancé showing up on the beach would be a start. Catching a murderer would be the jackpot. But as I walked into a morning briefing, I'd settle for apprehending a suspect.

"Investigator Cromwell, please give us an overview of where we are with the case," Captain Bradley announced.

I reluctantly plodded to the front of the room and placed my notebook on the podium. I didn't usually need the notes, but it served as a backup in case I stumbled across a hole in my memory. I'd tucked my instant pictures inside. It also gave me something to look at instead of facing a room full of men and women staring back my way. Most of whom had a photo of me dripping in tomatoes on their phones.

"We have three suspects in play, all of whom knew the victim,

Helena Redman," I began. "Top of the list is Chris Wendell, who is currently at large and ran when we tried to apprehend him."

I could feel the captain's glare as I used the royal "we" in my sentence.

"We have a BOLO out for Wendell," I continued. "In his possession was the vic's cell phone and a note asking her to meet at Doheny, which is where we're confident the murder took place. We also have video of him leaving the vic's place of employment shortly after she locked up and set the alarm on Tuesday night. Finding Wendell is priority one."

I dared a quick glance up at the room and found the faces looking back at me didn't appear as… well, I'm not sure exactly what I expected, but they seemed like they were just listening to the morning briefing. Except for Bradley. I shouldn't have looked her way. She still looked pissed off. I returned to my notes.

"Number-two suspect is Travis Redman, the vic's brother. We have him on video breaking into his sister's minivan, which was parked by Doheny. This was after the time we believe she was attacked. He has refused to give us a reason, so he's been charged with auto burglary, but we couldn't hold him."

"Worth another run at him?" Bradley asked.

"I believe so, ma'am. We'll track him down this morning," I replied.

I'd written the very same thing in my notes last night, but I knew she wouldn't believe me if I said we planned to find Travis that morning. I wouldn't believe me, either, if I were in her shoes.

"We have nothing suggesting those two were both involved together in some way beyond their presence in the area, but we're keeping it in mind," I continued. "The third suspect is the vic's former boyfriend and father of their teenage daughter. Darian Rutherford lives in Oregon but happened to be visiting the area last week. He's had no involvement in his daughter's life and told us he never speaks to his ex. He lied. We have a four-minute call on her phone logs from him on the afternoon of the murder."

"Anything on the phone records from the other two?" Deputy Ripley asked.

"Nothing from Wendell in the past few months and a handful of benign texts from the brother. Nothing odd or suspicious," I replied, and Ripley nodded.

"We believe Rutherford has left the area, and he didn't answer his phone yesterday when we tried him. We've reached out to local law enforcement in Oregon and they're visiting his address this morning for us. Although he's probably still driving north."

"Okay," Bradley said when I nodded, indicating that I was finished. "What do we need help with?"

"Finding Wendell," I replied. "Last seen in Newport Beach, where he'd either ridden his bike or taken it on the bus from Dana Point. He doesn't have his bike anymore, but we believe he has more connections here than in Newport, so he may well show up in town."

"Anything else, apart from the obvious?" Bradley asked, and a few snickers came from the crowd.

I balked for a moment, but pressed on as I felt the detail could save us time chasing ghosts. "If you get a report of Wendell in possession of a guitar, the sighting will be before he visited his cousin in Newport Beach. We know he had it with him from his home in Dana Point and left it behind at his cousin's when he ran."

"Sounds like a Rodriguez movie," one of the deputies joked and everyone laughed.

"So I've heard," I commented and Fuentes grinned at me. "If someone can find Darian Rutherford's stepmother and verify his story about coming down here to move stuff out of a house she's selling, that would be a great help."

Ripley raised his hand, and his partner, Hanson, rolled his eyes. Apparently, his cohort wasn't as eager to help.

"We can do that," Ripley volunteered. "Give us what you have to go on."

I smiled and nodded my thanks.

"Okay," Bradley said, taking over again. "More trouble with

teenagers on e-bikes, people. A handbag grabbed yesterday, and two younger kids on regular bicycles reported they were harassed and run into a ditch by a group of four youths. Keep your eyes open and be safe. That's it. Find Christopher Wendell for me, please. Let's get to it."

As the room cleared, I gave Ripley the name and address info I'd found for Rutherford's stepmother.

"Thanks for doing this," I said, noticing his partner had already left.

When I walked to the hallway, Fuentes had stopped Hanson.

"Is there a problem with helping us out, deputy?" Fuentes was asking in a less-than-cordial tone.

The man snorted. "Not at all."

I noticed he'd left off the "sir" part, which I figured wouldn't go down well with the investigator who was the man's senior in every sense of the word.

"Then you must have a problem with your eyes," Fuentes continued. "Need some drops, or maybe an eye wash? My apologies if that's a nervous tic you have that causes your eyes to roll like that when asked to do police work."

"What the hell's your problem?" the deputy snapped, puffing out his chest.

He wasn't a particularly large man, maybe an inch shorter than my partner's 5-foot-10 frame, but he appeared to be in good shape.

"What the hell's your problem, *sir*?" Fuentes rebutted, unfazed by the deputy's aggressive stance. "We're a team here, Hanson."

To be honest, I was surprised he knew the man's name, although he could have been reading his badge.

"We help each other out," Fuentes continued. "Understood?"

Hanson let out an angry groan and pushed past my partner as he stomped off down the hall.

"Shit, I'm sorry about him, sir," Ripley said. "He's had a hard time of things lately. He's not usually like this."

"We all have things we're dealing with," Fuentes replied. "He should take leave if he needs time to handle it. If he's wearing the badge, there's no place for that bullshit." He looked at me. "You have to be able to separate personal challenges from what we do on duty."

"I'll talk to him, sir," Ripley said, then lowered his voice, although we were the only ones left in the hallway. "His wife just left him, sir. Bad deal. She moved in with someone else."

Fuentes nodded, and Ripley left, chasing after his partner.

"Can't say I blame her from what I've seen," Fuentes said after Ripley was out of earshot.

"Women," I scoffed, then grinned. "I'd steer clear of them if I were you."

"Very funny," Fuentes grumbled.

Apparently, our relationship wasn't ready for my humor quite yet.

I finalized my report from Saturday night's Newport Beach adventure and hit "Submit" on the computer with a mixed sense of relief and dread. I'd worked on it all Sunday afternoon and too long again this morning, so I was glad to move on.

It was mid-morning when, to my amazement, Travis Redman answered the phone when I called him.

"This is Travis," he said, and by the way he answered, I presumed he didn't realize it was me.

"Investigator Cromwell," I replied. "Good morning, Mr. Redman. We'd like to speak with you again as soon as possible. Can you come to the station?"

He didn't say anything for several seconds, and I heard other people moving about in the background and bottles clinking.

"What for?"

"We have new evidence we'd like you to help us with. When can you come in?"

"What kind of new evidence?" he asked. I heard more crashing and banging, then it sounded like he walked outside where the ambient noise switched to traffic.

"Happy to share all that with you here at the station."

"I'm working. I have to make a living, man. I can't keep running to the cop station every day."

"What time do you finish work?" I asked. "Maybe on your lunch break? This is important, but if you're not interested in helping us find your sister's killer, then our investigation will drag on longer."

Another pause, and I listened to the sound of cars driving past. "I'll come by after five," he finally said, then ended the call.

"He said he'll come by at five," I reported to Fuentes.

"Be nice to talk to him sooner than that."

"Agreed. I was thinking we might take the video of Wendell's Jeep and show it to the staff at Capistrano Bay Tavern. See if anyone remembers seeing it around on Tuesday."

My partner stood and grabbed his jacket. "Better than sitting around here."

I quickly gathered my stuff and considered the background sounds I'd heard on the call. "I have a feeling we might run into Travis as well."

As we drove down the hill to the restaurant, Deputy Ripley rang me. I answered the call, which came through on the car's speakers.

"Get anywhere?" I asked.

"We just left the stepmother's place. Without prompting, she told me Rutherford was there last week moving his crap out of her house. There's a 'Sold' sign out front, and she has a detached garage with extra room, so it adds up."

Or they aligned their stories, I thought.

"Ten-four," I replied. "Thanks for doing that for us."

"Anything else we can do, just let us know," Ripley replied.

I thanked him again and hung up as I turned into the small parking lot by Capistrano Bay Tavern.

"How do you feel about pressing Felix Russo a little more about his former bartender?" I asked Fuentes.

He climbed out of the car and waited for me to do the same. "You want more suspects in this mess?"

I chuckled. "I'd love to have one, as long as it's the right one."

My partner almost smiled. "Press away. Not sure it has anything to do with Helena, but there's definitely dirt underneath his expensive clothes and slick haircut."

As we walked inside, I forcibly stopped myself from laughing at the irony of Hugo's statement.

Caroline Russo was sitting on a barstool inside with a laptop open in front of her.

"Mrs. Russo, Investigators Cromwell and Fuentes," I said as we approached her. "Would you have a few minutes for us?"

The woman finished typing something, then turned in her chair. "Hello. How's Helena's case coming along? Have you caught her killer yet?"

"We have several people of interest," I replied. "I believe we're getting close."

"Good to hear," Caroline responded, and slid from her barstool. "Can I offer you a water or soda?"

We both declined, and she led us to the same table we'd sat at before, taking her laptop with her.

"Is your husband here, Mrs. Russo?" I asked before I committed to sitting down.

"No," she answered. "I'm not sure where he is this morning. But I can call him if you need to speak with him, too?"

I looked at my partner, who gave me the slightest of headshakes.

"That's okay," I replied. "Is Travis Redman here?"

"Travis?" Caroline said, looking thoughtful. "He was a while back, but I believe he left. Felix keeps him busy. Poor guy."

"Travis, or your husband?" I asked, sitting down.

Caroline smiled. "I meant Travis. Must be awful to lose a sister."

"Let's talk about Chris Wendell," I said, watching Caroline's reaction.

Her left eye twitched. Again. Just like the first time Wendell's name came up.

"Is he one of your suspects?" she asked. "Seriously? I couldn't imagine Chris ever hurting Helena. But of course, they say you never know what love can do to a person."

"Do you think Chris was still in love with Helena?" I asked.

Caroline let out a long breath. "I suspect he was, but I couldn't say for sure. He hasn't worked here for a long time."

"Does he come by?"

Caroline shook her head. "Not really his sort of place when he's having to pay for his drinks."

I took out my phone and brought up the video from the security camera outside the gallery. Holding it for her to see, I watched her again. Caroline squinted at the screen.

"Is that Chris's Jeep?" she asked.

"It is. He parked across the road from your restaurant on the night Helena was killed."

Caroline frowned. "I honestly don't recall Chris being in here that night, but I suppose I could have missed him if we were busy."

"This is quite important, Mrs. Russo," Fuentes urged. "This video recording is from a few moments after Helena set the alarm to the restaurant."

Caroline raised a hand to her mouth. "My God. Did Helena leave with him?"

"Think back," Fuentes continued. "Are you sure you don't recall seeing Wendell or his Jeep that evening?"

She took her hand from her mouth and held her palm toward us. For the first time, I noticed a tattoo of a vine around her wrist with little white and red blossoms. It was elegant and pretty, yet deliberate and strong. Like Caroline.

I didn't have any tattoos. Paul and I had talked about getting matching ones with each other's names, but never did. I now took that as a lesson to never get a permanent marking on my body of someone I fell in love with. Life changes, but tattoos are forever. Maybe I should get a tattoo of a dog.

"As I told you before, I'd already gone," she replied. "Helena was locking up on her own. But I'm sure I didn't see Chris here before I left. His Jeep may have been over the road, and I just didn't notice it, but I know I didn't see him in the restaurant."

"And you'd remember any time you saw Chris, right?" I prompted.

She frowned at me. "I'm sorry, I don't understand."

"What I'm saying is that Chris Wendell was more than just an employee. Wasn't he?"

Caroline tried to feign a look of shock, but she couldn't pull it off. "That was all rumor and hearsay, which caused a great deal of tension in my marriage. I don't know who told you that, but none of it's true. And I don't see how harmless flirtations six months ago have anything to do with solving Helena's murder."

"When did Helena and Chris break up?" I asked.

"Before that," Caroline shot back. "Look, it was all a bunch of nothing. Certainly not worthy of your time in the middle of a murder investigation."

"Would your husband describe it the same way?" Fuentes asked.

Caroline glared at him. "Can I help you with anything constructive? If not, I have work to do."

I felt we'd pushed her as much as we should, and Fuentes rising from his chair suggested he agreed. We thanked Caroline, who returned to her laptop without saying another word.

We walked toward the car. I paused at the edge of the patio and took an instant picture, capturing Caroline at the table, then continued behind my partner. We both paused before getting in.

"She was keen to deny any affair," I remarked.

"Like a politician with pants around his ankles in a whorehouse." Fuentes replied.

I laughed. "That's quite a graphic analogy, Hugo. I assume you're saying you think she's guilty."

"Of screwing Chris Wendell, yes," he replied. "But I don't see that she has motive, opportunity, or means to murder our victim."

"What about the husband?"

"I think he had motivation."

"Sure, but to murder his wife or Chris Wendell, not Helena," I pointed out.

"Exactly. I don't see how either one of them had any reason to kill their valued employee," Fuentes said, and got in the car.

"Jealousy, perhaps?" I suggested once we were both seated. "You heard her. She thinks her lover may still have had feelings for their valued employee."

Fuentes thought for a moment. "I suppose it's possible. I mean, Helena was a nice-looking lady, but not in Caroline's league. Russo would be quite a catch for a beach bum like Wendell."

I nodded and started the car. "A politician with his pants down in a whorehouse," I repeated as best as I could remember his line. "You need to be careful, Hugo. Word might get out about your comedic side, and you'll lose your tough-guy image."

"I'm trusting you with all my secrets, Cromwell. Don't make me regret it."

"Mum's the word," I said, pulling a zipper across my mouth. "But I may book you a stand-up gig at the Holiday Inn."

23

———————

Chris Wendell was in the wind. I knew it wasn't hard to stay out of sight for a few days, but he'd have to show up sooner or later. He was without transport or a working credit card, and unless his cousin had lied to me and given him money, he didn't have much cash. Everybody has to eat, so Wendell would be forced to buy, beg, or steal food. If he tried using his credit card, we would be alerted. Whichever path he was forced down, it meant appearing in public where he could be spotted. And his face was now on the news, courtesy of Captain Bradley.

But being confident we'd find him was not the same as having the guy in custody, and it made me nervous. If he evaded us for weeks, another suspect in another case would be on the minds of the public and law enforcement, making it easier for Wendell to slip through our fingers.

I'd hoped we'd run into Travis Redman at the restaurant, but either he'd sensed from my phone call that I might come by, or by chance he'd left shortly before we'd arrived. The afternoon dragged on, with my concern growing over the Wendell situation, and dwindling over the chances of Travis actually showing up at five. After far too much time poring over the little evidence and paperwork we had on the case, the clock reached 5:10 p.m., and I tried Redman's phone. Which, of course, he didn't answer.

I was about to ask Fuentes how long he thought we should wait until putting out a BOLO for the bloke, when my phone rang and the front desk told me Travis was here to see me.

"I would have put money on him no-showing," Fuentes said as we walked to the doorway.

"Never a doubt," I replied. "No one breaks a date with me."

"From what you've told me, you *never* date," my partner replied.

"That's how no one ever breaks them with me," I quipped, pausing for a moment and lowering my voice. "I feel like Bradley would be happy for us to charge Travis and move on, but the DA would have a fit if he saw how little we had."

"It's too coincidental that he was there that evening, and too suspicious that he broke into the minivan for something he refuses to tell us about," Fuentes replied. "He's involved, but all we have is the auto burglary, and he could've beat that if he fought it."

"Agreed. That could be Hugh Jackman breaking in, for all we know."

"Your fellow countryman?" Fuentes commented.

"He's Australian, you geographically impaired American," I rebutted with a good-natured eye roll.

Fuentes grinned at me. "Your buttons are too easy to find, Cromwell."

"Very funny." I responded as we pushed through the door into the reception area, where Travis sat in a chair waiting for us. "Thanks for coming by, Mr. Redman"

I steered him to an interview room, which instantly made him uncomfortable.

"Last time I was in here, you charged me with something," he said. "You said you just wanted to talk."

"Last time, you were guilty of auto burglary, Mr. Redman," I replied. "Unless you're guilty of something else, we don't expect to charge you today. The interview room is simply a private area to talk."

"Do I need a lawyer with me?" he asked, hovering next to the chair without sitting down. "I can't afford it, man."

"I'm guessing your family helped pay for your counsel," I replied.

"Sure, but they can't afford it, either."

"Take a seat, Travis," I said, indicating the most uncomfortable chair in the building. "It's absolutely your right to have representation present, and we can assign a public defender to you if you can't afford your own. But our intention here is to find your sister's killer, and as long as that person isn't you, I don't know why you wouldn't help us in every way possible."

He sat down, wincing and putting a hand to his ribs as he did so. "I've already told you everything I know."

"There may well be details which seem insignificant to you, but could make a difference in our investigation. So humor us, Travis."

He nodded and looked in my general direction without making eye contact.

"How are those ribs?" I asked while I dipped a hand in my pocket to retrieve my pictures. Which weren't there.

My heart caught in my throat. Instantly, I went from confident and prepared to adrift. I'd left them all on my desk.

"They hurt like a bitch, thanks to you," he replied.

I looked at my lap where I'd usually hold the little bundle of photographs, ready to shuffle through them if my stupid brain wiring decided to glitch. I felt Fuentes's eyes on me, and Travis fidgeted in his chair.

I took a deep breath and looked up. "How well do you know Chris Wendell?"

Travis's eyes met mine for a split second, then darted away. He shrugged his shoulders.

"He dated Helena, but we didn't hang out or anything."

"Any idea where he might be now?"

"No clue," he snapped back. "I've seen the news. I know you're after him, and if he killed my sister, I hope you find the bastard."

"Do you think he could have killed your sister?" Fuentes asked.

Another shrug. "How would I know?"

"In the time you spent around Wendell, did he strike you as a man capable of murder?" Fuentes persisted.

"Hell, I don't know. He seems like a super chill, mellow guy, but who knows, right?"

My partner then sat back, which was my cue to resume. I'd been happy with him taking over, but I nervously picked up the reins.

"When was the last time you saw Chris?"

"Been a while, I think. Don't really remember," Travis replied.

"You didn't see him on Tuesday night?" I asked.

His eyes briefly caught mine again. "No."

So far, my mind was piecing everything together, and I began to relax. Although, I wasn't sure what to do with my right hand, which would normally be holding my safety nets.

"What time did you arrive at Doheny on Tuesday night, Travis?"

"I pleaded no contest, which my lawyer says means I'm not admitting to nothing. So I'm not saying I was there."

"We have you on video smashing her window at ten past midnight, Travis. Doesn't matter what you pleaded; this is a fact on record. We're not escalating the break-in charge. We're trying to establish your sister's movements that night to determine what time she was attacked."

He frowned and shook his head. "Maybe I should have my lawyer here."

"No problem, Travis," I replied. "Call him and get him down here. I'm sure he's readily available at 5:45 in the evening." I turned to Fuentes. "Do lawyers charge double time outside of regular office hours?"

"If there's blood to be sucked, I believe they take their fill," Fuentes obliged.

"Shit," Travis muttered. "I really don't know what time it was, but I'd just got there. I sat in my truck for a few minutes to see who was around, then I checked out her minivan."

"See, Travis, that's helpful to us. Thank you," I told him, although I wanted to see some other form of proof before I believed a word he said. "And when did you leave?"

"Right after that."

"Okay, so we can move on to more important matters, Travis. Can you now tell us why you broke into your sister's vehicle?" I asked. "There had to be a reason. What was in there you needed?"

Redman fidgeted in the chair and ruminated for a few moments.

"I'd left something I needed in her minivan, okay? It's not important. I tried calling her, but it went straight to voicemail, and I didn't see her there so I grabbed what I needed. Figured I'd buy her a new window."

We hadn't seen a call from Travis on Helena's call log, but we'd already ascertained that her phone was powered down at the time, so unless he'd left a voicemail, it wouldn't have registered.

I was on a roll now, doing fine without my pictures.

"May I look at your phone, Travis?" I asked, holding out my hand, finally giving it a purpose in the interview.

"Why?"

"To see the call attempt to your sister on Tuesday night. It'll corroborate what you're telling us so we can move on," I explained in what I hoped was a non-threatening way.

"I clear my call logs every few days," Travis replied.

"Why would you do that?" Fuentes asked without using a non-threatening tone.

"It's my business who I talk to, man. Nobody else's."

"I'm sure you can see how that appears suspicious to us," Fuentes rebutted. "The only people who clear call logs and search histories are trying to hide something. Innocent people don't clear their calls."

"Whatever. I don't want anyone spying on me, okay?" Travis said, waving his arms around, then stopping and clutching his ribs.

"It's my fucking phone, and my right to keep or erase whatever I want."

"Okay, okay," I interjected. "Don't get your knickers in a twist. Let's move on."

"Huh?" Travis said, frowning at me.

"Did you see anyone else while you were at Doheny on Tuesday night?" I asked, not bothering to explain one of my dad's favorite phrases.

"No."

"So, you were there for what appears, by your statement, to be ten to twenty minutes, and you saw absolutely no one?"

"Not that I remember."

"You didn't notice the car driving by, which recorded you breaking in on their dashcam?"

Travis shook his head, and I leaned forward.

"Your sister was murdered sometime between 10:30 and midnight, less than a hundred yards from where we have a recording of you breaking into her minivan, and you maintain that you didn't see anyone else there?"

His eyes grew wider, and I waited, holding my breath. I was sure I'd pushed him over the edge, and he was about to lawyer up.

"Help us rule you out of this thing, Travis," Fuentes added. "You're the only one we can place at the scene within the window of time Helena was killed."

Redman rubbed his face with both hands and groaned.

"Come on, Travis," I encouraged. "You've given us no plausible reason why you were there, or why you broke into her minivan. How did you even know your sister was parked at Doheny?"

The question came to me on the fly, and it felt like one of those huge gongs being hit with a mallet. We had no evidence of communication between Travis and Helena the night she was killed. Chris Wendell had written a note inviting her to the park, so how *did* Travis know she'd be there?

"If your call log's erased, you won't mind me checking something on your phone, right?" I asked. "Not going into your email, internet, or anything like that."

He looked at me suspiciously. "Then what are you looking for?"

"Let me see, and I promise I'll show you."

"Why don't you just ask me?"

"Because we're the police and we have to verify everything, Travis. That's how this works, yeah?" I replied. "Hand me your phone, or I'll bother a judge when he just sat down for a cocktail after a long day of locking up scumbags and get a warrant for your bloody phone. Believe me, he'll remember who that warrant was for."

Travis tentatively unlocked his phone. "Just tell me, and I'll look for you."

Fuentes rose from his seat. "I'll be back with a warrant. Sit tight for a couple of hours."

I held my hand out again, and this time Travis slapped his phone down in my palm. "This is bullshit," he mumbled.

I immediately went to his call history, and a quick scroll showed my missed call a little after five was the only one remaining. We had no way to tell if he made a habit of clearing the memory, but he'd certainly wiped everything before arriving here. I went back to the main screen and scanned his apps, swiping past the first screen of the standard stuff, a couple of dating sites, and a bunch of games. On the second page were more games and the Find My Phone app I was looking for.

"What are you looking for?" Travis asked, getting more agitated. "You need to give it back. I shouldn't have let you have it."

I ignored him and opened the app. He had two numbers belonging to other people's devices. They were saved as "Mom cell" and "Dad cell." I turned his phone screen to face him.

"Did you have your sister in here?"

"No."

"Then how…" I began, then paused, unsure of the question I was about to ask.

In the blink of an eye, my world had been turned on its head, and I couldn't breathe. Something had dropped from my neatly organized series of memories about the case, and I had no way of telling what detail was missing.

I turned the phone in my hand and saw the app open. *What the fuck was I about to ask him?*

Travis snatched the phone back from me and quickly locked it. Silence fell over the room, and I could hear my heart thumping in my chest. My puzzle wasn't just missing a piece; it had been scattered across the floor. An overwhelming feeling of panic crippled me from putting together the remaining memories so I could pull myself together.

"Then how did you know Helena was at Doheny?" Fuentes asked, to my relief.

"I happened to see her minivan when I drove by, alright?" he blurted. "I'm leaving now. All you keep doing is trying to turn this around on me, man."

"That's not true. You're helping us, and we appreciate that," I managed to say, but it didn't matter. It was too late.

"If you want to talk to me again, you need to call my lawyer," he huffed, and stomped toward the door with one hand clutching his ribs.

24
____

"What the hell just happened, Cromwell?" Fuentes fumed once he'd shown Travis out of the building.

I'd stayed in the interview room as I knew questions were coming, and I didn't want anyone else overhearing in the office.

"I was thinking about too many things at once," I lied. "Just a brain fart." Which was closer to the truth.

"You completely locked up, like you had no idea where you were," Fuentes pressed, his tone a mixture of anger and concern. In what ratio, I couldn't tell.

"It was nothing," I replied, hoping he'd drop the subject. I rose to leave, but he spoke again.

"You didn't have your bundle of photographs, did you?"

I stood by the doorway, fighting my own mixture of anger and concern. I was furious with myself for forgetting my pictures in the first place, then locking up when there was no need. I knew most of the case inside-out, so whatever aspect had glitched from my memory probably wouldn't have affected the interview. Until I let it. My concern was that Fuentes had immediately identified my momentary paralysis.

"What's the deal with the photos, Cromwell?"

My partner wasn't going to leave this alone.

"It's just my way of keeping a case organized," I replied, which was true. "Some people use sticky notes on a wall. I have my instant photos."

I heard him sigh. "And there's that trust issue again. If we can't be honest with each other, this is never going to work."

I still couldn't decide if Fuentes truly wanted me to fail, or if he was simply testing my mettle at every possible opportunity. Either way, the rollercoaster ride was exhausting. For us both. My neurological issue was a closely guarded secret I went to great lengths to conceal. Because my job depended on it. If my medical records hadn't been hidden from my youth, I never would have been accepted into law enforcement. After years of refining my system to deal with my problem, I felt I had enough of a handle on it that the positives I brought to an investigation outweighed my issue.

A belief that would not be shared by the captain.

But what about Hugo Fuentes? I looked him in the eye and tried to decipher whether he'd go running to Bradley if I told him the whole truth, or if he'd keep my secret and work with me.

The risk was too high.

"I was overthinking the situation, that's all," I said as casually as I could manage. "Trying to trick the guy into giving us the truth. I tripped over myself. Nothing to get wound up over."

Fuentes stared at me for a moment before shaking his head. "I'll see you in the morning," he said sullenly, slinging his jacket over his shoulder and pushing past me as he left the interview room.

I gave him a minute to grab anything he needed from his desk, before returning to mine. We were still spinning our wheels on the case, and now my relationship with my partner, which had made promising strides all day, was back on the canvas. Once he'd gotten over his hissy fit about my Newport Beach jaunt, he'd been almost likable. So much for that.

I busied myself at my desk for another hour, looking over the things I'd already looked over a dozen times. Just when I was about to leave, I noticed an email arrive from the Oregon police. It was a quick note saying they'd dropped by Rutherford's apartment several times but hadn't seen him yet. Not surprising, as he was probably still on the road.

Driving home, I swung by Taco Surf, a favorite restaurant of mine. It was located a little after PCH split in the middle of town. Well, it's where PCH used to split, but now remained on the inland side, and the coast side was called Del Prado. In the old days, before the traffic pattern changes, patrons who'd enjoyed a pitcher of tasty margaritas had a habit of turning right out of the Taco Surf parking lot, which led into the oncoming northbound traffic. Remarkably, I'd witnessed this occur on a weekly basis despite signs at the exit, yet I'd never seen an accident. Usually, the shouts from the patio crowd and the honks from the terrified drivers had corrected the error.

Taco Surf was my *Cheers*. My dad loved that old TV show, and I'd seen every episode over the years. Just like the regulars on the show, I knew all the waitstaff, had a favorite barstool, and the cook made some of the best tacos in town. A thumbs-up as I walked in set my usual order in motion without me saying a word.

My arse had barely hit my seat when my phone rang. I looked at the number. It was local, but not stored in my phone. I almost let it go, but I'd kick myself if it was actually something to do with the case instead of a recording of some woman calling herself Sarah, telling me my loan was a sure thing.

"Cromwell."

"I didn't kill her," came a man's voice that I instantly recognized. He sounded frazzled and tired.

"Okay, Chris. Then why don't you come in and explain your side of things? I'm ready to listen."

"I feel like I'm being set up," he mumbled, close to tears. "I'm scared, man."

"I promise I'm going to listen to what you have to say, okay, Chris? Where are you? I'll come to you."

"I'm so fucking tired," he muttered. "I don't know what to do."

"Whose phone is this, Chris? Tell me where you are?"

"Do you have my backpack?"

"Yeah," I replied, trying to listen for any background sounds that might give his location away.

"I need my pills. I'm freakin' out with all this shit going down."

"I don't blame you. It's all a bit too crazy, Chris. Let me come and get you."

"I've been walking for hours," he said, and I could hear traffic, which didn't help much. We were in Orange County, California. There was traffic everywhere.

"You have my bag, right?" he asked again.

"Yup. Let me pick you up, and we can get you your meds, Chris."

"I shouldn't have called, man," he said, suddenly switching his tone. "I gotta go."

"Chris, I found the other stuff in your backpack," I blurted in a last-ditch effort to keep him on the line.

He didn't hang up, but he stayed quiet.

"I found Helena's phone and the note, Chris. Tell me where you are, and I'll come and get you. We have to sort this out, mate."

"What do you mean?" he asked, sounding even more scared and confused. "Helena's phone?"

"All you have to do, Chris, is tell me where you are, and I'll be there."

"You have my phone, right? That's my phone in the backpack."

"Yes, I have your phone, too."

I'd be doing some fast-talking when I picked him up to explain how his backpack and all the contents were still at forensics, but I'd cross that bridge if and when I reached it.

"Too? Fuck. I went by there," he muttered, and I could tell he was pacing. "Fuck. You gotta help me, lady."

"I'll help Chris. Tell me where you are."

"Salt Creek," he finally said. "I'm in the parking lot for Salt Creek Beach. I screwed up, man. You gotta hurry."

"Don't worry, we'll sort it out. Stay on—"

But it was too late. He'd hung up.

"Bethany!" I shouted to the woman behind the bar, and she turned around from the register. "I gotta run! I'll be back, and I'll sort it all out…"

"No worries, Kat!" she shouted back as I barreled out the front door.

25

I sped north on PCH with the red and blue lights on while calling Hugo. It rang five or six times before going to voicemail.

"Hugo, Wendell called me. I'm meeting him now at Salt Creek. He sounded really freaked out, so I hope he's there when I arrive. Call me back when you get this."

Hanging up the phone, I sped on, pondering who else I should inform. Panda cars, as my dad called them, showing up with sirens wailing would send Chris running for sure, so I didn't want to call in the cavalry. I found Captain Bradley's phone number and called her instead.

"Cromwell?" she answered.

"Yes, ma'am. Chris Wendell called me. I'm driving to meet him now."

"Really? That's great news. Where?"

"Salt Creek. I'll be there in a few minutes."

"Is Fuentes with you?"

"No, ma'am. I left him a message before calling you."

"Do you have backup coming?"

This time, I'd expected the obvious question. "Not yet, ma'am. I couldn't reach Hugo, so you were my next call. It took a lot of persuading to get Wendell to meet me. He sounds like he's in quite a state. If he sees uniforms and squad cars, I'm sure he'll bolt again."

"I'm too far away, Kat. I can't get there fast enough," she replied. "But you need to have backup in place before engaging him."

I silently cursed. "I'm hoping Hugo gets the message, ma'am. But I'll call the station and have uniforms coming."

"I'll call and alert anyone close by to meet you at Salt Creek, and I want you to stand down until they're in place. Is that understood?"

"Yes, ma'am," I reluctantly agreed as I slowed for the light to turn left onto Ritz Carlton Drive. Before calling the captain, I'd already resigned myself to the fact that I'd be waiting, but it still sucked. I just hoped Wendell would still be there.

The semi-circular road led to the hotel, a park on the bluff above the beach, and finally a neighborhood of very expensive homes. The large, half-moon-shaped parking lot filled the land between Ritz Carlton Drive and PCH with a walkway to Salt Creek Beach through a tunnel ducking under the road.

"Radio in your position and status, then stand by," Bradley ordered.

"Yes, ma'am," I said again, and hung up more abruptly than she probably cared for. "Bloody hell," I swore as I pulled in, turned the lights off, and parked in the first section beyond the entrance on the left.

I radioed in my location to dispatch and asked for the ETA of whoever was closest. A patrol car identified themselves and told me they were a couple of minutes away. I got out of the car. The parking lot was a quarter full at most, with quite a few people loading up their beach and picnic gear or putting surfboards on roofs or in truck beds. In the middle of summer, the place would be packed until dark, but with the evenings still cooling off, it was mainly the hardcore surfers remaining.

I took out my phone and called back the number Wendell had used to reach me. After a few rings, a man answered.

"Yeah?"

"Hey, Chris, it's Kat Cromwell."

"Who?"

"Is this Chris Wendell?" I asked, now hearing it wasn't his voice.

"No. And who are you, Kat Cromwell?" the guy asked in a seductive tone.

"Did someone borrow your phone about fifteen minutes ago?" I asked.

"Yeah. Dude seemed kinda out of it. Said he needed to call for a ride. I let him use the phone."

"Okay, I'm with the Orange County Sheriff's Department. Do you still see the bloke?"

"Bloke? Where are you from, Kat the Cop?" he asked, laughing. "Australia, right?"

I wanted to strangle this idiot, but not causing a spectacle was a higher priority.

"What's your name?" I asked.

"Dylan," the guy replied.

"Well, Dylan, this is important. Do you still see the guy who borrowed your phone?" I asked, careful to switch up my vernacular.

"Errr, no," he said hesitantly, and I guessed he was looking around the parking lot. "I don't know where he went."

I tried to spot Dylan, figuring he was somewhere nearby, but the parking lot was huge, and trees and vehicles blocked much of my view.

"Where were you when you loaned him your phone, Dylan?"

"Salt Creek."

"Yeah, I know that, but where exactly? In the parking lot? North or south end?"

"At my car in the lot. Shit, I don't know if it's north or south, man."

"Well, Dylan, we're in California, so the Pacific Ocean is west," I explained impatiently. "When you're facing the ocean, if it's on your right, it's north. Left is south."

"Huh, that's cool," he replied. "I guess I'm parked north of the tunnel, then."

I was parked on the south side. "Great, thank you. But you don't see the guy now?"

"No. He bailed, but I didn't see where he wandered off to. Once he gave me my phone back, I was changing and didn't pay attention."

The radio on my hip squawked as the officers announced they'd arrived, and I turned to see them slowly driving into the entrance behind me. I waved a hand to identify myself, then noticed it was Ripley and his partner, Hanson.

"Dylan, what was the guy wearing?"

"Umm… I don't know, beach stuff, I guess. Shorts and a tee, I think. Like I said, I didn't pay much attention. I was just helping a brother out. He looked like he hadn't slept much, and at first I thought he was a homeless dude, but I didn't see a cart or anything."

"Okay. Stay by your car, Dylan, I'll be there in a minute. And call me on this number if you see him again, but do not approach the man, okay?"

"Who is this guy?" Dylan asked, but I didn't have time to explain and hung up.

"Thanks for getting here quickly," I said, turning to Ripley and Hanson, who'd parked and stepped from their car. "Wendell called me on a borrowed phone and told me he was here. The guy he borrowed the phone from is somewhere on the north side of the tunnel, and I told him to stay put. He doesn't know where Wendell went after making the call to me." I scanned the parking lot again, hoping to get lucky and see Chris. "Wendell is a mess. I'm pretty sure he won't show himself if he sees uniforms, so hang here for now, please, and I'll call you over the radio with updates, okay?"

"Sure, but I'd like to keep you in sight," Ripley said.

I was already walking away, but glanced over my shoulder. "I appreciate that, but just be low-key. I'm telling you, he may already have bolted."

I jogged north, pausing briefly past the restroom building as I looked down the lane to the tunnel. I squinted against the bright sun lowering in the evening sky, letting my eyes adjust. The wide tunnel, its white walls decorated with surfing-themed murals, was thrown into dark shadow, but I couldn't see anyone standing around. Two surfers carried their boards under their arms and chatted as they walked out of the gloom into the shade of the trees lining the pathway. I ran on, searching for Dylan.

Standing behind an older 3 Series BMW with a surfboard strapped to a roof rack was a man in his mid-twenties wearing loose cotton trousers and a blue hoodie.

"Dylan?" I asked.

He spotted me approaching and looked me over. "You Kat the Cop?" He grinned. "Maybe you should arrest me. I'll go willingly."

I ignored his comment. "The man was right here when he used your phone?"

"Yeah," Dylan replied, his tone turning more serious when he realized I wasn't amused. "When I came through the tunnel, I guess he was waiting cos he walked with me to my car asking if he could borrow my phone."

"Which I presume was locked in your car."

"Yeah. So, I said sure. I mean, he didn't look like he was in any shape to take off with my iPhone, so I figured why not? Help a dude out, you know?"

I looked all around from where we stood at the third row of parking behind Ritz Carlton Drive. Ripley was watching me from beside the restrooms, so I grabbed my radio.

"Ripley, this is Cromwell. Can you check the loos, please? Over."

Dylan laughed. "Loos?"

"Roger," Ripley replied over the radio.

I tried to use American English for anything official, like radio calls and paperwork, but I tended to slip when my mind was elsewhere. And at that moment, all I cared about was finding Chris Wendell.

"You sure you didn't see where he went?" I asked again. "Even if it's just an idea of which direction he started in."

Dylan thought for a moment. "Maybe toward the road," he said, clearly unsure. "Was it you he called?"

I nodded. "Yeah. And he said he'd meet me here."

"Ripley to Cromwell. Restrooms are clear. Over."

I gave the officer a thumbs-up. If Chris was hiding behind one of the cars or trees, he would have undoubtedly spotted the uniformed officers by now. I needed to get myself to a place where he'd feel more comfortable approaching me.

"Stay by your car," I instructed Dylan. "Call me if you see him, okay?"

"Sure. I can chill for a bit," he said, but his next words stopped me from walking away. "Maybe he had the other person he called pick him up?"

Bugger. "He made two calls?"

Dylan nodded. "I only noticed because after the first one, he paced around a bit and then pulled a card from his pocket to make the second call."

The business card was probably the one I'd given him. There hadn't been a wallet in his backpack, so I presumed he still had it with him.

"Did you hear anything from either conversation?" I asked.

"No. But I wasn't listening, and he was talking kinda quiet, you know?"

"Hand me your phone. Let me see the number he called."

Dylan unlocked his phone and handed it to me. I opened the call history and saw my number was the last one called. I used my own phone to take a picture of the number, then hit redial on Dylan's phone. While it rang, I waved at Ripley to come over. Hanson had stayed by the patrol car.

The call went through, but no one spoke. I could hear the drone of a car engine. Whoever I was on the line with was driving.

"Who have I reached, please?" I asked.

The person immediately hung up.

"Bollocks," I muttered, and showed Ripley the picture I'd taken. "Get a search on that number right now. The second number down. Wendell called them first."

Officer Ripley used his own cell to call the station while I dialed the number again. It was now unavailable. The person had either powered it down or pulled the SIM card.

"Stay with Dylan," I ordered Ripley. "We'll need a statement."

"Where are you going?" Ripley asked as I jogged away.

"The park," I called over my shoulder. "Tell Hanson to do something useful and catch up to me."

"Will do," he responded, then began calling his partner on the radio, but I was soon out of earshot and wasn't about to stop.

More people were leaving through the tunnel. Mostly teenagers and young adults who'd spent the afternoon on the beach with their friends. I was tempted to start asking if they'd seen Wendell, but I realized the description I could provide was useless. "Seen a surfer-looking bloke in board shorts and T-shirt?" They'd seen hundreds since arriving at Salt Creek.

I jogged out the other side of the tunnel into the sunlight. To my left, a set of steps led up the embankment to the road above. Stretching toward the beach, a brush- and tree-covered slope continued down the hill beside the pathway. A fence at the top prevented anyone from scrambling up to the grounds of the Ritz Carlton. To my right, the lawns of the park spread several hundred yards down the hill to the bluffs overlooking the sand and water. A handful of picnickers holding out for sunset sat on blankets or camp chairs on the grassy slope, and a group of kids were playing touch football farther down the hill where it flattened out near the basketball half-court. Smoke wafted from grills by the covered patios, where families reserved tables and benches for gatherings.

Scattered over the lawns were a few solitary figures, some reading a book or listening to headphones, others curled up asleep in the sun. I could tell by the bags around a couple of them that they were homeless folks. I ran a little farther down the hill and took the first pathway, which led laterally across the sloping lawn. In my hand, my phone rang, and I checked the caller ID as I continued jogging. It was Hugo.

"Hey," I answered.

"I'm sorry I missed your call. I can come now. Where are you?"

I spotted a lone figure without any bags or blankets who appeared to be sleeping on the grass closer to the top of the hill. Cutting right, I made my way up the slope toward them.

"I'm at Salt Creek. Ripley and Hanson are with me," I added before he jumped me about backup. And I'd just spotted Hanson ambling out of the tunnel, although he was hardly rushing to support me.

Jogging up the steep slope, I arrived next to what I now could see was a man lying on his side, catching some rest. He wore pale green board shorts.

"I think I just found Chris Wendell," I whispered.

"Is he giving himself up?" Fuentes asked.

I kneeled down on the grass. "Hold on a moment."

I placed my phone down and gently shook Wendell's arm. He didn't stir.

"Bloody hell," I muttered, picking the phone back up. "Dammit, Hugo, I'm too late."

"What do you mean?" Fuentes asked as I carefully held Wendell's head and turned his face my way.

"He's dead," I gasped, looking at the vacant look in the man's open eyes and blood all around the side of his face and neck, dripping to the grass. "Shit, Hugo. Someone stabbed him in the ear."

26

Once again, I held the distinction of most unpopular copper for an evening. All hands were called on deck to process the crime scene, canvass the area, and speak with anyone we managed to stop before they left. By the time I went to bed around midnight, all we knew was that absolutely no one we'd spoken to had witnessed anything significant, no CCTV or security cameras faced the top of Salt Creek Beach Park, and Wendell's second phone call had been made to an untraceable burner.

Needless to say, I didn't get a restful night's sleep.

In the morning, I badly needed a good workout to clear my mind, and by "workout," I meant punching the heck out of a big, heavy bag until everything hurt. But I didn't have time. Instead, I took a detour via Dippity Donuts on my way to the station, where I picked up a couple of boxes of delicious saturated fats and sugar, hoping to win back a few of the folks whose Monday night had been ruined.

I made a start on my report until 8 a.m., when Hugo arrived, shortly followed by Captain Bradley, who summoned us both to her office.

"I thought we were getting close, and now we have a second

body," she began, closing the door behind us. "Do we still think Chris Wendell killed Helena Redman?"

"He had the note and her phone in his possession," I replied. "And we know he left the restaurant around the time she did. But we still have Travis Redman as the only person we can prove was at the scene that night. Maybe they were involved together somehow, but if Travis knew it was Wendell, then why wouldn't he say so?" I considered the idea of two killers for a moment. "Wendell's murder could have been someone seeking revenge, or perhaps Wendell knew something about Helena's death and needed to be silenced."

"Hugo?" Bradley asked, looking at my partner. "Your thoughts?"

He looked at me for a moment before replying. "Odds are we're looking for one killer, but we should check on the Redman parents' whereabouts last night. I mean, the brother still has to be our number-one suspect for Helena's murder as Kat's right, he's the only one we can place at the scene. So maybe he killed Wendell to keep him quiet."

"What about the parents?" Bradley asked.

Hugo and I looked at each other. "The father has a quick temper, but hard to say if it's a violent temper," I offered, thinking about how quickly he'd snapped during our conversations.

"Would he have a motive to kill his own daughter?" the captain asked.

"He'd have plenty of motive to kill her murderer," Hugo answered. "And Wendell's name has been all over the news."

The thought that until now, we'd not seriously considered Bob Redman to be involved was a punch in the face. I should have had him on my radar.

"I have no idea what motive he'd have to kill Helena," I said. "But we don't have a clear motive for any of the suspects to have murdered her. The note, phone, and footage of Wendell potentially following Helena suggest he's our killer, and from what people have said, he was upset when Helena left him. Which would be motive if he couldn't take it anymore."

Our first conversation with Bob Redman came back clearly to me, which was good as I'd left my instant photo collection on my desk. Again. My second slip, which once more left me feeling naked when I searched inside my empty pocket.

Hugo looked down and surely noticed my empty hand fussing with my pants. Now I felt really stupid on top of uncertain, but I sensed the briefing was coming to an end, so I pushed on.

"Bob Redman was the first one to bring up Chris Wendell's name, too," I added, vividly replaying the man speaking in my mind. I let the memory roll like a movie, trying to pull out any other nuances I'd missed. Nothing stood out. But at least I'd had the correct memory on call.

"Start there," Bradley said with an air of finality. "See if he has an alibi for last night, then revisit the brother."

"Will do," I replied, and we hurried out of her office.

Making the short drive to the Redmans' house, Hugo didn't mention the pictures, but I couldn't help feeling like he'd logged another incident against me. Although, he seemed in a decent mood, so perhaps not.

We bantered more about the case, which was good, but we were still going around in circles with the same limited amount of information. We'd now passed the one-week mark from Helena's murder, and all we had to show for our efforts was a second body. In serial killings, new bodies were sometimes the only way to progress the investigation, but in Dana Point, two murders doubled our average annual number.

"How are you doing?" Hugo asked me as I turned into the cul-de-sac for the Redmans' home.

"It's frustrating," I admitted. "I wish we had more to go on."

"I meant, how are you doing having to deal with finding two dead bodies?" Hugo clarified, and his words surprised me.

I hadn't thought about it that way. I had been first on scene for both murders, and while our job meant that we'd see things we'd rather not see, I wasn't immune to the violence and tragedy. It bothered me. If I let it. My armor was staying focused on the unsolved case. My armor against everything. "Obsessed" might be another term a therapist would probably use.

My first reaction was to tell him I was fine and we had a job to do, but it wasn't lost on me that Hugo was being nice. He appeared to be genuinely concerned about me. This was uncharted territory in the time we'd known each other, and while it would be easy to chalk it up to him covering his own arse so I didn't reveal his secret, I didn't get that impression.

"Trying not to think about that side of things," I replied honestly, parking the car outside the Redmans' house. "But I don't know what's more jarring. Seeing a man I'd recently spoken to dead on the ground, or the fact that my mind immediately shoves that aside and begins wondering what the killer may have used as a weapon."

Hugo looked over at me. "The job does all of that to you, Kat. Don't let it numb you too much."

I nodded and managed a slight smile. I wanted to tell him it wouldn't, but I wasn't sure that would be true. *Thank you* hung in my mind, but the words didn't come out.

We both opened our doors and exited the car.

"A pen," I said as we walked up the driveway.

"Icepick," Hugo replied.

"Who the hell takes an icepick to the park?" I asked, pausing before ringing the bell.

"Someone who's willing to stab another human in the ear to murder them and doesn't want to get covered in blood," Hugo pointed out.

"That's a bit Agatha Christie, isn't it? And cold," I said as I pushed the doorbell button.

"I don't think Agatha Christie did it, Kat," he joked with a straight face. "And cold? I'd say stabbing someone precisely through their ear canal is pretty cold and calculated. Which would also take deliberate planning," he added.

I was about to respond, but the door opened. Sheila Redman stood before us, keeping their golden retriever at bay with her leg.

"I saw the news," she blurted. "Does it have anything to do with Helena's murder?"

We hadn't released Wendell's name to the media yet, but naturally, the incident involving an unnamed individual had already been all over the local news.

"There may well be a connection, Mrs. Redman," I replied. "Can we come in for a few minutes?"

Sheila backed the dog up and waved us inside.

"Who else is in the house?" I asked as we stepped into the living room.

"Just me and Bob," she replied. "He's in the backyard."

"Scarlett?"

"She's back at school this week," Sheila said, closing the door behind us. "Her choice. I think she needed to be around her friends."

"Could you ask Bob to join us?" I asked, walking through the open-plan lounge to the dining area beside the kitchen. French doors led to the backyard, and through a large window off the dining area, I could see a shed door ajar at the far end of the garden.

Sheila opened the back door and called to her husband. After a few moments, he poked his head out of the shed, and she waved him over to the house. He carefully closed the shed door and appeared to lock it before walking across the backyard and joining us. I quickly shuffled through my instant photos before tucking them away again in my pocket.

"What's going on?" Bob immediately asked. "Is this about that business at Salt Creek?"

"Let's all take a seat," I responded, pointing to the dining chairs. "When was the last time either of you saw or spoke with Chris Wendell?" I asked once everyone sat down.

The Redmans looked at each other, then back to me.

"I don't really know," Bob replied. "It's been a while, I suppose."

"We didn't see him that much even when they were dating," Sheila added. "Busy lives and odd schedules, I'd imagine."

"Have you found him?" Bob asked. "It's been all over the news that he's your suspect."

Of course, we'd never said that Chris Wendell was a suspect, simply that we were looking to speak with him in regard to an investigation. But it wasn't a leap for Helena's father to come to that conclusion.

"Yes, we've found him," I said, which was the truth. "So, to be clear, neither of you have seen or spoken to Chris over the past few weeks. Is that correct?"

They both nodded.

"Where is your son at the moment?" Hugo asked.

"Probably working," Bob replied.

"And where would that be?" I followed up.

"Varies. He does odd jobs and helps different people."

"Does that include the Russos and their restaurant where Helena used to work?" I asked.

Bob frowned. "I believe so. What's that got to do with Wendell? Sounds like you have your man."

"Were…" I began, and paused when I realized my error in tense. Which wasn't actually an error, but didn't fit our current line of questioning. "Are Travis and Chris close?"

Sheila went to answer, then stopped. We'd spoken to the couple enough to know by now that Bob liked to be the one handling their narrative, and his wife clearly knew it.

"Not that I know of," Bob replied. "I mean, they know each other, but if they spent any time together, I've never heard about it."

"Did Travis stay here last night?" I asked.

"No, and why are you asking about Travis again?" Bob responded, his voice already beginning to rise. "You've already cost me a bunch of money on a damn lawyer for no good reason."

"Our reason is that your son broke into your daughter's minivan on the night she was murdered, Mr. Redman," I replied calmly. "He was within a hundred yards of where she was killed around the time it happened, and he's yet to give us a good reason."

Sheila's head dropped into her hands, and she began sobbing. Bob's face turned red, and he placed an arm around his wife.

"That's ridiculous," he stammered.

"Ridiculous" would be to believe that the lawyer he'd hired hadn't explained exactly why Travis had been brought into the station. Travis may well have omitted to bring up the second time we'd interviewed him, but there was no way Bob Redman hadn't had a say in the no-contest plea. Or at least knowledge of the decision.

"Did Travis have a problem with Helena?" Hugo asked, and Bob shot to his feet.

"You need to leave! This is ludicrous. You have her killer. You know it was Wendell."

"You're going to great lengths in helping Travis cover up his reason for being at Doheny, Mr. Redman," I challenged. "If your son is innocent of any wrongdoing, we need to know so we can focus elsewhere."

"Elsewhere is exactly where you should be looking!" Bob shouted in return. "You need to leave."

"Oh, Bob," Sheila whimpered, but he waved her off.

We stood. "Were you both home last night, Mr. Redman?" I asked.

"Yes. Now damn well leave," he replied, wrestling with his temper and unsuccessfully attempting to calm his voice.

"All evening?" Hugo followed up.

"No," Redman replied, marching across the living room and expecting us to follow. "We went to dinner around 6:30 and were home by… I don't know. Probably 8:30."

I walked behind Hugo, who took his time catching up to Bob. Sheila remained at the table in tears.

"Where did you have dinner?" I turned to ask her.

She peered at me through damp eyes. "Salt Creek Grill."

My breathing skipped, but I tried my best not to let it show. The restaurant was a mile up PCH from where Wendell was killed in the park.

"Just the two of you?" I asked.

Sheila looked panicked, and her eyes shot from me to her husband's. She didn't answer, dropping her head again.

"Mr. Redman?" I said, turning his way.

He let out a long sigh. "No. Travis met us there."

27

———————

We sat in the car outside the Redmans' house for a few minutes.

"Maybe the Redmans planned it together," Hugo said. "Travis knew it was Wendell, told his father, and the two of them killed him in the park."

"While Sheila waited in the car?" I questioned.

"She seemed very upset this morning."

"True, but she's had a few things to be upset about lately," I pointed out. "Hard to say that's any kind of indicator."

Hugo nodded. "They said Travis met them there, so maybe it was Travis alone after leaving the restaurant."

"Boy, I'm getting tired of talking to Travis Redman with nothing but weak circumstantial evidence to throw at him," I said, as I started the car. "We have to do it, but having dinner in the same vicinity that a crime took place is about as thin as it gets. I wish we had CCTV from the park or even the parking lot."

I turned around in the cul-de-sac and drove to the stop sign for Camino Del Avion.

"We could check the intersection at PCH and Ritz Carlton Drive," Hugo suggested. "There are businesses on opposite corners. Maybe one of them has a camera facing PCH. If we see the Redmans and their son drive past, it might help clear them."

"Or, if we see them rejoining PCH from Ritz Carlton Drive, it would mean they made a stop on the way home," I finished for my partner.

"Yup," he said, already calling Sergeant Martinez at the station.

I drove to Golden Lantern and waited at the left turn light. Our conversation before we'd visited the Redmans came back to me, and I thought through what Hugo had said about a cold, calculated method of killing someone. He was right. Unless the killer made an extraordinarily lucky strike, Chris Wendell had been killed by a precise and instantly lethal stab. One that would be hard to execute without being physically close to the victim, who would need to remain still. Maybe the toxicology report on Wendell would show a tranquilizer in his system, but I knew from seeing him up close that the only trauma to his head was the wound that surely killed him. He hadn't been forcibly knocked out, and there were no marks around his neck, so he hadn't been choked into unconsciousness.

I thought about my conversation with Wendell, which was fortunately staying with me as I had no way of using my instant pictures to jolt my memory of an audio conversation.

The light turned green, and I turned, continuing down Golden Lantern towards the station as Hugo wrapped up his phone call.

"You're right, Wendell knew his attacker," I said. "It had to have happened quickly and quietly for no one to notice, and for it all to take place before I got there. I bet the killer was only just leaving when I arrived."

Hugo thought it over while I turned left on Acapulco Drive, then immediately left again into the city buildings' parking lot housing the station, amongst other official offices.

"No signs of defensive wounds, so there's nothing to suggest he struggled," Hugo said. "I'm guessing he didn't suspect the killer would harm him."

"I suppose Wendell could have been asleep," I mused. "He sounded exhausted on the phone."

"So he got off the call with you, walked through the tunnel into the park, laid down, and went to sleep?" Hugo questioned. "Possible, but I think it's more likely he met someone who he trusted."

"I agree," I acknowledged. "Yet, no one so far, including Travis himself, has admitted that he knew Wendell beyond a casual knowledge of each other through Helena."

I parked the car, and Hugo opened his door.

"Are you coming?" he asked when I didn't do the same.

"I'll be a few minutes behind you, if that's okay?" I said as an idea popped into my brain. It was a long shot but would only take a few minutes.

Hugo looked at me suspiciously.

"I'm going to see if I can speak with Scarlett Redman," I explained, looking up her number I'd saved in my phone.

Hugo hesitated, then nodded. "Okay. I'll try calling Travis Redman and follow up with Martinez on the CCTV. Join me after you've called the kid."

I was about to explain my thinking, but he'd already swung the door closed and was walking toward the office. I typed a quick text to Scarlett.

"This is Kat, the investigator on your mum's case." I paused and was about to delete and type "mom" instead, but then decided it didn't matter as I was pushed for time. *"Could you chat for a few minutes if I come to the school?"*

I got out of the car and made my way to the crosswalk, hoping she'd be available, and just as the light flashed for me to cross, she answered.

"Sure. Study period. I'll step outside."

Striding quickly across Golden Lantern, I jogged over Acapulco without waiting on the crosswalk. By the time I walked to the parking lot, another ping sounded on my phone. Scarlett had dropped a pin in the map app. I knew just where she was waiting for me. Lots had changed since I'd left the high school, but the main buildings hadn't.

"Hey," I greeted her a few minutes later. She was waiting for me in the shade. "Sorry to spring this on you."

"That's okay. Have you found them?" she asked.

"We don't have anyone in custody yet, I'm afraid, but I believe we're getting closer."

"Oh," she responded, and by the look on her face, I could tell I'd dashed her hopes.

"Are you comfortable chatting with me without a teacher or your…" I hesitated as I realized I'd been about to say "parents." "…Grandparents present?"

Scarlett shrugged. "I don't care. I don't mind talking to you."

I wasn't required to notify a parent or guardian, as Scarlett wasn't in custody, but I didn't want to add to the kid's trauma. Or give Bob Redman something else to shout about.

"I had a couple of things I thought you might be able to help me with," I explained.

She nodded, so I continued.

"I know you said your mum had seemed normal in the time leading up to last Tuesday night, but is there anything, upon reflection, you've thought of since we last spoke that strikes you as odd?"

She shook her head, then looked at the ground.

"What is it, Scarlett?"

The teenager didn't respond, and for a moment, I wondered if my presence and bringing up her tragedy once more was too much for her. A pang of guilt hit me. My driving need for answers suddenly felt reckless and insensitive.

She looked up with tears running down her cheeks. "I honestly don't know what she had going on," Scarlett sighed, her voice low and ragged. "I was too worried about stupid crap in my life while she did everything she could to be there for me. We had so little time together, I didn't ask about *her*. She'd get in late from work, but always woke up early to have breakfast with me and take me to school. 'Our time' she called it…"

There was more, but the girl broke down. I reached an arm

around her, and she clutched onto me, sobbing. I felt like a complete arse. The only reason I was now comforting Scarlett was because I'd shown up there in the first place. If I'd left her alone, she would have carried on with her day, getting by as best she could with her grief.

"I'm so sorry," I whispered, and held her close.

After a minute, her sobs turned to sniffles, and she released me. "No, I'm sorry," she said, wiping her face.

"Don't you dare apologize to me, Scarlett. I shouldn't have dropped in like this."

In theory, nothing within the law was out of bounds when pursuing a murder suspect, but this felt like I'd made another poor choice.

"It's okay," she said, and took a deep breath, letting it out slowly. "I'm good now. Ask what you need to ask. I want to help."

"Are you sure? We can do this at your grandparents' house later if you'd prefer."

She quickly shook her head. "No. Go ahead."

I ran through the questions I'd listed in my mind while walking over and tried to prioritize and filter them, feeling like I should only ask a couple of the most important ones. The damage was done, so I figured I might as well salvage something from my clumsy attempt at moving the case forward. Leaving with no answers would be worse at this point.

"Has Darian Rutherford tried to contact you since the other day at Doheny?"

"No," she answered flatly, and I couldn't tell whether she was resentful or simply didn't care.

"Do you know if your mum and your Uncle Travis ever had disagreements?"

Scarlett laughed. It was short, hollow, and without much humor, but she did grin for a second afterward before her face was consumed with sadness once more.

"Mom always said it was normal sibling stuff, and I kinda see that with brothers and sisters at school. But what they had was different. She was a lot older than him, so Mom was a bit like another parent to Travis. One he could actually come to for stuff."

"I'm guessing your grandparents are wound a little tight," I observed, and she rolled her eyes.

"More than a little. And I know they're way easier on me than Travis."

I noticed she didn't use the "uncle" prefix as I had. Maybe that wasn't weird, as he was as close to Scarlett's age as he was to Helena's.

"That's probably from the accumulation of stuff over the years," I pointed out.

She nodded. "No doubt. So, I guess you could say they fought, but mainly Mom straightened him out and Travis apologized a million times, then screwed up again a while later, and they'd do it all over again."

"But nothing that stood out lately?"

Scarlett shrugged. "No, but I hadn't seen him much in the past few months. He needed money for something, like maybe three or four months ago, and she said no. It was part of their thing. He'd be mad at her and stay away for a while, then Nana and Gramps would find a way to get them together at a dinner or something, and then it'd be fine for a while, until it wasn't again."

"So they had an argument a few months back, and you think they hadn't reached the resolution stage yet?"

Scarlett looked at me, unsure, or perhaps trying to figure out where I was heading with my questions.

"I guess, but Travis would never hurt Mom," she said as though the idea was unthinkable.

Murder, especially killing a family member, was unthinkable to most loved ones… and especially their victims. I moved on.

"Did Travis and Chris Wendell hang out at all?"

Scarlett thought my question over for a few moments. "They knew each other, for sure, but I don't really know how well. I mean, I remember Travis talking about the band Chris was in one time, like he'd seen them. But they were never both over for dinner or anything like that."

I kept thinking of more questions, but knew I needed to wrap this up. For Scarlett's sake, and to get back to Hugo at the station as I'd left him with a lot to do.

"Last questions, Scarlett, then I'll let you get back to class. How did you get along with Chris?"

She looked at the ground and then back up at me. "Do you really think he killed my mom?" she asked instead of replying.

I felt another pang of guilt for not telling her that Chris was dead, but I couldn't. I liked Scarlett, and my heart went out to her for losing Helena, but she was still a teenager. She'd have to tell her best friend, and all it took was one more, "I'll tell you, but you can't say anything to anyone else," and the story would be out before the family had even been informed.

"There's evidence to suggest he was in the vicinity at the time, Scarlett. Did he have a hard time when they broke up?"

She nodded. "I think so. Mom never knew, but he texted me for a while afterwards. I like him. He's always been cool to me, and he didn't try to buddy up, or be a dad, or anything like that. He was just a cool guy, and I was bummed they broke up."

"Even though he forgot to pick you up?"

Scarlett laughed. "We live in Southern California. It wasn't like I was abandoned at night in a snowstorm. It was no big deal to me."

"Was he angry about the breakup?"

Scarlett shrugged again. "He was upset, but he knew it was his fault. He apologized to me, and I told him I didn't care, but we both understood why Mom got mad about it."

"So Chris was upset, but understanding?"

"I guess," she said thoughtfully. "I think he knew it would always come to an end at some point, you know? It was like he knew he'd screw it up beyond repair one day. It was just a matter of time."

"Have you texted with him lately?"

Her head dropped again. She stared at the ground for a moment and sighed. "The Sunday before… you know." She lifted her head and gulped back the tears that were ready to flow. "We hadn't spoken in ages, so I was surprised he texted me. Said he really missed us both. I replied and told him I hoped he was okay, but that was it. He didn't send anything back."

Scarlett took out her phone, and with the lightning-fast thumb speed of every modern teenager, she typed, swiped, and scrolled, then showed me her screen. She'd relayed their short text exchange almost verbatim. I noticed the previous text was dated three months earlier.

I'd already been at the school longer than planned and put the kid through enough.

"You've been a big help, thank you," I told her. "I'll let you get back to study."

"Okay," she said, but I got the sense that she'd needed to talk about her mother. I could imagine her grandfather being the "let's not talk about it and put it behind us" type, so maybe Scarlett needed the conversation, even if it was with a relative stranger. Perhaps *because* it was with a relative stranger.

"I have one more request before I go," I said, wincing as I pulled my instant picture camera from my back pocket. "Mind if I take a quick photo?"

Scarlett rolled her eyes. "I look like crap. Do you have to?"

"It helps me remember everything we discussed," I offered, which always sounded like a weak reason but was more genuine than anyone ever realized. "It's okay if you don't look right at the camera."

I quickly snapped the picture as she glanced off into the distance, then thanked her again before walking away.

Starting back to the station, I was eager to tell Hugo what I'd learned, but it was good that it took me a few minutes. I spent the whole walk deciding exactly what it was I *had* learned. I wouldn't classify what we knew as a strong motive, but it seemed a step more believable to me that either man could have killed Helena if a confrontation had gone awry. Helena had been on Chris Wendell's mind lately, and he had the note he'd used to lure her to the park. It wasn't a stretch to imagine her rejection flipping a switch in his head and things ending badly.

I marched into our offices, where Hugo briefly glanced up as I approached, then continued with what he was doing.

"We need those records from Wendell's phone," I announced. "They must have cracked his password by now."

Instead of replying, Hugo slowly stood and walked around the desks. I jumped when he slapped a piece of paper face down next to my keyboard.

"I'll never fucking trust you again, Cromwell," he growled. "I came back to this taped to my monitor."

Hugo stomped away, leaving me stunned and speechless. I picked up the paper and turned it over. It was a poorly patched-together, cut-and-paste job, but my heart sank.

The photo was Hugo's official department headshot taken from our internal system. It had been pasted into the profile page of a gay dating site.

28

I stared at the piece of paper in my hand, baffled as to what I should do. Surely he didn't think I did this? No, I figured, but he'd definitely think I told someone, which was what led to the childish prank. I slid my chair back and was about to head for Captain Bradley's office when an email alert pinged on my phone. I shuffled the chair back closer to the desk and logged into my computer so I could read the email on the monitor. It was from forensics and contained several reports.

There was no question I was hanging too much hope on what these documents contained. We could come up with theories until we were blue in the face, but what we lacked was useable, incontrovertible evidence. Anything in these reports that tied the killer to the actual attack could be just what we needed.

I already felt sick over the Hugo drama, and now the nervous anticipation of opening the files added to my unsettled stomach.

I looked over my shoulder to see where Hugo had gone, but he was nowhere in sight. Things had been going so well with him, and now, just as I felt our case might gain a little momentum, some inconsiderate wanker pulls a pubescent stunt. But going to Bradley would probably make things worse, so I was glad the email had distracted me. Steaming in to see her would be the correct and appropriate thing to do, but it would also escalate a situation Hugo may well wish to squash in his own way. Which, of course, I couldn't know as he'd disappeared.

I opened the first report, which was Chris Wendell's phone records. They'd cracked his password, or whatever they did to get the info. The phone hadn't been powered down, so even missed calls after I'd taken the backpack showed up. Several were from Douglas Ashley, who I guessed to be the drummer from Wendell's band I'd spoken to, but multiple calls over the past two weeks were from a number I instantly recognized. It was the burner he'd called from Salt Creek on the surfer's phone. The person who'd hung up on me had then deactivated the number.

One thing I couldn't find was any recent calls to Helena, at least not to her cell, although I found the text exchange with Scarlett. A thought occurred to me. What if the burner phone had belonged to Helena and now the killer had it? But why would Chris Wendell call the burner number of a dead woman? Unless he was somehow involved.

"Bloody hell," I muttered aloud.

Wendell and Travis Redman were both complicit in Helena's murder, and Travis then killed Wendell when he thought he was about to tell me something. Travis had the burner phone that Chris called, and he was conveniently a mile up the road at the restaurant. That's how Travis beat me to Salt Creek Beach Park.

A wave of excitement hit me as I sensed I was finally onto something that made sense, and I jumped up. All I needed now was my partner back in the game, and some shred of solid evidence.

I marched from the office into the reception, looking for Hugo. I then checked the break room. He was nowhere to be seen, so I tried his phone, which rang twice before going to voicemail. Which likely meant that he'd seen it was me and declined the call. I hung up and texted him instead.

"I didn't tell anyone. Whether you believe me or not, we have a case to work. We have new reports, and I think I know what happened."

Perhaps it was because my parents didn't get me a cell phone until I was fourteen that I didn't grow up with turbo-charged thumbs, but I typed only marginally faster on a phone keyboard than my mother. My dad's thumbs were the size of small bananas, so he tended to hit four letters at a time, and his messages made no sense. I looked at the screen, hoping for the little dots to appear, telling me Hugo was typing a reply. After a minute of staring at my phone in the reception area like a lovesick teenager, I went back to my desk and opened the next report. It was the detailed forensics report on the evidence taken from Helena's body. Clicking it open, I began reading, but was interrupted by my phone ringing. Thinking it was Hugo calling, I grabbed it and answered.

"Hey."

"Is this Detective Cromwell?" a man asked.

"This is Orange County Sheriff's Department Investigator Cromwell, yes," I corrected him.

"This is Sergeant Calderone with Astoria PD in Oregon. You'd requested we keep an eye out for one Darian Rutherford."

"That's right. Thanks for calling. Have you found him?"

"I'm standing next to him, ma'am. Shall I put him on the phone?"

"That would be great, Sergeant, thank you," I replied in surprise.

"What now?" Rutherford greeted me.

"You lied to me, Mr. Rutherford. Again."

"Oh, yeah?" he replied. "I probably just forgot or something. What about?"

"You called and spoke to Helena Redman on the day she was murdered," I said. "Are you telling me you forgot about that?"

The line was quiet for several moments. "No, I chose not to tell you that."

"That's an important detail, Mr. Rutherford. Care to tell me why you omitted to let me know the two of you had spoken?"

"Cos it didn't have anything to do with her getting murdered, and you were already wasting your time looking at me," he snapped back. "I told you, I have a gig starting up here. I figured you'd pull some bullshit and keep me in Dana Point if I told you."

He wasn't wrong, but I was still annoyed he'd lied. But of course, if only the guilty ones lied, our job would be a lot easier. Unfortunately, most people were hiding or embarrassed about something, so they tended to lie or omit useful information with the police.

"What did you discuss?" I asked.

"Not much," he scoffed. "She didn't want to have anything to do with me."

"Okay, let me ask you a different way. Why did *you* call her?"

"I was in town. Honestly, that was it. I hadn't been back there in years, and it felt weird to be there and not at least say hi, you know?" he replied, his voice losing some of the animosity it had been laced with from the first time I'd spoken with him. "I wanted to see how Scarlett was doing."

"Did you ask to see Scarlett?" I asked.

"No, no. When I say I wanted to see how she was doing, I just meant to ask after her, I guess."

"And what did Helena say?"

"She told me they were both fine," he replied curtly. So much for the softer tone.

"And?"

"What do you mean?"

"I mean, what else was said?" I clarified. "What you just told me takes no more than twenty or thirty seconds, but your call was four minutes long. So, what else did you discuss?"

As Darian began replying, Hugo walked by our desks and took his seat. I forced my attention back to the call.

"We just bickered with each other. I told her I had a right to ask how the kid was doing, and she told me I didn't. It went back and forth until she said she had to go and hung up."

I felt like pointing out that referring to their offspring as "the kid" was probably part of the problem, but I let it go.

"Mr. Rutherford, please answer if I call you again so we don't have to involve the local authorities in tracking you down, okay?"

"Well…" he began, then stopped.

"I know. You have a gig, so you'll be on a boat for a while, right?"

"Yeah. We don't get cell service in the Pacific."

"Text me the name of the boat and its home port, okay?"

"Yeah, sure. Here's your buddy."

The phone was handed off, and Sergeant Calderone came back on the line.

"Anything else you need?" he asked.

"He's supposed to be texting me the name of a boat and its port," I said. "If you could make sure he does that, then we're all set. I really appreciate you guys helping out. Shout if we can ever be of assistance to you in return."

"Sure thing, ma'am," he replied, and we ended the call.

I put my phone down and took a deep breath.

"Hugo," I began quietly, "you have to know I had nothing—"

"Cromwell, stop," he interjected. "I don't *have to know* shit. But we gotta work the case. So, let's work it."

I still had a knot in my stomach, but I couldn't force him to listen to me. Or believe the words I said. So I pressed on.

"That was Darian Rutherford. Obviously, he didn't commit the second murder as he's in Oregon, but he had a story about the phone call with Helena on the day she was killed. Told me he didn't mention it because he figured we'd keep him here."

Hugo didn't say anything or react in any way. He remained hidden behind his damn monitor where I couldn't read his face. Not that I needed to. His anger permeated every inch of the room.

I rattled off my theory about Chris Wendell and Travis Redman, to which he also didn't say a word. I couldn't believe Hugo and I were back at square one. Actually, worse than that. He now actively hated me instead of harboring a snobby indifference. I reminded myself again that I couldn't fix it right now, and returned my attention to the forensic report.

Pages of comparisons, technical and scientific details, and measurements made very little sense to me, and I did what most law enforcement officers do: I skimmed until I found the conclusion for each section. The dirt in the rope wound was unlikely to have come from Doheny Park. There were almost no sand particles present, but there were traces of potting soil.

Even more pages were dedicated to the oil and other chemicals deposited. All to render the conclusion that the rope used had likely been in an environment where it had picked up very small amounts of a variety of marine and/or automotive oils and lubricants, including 10W-30 synthetic engine oil, marine grease, WD-40, and a few others. Meaning, the rope had sat on the floor or bench in a workshop, or been tossed into a boat locker, which all the chemicals mentioned had frequented at some point. The main thing I took from this section was that it was unlikely the rope used to strangle Helena came from the new length of rope we took from Darian Rutherford's friend's boat. And we'd seen the old one he'd replaced it with, which hadn't been cut up.

As I moved to the next page, the text immediately caught my attention. They'd found a strand of hair. I scanned through the extensive measuring and references they'd made and stopped when I realized what they were talking about. It wasn't a human hair. It was from a dog.

"Hugo!" I said, and the lack of response reminded me that he still hated me. "The hair, Hugo," I said, trying again.

"The Redmans have a dog," he said flatly.

"And Wendell."

"All they say is that it's from a mid-to-large-sized breed with medium-length hair," Hugo added.

That was progress. A full sentence.

"Maybe we should check the garage and the garden shed at the Redmans' place," I said, mulling it over. "I'm sure the guys looked in both when we served the warrant, but they were looking for a piece of rope, not what a piece of rope might have laid in for a while. I hate to say it, but I think it's time to get

Travis back in here once more. Really lean on him. What do you think?"

"I think you haven't read the final report," Hugo replied.

I went back to the email and opened the third report. This one, I hadn't expected. We'd sent the note in to see if anything could be pulled from the paper or something unique about the ink used, but that all came back with nothing useful.

The handwriting, however, was positively not Chris Wendell's. It was a 97-percent certainty match with Travis Redman's.

29

Needless to say, Travis Redman didn't answer his phone when I called. I sent him a text suggesting there was one loose end he could help us with, hoping I'd bluff him into calling me back. He didn't.

After checking in with Captain Bradley, we put out a BOLO for Travis, then walked outside to the car. I hit the unlock button on the remote, but didn't get in.

"Let's get a sample of dog hair from Wendell's place first," I suggested to Hugo across the roof of the car. "Take a swab from the carport as well. It wasn't very clean, from what I recall."

Hugo stared back at me. "Okay," he mumbled unenthusiastically.

My frustration returned in a wave, and I couldn't help myself. "Dammit, Hugo, I swear I didn't tell anyone! I'm sorry this has happened, but I had nothing to do with it. Why would I?"

His blank look quickly turned to anger. "You're saying it's a total coincidence that no one knows anything about my personal life for years, and a few days after you find out, the world knows, yet that has nothing to do with you?"

"I'm saying exactly that! I didn't tell a soul, I promise you. You should take the note to Bradley so she can figure it out. The idiot was probably stupid enough to make it up and print it from a work computer. She can have IT take a look."

"Now you want Bradley and the IT department involved?" Hugo shot back. "Fucking perfect. Maybe we should bring it up in the next briefing. Ask if anyone knows anything about it. Think that's a good idea? You don't get it, Kat!" he fumed.

He was right. I didn't. I was made to feel like the rookie all the time, with eyes on me and a black cloud hovering over my fiancé's case, but that wasn't the same. This was as personal as it could possibly get for Hugo. I was incredibly pissed off, but still self-aware enough to know my anger was about the situation and the prick who did this, not Hugo. I couldn't blame him for being furious.

"Hugo, I don't know how whoever did this found out, or whether they simply took a lucky shot in the dark, but it didn't come from me. I haven't had a conversation, phone call, text, or anything which even mentions you, and certainly not…" I lowered my voice. "I've certainly not spoken a word about what I saw."

"Of course you'd say that," he responded, slapping the roof of the car. "But the timing is far too coincidental." He stepped back from the car. "Let's split up. It'll be more efficient. You go to Wendell's. I'll check Travis Redman's digs in San Juan Capistrano."

Hugo walked away, and I could tell there was no point trying to further the conversation or chase after him. His heels were dug in, and all I could hope was he'd calm down given time. Maybe then he'd consider the notion that it wasn't me who'd ratted him out.

Adding to my frustration was the knowledge we were back to operating as a divided team. The past few days hadn't been perfectly smooth, but at least we'd been communicating, and now that was out the window again. It was unfair to Helena Redman. And Scarlett.

I climbed in the car and left the station, heading for Beachwood Trailer Park while trying my best to put the situation with my partner out of my head. We were close on this case. I could feel it.

The forensics hadn't handed us a knockout punch but certainly added fuel to the fire of my Wendell and Travis Redman theory. As unfathomable as it was to think Travis had been involved in the death of his own sister, the evidence didn't lie.

Parking in front of the mobile home, I walked up the steps to the door and knocked. As he worked nights, I suspected Wendell's roommate, Manny Rubio, would be home in the early afternoon, but I might have to rouse him. After three rounds of hammering on the door without a response, I dug his phone number out of my notebook and called.

A sleepy voice answered just as I thought it was going to voice-mail. "Yeah?"

"Sorry to wake you, Mr. Rubio. This is Sheriff's Department Investigator Kat Cromwell. Would you mind coming to the front door?"

"What? How d'you find me, man?"

"Are you home?"

"No. What's happening, man?"

I'd weighed calling ahead, but people often had a habit of making sure they weren't home if you warned them you were coming by.

"Where's your dog?" I asked, having not heard any movement or barking from inside.

"He's with me, man. Why the hell are you interested in my dog? You with animal services now?"

"No, nothing like that, Mr. Rubio," I replied, trying to think of a way to get what I needed without having to come back. "Are you close by?"

"No. I'm in Costa Mesa right now. I ain't coming home before work tonight."

"All I need to do is check one thing in Chris's room, Mr. Rubio," I said, figuring I'd make one last effort. "Does a neighbor have a key, by any chance?"

"Quit calling me Mr. Rubio," he mumbled. "You're freakin' me out like my ol' man's here. There's a key under the white rock. Left of the porch step. Lock it when you're done."

I scrambled down the steps to find the key and thought he was going to hang up, but he carried on, sounding a little panicked.

"And you don't have no permission to go into my room, man! That ain't the deal, right?"

I laughed. "You have my word. I'll be in and out. Thanks for your help, Manny."

"Later," he muttered, and hung up.

I found the key, hidden where no one in their right mind would hide a house key. Under the most obvious object near the door. I went inside, greeted by the stale smell I recalled from before, and quickly donned my nitrile gloves to protect myself from whatever festered on every unclean surface.

It wasn't hard to find samples of dog hair as it was everywhere. The couch alone provided all I needed, so I sealed and labeled the evidence baggie. It was tempting to poke my head into Manny Rubio's room, but I resisted. I was sure I would find drug para-phernalia and probably illegal narcotics, but that wasn't my mission. And I'd given my word. Chris Wendell's room was exactly as we'd left it a few days ago. Nothing appeared to have moved.

Locking the front door, I replaced the key under its rock and moved to the carport. With the Jeep gone, I could see they kept the outside of their home in the same state as the interior. Which meant there was automotive junk along the back edge, and a grubby mess from spilled oil that had mixed with dirt and other grime. I took a photograph with my phone, so I could email it, then scraped up a sample of the muck from three different spots and labeled the baggies. There were no obvious marks, indents, or discoloration to suggest a coil of rope had spent time anywhere I could see. But if the length used on Helena Redman had been dropped on the ground in the back of the carport, it could easily have picked up the residue found on her neck.

Back in the car, I texted Hugo and reported that I'd collected samples from Wendell's and was now heading to the Redmans' house. He didn't reply. I felt myself tense once more in frustration.

As I began driving, an idea resurfaced, and as much as I tried to beat it back where it belonged, the thought grew like ivy until it consumed me. I texted Hugo once more.

"I have something. Meet me at the grocery market parking lot, Stonehill and Del Obispo."

The location was somewhat between us, and on Hugo's probable route back to the station. I headed that way, waiting for a response. I was already parked before a reply arrived. Or, more accurately, *he* arrived.

Pulling up alongside me, he lowered his passenger-side window. "What is it?"

"Come over here, and I'll explain," I said, moving my bag to the back seat to make room. "We shouldn't be shouting across the parking lot."

Hugo didn't look the least bit interested in joining me, but after a few moments of contemplation, he opened his door and walked around.

"Okay, what do you have?" he asked as he sat down and closed the passenger door.

I took a deep breath. This felt like the most impetuous move I could make, yet a powerful urge from within started me talking. Albeit awkwardly.

"You've been asking, and I haven't been telling you everything," I stumbled. "About my pictures."

Hugo stared at me with a frown creasing his brow. He didn't say a word.

"You've been talking about trust," I soldiered on, the powerful urge receding as a sense of impending doom took its place. "And you're right. We have to be able to trust each other."

Still no response.

"I get that you're having a hard time believing me about your secret and that stupid prank at the office, and I get it. Sort of. But I figured the best way was to even the playing field."

"What the fuck are you talking about?" Hugo snapped.

My hackles instantly went up. "Will you stop being a pissed-off dickhead for one minute so I can tell you this?" I barked back.

His hand moved to the door, but I grabbed his arm before he could leave. "Hugo! Please. Hear me out. This isn't easy for me."

His expression didn't exude sympathy, but he stayed, and his hand returned to his lap.

"I have a neurological disorder, alright?" I blurted. "That's why I need the pictures."

Hugo stared at me for a moment. "What? Does Bradley know?"

My heart sank. His first response was whether the powers-that-be knew I had a condition that would prohibit me from wearing a badge.

"No," I replied. If it was time for honesty, then there was no point telling half-truths or lies. "Nobody knows, except my parents, a handful of doctors I haven't seen in years, and now you."

We looked across the car at each other and I held my breath, waiting for my partner's next reaction. He held my career in his hands.

"What kind of neurological problem?" he asked.

I drew a breath. I was far from in the clear, but Hugo hadn't immediately left to report me, so there was still a chance this ridiculous gamble could work out.

"Do you know much about how human memory works?" I asked.

He shrugged his shoulders. "You mean like short-term and long-term?"

"Let's start with them," I replied, and prepared myself to relay the explanation a doctor had once given me many years ago. "You know how you'll be sure you know the answer to something, but you can't recall the name or the place?"

"On the tip of my tongue, and all that?"

"Exactly. Well, think of short-term memory as being the front desk, and long-term memory as being a poorly organized filing room in the basement. Short-term only lasts a handful of seconds before it's sent down to the basement, so after that, the little old lady at the desk has to trot downstairs and retrieve whatever it is you're looking for. If it's something recent or you often think about, it's easy to find, and she's back in a heartbeat. If it's a memory you haven't considered in a long time, then she has to hunt for it."

Hugo appeared to be listening intently, so I carried on.

"So that phenomenon you mentioned about something being on the tip of your tongue, you'll often picture a place, or come up with the first letter of a name, right?"

He nodded. "Sure."

"That's the front desk lady running up and down the stairs, finding bits and pieces from the file you're looking for, slowly gathering enough information until the memory becomes clear."

"So, some part of your system doesn't work?"

"My old lady trips down the stairs sometimes."

"Meaning what? You can't recall anything? So you lock up like you did in the interview room?"

"Yes… well, no. That was more me freaking out when I realized I didn't have my pictures to back me up. I was missing one detail, and I let it derail me. Dropping a particular memory only happens occasionally, and I don't lose everything, just the one scene or situation. The pictures act like a trigger. It's a form of something called synesthesia, which is more commonly where one sensory input produces another. Meaning, a picture of a rose will make the person feel like they can smell the flower. Or the sound of coffee brewing makes them actually taste the drink. For me, the picture recalls the memory surrounding the scene I'm looking at."

Hugo looked puzzled again. "Do you suddenly forget how to do regular things? Like driving, or where you live, or how to wipe your ass?"

I laughed. "Those are learned functions and become automatic, unconscious thoughts. The old lady up and down the stairs analogy represents the system of neurons and synapses, and those are fixed in place, providing you regularly use the function. Believe it or not, I can wipe my own bum."

Hugo allowed himself a brief smile.

"Written documents stay with me, too. I actually have a really strong memory for details, so I'm fine studying for exams and recalling reports, but lectures in university were hit-and-miss for me. I had to take a lot of notes, as the picture triggers could get confused over which lecture I was trying to recall from that professor."

Hugo nodded slowly. "How can Bradley not know? Surely all this shows up in your medical records?"

"My parents stopped taking me to the specialists when I was twelve. My case was unique, as it's slightly similar to a weird form of seizure called TEA, which is transient epileptic amnesia. They tested me every which way for seizures, but I don't have them. I'd become nothing more than a neurological case study and a lab rat. None of the medications they tried did anything but make me feel like crap, so my dad stopped taking me and convinced a doctor friend to close out the files. We lied and said I'd grown out of the problem. Now my issue doesn't show up as an ongoing condition, so it never came up when I applied for the sheriff's department."

Hugo thought for a few moments. "What is your condition called again? Syntha-something?"

"Synesthesia isn't my condition. It's just a part of how it manifests," I explained. "What I have doesn't have a name. If I'd allowed them to prod and poke me for a few more years, it would probably be called Cromwell syndrome, but I can live without a medical problem named after me."

Hugo rubbed his chin and thought some more. "What happens when one of these episodes hits you in the middle of a situation?"

"That's never happened."

"But it could."

"We're investigators, Hugo. We leave the car chases and running around after the baddies to the uniforms."

"You don't seem to," he countered.

He had a point.

"I was on patrol as a uniform for three years," I reminded him.

"It never caused a problem. And on the positive side, I have a significantly above-average memory for detail."

"Providing you can recall that memory."

I took my instant pictures from my pocket and held them up. "No problem."

"If you remember to have them with you," Hugo pointed out.

I felt my cheeks blush.

"Why the hell don't you use your phone? You can store a bazillion pictures on there."

"Habit," I replied. "We discovered my disorder when my parents bought me a Polaroid camera when I was young. Until then, they thought I had some sort of learning disability. I was super smart about most things, but couldn't answer the simplest question about certain lessons or experiences. If I had a picture, I could tell them everything about whatever happened around that time. The cameras have evolved, and now they make one that you've seen fits in my pocket." I held it up to prove my point. "I tried using a cell phone, but for some reason, looking at the screen instead of the actual photograph doesn't always work as well. That, and I have a bad habit of losing or breaking phones, so I've never trusted myself enough to switch."

"You could lose your instant photo gadget just as easily," he pointed out.

"I didn't claim my system is perfect or makes the most sense," I replied, sticking with the complete truth. "But it's the habit I've built and come to rely on."

Hugo nodded and thought for a while until he spoke again. "Okay."

I waited, but he didn't elaborate. "Okay, what? We're okay? Or okay, you're heading straight for Bradley's office?"

He glanced at me, then looked away. "I don't know. This is a lot to take in, Kat. I appreciate your honesty, but that doesn't make everything alright, does it? I need to think this through."

Impending doom felt better than having a knife held to my throat, but I knew I had no choice. Pushing him for a response or answer right now was more likely to result in the words I didn't want to hear.

"I'm heading to the Redmans', then," I said, and Hugo opened the door.

"You should have uniform backup," he said, peering back inside.

"Travis won't be there," I responded.

He nodded again. "True. I'll drop the evidence bags I gathered from Travis's place at the station and bang out some paperwork."

I reached over to the backseat, then handed him my evidence bags from Wendell's. "If you wouldn't mind. Might as well send these in at the same time."

He took them, and I watched as my partner and possible executioner walked back to his car and drove away.

It was hard not to feel like my law enforcement career was about to be ordered out of the ring.

30

After spending half the drive calming myself down, I switched to thinking about my approach with Bob Redman. I truly wasn't expecting Travis to be there or for them to know where he was—or admit to it, at least—but I didn't want to leave there without getting the forensic evidence from the dog and the garage. We'd already executed our search warrant, so Bob was under no legal obligation to allow me on the property and could turn me away. I couldn't lie to him, but I hoped he wouldn't realize that fact and allow me to poke around.

After thoroughly preparing myself for the father, I was taken aback when Sheila Redman opened the door and informed me that she was home alone. Apart from the dog, who did his usual ducking and diving move behind her defensive leg. I decided to wait to bring up Travis's name.

"With new forensic evidence which has come to light," I began, adjusting my practiced speech on the fly to a softer version, "I need to grab a couple of samples from your house. I promise it'll only take a few minutes. The purpose is to rule out any connection between your home and the additional evidence. Purely routine, Sheila, and it'll help us focus on other areas."

"Oh… I see," she responded. "Bob usually handles this sort of thing, as he understands it all. Could you come back when he's home?"

"When will that be?" I asked, keeping my fingers crossed.

"He's playing golf," she replied, looking at her watch. "His tee time was 1:15, so 4:30 or 5, I'd expect."

It was already a few minutes after two, and the day was rapidly escaping me.

"I could, but it will create a lot more running around for me, and quite honestly, this is just a formality. I need to tick a box on a list."

"What exactly do you need?" she asked hesitantly.

"Actually," I said with a smile, pointing to the golden retriever, "I need a sample of your dog's hair, and then a swab from the garage and the garden shed."

Sheila looked shocked. "What on earth do you need those things for?"

"Like I said, we have forensic evidence tied to your daughter's case, and it would be incredibly helpful to rule out your home as the source so we can look for a different location."

Slowly, Sheila backed up and guided the dog into the living room, allowing me inside.

"What do you have to do to Hobson?" she asked, gesturing to the dog.

"Cool name," I replied, closing the door behind me. "From the movie *Arthur*?"

Sheila nodded, still looking worried.

"One of my dad's favorites. Don't worry, all I need are a few samples of hair. Do you have a brush you use on Hobson?"

The dog watched me and wagged his tail every time I mentioned his name. Sheila went to the kitchen and came back with a dog brush, handing it to me. I removed a few stray hairs left on the brush to make sure all the evidence gathered belonged to Hobson, then petted him a few times before running the brush along his back. He was disappointed I stopped to transfer the hair into a plastic bag after what he considered to be a minimal amount of attention. I handed the brush back to Sheila.

"Garage next, please."

"The garage?" she questioned, but led me to a door off the kitchen.

Parked inside the expansive double garage was an older four-door car. I couldn't tell what brand it was without seeing the badge, as for the last twenty years, it seemed every mid-sized car looked exactly the same. It was silver. I could identify that much.

A quick walk around the garage told me the residue found on the rope hadn't come from there. The place was immaculate. I didn't see any trace of automotive parts or lubricants, and at a guess, I'd say Bob Redman had his cars serviced at a dealership.

"Last thing is the garden shed, please, Sheila," I said, deliberately using her first name to make it all sound more amicable and routine.

"That's Bob's man cave," she replied, not moving this time.

I wanted to say that I didn't care if it was Bob's harem of nubile virgins and fire-breathing dragons, but I reminded myself I was gaining access by permission rather than a warrant.

"It'll be a quick look, Sheila. Just need to poke my head in the door."

I walked through the kitchen to the French doors leading to the backyard, Hobson following me. Mrs. Redman didn't appear as eager.

"Can Hobson go out?" I asked, looking for an excuse to keep moving.

"Okay," Sheila said hesitantly, finally joining me as I left the house.

The dog took off, finding a well-slobbered-on tennis ball behind a row of neatly pruned shrubs along the wooden fence dividing the property from the neighbor. Hobson brought the ball to me as, apparently, one brush stroke made me his new best friend. Hobson was the kind of dog I needed to greet me when I came home every day.

"It'll be locked," Sheila said as we crossed the backyard.

"Do you have a key?" I asked, hoping she wasn't trotting along behind me without a means of accessing the shed.

"It's a combination," she said at the same time I reached the door and noticed the padlock.

I stepped aside so she could enter the code on the tumblers. Sheila just looked at me.

"I don't know it," she said. "I told you, he calls it his man cave. I don't go in there."

"What does he use it for?" I asked, noting the single window had blinds tipped to allow in light, but block any view of the interior.

"I don't really know. Gardening stuff. He does woodwork some-times. Bob's pretty handy with that sort of thing."

I held the three-number lock in my hand and looked at the numbers. 4-7-3.

"Any guesses at what your husband's code might be?"

Sheila shook her head. "I'd prefer you wait until he's here, anyway. I don't know what it is you're looking for, but I don't see how it would be in his shed."

I had a pretty good idea of how that conversation would go once Bob Redman came home. If he kept his own wife from snooping around his *man cave*, he wouldn't want me looking inside. Not that I thought I would find a messy surface covered in oil and grease. Going by everything else I'd seen, the man was a neat freak. But I still wanted to look.

Placing my thumb on the tumblers, I rolled them all backwards two digits, knowing most people spun combo locks using that method in the opposite direction when locking them. 2-5-3. It didn't open. I rolled the last tumbler another digit. 2-5-2. To my surprise, and Sheila's, the lock opened. Apparently, Bob liked to give the last digit an extra roll for good measure.

Slipping the lock from the latch, I paused before opening the door. "You've never been inside here?" I asked.

Sheila shook her head. "Not for years, anyway."

"Why don't you step over there for a moment while I have a quick look," I said, nodding toward the house.

For the same reason I resisted going into Manny Rubio's room at the mobile home, it dawned on me that Bob might have a less-than-savory reason for keeping his wife out of his shed. I didn't need the distraction of the two of them having a domestic dispute if Sheila found fuzzy handcuffs and whips or a *Penthouse* poster on the wall in Bob's playroom. She moved back a few paces and petted Hobson, who was the only one of us who didn't appear concerned.

I put on gloves and eased the door open. The inside of the shed was spotless and tidy. A metal-topped bench was void of any clutter, and a red rolling cabinet stood at one end with a matching red tool chest on top. On the back wall, a custom built-in cabinet ran from end to end with a pair of shelves above. On the shelves were several wooden carvings of birds, two models of navy ships in display cases, and assorted framed pictures of family outings. Not a hint of oil, dirt, or grime anywhere.

As I doubted I'd have another opportunity to look around, I began opening cabinet doors, although I was sure I wasn't about to stumble across a length of rope. Inside, I found various power tools, still in their plastic cases, along with an impressive collection of clamps and an assortment of glue, varnishes, and stains. I moved to the tool chest and lifted the lid, which released the lock holding the drawers closed. I opened each one in turn. Every wrench—or spanner, as my dad called them—had a place in a rack, and every socket had a peg on which it sat.

I pulled on the top drawer of the rolling cabinet, but it was locked. I was ready to leave, but it was too odd that the top box would be unlocked, yet the roll cab wasn't. It was inconsistent, and Bob didn't strike me as a guy to skip a detail. I'd probably just stumbled on his hiding place for his fuzzy handcuffs, but my curiosity wouldn't let it go. I looked around for any keys hanging on a peg, or an obvious knickknack tray, but didn't see anything.

"Are you about done in there?" came Sheila's voice from outside.

She'd stayed clear, which I found amazing. If my husband had a secret spot within our home, I didn't think I'd be able to resist a peek if the opportunity arose. But I didn't have to worry about that. My husband-to-be was washing up on the beach one piece at a time.

The thought caught me off-guard, and I skipped a breath or two.

"Be out in just a minute," I called back, looking at the top of the tool chest again.

On the right side, in a small partitioned-off section, there were two little bottles of thread lock, and a tin of breath mints. I picked up the tin and shook it. The metallic sound from inside was not that of chewable tablets. Popping the lid, I found the key and unlocked the rolling cabinet with a clunk of the mechanism. *Bingo,* I thought, opening the top drawer.

It appeared Bob Redman's pornography of choice was some form of leg or foot fetish. I was glad I had gloves on. Although the guy was so fastidious, I was sure he mopped up after himself.

The next drawer contained more tools. Pliers, snips, and cutters were all neatly arranged across the drawer, which I closed slowly, careful not to send his hand tools rattling around. I opened the third drawer and stared in surprise. A wooden case had its lid removed to reveal a set of very expensive-looking wood carving chisels nestled inside a custom insert. They ranged from wide blades on the right to narrow on the left. The smallest chisel in the tray had a slightly curved blade no more than a quarter of an inch wide. Its neighboring slot to the left was empty. The insert showed the outline of what would be a slender handle with an even thinner, curved blade.

I stepped back, took out my instant camera, and snapped a shot of the missing tool, which appeared to be remarkably similar to a sturdy icepick.

<h1 style="text-align:center">31</h1>

Bob Redman was wholly unimpressed to be pulled from the golf course in order to answer our questions about the tools in his man cave. He was spitting mad at me, and just as furious at his wife for voluntarily allowing me into their home. By the time he showed up, the forensics team was already busy in his garden shed, and red-faced, he ranted for several minutes before telling me he wouldn't answer a word until his legal counsel was present. I finally managed to steer him into a corner of the living room, away from everyone else.

"Mr. Redman," I said in a low voice. "We have no interest in your... the things I'm sure you're worried we found. I'm looking for a murderer, not a bloke who occasionally *amuses* himself in private. Otherwise, I'd be questioning the whole male population."

He frowned at me but didn't protest.

"You can call your lawyer and take up a bunch more of my time, during which I might as well have the team empty out the contents of your man cave and spread them across the lawn to make sure we catalog everything in detail. Or you can answer my questions now. If you have a good explanation that covers my concerns, then we'll button up here in no time. The other way means you and I are heading to the station."

Bob gritted his teeth and rubbed his forehead as though he had a terrible headache. Which he may have had, but I hoped I'd convinced him that I could make it feel far worse if he didn't play ball.

"You've been aiding Travis in avoiding telling us the truth," I continued. "So you'll really be digging your family a hole if you choose to further impede our investigation."

I really wished I hadn't used the phrase "digging a hole" to a man who was about to bury his daughter, but he didn't appear to notice.

"What do you want to know?" he asked.

"Where's the missing chisel from the set in your tool chest?"

Usually, I'd build up to the big question, sneaking around with innocuous queries to lead the suspect or witness around the garden until they were feeling more comfortable. It held a higher risk, but every once in a while, coming out of your corner with a knockout punch worked, too. Especially as I was feeling pressured on time. Despite the second murder, the case was on the brink of falling into a long-term affair unless I turned one of these leads and sprinkles of evidence into a prosecutable suspect.

Bob stared at me with his mouth slightly open. "What?"

"The set of chisels in your tool chest, Mr. Redman. Below the drawer containing your reading materials. The chisel set has one missing. Where is it?"

"Why on earth would that be of interest to you?"

In his annoyed and paranoid state, it was hard to read if he was being cleverly evasive and acting confused, or truly felt perplexed.

"Where is the chisel?" I repeated.

He thought for a few moments. "I broke it a little while back."

"Did you throw it away or send it out to be repaired?"

"I threw it away."

"When was this?"

"I don't know," he replied, thinking again. "A month. Maybe six weeks ago."

"Why haven't you replaced it?"

"Why are you so interested in a damn carving chisel from my shed?" Bob fumed, growing angrier again.

The man's response to everything appeared to be varying levels of temper.

"If you stick to answering the questions, this will go a lot smoother and be over with before you know it, Mr. Redman."

He shook his head and sighed. "I didn't replace it because I've been looking at buying an upgraded set. Didn't see much point in getting one when I would have that size in the new set."

The forensic crew would check the shed for traces of blood or any other link to the killings, but as neither crime had happened there, the team was unlikely to find any. If Bob Redman had used the chisel to kill Chris Wendell, then he'd have been stupid to bring the weapon back home, and I didn't think the man was stupid. Although hot tempered and capable of the revenge murder of his daughter's ex-boyfriend was fresh on the menu. Regardless, with what seemed to be our current trend, I had no smoking gun or justifiable reason to take this any further at the moment, so I switched tactics.

"Where's your son, Mr. Redman?"

"I have no idea," he replied quickly, looking momentarily relieved I'd changed subjects. Until it dawned on him that we were still chasing his son. "You can't possibly still believe Travis has anything to do with Helena's murder. Why must you persist on hounding him?"

"There's no question your son was involved in events on the evening of Helena's murder," I replied. "We have irrefutable evidence of the fact. But unless he turns himself in and explains his side of the story, we can't rule out that he did indeed murder his sister. So, where is he?"

"That's ludicrous. And I told you, I don't know."

"Are you saying if I get a warrant to seize you and your wife's cell phones, I won't find any calls to him?"

"You'll find calls to him, but none that were answered," Bob snapped, taking his phone from his pocket. "His phone's been off. Here," he said, unlocking the screen, opening his call history, and holding it up in front of me.

I took the phone from him and found eight calls over the past two days to his son's number. None of them had been longer than a few seconds.

"If Travis makes any form of contact with you, please advise him to hand himself in," I said, giving the father back his phone. "The longer he runs, the worse it looks for him."

Bob nodded, but I didn't hold out much hope. Blood was thicker than water, and Redman Senior wasn't exactly pleased with the Orange County Sheriff's Department at the moment.

"One last question," I said, and his brow furrowed. "Does Travis know the combination to the lock on your shed?"

Bob froze like a deer in the headlights. I'd either hit the mark, or the idea hadn't occurred to him before and had taken him completely off-guard.

"No," he finally said. "No, he doesn't."

"Thank you for your cooperation, Mr. Redman," I said. "We'll be out of your house as soon as the team is finished with the shed."

I walked to the back door without mentioning how I'd broken his lock code in a few seconds, so his son undoubtedly could have done the same. In the back of my mind, I wondered if Travis could have taken the chisel and Bob was covering for him. But Bob had come up with his story about the tool awfully quickly and had no way of knowing how Wendell had been killed. Unless he did it, of course. Or knew how Travis had.

32

The remainder of the afternoon and early evening evaporated in a stream of procedural BS at the station. The forensic team had wrapped up pretty quickly at the Redmans, and I'd given them the samples I'd taken before their arrival. Hugo had driven our earlier evidence straight to the lab. He said he'd done that to expedite things, but I knew it was more about avoiding me and the station for as long as possible. He then followed up on a possible Travis Redman sighting in Laguna Niguel, which, of course, turned up nothing, but gave my partner an excuse to stay away until it was time to go home. At least I knew he wasn't standing in Captain Bradley's office unveiling my career-ending secret.

Travis Redman was nowhere to be found. His Ford Ranger pickup truck was in the sheriff's department yard as it hadn't been returned yet from when we took it under our warrant. He could have borrowed a vehicle, but he hadn't rented one as we'd checked. Neither had he bought a train, bus, or air ticket unless he'd used someone else's credit card or ID. Having sat in a room with the guy for several interviews, I knew he'd be beside himself at this point, and was surprised he hadn't reached out to his parents. He had a history of running to them when he screwed up, but maybe he'd crossed a line this time and knew he couldn't.

A few minutes after 7:30 p.m., I gave up on the day, slid my laptop into my backpack, then gathered up my keys, pictures, and phone before heading out. Everything always took longer than hoped with police work, yet every minute counted in many situations. The dichotomy of the job drove me nuts, especially as patience wasn't high up on my list of talents.

I unlocked my car, tossed my backpack on the passenger seat, and was about to get in when I remembered I'd left my travel coffee mug at my desk.

Walking back inside to reception, I saw Deputy Ripley chatting with Sergeant Martinez at the front desk. They both turned around when I entered.

"Change your mind, Cromwell?" the sergeant joked. "Pulling an all-nighter?"

"As much as I'll miss your stellar company, I just forgot something," I replied.

The lights were off throughout the rest of the building, but when I walked into the office Hugo and I shared with several unassigned desks, I abruptly stopped. From the faint glow of the tiny LEDs on a variety of electronics, I caught someone moving. Flicking on the fluorescent lights, Ripley's partner, Deputy Hanson, stared back at me from behind Hugo's desk.

"I was just leaving you guys a note," he said as I walked over.

He was partially hidden behind our monitors, but he reached to the side, peeled off a sticky note, and picked up a pen.

"Don't waste the paper. I'm here, you can just tell me," I said.

"Of course," he muttered, and put the sticky note back on the pad.

I grabbed my travel mug and waited, but Hanson shifted from foot to foot, not saying a word.

"Well?" I asked.

"It was about the lady you had us visit the other day," he replied. "Wendell's stepmother. I was just going to tell you she seemed to be telling the truth. We didn't get the impression she was hiding anything."

I looked the deputy in the eye and smiled. "Good to know. Thanks."

He moved from behind the desk, but I stepped in front of him, blocking his path.

"Give me that sheet of paper you just pulled off Fuentes's monitor," I demanded.

"I don't know what—"

"Bullshit, Hanson. Give it to me."

"You should get out of my way," he warned through gritted teeth.

"Or what?" I replied, grimacing inside as I sounded a bit like a teenager in a playground stand-off. But I wasn't backing down to this wanker. "You can hand it to me, or I'll call Sarge and get him involved. Your choice."

Hanson glared at me. "Your partner's a fucking prick, and I'm sick of his shit," he fumed. "He even treats you like shit, so why do you care?"

"Because you're being a bigger prick," I said, and held out my hand.

He shook his head and dipped his shoulder, striding forward in an attempt to barge me aside. I'd guessed it was coming, and he made the mistake of not anticipating physical resistance. Sweeping my arm across his throat, I pulled hard and kicked my right leg out, effectively clothes-lining him. Tripping backwards over my calf, he hit the floor with an audible thud, letting out a deep groan as the air left his lungs. Before he had time to react, I dropped my knee to his chest and pulled the paper from his right hand, tearing half of it away as he desperately tried to keep hold.

I stood and looked at the torn sheet in my hand. It was a version of the movie poster for the movie *Brokeback Mountain* with another amateur cut-and-paste of Hugo's face in place of one of the actors.

I scoffed. "What are you, twelve years old, Hanson?"

He regained his breath and struggled to his feet, throwing the other half of the paper at me. "Fuck you, Cromwell. You're as bad as him if you're gonna defend the asshole."

"I'm not defending his snarky tone, but trying to spread bullshit rumors about the bloke isn't an acceptable response," I replied, searching his face.

"Who says it's bullshit?" Hanson retorted.

I fought to keep my expression even. "The guy was married, you idiot. Have you seen a picture of his ex-wife? She's bloody gorgeous."

Hanson looked confused for a second, then regained his conviction. "Look at the way he dresses. His hair. No self-respecting red-blooded man spends that long on his fucking hair, Cromwell."

Inside, I breathed a sigh of relief. Hanson didn't know. Or at least he didn't have any verifiable proof.

"You're a bigoted idiot, Hanson, and I should report you to Bradley."

He threw his hands up. "Seriously? You'd do that to me? You're unbelievable."

"What's unbelievable is how petty you are. Not to mention prejudiced. You're a disgrace to the uniform," I snarled, forgetting my relief and feeling outraged at the man's archaic attitude. "You'll apologize to Hugo in person, man to man, or I'll haul your arse into Bradley's office myself."

"You might as well, cos that's what Fuentes will do."

"Your choice, Hanson. Apologize and take your chances with Hugo's mercy, or I guarantee you I'll have you in front of Bradley by break tomorrow."

"You're a bitch," he muttered, and gave me a wide berth this time as he stomped away.

His insult made my blood boil, and I swung around to do something about it, then stopped. After another minute spent bouncing between fuming and calming myself down, I'd settled my emotions enough to leave. When I did, no one was in the reception area, and I realized I'd been the only witness to my outstanding display of composure. Calling me a bitch was grounds for being put on the floor for a second time, but I'd let him go. I felt like sending Bradley and Hugo an email announcing this Olympic feat of self-control, but instead, I quietly made my way to my car.

Driving down Golden Lantern, I stopped at a red light. Shifting uncomfortably in the seat, I realized I still had my hip radio clipped to my belt, which dug into my bum. I unhooked it and dropped it in the cupholder. Pulling my cell phone from my pocket, I took the opportunity to call my partner. He didn't answer, of course, and it went straight to voicemail.

"Hey, it's Kat. I've found your secret admirer at the office. Call me back, and I'll explain. I think you're in the clear."

I hated to be so cryptic, but I didn't want to leave any incriminating words on a recording for him to come back at me with. I'd tell him to his face. If I ever had the chance. It shouldn't be that way, but nothing about Hugo's situation should be the way it was. I'd told Hanson I'd put him in front of Bradley if he didn't apologize, but the truth was I'd have to defer to whatever Hugo chose to do, regardless of whether Hanson said he was sorry or not. It was Hugo's life, and his call to make.

Arriving at a red light for PCH, I realized I'd driven well past my turn to go home. Maybe my stomach had taken over the controls, as it groaned to remind me that I was starving, and it dawned on me that I'd skipped lunch. The light turned green, and I drove straight, undecided where to pick up food.

An idea fell into my head, so I slowed and turned right, driving down the unnamed alleyway behind the businesses fronting Del Prado. The first parking lot on the left was for Capistrano Bay Tavern, and I pulled in, surprised to find an open spot at almost 8 p.m.

The last glow of sunset kept the western sky a deep shade of blue, while darkness enveloped the hillside to the east. Streetlights bathed the parking lot in an orange hue, and a cool breeze made me reach back inside the car for my jacket. It was a long shot that the Russos had seen Travis, but I'd planned on dropping by after the Redman visit until that venture had soaked up my whole afternoon. *Maybe I'll order something to go from here*, I thought as I walked toward the awning over the customer's rear entrance to the restaurant.

Halfway there, I paused. Parked in a spot near the building was a dark blue pickup truck. If I studied all the vehicles in the lot, it was likely I'd see five or six more pickups, but this one was different. It had the restaurant's logo on the doors.

I walked over and looked in the bed. I was just taking my phone out to use the flashlight function when the device buzzed.

"Bollocks," I muttered, seeing I had a missed call and a voicemail, both from Hugo. I'd turned the ringer off earlier at the Redmans, then missed it vibrating while I'd been driving. I hit play on the voicemail and put the phone to my ear.

"Calling you back," Hugo said. "If you haven't recently, check your email. The IT guys sent us a clip from the art gallery's camera. It's from last Thursday night. Their facial recognition picked up Chris Wendell as he cycled by the gallery. He'd just come from Capistrano Bay Tavern."

The message ended at that. No "talk to you later" or "try me back." But the fact that he'd called at all was promising, considering our current state of affairs.

I ran the new information over in my head for a moment. Manny Rubio, Chris's roommate, had told us he hadn't seen him in a couple of days. That was on Saturday. Wendell must have stopped by the restaurant on his way north to his cousin's place. He should have been easy to spot with a guitar strapped to his back. The timing fit.

I closed out of voicemail and switched on the flashlight function, aiming it at the bed of the pickup. It looked clean, or at least a lot cleaner than the scrapes and dings around the rest of the work truck. I checked the corners of the bed and found dirt and grime packed into those hard-to-reach nooks and crannies. Someone had recently power-washed the bed, but there was no way to get to those tricky spots.

Moving to the window of the extended cab, I shone the light

inside. A few fast-food wrappers and paper bags littered the floor, and a couple of cardboard boxes containing cocktail mixers rested on the backseat. The interior looked worn and grubby, and I guessed it had been used far more for the liquor stores than the restaurant. I focused the light on the seat fabric right below the window, which was threadbare and covered in hair. Whoever had power-washed the bed hadn't taken the time to vacuum the interior. Looking more carefully, I realized I was most likely seeing dog hair.

My mind raced. I needed access to this truck immediately to get samples, but no way could I get a warrant until the morning. I turned off the flashlight, swiped back to my call log, and was ready to click on Hugo's name when I glanced up, sensing movement in the alleyway. Travis Redman appeared in view and stopped dead in his tracks as we both recognized each other.

"Travis," I said on reflex. "We need to talk."

But Travis didn't want to talk. Travis wanted to run.

33

———

Cursing myself for leaving my radio in the car, I hung on to my phone as I took off after Travis Redman. He ducked right, moving through a smaller parking lot between two buildings with a fifteen-yard head start on me. Housing businesses and offices that were all closed for the night, the lot was unlit, and my eyes strained to adapt. I needed to call for backup, but dialing phones and chasing people in the dark didn't go well together. I glanced at the screen, which was still on my call log, and scrolled away from Hugo until I found the station. As I attempted to touch the screen with my thumb, I kicked the corner of a concrete parking block.

Somehow, I stayed on my feet, but my phone skittered across the sidewalk as I tried to regain my footing on what had become wet and slippery pavement. Cursing whoever it was who'd decided to run their sprinklers nearby or wash their car, I wind-milled my arms before finally crashing to the ground. Wincing, I looked up and saw Travis running west down San Juan Avenue, a narrow lane between more buildings. I quickly looked around in the dim light, but I couldn't see where my phone had landed. It didn't matter; recovering it would take too long.

Getting up, I noticed a bunch of notecards, or something similar, washing away in a stream of water as I launched into a sprint. Ahead, I watched Travis turn right again, cutting through the parking lot for Harbor House Café, an old-school diner that had been there my whole life.

As I made the same turn, I could see Travis at the far end of the lot, bathed in the streetlights of Pacific Coast Highway. He looked over his shoulder, clutching his injured ribs, and saw me still in pursuit. We both knew he had a tough choice to make. Take off down the sidewalk under the lights, or risk four lanes of evening traffic to reach the residential Lantern District. Travis Redman had made plenty of poor decisions in his twenty-six years, but I didn't think he was completely stupid. Crossing the highway was the riskier option, but also the better choice.

Horns honked and tires screeched as he dodged between vehicles whose drivers swerved and slammed on their brakes to avoid him. By the time I arrived, traffic had begun to move once more, and I waved a hand in the air to get the drivers' attention. Maybe they were annoyed by Travis's interruption of their evening, but no one seemed keen to stop their cars a second time for me, and I was lucky they were moving slowly enough that I could weave between them. In the last lane, a guy in a large black SUV with ridiculous-looking chrome wheels on super low-profile tires honked as he braked hard not to hit me. I thumped his hood with my fist as I leaped to the sidewalk, relieved to have made it one piece.

Travis was already out of sight, but I'd caught a glimpse of the direction he'd headed, and set off that way. Running between the little car wash and a bank, a dumpster blocked my view beyond, so I had to guess which way he'd chosen from there. To the left was Violet Lantern, which ran dead straight up the hill to La Cresta Drive. If he'd gone right, he'd end up in the well-lit La Plaza Park marketplace area with Hennessey's on the corner.

I dodged around the dumpster and jogged slightly right, aiming for the alleyway behind Hennessey's and the other businesses in the plaza. Up ahead, I could see Travis checking over his shoulder once again.

As I tried to predict his next move, my mind kept bouncing back to the dark blue pickup at the restaurant. Travis worked for the Russos, so undoubtedly drove the truck. But we knew he'd been at Doheny in his own vehicle just after midnight when he'd broken into his sister's minivan. *Had Wendell used the restaurant's truck?* We had his Jeep on film leaving the tavern at the same time as the victim, so that didn't jive, either.

Travis ran straight across La Plaza, cutting left around a row of shrubs into the parking lot of a dentist's office. As I reached the same point, I saw why. The parking extended along the side of the building, which was beyond the reach of the streetlights and consumed in shadow. He was scrambling over a five-foot-high vine-covered wall. I was only six feet from him when he dropped to the other side. After one more stride, I launched myself at the wall, leaping as high as I could. Latching my arms on the top, I swung my right leg over and dropped, praying I wasn't about to land in another vegetable garden.

My feet stung as they hit concrete in the parking lot behind a large building of either condos or offices—I couldn't tell which. Travis was already alongside the building, heading down the sloped driveway to La Cresta. I guessed he'd been hoping to stick to alleyways and pathways between homes, but now he found himself back on a major, well-lit street.

I sprinted after him, having gained a few more yards over the wall. If he stuck to a straight run, I knew I could catch him, but he had to have come to the same conclusion by now. And surely he was in agony with the cracked ribs? Though, maybe he was amped up on pain pills.

A car shot by, causing Travis to check up for a second, and I watched him search for an escape route across the road between the homes. He angled left as a motorcycle approached from our right side in the far lane. Both Travis and the motorcyclist hesitated, but I didn't. Just as my suspect timed his run to miss the back of the bike, I hit him from behind. We both tumbled forward, which caused Travis to clip the back of the motorcycle. The collision momentarily checked Travis's forward progress, and I smashed into him again on our way to the ground. From a few yards away, an awful scraping sound, joined by the motorcycle's engine revving loudly, told me we'd taken out the unfortunate rider as well.

Travis's body broke my fall, and I was quickly back on my feet as a car screeched to a halt beside us. Travis lay on the ground, groaning and holding a hand to his face. On my left, the motorcycle rider was unsteadily picking himself up. He looked at his bike, which was idling on its side.

"What the hell just happened?" shouted the driver of the car as he stepped out.

"Police," I spluttered, out of breath. "Call 911."

I looked down as Travis rolled over on the ground. The side of his face was badly grazed, having used the road to arrest his fall, and he now held his left arm with his other hand. Judging by the extra joint mid-forearm, I could tell he had more broken bones to go with his ribs.

"Tell them we need an ambulance," I added to the motorcyclist.

Travis moaned and muttered by my feet.

"Let's get you to the sidewalk," I said, and reached down to help him up.

He yelped as soon as he moved. "I think my arm's broken," he wheezed.

"I know your bloody arm's broken, mate. Now quit crying and get up so I can help you out of the road."

Grunting, groaning, and wincing, he let me assist him to the sidewalk.

"Are you injured?" I asked the motorcycle rider, who was looking forlornly at his bike on the ground. He'd turned off the engine but didn't look ready to pick the bike back up. It was a Harley of some sort with lots of chrome parts, so I was sure it weighed a ton.

"I think I'm okay," he replied, slipping off his helmet. "But look at my bike. What the fuck were you doing?"

Sirens started in the distance, so I knew the cavalry wasn't far away.

"Sir, why don't you sit down for a minute until I can get you some help?"

The man, who I could now see was probably in his forties, nodded and wandered to the curb. I returned my attention to Travis.

"You're in deep shit, sunshine," I said, sitting next to him. "It looked bad before, but on top of everything, you decided to run. Add that to the note you wrote luring your sister to Doheny, plus me finding the restaurant's pickup truck, and I'd say you're cooked."

Travis looked at me forlornly. The abrasion on his face must have hurt like hell, but his arm was probably worse. Or it would be when the adrenaline stopped flowing.

"The forensic evidence from the truck will tie you to the murder scene, Travis," I said, looking for his reaction. "You should have done a better job cleaning out the truck bed."

His eyes darted up to meet mine, then shot away again.

"Your own sister, Travis," I pressed. "How could you? All she ever did was help you."

"I would never hurt her," he mumbled. "Never."

"Evidence is stacked against that statement. You're going to have a tough time proving you didn't do this, mate."

"It wasn't me," he repeated.

"How does Wendell play into all this, then? Were you two in this together?"

He twitched, but stopped himself from looking my way this time.

"He's dead, Travis, so you might as well tell me how he fitted into what happened. Did he kill Helena, and you helped him clean up the mess?"

I heard Travis gasp, but I couldn't tell if it was in reaction to learning Wendell was dead, or simply the pain from his various injuries.

There was no doubt Travis Redman was tied up in these murders in some way, but I still struggled to picture him killing his own sister. Not because such things never happened, as they unfortunately did, but telling him "No," like she'd apparently done many times before, didn't feel like a strong enough motive. It was worth letting him think I didn't suspect him of killing Wendell if I could get him to give me something about Helena.

"What's your connection with Chris?" I asked.

He just shook his head and clutched his arm, wheezing and fighting for breath. The sirens were getting louder. Once the ambulance arrived, I'd lose my chance as I couldn't deny him medical care.

"Your choice, Travis," I told him. "Mummy and Daddy won't be able to get you out of this one. My captain's taking a lot of heat to wrap this case up. Bad for tourism. She'll want to serve you up, mate. Feed you to the lions and all that."

I started to get up.

"Russo made me do it," Travis hissed under his breath, and I sat back down.

"Russo made you kill Helena?"

He glared at me. "No! I'm telling you, I would never harm Helena. Russo made me write the note."

"Was the note in her minivan? Is that why you broke in?"

Travis began sobbing, his body convulsing. He shook his head again. "I broke in to get her phone. Russo told me I had to get her phone. But the note, I wrote it and have no idea what happened to it after that. I didn't know Helena was dead until the next day. I swear I didn't know."

"Why would you do any of this to your sister?" I asked in amazement.

Travis groaned. "They had me by the balls."

"Had you how, Travis? She's your bloody sister."

"They caught me taking cash from the restaurant, alright?" he shouted, glaring at me. "If they turned me in, I'd be screwed. I had no idea any of this shit would happen, I swear."

My mind was racing, trying to keep up. I looked up as sirens echoed off the buildings. The scene had turned chaotic, with traffic backed up both ways. A patrol car arrived at the same time an ambulance stopped by the downed motorcycle, parking on the wrong side of the street.

"Did Russo have Chris Wendell kill your sister?" I asked, but I was pretty sure I already knew the answer.

"You should talk to Russo, man. I'm not saying another word," Travis muttered as the ambulance crew rushed over.

"Did Russo kill her, Travis? You have to tell me," I urged.

But he shook his head one more time, and then I lost him to the EMTs.

I needed to find my phone. Hopefully, Hugo was ready to put his grudge aside and join me in picking up Felix Russo.

34

Much to my relief, my instant camera was still in my back pocket and had survived my tumble. I snapped a shot of the scene as the EMTs wheeled Travis away on a gurney. Leaving the uniformed officers amid the pandemonium on La Cresta Drive, I walked down the hill, crossed PCH in a safer manner this time, and returned to San Juan Avenue, where I'd lost my phone. Tucking my camera away, I shoved the processed picture into my front pocket, which was when I realized that my collection was gone.

Checking all my pockets a dozen times, I tried to recall if I'd left all the pictures in my bag, but I was sure I'd kept all the key ones with me. Trying not to panic, I searched for my phone, which I found under a parked car that fortunately had not backed out of the spot and run it over. The water that drained down the edge of the street and the parking lot had mostly been close to the edge, so my phone was dry. The screen was cracked, but the device appeared to still work. Like I'd told Hugo, I was tough on cell phones.

Using the phone's flashlight, I began looking around and soon found one or two of my instant pictures. It hadn't been notecards

I'd seen floating away. Every photograph I found was ruined. Soaked through.

I felt sick to my stomach. I used the instant pictures because I'd always used them. It was my system that had worked for me for twenty years. I was so paranoid about losing pictures if I used my phone, that I'd stubbornly stuck to my tried-and-true method. Which had finally failed me.

My mouth turned dry, and my legs felt weak. I needed to pull myself together.

I called Hugo, cursing out loud when it went to voicemail.

"Hugo, call me back," I said, out of breath. "I have Travis Redman, but I don't think he killed his sister and maybe not even Wendell. He told me Russo made him write the note and he broke into the minivan to get her phone… anyway, I'll explain the rest when you call me. I'm at the tavern. I'm going to speak with Felix Russo."

I wanted to add "I need my partner" but I resisted and hung up. After walking back to where I'd parked at the Capistrano Bay Tavern, the first thing I noticed was that the dark blue pickup truck was gone. Perhaps it was coincidence, but I suspected someone besides Travis had seen me looking in the windows. Either way, my newfound evidence was in jeopardy.

I went inside the restaurant and looked around for either of the Russos. The place was busy on the patio, but the inside tables weren't set up. The bartender, who I recognized from before, looked up at me.

"Are Mr. and Mrs. Russo here?" I asked.

"Caroline is," he replied. "She's in her office, I believe. Want me to tell her you're here?"

"That would be great, thanks," I replied. "Was Felix here earlier?" I added before he'd made it to the kitchen.

"You missed him by maybe thirty minutes or so," the bartender replied, then continued through the doorway.

I stood by the bar waiting while a sense of urgency welled inside me. If Felix had seen me chasing Travis, then he could well be running himself. And where the hell was Hugo? Honestly, I couldn't blame him if he was a few drinks into an evening, trying to forget the day, but I'd feel better having him around. Which, in itself, was a good and a bad thing. Good, as I still looked to him as my partner, yet bad, as he was undoubtedly feeling the opposite.

Caroline appeared through the doorway and smiled, although I could see concern in her eyes. "Good evening, Miss Cromwell. You wanted to speak with me? Where's that handsome partner of yours?"

"I was hoping to chat with you and your husband, but I understand he left a little earlier," I responded, ignoring her compliment of Hugo. Partially because I didn't know where the bugger was.

"Yes, he dropped by so we could eat dinner together. He often does."

"Does Felix usually drive the blue pickup truck?"

Caroline looked surprised. "Sometimes. We use it for all sorts of things between the restaurant and the liquor stores. Staff members are mostly driving it. Running errands and what have you."

"But your husband's driving it this evening?"

"Umm… I don't know, to be honest," she replied. "I didn't see what he was driving."

"Was Felix heading home when he left here?" I asked.

Her brow furrowed. "That's what he said."

"Dog probably needs a walk, right?" I asked, verifying my assumption that they indeed owned a dog.

"I dare say," she replied. "Why all this interest in my husband and what he's driving?"

The bartender had reappeared and began cleaning glasses, so I beckoned Caroline to join me.

"Why don't we talk over here," I suggested, moving to the table we'd sat at before, but I didn't sit down. Neither did Caroline.

She lowered her voice. "Can you tell me what's going on, please?"

My hand reflexively fell to my pocket where my collection of pictures should have been. Now there was only one. Without my partner or my photos, I felt incredibly vulnerable, but my mind was clear on the current objective.

"We've arrested Travis Redman for his involvement in his sister's case, and for the Chris Wendell murder," I explained, watching for her reaction. "Based on what he's telling us, we need to speak with your husband."

Caroline's mouth hung open. After a few moments, she managed to speak.

"Wait, Chris is dead? That's awful. Why Felix? Travis thinks my husband has something to do with all this?"

I didn't respond and let her process her thoughts for a few moments. Something appeared to click in her mind, and her expression changed.

"Oh my God," she whispered.

"Mrs. Russo?" I questioned. "Do you have something to tell me?"

The woman began pacing and rubbing her forehead with both hands.

"If you have something to share, now's the time, Caroline," I prompted.

She stopped and looked at me in disbelief. "I need to talk to my husband."

"To discuss what?"

"No," she said, waving a hand at me. "This is ridiculous. Travis is making things up, I'm sure of it." She took a deep breath. "I can't believe Chris is dead. How?"

"Caroline, I need you to tell me what's on your mind," I urged. "There's probably a perfectly good explanation for the situation, but the more I know, the more I can help."

They taught us to say things like that, but it always made me cringe inside. Our singular goal was to find guilty parties, so our ability and willingness to *help* started and ended with whether who we were talking to was actually involved. If they were, a confession made my life easier, but the district attorney would decide if it earned them any leniency. In this case, I was trying to persuade a woman to give me information that may help me arrest her husband. I needed her to think her help might clear him rather than confirm his guilt.

"Look," she replied, pulling herself together and becoming more resolute, "I don't think there's any way Felix was involved in either murder, but I have a feeling some things may well come to light. Especially if that idiot Travis is running his mouth."

"Okay, go on," I said.

"I did not have an affair with Chris," she said firmly. "He flirted. Maybe I flirted back a little, but nothing ever happened, I swear. Felix had a hard time believing me. Chris was a good-looking, carefree guy, younger than my husband, and I can see why he was jealous. But it was over nothing. I wouldn't risk everything we have on a meaningless fling."

She paused for a moment, so I spoke. "I should tell you that we already surmised all of this, Caroline. It wasn't hard to see. So what are the blanks that Travis will be filling in? It's better if I hear them from you."

Caroline nodded. "Travis may tell you what he thinks he knows," she scoffed. "But I can tell you the truth. For a while, Felix and I went through a rough patch. Even after we let Chris go, my husband was still upset and was far too worried about what the staff thought. Helena was an absolute sweetheart, she was everybody's friend, but I noticed Felix was talking to her more and more. He swears to me that nothing happened between them, and I'd like to believe him, but it created a unique position for us both."

"You now had the same suspicions that he'd gone through about Chris," I filled in for her. "But you still haven't explained your *aha* moment a little earlier."

Caroline rolled her eyes and waved a hand again. "It was just a silly notion. Now I've explained what took place, you can keep things in perspective when Travis spouts his theories."

"What is it you think Travis will say?"

"I have no idea," Caroline scoffed again. "But I'll tell you one thing I bet he doesn't mention."

"Okay. What would that be?"

"That he's always had a thing for me," she replied. "I suppose he was one of those who believed the stupid rumors about Chris and me, because he hated Chris."

"But why would he be angry enough at his sister to harm her?" I asked.

Caroline shrugged her shoulders. "I really don't know, but Helena did mention a few weeks back that they'd had a falling-out."

"I don't think that was unusual," I pointed out. "From what I've learned, their relationship was a constant cycle of falling out and making up."

"According to her, this one was different."

"And you're just mentioning this to me now?" I challenged.

"It seemed insignificant before," Caroline replied. "I hadn't given it much thought. Helena had mentioned their disagreement as a passing comment, and when we spoke before, I didn't think Travis was really involved. But it appears he is, so I'm sorry. I should have said something."

I touched my hand to my pocket once more and felt the lone picture. My throat tightened, but it also reminded me of something.

"What can you tell me about Travis stealing from you?"

Caroline rolled her eyes. "The idiot. I was pissed about it, but Felix wanted to give the kid a break. Said he'd be a perfect employee from here on out. Like we had something to hold over his head."

"You didn't agree?"

She shrugged her shoulders. "I didn't like the idea. I told Felix we should let him go and move on if we weren't going to get the police involved."

I thanked Caroline for her time and left, sensing the urgency to find her husband. My head spun as I walked to the car. I checked my phone, but I hadn't missed a call from Hugo. I wished I had more self-confidence, but I felt like I needed a sounding board to bounce these thoughts and theories around with. And I was terrified my stupid brain was forgetting a crucial piece of the puzzle.

It was hard to believe everything Caroline had told me, but I figured she'd spoken a few truths. My gut told me she'd had an affair with Chris Wendell. If nothing else, she wouldn't have used his first name when she spoke of him if her goal was to dispel rumors. She'd also served up a motive for her husband to be involved, if he'd indeed retaliated and had an affair with Helena. Which wasn't unbelievable. Helena was a nice-looking lady. But the Russos had both done a superb job of hiding their affairs if, in fact, they'd ever happened. Perhaps Helena had threatened to tell Caroline, and Felix needed to keep her quiet?

Travis had now admitted to his involvement at the scene in some capacity, and what he'd said fit with Felix pulling his strings. Both Felix and Travis had reason to hate Chris Wendell, so my next step had to be finding Felix.

Back in the car, I looked up the home address we had for the Russos, and left the restaurant. As I pulled up to PCH, I plucked the radio from the cupholder, but before I could key the mic, a call emitted from the speaker.

"All units in the area. Reports of a car fire near the lumberyard off Stonehill Drive. Repeat…"

I hung my head and thumped the steering wheel. I already knew which vehicle would be burning.

"Bugger," I muttered, and when the radio fell quiet for a moment, I asked dispatch to issue a BOLO for Felix Russo.

I sat at the intersection, fuming. The Hugo situation was starting to really piss me off. In his own words to Hanson, our personal bullshit shouldn't interfere with the job, yet he was now MIA when we were on the verge of catching our murderer.

I texted again. *"Need backup. Where are you?"* Hitting send, I angrily tossed my phone onto the passenger seat.

Picking up the radio once more, I verified with the deputies on scene that it was indeed a dark blue pickup truck smoldering. With that news, there was no point going to Stonehill Drive. Instead, I began making my way toward the Russos' home above Dana Strands Beach.

The hillside had been carved into tiers, and a gated community of luxury homes on large lots—by coastal Orange County standards—had been built over the past ten years. I pulled up to the security gate building, which was about the same size as my house, and put my window down.

"Orange County Sheriff's Investigator Kat Cromwell," I said, holding up my badge.

The security man, who looked to be in his fifties, studied my credentials. "May ask the nature of your visit, ma'am?"

"I'm here to speak with someone regarding an ongoing case," I replied, waiting for him to lift the gate.

Which he didn't do. I wasn't having much luck with gate guards lately.

"Are they expecting you, ma'am? I don't see you on my guest list for this evening," he said, looking at a clipboard in his hand.

"No. But time is of the essence… Robert," I said, reading his badge. "So how about you open the bloody gate?"

"Ma'am, I'll need to know which residence you're visiting. It's a requirement for our residents' privacy and security."

"So, Bobby, you think the person I'm visiting would like for you to know that I'm questioning them in regard to a double murder investigation?"

His eyes widened. "No. I suppose not, ma'am," he muttered.

"Open the bloody gate," I snapped, and this time he did.

I sped through before he could call someone higher up the food chain who might insist on a warrant before I entered a private community. Once I rounded the first corner, I pulled over and parked, turning my headlights off. I retrieved my phone and checked for messages. Still nothing.

"At Russo's house," I texted Hugo, holding out little hope of a reply.

"Dispatch, this is Sam 54," I said, switching to the radio. "Request backup at The Strand, asap. Over."

"Sam 54, this is dispatch. Hold tight for backup. No units currently available. Over."

"Bugger," I vented, and slapped the steering wheel again.

I took a breath before keying the mic. "Dispatch, this is Sam 54. Copy. Over."

Every part of me itched to continue down the hill to the Russos' house. This potentially disastrous delay was all Fuentes's fault, but I knew that wouldn't hold water in Captain Bradley's office. I had to wait for support. It was one thing approaching a witness alone at a place of business, but a murder suspect's house was out of the question. I understood and agreed with the rules, but it didn't keep me from being furious with the delay.

My anxiety level wasn't helped by the loss of my instant pictures. I ran the case through my mind in chronological order, starting with finding Helena Redman's body at Doheny Beach. Giving the death notice to Scarlett and her grandparents remained clear in my mind, and details involving Travis Redman and Darian Rutherford fell into place. Visiting Chris Wendell at the mobile home he shared played like a movie, and my confidence began to grow once again. Everything felt like it made sense through my pursuit of Travis earlier in the evening.

But Chris Wendell's name hung in my consciousness like a puzzle piece without a vacant slot. What was I missing about Wendell? My sortie to Newport Beach held a place in the timeline, but why did I know that Wendell was dead?

All the panic and anxiety returned in an avalanche of doubt as I realized I was missing a vital memory. I knew Wendell was dead, but I had no clue why, where, or how. I desperately needed my pictures, and the only one I had didn't help.

I jumped when my phone chirped. It was a text. Finally, Fuentes had responded.

"Sorry. I'm here. I'll cover back, you knock on door. Keep radio silence."

It felt like the world had been lifted from my shoulders. I had a partner again. Someone I could rely on. At least for now, and we could sort out the other shit later. I didn't have my pictures to rely on, but I knew we were pursuing Felix Russo as a murder suspect, and that was all that mattered at this very moment. Hugo was ready to cover the back of the house, which verified I was doing the right thing.

"*Roger,*" I texted back, and started the car.

The Russos' home was big, modern, and located in the last lot of the row, with what I expected were stunning ocean views. I parked at the end of the cul-de-sac and walked up the short driveway, where three black garage doors contrasted against the white stone exterior and frameless glass. Perfectly located lighting accentuated the angular features of the home and lit the path to the all-black front door, set back to the left of the garages.

Turning my radio down in case calls regarding backup came in and blew the conversation I was planning to have with Felix Russo, I stood at the front door.

I texted Hugo. "*Knocking.*"

He quickly replied. "*In place.*"

Pressing the doorbell, I unclipped the strap on my holster while I waited. For a moment, I considered if I'd beaten Felix Russo back home, but then I heard a voice shout from inside.

"I'll be right there!"

After a few more moments, the extra-wide door opened, hinging from a quarter of the way along the frame instead of at the end. Felix stood before me in a silk bathrobe, his hair wet.

"I'm sorry," he said. "I was taking a shower. Wasn't expecting you here so soon."

"You were expecting me?" I asked.

"Not you, per se, Miss Cromwell, but the police. I'm surprised you'd be dealing with something as trivial as this," he replied. "I just reported my company truck stolen about ten minutes ago."

35

As I followed Felix Russo inside his palatial home, I quickly texted Hugo.

"Inside. No trouble."

Although the lights inside the home were dimmed, casting a soft taupe hue across the stark white cabinetry with stainless steel features, the glass front revealed nothing beyond the pool on the patio. A bearded collie wagged its tail at me as it paced back and forth with its nose on the glass, and I wondered if any remnants of hair had survived the pickup truck blaze. Regardless, I made a mental note to take a sample from the Russos' pet.

It was too light inside and too dark outside to see the ocean, but I could hear the waves reaching the beach and the bottom of the bluffs. The thought of Paul's arm flashed through my mind, and I hoped the rest of him was safely nestled on the seafloor somewhere. Where they'd remain.

I pushed those thoughts aside in favor of trying to guess where my partner might be hiding. I didn't feel threatened in any way by Felix. If he had a weapon hidden beneath his form-fitting bathrobe, he'd nestled it somewhere uncomfortable and inconvenient to retrieve.

"Drink?" Felix asked. "I mean, a water or soda or something. You're still on duty, right?"

"I am, but I'm fine, thank you," I replied, although a coffee sounded good about now. "Can I ask how you got home if you didn't drive the truck?"

"Sure. E-bike," he replied without hesitation. "I'd had a couple of drinks, so I decided to ride the bike. It needed to be brought home, anyway."

"You can get a DUI on a bike," I reminded him.

He laughed. "True, but I probably wasn't over the limit, and like I said, the e-bike needed to be brought back to the house. I'd used it to ride down to the restaurant one afternoon, then came home with Caroline."

"I see," I said amiably as he poured himself a glass of wine. "Why was it you who reported the truck missing? You said it was taken from the restaurant."

"Caroline called me and asked me if I was driving it. She mentioned you'd been by. I told her I'd ridden home, so when she said it wasn't parked outside, we realized it must have been stolen. She's busy at work, so I said I'd report it." He took a sip of his wine before continuing. "Have you found it already?"

I ignored his question. I wasn't ready to discuss the truck fire just yet.

"We have Travis Redman in custody," I said instead.

"Caroline mentioned that."

"He claims he was put up to breaking into his sister's minivan," I continued. "By you."

Felix Russo's expression immediately changed. His relaxed posture as he leaned on the kitchen counter quickly switched to a tense stance.

"Why would he say that?" he responded. "I did no such thing!"

"Any idea why he might tell us that you did, Mr. Russo?"

"None at all. I've been nothing but supportive of that kid. Especially after what happened to Helena," he replied before going quiet as he thought for a few moments. "What did he say, exactly?"

"He told me he was instructed by you to retrieve Helena's cell phone, and that's why he broke into the minivan."

Felix shook his head. "That's a lie. I never told him to do that."

"Do you also deny telling Travis to write a note to his sister?"

"A note? I don't know anything about any notes. A note about what?"

"Okay, Mr. Russo, let's talk about your wife's affair with Chris Wendell," I said, figuring I needed to get the guy wound up to make a slip.

Felix glared back at me. "That was all bullshit rumors."

"Pretty good motive to kill the bloke," I pointed out.

"What? Caroline told me Wendell was dead. You're accusing me of killing him?" he replied, raising his voice. "That's ridiculous."

"We're investigating all possibilities, Mr. Russo. I'm just saying jealous husbands are number-one suspects."

Wine spilled from his glass as he swung his arms in frustration. "This is insane. If you're going to accuse me of every crime in town, I'll have to ask you to leave. You can have my attorney's number."

"I didn't mean to upset you, sir," I said, thinking up another approach before I'd be forced to officially detain him. "Your wife seems to think you and Helena may have had an affair as well."

"What are you talking about?" he demanded, smacking his wine glass down on the counter so hard that it broke the stem. "Fuck!" he shouted, and tossed the broken piece he was still holding into the sink. It shattered into a hundred pieces.

Felix was facing away from me, but when he held up his hand, blood dripped from a cut on his fingers. "Dammit," he swore, snatching a tea towel from the back of the counter.

I was pretty sure the one he chose was a decorative item not intended for drying dishes or mopping up blood, but he could debate that with his wife later. Amongst the many other touchy subjects I'd stirred up.

"Can I get you something for the cut?" I asked. "Is there a medical kit around?"

The radio vibrated on my hip, and I barely made out the dull murmur of a voice mentioning my name. Dispatch was probably wondering where exactly to send the backup I'd requested. The safest play now was to take Felix into custody before I was accused of attacking him with a bloody wine glass.

"I'm fine," Felix said as I took out my phone.

I typed out a quick text to my partner. *"Come inside."*

Outside, the dog barked a few times and ran more frantically to and fro. It was wagging its tail, but I figured it sensed its owner's distress. Or perhaps Hugo's presence.

But that wasn't why.

"Mr. Russo, I'm—" I began, just as I heard the buzz of a phone receiving a text message behind me.

Before I could turn, a sharp pain shot through the back of my head, and the world spun like a top. I was aware of dropping to the floor, but could do nothing about it. My body met the cold ceramic with a painful thud, and my cheek landed on my arm before sliding to the tile. The large white squares wouldn't stay still, and the cabinets distorted and morphed into shapes and colors I couldn't identify. A dark blotch on the floor may have been my phone, and I vaguely considered the fact that I may have killed another cell phone.

Rain lashed down, striking my face, yet logic told me I was still in Russo's kitchen. The floor lifted and dropped on the backside of a wave as the somber hues became the blue steel colors of a storm. *The* storm.

My body turned to where my fiancé, Paul, stood behind me, his hair wet and rain jacket shedding water in a million rivulets that whipped away in the wind. His face, staring at me through the squall, was full of anguish.

This was my final memory of the man I'd once adored. An image cemented in my brain for the past eight months through nightmares. The exact moment the movie reel always stopped playing in my mind.

Until now.

"You couldn't help yourself, could you?" Paul yelled above the raucous pounding of the waves and swirling winds. The movie was finally rolling on, and instead of wishing I could wake up, I desperately wanted to stay inside the memory vault my conscious brain refused to show me. "You had to play detective in our personal lives!"

"And look at what I found, you cheating prick!" I heard myself scream back.

"You have no idea what you've done!"

"Why her?" I pleaded. "Of all people. Why would you choose her?"

"It had to be her!" Paul yelled, as though the reasons were obvious. "How can you not see that?"

The boat rocked violently, and I hung on to the helm, where I'd been keeping the bow facing the incoming waves as best I could with the sick engine delivering a fraction of its capable power. When I turned back again to look at Paul, he lunged toward me.

Then the movie faded, until it vanished into a hazy darkness.

"...because I always have to handle everything," came Caroline Russo's voice, reaching my groggy mind as though the volume in the here and now was slowly being turned up.

"She's a fucking police detective," Felix Russo growled. "This has gotten completely out of hand."

Investigator, I wanted to correct but was currently incapable of saying anything. My head throbbed, and I wanted to reach back and check the extent of my injury, but I was also fighting the urge to vomit. My stomach churned, and every inch of my body ached. I kept my eyes shut and listened, praying the dizziness and nausea would pass. If I could regain my bearings enough to stand, I had my gun in the holster on my hip. Providing they hadn't taken it while I'd been busy swimming in memories from eight months ago.

Had I dreamed the scene on the boat with Paul? Had my mind

made it up? Or was my subconscious finally revealing more of the missing events to me? If it took a brutal bash to the head to jolt a few more seconds of the memory free, I didn't think I could survive discovering much more from that day.

"Pick her up by the legs," I heard Caroline order.

"I'm still bleeding," Felix complained.

"Don't be such a fucking pussy. Pick her up," she demanded.

I felt hands wrap around my ankles. The movement turned my stomach over, and I desperately fought back another wave of nausea. More hands grabbed my wrists, and I felt myself lifted from the tile floor. My head flopped limply backwards, so I let it fall to the right and cracked an eyelid open. In a hazy, filtered view, I looked at my arm and Caroline Russo's determined face passing beneath recessed ceiling lights that blinded me every few steps. I noticed the tattoo around the woman's wrist, below the lean, tight muscles of her toned arms that appeared to effortlessly haul me away. Strength enough to manhandle the petite body of Helena Redman all on her own?

It was then that I realized Travis had meant *Caroline* Russo, not *Felix*.

She pushed through a door and a bright light came on, causing me to squeeze my eyes tightly closed once more. Felix grunted and moaned as the two of them carried me across what I presumed to be their garage. She let go of my wrists, and I dropped to the concrete floor with another stunning whack to the back of my head. My legs followed, but I barely noticed.

"What the hell are we going to do with her?" Felix asked.

"I don't know!" Caroline barked back, her voice moving farther away. "But we need to buy time."

"Time for what? This is all madness, Caroline. It has to stop."

I heard the rattle of what I guessed to be car keys and a few beeps from beside me. Locks clicked open. *Where the hell was Hugo?*

Then it came to me. In my relief at hearing from my partner, I'd overlooked the odd nature of his texts, and his departure from standard procedure. The messages had come from my partner's phone, but not my partner. Caroline had Hugo's phone. It had been my own message buzzing on Hugo's phone behind me right before she'd blindsided me.

Which meant no one knew exactly where I was. I'd only told dispatch The Strand.

"You don't get it, do you?" Caroline said, her voice closer once more. "We're done here. All we can do is run. They have Travis."

"But he's telling them a bunch of lies—" Felix began, but she cut him off.

"Are you really that stupid?"

Another click, and a door swung open. I guessed it was the tailgate of the vehicle. My head had cleared enough once more to crack an eye open. I was lying by the tire of a large SUV.

"I can't believe it," Felix, who'd changed into sweatpants and a T-shirt, replied meekly. "Please say it's not true, Caroline."

"Which part?" she snapped back. "Pick her up. We're wasting time."

"All of it," he replied more boldly as he roughly took hold of my ankles. "Actually, that's not true. I know you've been fucking Wendell all along. That part, I believe, damn you. But killing Helena? My God, Caroline, why on earth did you do that?"

Caroline snatched up my wrists, and the two of them threw me into the back of the SUV. Everything was still swaying, although I was slowly regaining enough strength to help myself. But I needed to wait. I wanted them to keep talking while they thought I couldn't hear them, and once they sat up front, I could pull my gun and have the upper hand. From the pressure around my waist, I could tell I was still wearing my belt, but I was gambling on them having overlooked my sidearm.

"I don't get it," Felix continued. "Why she had to die."

"None of that matters anymore, Felix, for fuck's sake," Caroline rebutted, then calmed herself and continued in a more subdued voice. "There were too many rumors and bullshit going around. It had to stop."

"You mean you were scared Helena would tell me you and

Wendell were still sneaking around behind my back?" Felix shouted back as the rear door closed. But they were arguing loudly enough that I could still hear them.

"No!" Caroline fumed, her voice shaking. "He told me he was still in love with her!"

"Perfect!" Felix shouted, his voice cracking. "You were jealous of your boyfriend's hang-up over an old flame. Unbelievable, Caroline. You know what? I'm done, dammit! We're done."

"Don't be naïve, Felix. What will the police think when they place your old pickup truck at Doheny that night?"

"I was at home!" he shouted.

"Prove it," Caroline challenged. "I'll swear you weren't."

Footsteps on concrete told me they were walking to the front of the SUV, and I could still hear them bickering. I shifted and felt for my gun.

It was gone. That changed everything. Not only was I weaponless, but they were now certainly armed. I should have made a move earlier, but with as little strength as I still had, I doubted I could have done anything.

They hadn't opened the front doors of the vehicle, so I propped myself up to see what was going on. I couldn't see Caroline, but Felix was rummaging through a drawer in a built-in cabinet down the side of the garage. He turned, holding zipties in his hand, so I knew what was coming next. I dropped back down, hoping the tinted side windows hid my movement.

A few moments later, the tailgate unlatched, and I waited, listening to it slowly swinging up. A hand grabbed my left arm, and as he pulled me over, I jabbed with my right fist. The blow lacked my usual snap, but it knocked Felix backwards, stunned by the punch. I urged my body to cooperate, but I was mired in slow motion. By the time I swung my legs out the back, Felix had recovered and was stepping toward me. I threw another punch from the seated position, which hit his arm as he defended himself.

Behind him, the garage door was rising, which momentarily stole his attention. I dropped my feet to the floor, swinging again.

My legs were unstable and offered none of the drive I needed for a solid punch, but I connected with his chin, and his head snapped backwards. Felix clattered against the rising door, and I willed my sluggish feet to step forward, determined to finish him off.

"Enough!" I heard Caroline yell, and I froze.

Turning slowly, I saw a gun pointed at my head. It must have been hers, as it wasn't my sidearm. The garage door rattled and whirred its way up until it clunked to a stop.

"Why did you open the damn door already?" Felix muttered, touching his face where red blotches marked my hits.

"Because you should have been done by now," she chided. "You're fucking useless, Felix." Her focus turned on me. "Get in the back."

"Calm down. Let me put these on her first," Felix said, still holding the zipties, but his wife shook her head.

"We don't need those," she growled.

Keeping Caroline in my sights in case she came close enough for me to lunge for the gun, I took my time sitting in the back of the SUV. Her plan was clear. There was only one reason why she didn't need me restrained anymore. Resigned to the fact we'd caught up to her, she no longer worried about one more body, or the mess my execution would make in the back of their expensive vehicle.

"Caroline…" Felix said, but by now it was clear he had no influence over his wife.

I wondered if my compatriots would ever find whatever icepick or sharp instrument she'd used to kill the man she'd been sleeping with. I was certain now that she'd killed both Helena Redman and Chris Wendell. Travis had been nothing but a pawn. Her husband had been some combination of oblivious and unwilling to accept the truth. Caroline had taken Travis's note off Helena's body before dumping her in the sea, and Travis himself had brought Caroline Helena's cell phone later that night. Caroline may have panicked when she realized the phone was missing and she hadn't taken the time to check the minivan. She wouldn't have known there was nothing incriminating on it. Travis had allowed his own selfishness to make him an accessory to his sister's murder.

Chris Wendell had been guilty of sleeping with a married woman, then making the mistake of stopping by the restaurant as he fled from the police, scared he'd be wrongfully accused. Caroline must have slipped Helena's phone and note in his bag before sending him on his way. Maybe she trusted him to stay quiet about her, or perhaps she couldn't risk taking care of him there at the restaurant. Either way, something changed by the time he called her from Salt Creek. I wondered if she cradled her lover in her arms before driving an icepick into his brain. Beyond cold.

"Get all the way in," Caroline ordered.

I looked past her, down the driveway to the cul-de-sac beyond. My car sat under a streetlight, and I contemplated what her plan might be to hide it. Not that it would matter to me in a few minutes. I slid back into the luggage area and lifted my feet inside. Caroline lined up the sight, aiming at the center of my face.

"Put the weapon down!" Hugo's voice boomed, and Caroline swung his way.

My partner stood just beyond the garage door, his own weapon trained on Caroline Russo. He looked remarkably unkempt with ruffled hair and his tie askew. Deputy Ripley stood off to the side, several yards away, his gun also trained on the woman. She began raising her hands, but I seized her wrist while it was still within my reach and disarmed her.

"You okay, Kat?" Hugo asked.

I slid from the SUV and pushed the Russos to the driveway, where we made them lay down with their arms behind their heads.

"Yeah," I finally replied. "Where have you been?"

Hugo raised his eyebrows. "Tied up in the trunk of her car until Ripley let me out," he replied, nodding at Caroline. "She pulled a gun on me in the parking lot outside the tavern. Ripley found your car from your vehicle's GPS tracker, then heard me banging from the trunk of Caroline's vehicle. You sure you're okay? Your head's bleeding."

I touched a hand to my scalp and winced. He was right. "My skull is resilient, but if you're lucky, she might have knocked some sense into me."

Hugo scoffed. "I doubt it. Besides, you probably won't remember by tomorrow."

But then I swear he smiled.

36

Not that I was about to admit it, but I was dog-tired. I'd spent the night in the emergency room where they wouldn't let me sleep, as they'd diagnosed me with a concussion. My head throbbed, and my eyes hurt, so I'd say they were right. It was a good job my dad had convinced his doctor friend all those years ago to close out the files on my wiring issues, or the specialists would have swarmed me and never let me leave.

My mum had picked me up to drive me home, but I'd convinced her I had to stop by the station on the way. Reluctantly, she'd dropped me off and continued to my house to make soup for lunch. I'd told her a deputy would bring me there shortly, but that had been an hour ago. She was now texting me every five minutes with notes of motherly concern, urging me to come home as the doctor had ordered. Her last message threatened to send my dad around to give me another concussion unless I showed up right away.

Currently, I was standing next to Hugo in Captain Bradley's office, wishing I'd gone straight home. The captain had begun by asking about my head, but quickly moved on to last night's situation at the Russos' house.

"Can you explain to me how you ended up at a murder suspect's home on your own, Cromwell?"

"Well, ma'am," I began, trying my best to reassemble the evening through my foggy, sleep-deprived, and concussed brain.

I then rambled on about Travis Redman, the dark blue truck, its subsequent demise, my pursuit of Felix Russo, and the text messages. Bradley stared at me the whole time. I had no way of knowing exactly what she was thinking, but I got the impression she was pulling apart my words to either make sure the department wasn't in trouble, or to find the key elements she'd use in my dismissal.

When I was done, she nodded slowly. "So, against procedure, again, you entered a murder suspect's property alone. Where you were subsequently assaulted, disarmed, and taken hostage. Why didn't you wait for uniform backup? Or insisted your partner enter the premises with you?"

"That's my fault, ma'am," Hugo replied before I could say anything.

Captain Bradley and I both looked at him in surprise.

"Kat tried to keep me informed the whole evening," he went on, "but we kept missing each other. She told me we needed to arrest Felix Russo, and I went to the tavern to join her. Kat only entered the property when she thought I was backing her up. If I hadn't let Caroline Russo jump me, I would've been there."

The captain stared at my partner, her laser vision boring into his skull. "Is that so, Fuentes? So, this woman got the better of both of you. While you weren't together as you should have been."

"You'll see calls and texts back and forth all evening, ma'am," Hugo replied with more confidence than I felt.

Sure, we'd traded voicemails, and I'd sent texts, but he was stretching the truth to the breaking point on my behalf. Well, on both our behalf, I suppose, but I still wasn't sure why he was doing it. Eighteen hours ago, our relationship had been teetering over a precipice.

Bradley shook her head. "Once again, chaos reigns around you,

Cromwell," she said, shifting her focus my way again. "But it appears we have our killer, so I suppose I must congratulate you both."

Her words were nice, but she still didn't look to be in a congratulatory mood.

"And you think the wife committed both murders? Yesterday, you had forensics tearing a garden shed apart looking for a wood-carving chisel belonging to Mr. Redman."

"Autopsy report on Wendell came in this morning, ma'am," I told her, having read the report on my phone from the hospital bed. "The instrument used to kill him was a slender, sharp rod, such as an icepick. It didn't have the crescent-moon profile of a carving chisel."

"Anyone can buy an icepick or a mechanic's pick, Cromwell," she rebutted. "That's hardly irrefutable proof, is it?"

"No, ma'am," Hugo interceded again, "But we have a solid case against Caroline Russo through Travis Redman's testimony, and we now have Russo's SUV on CCTV entering and exiting Salt Creek at the time of Wendell's murder. We're also revisiting CCTV to place the dark blue pickup in town on Tuesday night."

"We do?" Bradley and I asked simultaneously.

"I spent a while last night going through the footage uniforms brought us from a business at the corner of PCH and Ritz Carlton Drive," Hugo explained.

"I thought we sent that out to the IT guys," I said.

"We did," Hugo replied. "But I knew they'd be awhile, so I took a look myself. I've sent a small clip out to be enhanced, but it's Caroline Russo at the wheel with no one in the passenger seat."

I smiled at my partner, but he kept his eyes straight ahead as he continued speaking.

"I also have uniforms looking for private security footage between the lumberyard off Stonehill and the Russo's residence. It'll prove Felix Russo torched his own vehicle."

Hugo was full of surprises this morning.

"But you don't think the husband committed either of the murders?" Bradley asked.

"I don't, from what I heard him say in the garage, ma'am," I replied, my fingers resting on the instant picture in my pocket I'd taken at the Russo's before the EMTs had hauled me off to the hospital. "Furthermore, I think he'll spill his guts in exchange for leniency."

"Why's that?" she challenged. "She's still his wife."

"Because she was screwing Chris Wendell, and the only reason she killed both Wendell and Helena was a mixture of jealousy and keeping them quiet," I responded.

"You think Helena Redman was going to tell the husband?"

I paused for a moment to consider the question, although I'd spent much of the night mulling over the same point.

"I'm not sure I can prove whether she was about to or not, ma'am, but I'm convinced she was murdered because Caroline Russo couldn't stand the fact that Wendell was still hung up on Helena. And she believed Helena *might* tell her husband. Felix had the money, but the restaurant was Caroline's project. She knew if he found out for certain that she'd been screwing around, there'd be no more restaurant."

Captain Bradley let out a long sigh. She looked from me to Hugo, then back to me.

"I believe Caroline killed Chris Wendell because he was about to tell me what he suspected," I offered, predicting what the captain's next question would be. "His mistake was calling her first. He didn't know it when he called her, but she'd slipped the note and Helena's cell phone into his backpack when he stopped by to see her while he was cycling north to his cousin's place in Newport. She got to Salt Creek first. My guess is, they were laying down together on the grass when she jammed an icepick in his ear. The accuracy suggests it had to be somebody who was very close to him while he wasn't moving."

"Can we prove any of this?" Bradley asked.

Hugo shrugged. "We have her on attempted kidnapping and attempted murder of a police officer, so she's not going anywhere. Between Travis Redman and the husband, I'm confident we'll have statements regarding the parts she had them play. We also have a burner phone we found in her SUV, although the SIM's gone, ma'am. By the time we're done, we'll be giving the district attorney a strong case."

Captain Bradley nodded again and picked up her pen. "Alright. Thank you both for the update. Good work." She turned to me. "Go home, Cromwell. I need a doctor's note signing you off as fit to return to work before I see you again."

"Yes, ma'am," I said, and Hugo and I scurried out of her office before she came up with another way to question our case.

Hugo sat in his chair and leaned back. I perched on the corner of his desk.

"You didn't have to do that in there, Hugo. I don't want you having to embellish things for my sake."

"It's what partners do," he replied, looking up at me. "I should have been there with you last night, Kat. It was my fault you were on your own."

"You were there when it really counted," I quickly replied. "She was going to shoot me. You saved my arse."

"It never should have come to that."

"Well, I was about to get shot making a low-percentage move on Russo when I saw you outside the garage. I have to say you were a sight for sore eyes."

"I didn't know it, then," he replied. "But I owed you one."

"How come?" I asked. "The way I figure things, I'm indebted to you until who knows when."

Hugo smiled. "We'll call it even. Hanson came by this morning and apologized. I assume from your message last night that you had something to do with that."

"I might have," I said with a grin. "Did he mean it?"

Hugo laughed. "Not in the least bit. But he assured me it would never happen again, and said he'd do his best to quell the rumors he'd started. So you and I both dodged a bullet."

"I think the one you saved me from was going to have more long-term consequences," I joked.

"Don't be so sure, Kat," he replied without smiling this time. "The world is slowly changing, but we're not there yet." He patted my leg. "Go home and rest, Kat. I'll start on the paperwork."

I stood to leave, then paused. "What about... you know, the other thing?"

Hugo furrowed his brow. "What other thing?"

I sighed and kept my voice low. "My camera thing."

"Oh, that," he said far more loudly than I would have liked. I checked over my shoulder. Thankfully, Bradley's office door was closed.

"I'm thinking I might get me one of those Polaroid-type cameras too," Hugo continued with a grin. "I kinda like having that instant picture of the scene."

I smiled all the way to the deputy's car waiting to take me home. I made it halfway to my mum's soup before my stupid brain decided to replay the words I'd heard after being hit on the head by Caroline Russo.

"It had to be her."

Those were the words my fiancé Paul had used.

What on earth could that possibly mean?

Thank you for reading *Why She Had To Die*, I hope you enjoyed it!

Looking for more from Kat Cromwell?
For those of you interested in joining my monthly newsletter, I've
created a fun bonus you'll find by using this QR code…

Don't forget to grab the next book in the series,
Her Last Breath At Dawn

ACKNOWLEDGMENTS

My heartfelt thanks go to:

My incredible wife Cheryl, our family, and great friends for their unwavering support, love, and encouragement.

The fine folks at the Orange County Sheriff's Department who met with me, emailed, Zoom called, and provided their wonderful advice and knowledge. Any variances from procedure and law enforcement facts are strictly on the author by error or to enhance the story.

Peter Carey of Capistrano Boxing Gym for taking the time to help me with the boxing scenes. Again, any errors in this regard are solely on the author.

My marvellous editor Chelsey Heller for her diligent and detailed work.

My beta reader group for their wonderful support, feedback, and keen eyes, which make each book better before reaching you.

Above all, I thank you, the readers: none of this happens without your choice to spend precious time with my stories. I am truly in your debt.

LET'S STAY IN TOUCH!

To buy merchandise, find more info, or to join my newsletter, visit
my website at
www.HarveyBooks.com

If you enjoyed this novel I'd be incredibly grateful if you'd consider
leaving a review on Amazon.com
Find eBook deals and follow me on BookBub.com

Catch my chat show, The Two Authors' Podcast with co-host
Douglas Pratt

Visit Amazon.com for more books in the
Investigator Kat Cromwell Mystery Series,
Nora Sommer Caribbean Suspense Series,
AJ Bailey Adventure Series,
and collaborative works:
The Greene Wolfe Thriller Series
Tropical Authors Adventure Series

ABOUT THE AUTHOR

A USA Today bestselling author, Nicholas Harvey's life has been anything but ordinary. Race car driver, motorsports professional, adventure traveller, divemaster, and since 2020, a full-time novelist. Raised in England and resident in America for many years, Nick and his amazing wife, Cheryl, now base themselves in Grand Cayman from where they travel the globe in search of new plots for his novels. He is the author of the Nora Sommer Caribbean Suspense series, Investigator Kat Cromwell Mysteries, and AJ Bailey Adventure series, along with multiple collaborations.

For more information, visit his website at HarveyBooks.com.